W9-CLU-861

IN A
DARK
WOOD

BY AMANDA CRAIG

Published in Great Britain

Foreign Bodies

A Private Place

A Vicious Circle

IN A DARK WOOD

a novel

AMANDA CRAIG

NAN A. TALESE

DOUBLEDAY

NEW YORK   LONDON   TORONTO

SYDNEY   AUCKLAND

PUBLISHED BY NAN A. TALESE

an imprint of Doubleday
a division of Random House, Inc.
1540 Broadway, New York, New York 10036

DOUBLEDAY is a trademark of Doubleday
a division of Random House, Inc.

First published in the United Kingdom by Fourth Estate

Book design by Marysarah Quinn
Title page illustration by Mike Rejto

Library of Congress Cataloging-in-Publication Data
Craig, Amanda, 1959–
In a dark wood: a novel / Amanda Craig.—1st ed. in the
United States of America
p. cm.
1. Fairy tales—Appreciation—Fiction.   2. British—South
Carolina—Fiction.   3. Manic-depressive persons—
Fiction.   4. Maternal deprivation—Fiction.   5. Motherless
families—Fiction.   6. Mothers and sons—Fiction.
7. Suicide victims—Fiction.   8. South Carolina—
Fiction.   9. Divorced men—Fiction.   10. Women artists—
Fiction.   I. Title.
PR6053.R25 I5 2002
823'.914—dc21   2001035247

ISBN 0-385-50262-1

PRINTED IN THE UNITED STATES OF AMERICA

February 2002

First Edition in the United States of America

1   3   5   7   9   10   8   6   4   2

To Susannah Fiennes, Emily Patrick, and Jenny Wright—

THREE GRACES

Midway upon the journey of our life
I found that I had strayed into a wood
So dark the right road was completely lost.
How hard a thing it is for me to tell
Of that wild wood, so rugged and so harsh—
The very thought of it renews my fear!
So bitter is it, death were hardly worse.
But to explain the good I found therein
I will relate the other things I saw.

Dante,
THE DIVINE COMEDY, HELL, CANTO ONE

My mother said, I never should
Play with the gypsies in the wood;
If I did, she would say,
Naughty girl to disobey.
Your hair shan't curl,
Your shoes shan't shine,
You naughty girl you shan't be mine.
The wood was dark, the grass was green,
Up comes Sally with a tambourine.
I went to the river—no ship to get across,
I paid ten dollars for an old white horse,
I up on his back and off in a crack—
Sally, tell my mother I shall never come back.

FOLK RHYME

Wood 1. (n.) *A collection of growing trees: the hard part of the substance of trees*

Wood 2. (adj., Shak., Scot.) *Mad, fierce, furious, rash or reckless, vehemently excited*

ONE

THE BOOK, *her* book, was bound in black, with the words *North of Nowhere* indented in worn gold on the spine. Dirty and dusty, the boards loose under the cloth, it resembled a kind of withered bat. I looked at it with vague distaste. Then, almost as if it had suddenly come to life, it slithered out of my grasp, jabbed my foot, bounced and splayed open. I picked it up. I didn't know then how dangerous fairy tales can be.

I was trying to separate my possessions from those of my wife, Georgina. A biography in books, this is why some people scan your shelves, in the manner of a Roman seer gazing at entrails. There were duplicate editions of T. S. Eliot and Shakespeare, of Beckett, Pinter, and Joyce. My own copies of Conrad, Dostoevsky, and Waugh jumbled up with her Austen, George Eliot and the Brontës—the male versus the female canon. The plays I had been in, with my parts underlined in lurid orange. Her university texts, with notes scribbled in pencil or biro. Then single volumes, signifying union: paperbacks stained with the oils of lost summers, whose cracked spines still released cascades of fine sand or faded blades of pale grass; hardbacks generously inscribed to mark birthdays or Christmas, passed from one to the other at bedtime as a preliminary to love; bound proofs of new books, battered ghosts of old ones. All of these, left to me to divide and put into boxes. She had taken the children's books, as she had taken the children. We had been separated now for over a year, and were getting divorced.

I had been astonished by how much suffering this had caused, and was now weary. My body had taken on a life of its own, in which it wept while I remained an embarrassed parent, unable to control its excesses. She had gone and I had stayed. It wasn't just because I'd been determined not to relinquish this house. I had been unable to do anything. Once a fortnight, I would emerge to buy groceries. Otherwise I slumped in an armchair, without hope or energy. Some days, I couldn't remember how to talk. On really bad days, I couldn't even walk either. Eventually, after a bout of snarling by lawyers, we had agreed to sell and split the proceeds. The new owners were people who would paper over the walls and drain the Japanese pond I had made in the garden (I had heard them agreeing on this in loud voices, when they walked round with the estate agent). Several other prospective buyers had dropped out even as they walked to the front door. I had heard stories of divorcees who had bought a dog just so it could crap over all the carpets and drive the price down, but my neglect wasn't calculated. I had given up washing anything, including myself. The small, synchronized actions to get to the bathroom were too much for me. I knew the new owners would think I was crazy anyway. People always think this of the person who lived in their house before them. It's a way of pretending you never existed.

In every room, packers were entombing our furniture, wadding it in transparent, silvery bubbles that, they assured me, would protect the most fragile of objects. If I stood still for long enough, there was even a chance they might do the same to me. I shivered. The front and back doors were open, the heating switched off. What had been my life, our life, was finally ebbing from this place. Already, the house was acquiring a hollow sound, motes swirling in weak sunlight as if the very atoms of my existence were being sent into Brownian motion. There was nothing but boxes and dust, and these, too, would go—a ghostly picture here, a chair there, wiped out, painted over, forgotten.

I turned over the book I held. The pages were spotted like elderly hands. I began to read, mechanically.

"At least tell me the way," she said, "and I will seek you—that I may surely be allowed to do?"

"There is no hope, not unless you wear out an iron staff and a pair of iron shoes in searching," said he. "The troll witch lives in a castle which lies East of the Sun and West of the Moon, and there too is her daughter the princess with a nose three ells long, and she is the one I now must marry."

Then the girl fell into a deep, deep sleep; and when she awoke there was no prince or castle, only a little patch of green on which she lay and the great dark wood all around. By her side was the same bundle of rags that she had brought with her from her own home.

Why should these words have affected me so deeply? Perhaps it was seeing my own home vanish, like that of the girl in the story. Perhaps it was knowing that I was heading North of Nowhere, too. Or perhaps it was the drawing beside it, occupying almost the whole page, and executed in black ink. There was an ornate frame just inside the margin of white, made of intertwined thorns, and then the illustration itself.

What I saw was a girl, waking up in a tiny clearing almost completely overgrown by black brambles and branches. There was no visible way out, just a shaft of sunlight coming down on her like a spotlight in a theatre. Her face was a white wedge of misery. The darkness pressed in upon her, wave on wave of chaotic, seething undergrowth: yet was repulsed. You could tell, I don't know how or why, that this wasn't going to be the end of the story, that she was going to get up and put on those iron shoes and find the happiness she had lost. She looked the way I felt, or wanted to feel.

High on an empty bookcase, a telephone rang. It would not be cut off until noon. I closed the book with an effort and thrust it into the pocket of my jacket.

"Oh, hi, hi, it's me. I was just wondering how you *are*." This was Diana, one of several single women who had decided that my emotional, psychological, and gastronomic well-being was of particular concern to her. Diana was the most persistent.

"Fine."

"I just wanted to know if there's anything I can do. I could get a couple of hours off work, to help you pack, you know? It must be so difficult for you."

"It's done. Thank you."

I forced myself to sound a little less churlish, and immediately a tin of syrupy concern oozed towards me.

"Are you sleeping OK? Eating? You know, any time you want something cooked, let me know. You need to look after yourself, Dick."

As I lied that I was not drowning but microwaving my Meals for One, the line began an insistent chirping. This was my excuse for ringing off, in case it was my agent.

"Hallo? It's Sarah? I suddenly realized you're about to have a new number. I'm having a drinks party next week. Would you like to come?"

They were all so hesitant, these Cinderellas of the mating game, it was difficult to see them as predatory. Something had gone wrong in their lives—they had worked too hard, or played too fast, or been too soft or stayed too long—and now they were desperate, strung out, seeking salvation at the eleventh hour before the biological clock struck midnight. It was not myself they wanted so much as any half-decent heterosexual husband. They had hearts overflowing with love, yet they woke up every morning and saw the gradual withering, the shriveling, the advance of age that only marriage and childbearing could make tolerable. I felt sorry for them, but fed up. I wasn't the solution to anybody's problem, any more than they were to mine.

Upstairs, the packers grunted. The tape they carried in large reels thrummed and shrieked; they would cut the right length with keys—keys, presumably, to their own homes. The dismantling of my own would not take much longer, I knew. Boxes were stacked like battlements on either side of me; I envisaged Georgina and myself crouched down behind our respective barricades like two feuding medieval barons, sniping at each other.

As if in response, the telephone rang again. My wife's voice. I imagined it being bounced down from space, as heartless and cheerful as a goddess speaking from her oracle. "How's it all going?"

I gritted my teeth, and tried to keep my voice even and light. Years of training, and in a situation like this I still start to hyperventilate. "Like a nervous breakdown in slow motion."

She laughed. All my life I had tried to be funny, and nobody laughed. Now I told the truth and everything I said was amusing.

"Bad luck."

"All these *women* keep ringing up. Single ones."

"Why don't you try going out with one of them?" said Georgie.

"There's always a reason why they're still single."

"Nonsense. They're lovely girls. Clever, pretty, successful, nice, good cooks—what more d'you want?"

"They aren't *you*."

I knew at once that I'd overstepped the invisible line that had to exist between us.

"Oh, Benedick, you are sweet. You never said anything as nice to me when we were married."

"We're still married."

A large part of my wife's attraction is that she treats my sex as though we're children to be managed. She used to enjoy this. Then she had Cosmo and Flora.

"You should be out there, enjoying your freedom."

I knew this was true. In fact my first reaction when she left me was a kind of elation. If you've been with the same person for most of your adult life, you can't help feeling curious. All those girls you haven't slept with, the parties you haven't gone to, the offers you've turned down.

A year ago, my new situation had seemed like a sort of holiday. Furious, but elated, I raced about going to films and plays and parties as if released from bondage. I had kept my wedding ring on, largely because it had become too tight to remove, but I was free. I would stand in front of the mirror, with the theme tunes to the James Bond movies playing very loud, drawing an imaginary gun from a holster. I could go to the gym, travel the world, buy designer clothes, have affairs—

It took about three months for this tawdry fantasy to come crashing down. Most of the people I knew were just as I was—exhausted, poor, harassed, and prematurely aged by parenthood. The unmarried looked better but behaved worse. Everyone who was still single came trailing a history of romantic disappointment. In my twenties parties had been casual, raucous, bring-a-bottle events. Now, as forty approached, there was champagne, cocaine, and utter desperation. I was actually frightened by the intensity with which I was pursued. One woman I had hardly even spoken to came up to me and said, "I don't want a relationship. Let's just fuck."

I stopped going out, but not before my name and number had been entered in too many address books. Now Georgina had joined in the game of pairing me off. "What about Amelia de Monde?"

"You must be joking. The last thing I want is another divorcee. Or another hack, for that matter."

My wife ignored this. Just before she left me, she had been writing a column about her life, in which I had featured largely as a neurotic layabout who spent all our money on absurdities and left her to cope with the ensuing disaster. It was hugely popular—thousands of women apparently wrote in to say their own lives were just the same. No, I did not want Amelia de Monde.

"Candida?"

The vision of Candida Twink flashed before me. "Horrible scent."

"Pity. I know what you mean, though. Marvelous for clearing a corner in a crowded restaurant. Natasha?"

"Laughs like a donkey, and has a gap in her front teeth."

"Only a small one."

"Every time she smiles it makes her look like a piggy bank."

I wouldn't normally say things like this, but I knew my audience. I had heard too many conversations in which my wife and her cronies assessed the physical assets of single women they all knew, seeking the tragic flaw. One girl, an ex-model, was dissected for hours until Georgina's friend said triumphantly, "You know, *she has varicose veins!*"

"Well, at least it's been crossing your mind."

"It hasn't. That's the point."

Georgina changed tactics. "When are you going to come and see the children?"

I took a deep breath, and said, "How are they?"

"They're fine. Apart from missing you."

"Look, I just . . . sorry, dust everywhere. How are they other than that?"

She said, in a slightly more subdued voice, "Well, Cosmo

isn't enjoying his new school very much, but Flora is bouncing about."

"That's what children her age do." There was a long pause, in which all that had gone wrong between us seemed to echo down the line. I knew that this could not be easy for her, either, except that it was she who had done this dreadful, selfish, incomprehensible thing of having an affair. Her lover was her publisher. She had moved into his house in Notting Hill with our children. I hadn't seen them since Christmas. Often, I wondered if I should simply reject my children altogether. A uniquely modern form of torture, this: you hate someone, yet have to go on seeing them for the rest of your life because of what you once made with love. I wondered whether my own father felt this way about me.

"What's wrong with Cosmo's school?"

"Nothing," she said defensively. "He's just taking time to settle down."

"Is he being bullied? If he's being bullied, I insist he's withdrawn at once."

"No. Look, calm down."

"How can I calm down? I'm his *father*. Have you told them why I'm not there? Or are you blaming it on me, as usual?"

"I'm sorry you feel this way, Dick," said Georgina, politely, and hung up.

"Ha!" I shouted, punching the air. "Bitch!" A moment later, I caught sight of where we had marked the children's heights on the wall a year ago, and put my head in my hands. It felt like a very heavy bomb that was about to fly apart.

There is no hope, not unless you wear out an iron staff and a pair of iron shoes in searching.

I had been much more in love with my wife than she with me, that was all. Somehow, you were supposed to be ashamed of this, as though love were a perpetual jostling for the roles of pursuer and pursued. As if it didn't take more courage to admit that someone held your hopes of happiness in their hands. As if it were a choice.

"Don't you hate Bruce?" people asked. "Don't you want to *kill* him?" Actually, I had once liked Bruce. He'd always seen the latest plays and films, never had an original word to say about any of them, but exuded an air of pleasantness that, coupled with all his money, passed for charm. He read the papers and knew interesting people, he played poker and had a rich, catarrhal laugh that spoke of a lifetime of scoffing *pâté de foie gras* to the sound of trumpets. He had had his house *feng shui*ed; there were silk rugs on his floors and a complete set of Penguin Mini Classics in his downstairs loo. Compared with our own hand-to-mouth existence, he represented civilization; it never occurred to me to doubt my wife on the occasions when she chose him, rather than me, to go out to certain kinds of party with. He owned the publishing firm of Slather & Rudge; but he'd have gone into manufacturing breakfast cereals in the same spirit. You could enjoy his company without ever getting below the surface, assuming there *was* anything below the surface. The complete public schoolboy: not entirely stupid or wicked, just utterly lacking any glimmering of an inner life. The best screen actors, I kept being told, are those who don't bother to work out what they are supposed to be feeling and thinking, but who just say their lines. It's the same, apparently, in life.

It wasn't even Georgina I missed so badly; it was the children. You can never be too depressed with small children; they are so intensely alive, like animals. To think of them now, wriggling in Bruce's bed, actually gave me more pain than to imagine my wife there.

One of the packers poked his head round the corner. "Just letting you know, we're leaving the door on the latch, mate."

"Oh?"

"In case your dog gets out."

"I haven't got a dog," I said.

"Haven't you? Thought I heard—" The packer broke off, seeing my face. "Divorce?"

I nodded.

"Bad luck," said the packer kindly, ducking out. "Happens to the best of us."

I knew this tender dolt meant to comfort me, but the banality of my situation only added to its misery. If only I could be in a uniquely horrible situation, I thought, there would be a kind of distinction to it all. As it was, I had to accept my predicament with humility, and this, too, was unbearable. Nobody tells you how ridiculous depression is, how ludicrous it makes you. My mother's solution to being left had at least had a kind of grandeur, even if it hadn't been good for me. I could feel the outline of her book in my pocket, like a vague ache. I wanted to look at the girl in it again.

I filled the last box, wrote B. HUNTER on it, saw the packers out, loaded the car with a couple of suitcases, and dropped the keys off at the estate agent's. At least I could keep the car. I couldn't read, watch TV, or talk to people, but driving took just enough concentration to keep my mind off the other things. How many people in London drive simply to keep sane? The tower blocks rose above Georgian houses like my own; brooding ant's nests. Hundreds of families, misery stacked on misery. There were so many people living worse lives than mine, and yet it was like thinking of starving children in Africa when faced with a horrible meal. It didn't help.

The Thames opened ahead, the sky above stretching into a streaky winter sunset like a cheap balloon. Over Chelsea Bridge, its gilded galleons shining red.

Then, out of the corner of my eye, I caught sight of a figure falling from a dark tower, plunging head first through the air, screaming, the hair streaming out like the roots of a tree. A woman. Down, down, down she hurtled, over the glaring waters of the Thames. I gasped, braked, covered my eyes, and felt my own body thrown forward with sickening force.

When I dared look up, horns blaring behind me in a discordant chorus, I saw the woman was no longer falling. Miraculously suspended in midair, she hung between heaven and earth, bouncing gently. Now I saw that her feet were attached to the end of a long, striped elastic rope, which gave her the appearance of a child's toy. There were cheers and claps from onlookers as she was hauled in. She stood up and waved. Upright, the woman was a man. The thick bright cord was hooked up to a new figure. I didn't want to see it all over again. Shaking, I restarted my car, and drove on.

T W O

PEOPLE DIDN'T TALK about my mother. Yet everybody knew about her, it seemed. Complete strangers, people to whom my private life should have been a blank, pitied me, told me at the end of a job that I deserved a rest, afraid perhaps that I, too, would do something terrible. It was not rest I needed, though, or pity, it was work; and work was what I couldn't get.

Some people, perhaps those with more dignity or less rage gnawing at the roots of their being, are nicer as failures. For me, it was like descending a deep pit that had no bottom. Most actors are created by damage; but even with all the obstacles placed in your way from the beginning, it doesn't occur to you that you could really fail until it's too late. Every day, I thought I could sink no lower, yet every day I felt that lurch of uncontrollable terror, that feeling some people get momentarily when falling asleep—except that I had it for hour after hour when I woke up.

I had always been failing and falling, it seemed, just as my father had always been succeeding and rising. Every other week, he rang me to underline this fact, and to tell me I was (by implication) a worthless and foolish human being. He is a columnist, so judging others comes naturally to him. I've never been sure what to think, especially about people. How could I be, when I myself am so easily molded into the shape of another? I accepted long ago that I can never win any debate. Even when he's arguing in favor of the most terrible things, things you know unequivocally to be wrong or evil or just stupid, Howard manages by sheer energy of personality to defeat the opposition. It is this vigor that makes him so attractive to women, apparently. The one real blot on his career was my mother's suicide.

Of course, as Laura's reputation grew, so did curiosity about her. From having been completely obscure during life, she has risen to become a minor cult figure, particularly among my generation. Academics from Germaine Greer to Marina Warner have written about her pictures; the originals are now worth a small but increasing fortune. Only a handful of her books remain in print, but *In a Dark Wood* and *The Angry Alphabet* are now somehow as much a part of every middle-class child's birthright as Beatrix Potter or Sendak. Alas, she didn't go in for anthropomorphism, so there are no toys or mugs to cash in on. Even so, most years, my entire income has come from my share in her estate. Without Laura's legacy, I wouldn't have had the luxury, or the nerve, to stick at acting.

Georgina always wanted to know about her. In the beginning, she found my semi-orphaned state romantic. Later, she became angry. To my father's generation, discretion was a virtue; to mine, it is the sign of emotional repression. I argued that there was a lot to be said for leaving things unsaid. She believed it was Laura, rather than her own restlessness and ambition, that poisoned our relationship.

"Why can't you say what you feel?" she asked. "Why can't you *talk* about her?"

"Because I can't—I don't, OK?"

"You're like all men, struck dumb by testosterone. You never talk about anything that really matters. The only time you cry is when you stick a tube of menthol under your eyes for a performance."

"I don't remember what life was like before I was six," I said; and it seemed better, from what I did know, to keep it that way. When Cosmo and Flora were born, looking so unlike either of us (looking, in fact, like homicidal boiled eggs) I had been briefly curious to know if they resembled Laura. It was hard to tell from the one, standard picture. There were no others. I knew, because I once found a photograph album of my parents' early life. It was full of tiny black-and-white pictures, the sort that always make the past look so much more attractive than the present. In every one, my mother's face had been meticulously removed.

As far as I was concerned, my real mother had been neither Laura nor my stepmother, Nell, but Ruth Viner, with whom I was now going to stay.

The Viners had once been neighbors of ours in Primrose Hill. Tom Viner and I had played, fought, and been taught together; at twelve and thirteen respectively, we had been sent to the same progressive co-educational boarding school, Knotshead, in Devon. By then, my father and Nell had moved to Notting Hill and the Viners to Belsize Park, but it made little difference. During the holidays, I spent so much time at Ruth's house that most nights, I never went back to my father's. There didn't seem to be much point.

"Your foul-weather friend," Georgie would call Ruth, implying that she was only interested in me when I was in trouble. It was true I could never understand why she was so kind to me, unless she had a soft spot for the kind of ugly ducklings who turn into lame ducks. I was as unsuccessful at Knotshead as Tom and Josh were successful, but it didn't seem to matter to her that at eighteen I still hadn't lost my virginity or found anything other than a vocation to be an actor. Twenty years ago, when my father had cut off every vestige of support, Ruth had given me a room in her house, food, and, most importantly, encouragement.

Yet I hadn't seen her for such a long time—at first because I had been consumed by being in love with Georgina, and then because Georgie had made it very clear that she didn't like Ruth. I hadn't seen Ruth, in fact, since Flora had been born, and that was only because she made some effort to visit us in Stockwell. She had called me a month ago, to offer me back my old room while I looked for a flat to buy when the house was sold. I had been too wretched to think of calling her. I hadn't wanted to inflict my self-pity on anyone.

When I thought of Ruth, I always saw her sitting in her chair on one side of the fireplace, listening, while I sat hunched up on the other, talking. She would sit beneath a cobwebbed spotlight and sew pieces of ivory-colored cotton around what looked like an interminable supply of thin cardboard hexagons. In time, these formed a vast patchwork quilt that spread and pooled over her lap and beyond her feet. The quilt made a pattern of boxes, apparently in free fall with the lid open. If you stared at them, the boxes became stars, then boxes again. I was never sure if it was the same quilt she was sewing, like Penelope in the *Odyssey,* or if she made several, all identical. I used to believe that this quilt was a sort of receptacle into which I could pour my callow woes. Later, I realized her sewing was a kind of trick. You always tell somebody more if they don't look you in the eye; and of course, Ruth was a professional listener just as, for very different reasons, I am.

I pushed open the ornate iron gate in Belsize Park. Ruth's house was even more festooned with ivy than I remembered. Long strands of it hung down to touch my head with a ghostly caress as I walked up the path to the front door. Most gardens are dead at this time of year, but here green flowers erupted from jagged hellebore leaves, and a lemony scent gusted from a bush pricked with small white blossoms. Beneath a corkscrew hazel tasseled with stubby yellow catkins, a naked stone infant clutched a squirming fish. I looked at its sightless eyes. There were tears of dirt below them, but the child's face was serene, its round cheeks bunched in a faint, mysterious smile. A piece of Victorian kitsch; yet seeing it, I felt almost comforted.

To say I loved Ruth was to use too simple a word for the mixture of gratitude, affection, trust, and unease she aroused in me. She had been a friend of my mother's and was, like her, American. I always assumed they were drawn together by virtue of this. Or perhaps it was an attraction of opposites, as true in friendship as in love affairs. Laura was tall and dark, Ruth is small and red-haired. Laura had been beautiful, it was said, whereas Ruth is not. For a time, when I had been a teenager, embarrassment had leapt from pimple to pimple whenever she addressed me. Even now, something of that remained. Sometimes, she seemed the most attractive woman I'd ever seen; and then, in the blink of an eye, she could look like a troll. It was another thing my wife had held against Ruth, and, ultimately, myself. Georgina likes people to be consistent.

I pressed the bell. Once, I had had to stand on tiptoe to do so. Cosmo is that size now, I thought. I had been just the age my son was now when my mother died.

The garden suddenly grew and loomed, expanding as I shrank. It was vast and dark, raking the air with long skinny claws. Cold struck up through my thin soles like a blow. The world was black and gray, every tint of life leached out of it. Terror boiled and surged to my throat. Then, as suddenly as it had come, it subsided. The shaking, shrinking sensation stopped, though the hopelessness remained. When I was twenty, I had always imagined my thirties would be a time of calm and maturity, not this vertiginous sense of being a hinge, swaying between past and future, crushed between both. I waited until my second fit of trembling passed, then pressed the bell again.

Ruth opened the door, cats wreathing and coiling round her ankles. I thought she, too, looked curiously bleached. Then I realized she was older. All age is a kind of tiredness, I think. When you're young, the lines never show. Every morning you wake up unmarked, wiped clear by sleep. One day, though, you see lines that itch, as though some crumb of existence has been creased into your skin. They can never be smoothed away, and after a while you forget that this heavy, irritable feeling wasn't always there.

"Benedick, sweetheart," she said, hugging me. "It's been too long."

"I'm sorry. My fault. It's good of you to have me now. I've been so bad at staying in touch—"

"You can have your old room back again. Grub's friend Alice had it for a while, but they've bought a flat together now."

"So you've got an empty nest."

She smiled. Ruth would never lack for friends, or guests. "I saw you the other night on TV. In a thriller."

"Oh, that," I said unenthusiastically. "That was made last year. I'm always cast as the best friend. The eternal side-cock. I mean, kick." I always found myself making Freudian slips of this kind with Ruth, out of sheer self-consciousness.

"Well, you were *good*."

"I haven't worked for eight months. Except for one day on a drumstick job."

"Drumstick?"

"Period film. There's always some bloke with a chicken bone in his mouth, saying, 'Indeed, my lord Bishop.' Sometimes he sneers and sometimes he grovels. I did mine with a sneer."

Ruth laughed. "Well, good for you. I saw your Mercutio at Stratford, too. Last spring."

"Ah. That was better. I hated doing it, but it was better." I was silent. That had been my big chance, and I'd been good, really good, before I'd blown it. "My Touchstone wasn't too bad, either. You should have come round to the stage door."

She shook her head. "Not my style. So. Anything else in the pipeline?"

It wasn't as though I led an exciting life as an unemployed actor, but that's the odd thing about it. I mean, nobody asks accountants if they've got any big fraud cases coming up, do they? Which would probably be far more interesting.

"I did three days as a cross-dressing, upper-class coke dealer in a Brit-flick about drug addicts just after Stratford. It was made on a shoestring; it'll probably never even be screened. Otherwise, there's bugger all. You want to know the sort of thing I'm up for? My agent's sent me the pilot for a new TV series called *Jigsaw*. It's about an interior decorator who's also a detective—you know, sort of *Home Front* meets *Morse*, so that viewers can pick up tips about gilding candlesticks with a couple of corpses thrown in."

"Sounds a scream," said Ruth.

"Yes, well, that is the correct word."

"Cup of mud?"

"Please."

We went past racks of drying laundry—Ruth is a great one for washing her clean linen in public—to the kitchen, a warm, dark half-basement that smelled of cats and fried onions and herbs and soap. It was just as it had been all my life except that the faded daubs she had stuck to the ceiling during my own childhood now had bright new additions.

"Hannah," she said, following my gaze. "Isn't that abstract style great?"

I'd forgotten there would be other children living here. Josh, Tom's middle brother, had done some complicated thing buying the top floor of this vast house and making it a separate flat to free up some money for the other brothers. He was a private GP in the City, and the only one so far to have married and had children. It was weird to think of him being more or less at the same stage of life as I was; to me, he'd always been Tom's kid brother.

I could imagine how Ruth would dote on grandchildren. There were the usual pieces of brightly colored wood and plastic scattered around, now I looked: a smiling Russian doll on the mantelpiece, an ancient dappled rocking horse, an easel from the Early Learning Centre.

"What's wrong?"

"I'm not sure I can handle living with someone playing Happy Families."

Ruth looked at me, and raised her eyebrows. "It's not playing."

"Oh, sure. It never is, until it all ends in tears."

I wondered if she understood what had happened to me. I hoped, yet doubted this. I was back where I had started. Seventeen years ago I had left this house and moved in with the woman who became my wife. I had a terrible sense of slipping back in time. What frightened me most was, I could no longer believe in my own life as a story. Everyone needs a story, a part to play in order to avoid the realization that life is without significance. How else do any of us survive? It's what makes life bearable, even interesting. When it becomes neither, people say you've lost the plot. Or just lost it.

"So, tell me how you really are," said Ruth, putting the kettle on to boil. A stew popped quietly on the other plate of the cream Aga. She lifted the lid with a brisk motion and stirred. I had a sudden vision of something indescribably vile, surrounded by heaving green and yellow jealousy. I blinked, and the convoluted twists resolved themselves into a stew.

"Doctor, doctor, I feel like I've had my entire adult life surgically removed."

"Yes. It's nearly always that way. You aren't going to get over it for about two years."

"Really? I was thinking that I'd be skipping about like a spring lamb in a couple more weeks." I couldn't help the sarcasm.

"What does your father think?"

"Does it matter what Howard thinks?" I asked angrily; then, when Ruth did not react, sighed. "Yes, of course it does. I wish I could grow out of it. He thinks Georgie leaving me for another man must be my fault, of course. He thinks that if only I'd gone to Oxbridge and chosen another profession . . ."

"He still doesn't accept what you do?"

"When Georgina and I got engaged," I said, "Howard took us out to dinner at some posh place in Mayfair. He said it was the only sensible thing I'd ever done in my life, so we'd better celebrate before I screwed up. He wasn't even proud I'd just got that small part in *Another Country,* remember? Straight out of Webber Douglas, and God's gift to the world. I was on such a roll, I must have been unbearable."

"You were just young," said Ruth, mildly.

"I thought, Maybe now he'll treat me as an equal. Or at least as an adult. Instead of which . . . it matters so much, acting, and yet I can't take it seriously."

"Why not?"

"It isn't brain surgery, is it?"

Ruth cried, "Why should the *only* thing in the world that's taken seriously be brain surgery? Brain surgeons go to the theatre, you know. Just like anybody else."

Now it was my turn to laugh. I had forgotten how passionate the warmhearted are. "Ruth, entertaining people isn't a manly thing to do."

"You think you should be out there hewing wood?"

"Yes. No. It's what you *do* that makes you interesting."

Ruth said, "You should think more about what you *are,* not what you do. Why do you think people resent actors so much?"

I shrugged. "Georgie said that an actor's vanity is so much beyond that of any ordinary person's it was almost an affliction."

"I scarcely think vain people expose themselves to the possibility of failure quite so assiduously," said Ruth.

"If you fail, as the child of somebody successful, you're never *more* than that. You're never allowed to grow up. Can't you see?"

Ruth was so intelligent, and yet so dense at times. She believes that people are basically benign, basically salvageable. I began to wonder whether I had made a bad mistake. I had spent so long in the lethargy of despair that I had accepted her offer to stay without thinking. Now something mocking and malignant was waking in me, almost as if I were being invaded by another presence.

"You knew it was a tough way to make a living," said Ruth, with mild reproof. She heard, as I did, the whine creeping into my voice.

I swallowed, and said in a rush, "I have this awful suspicion that absolutely everyone is better than I am. They look better, talk better, act better. I'm terrified of the ones who've been to real drama school for three years; I keep feeling I'm a fraud. You've no idea how many people hate you now if you're a white, heterosexual ex-public-school man. They think I must be either a fascist snob, like Howard, or a complete twit. I probably am, too. I know so little about anything, even myself. And yet the one thing I do know is that I *must act*. People think that's terribly funny. They'd understand a musician saying he must play, or a painter paint or a writer write. But acting is all supposed to be this gigantic ego trip. And oh, God, it isn't. It isn't."

Ruth poured coffees. I didn't really want mine, but sipped it anyway. It was good. Her coffee is always good and strong. My irritability subsided. I couldn't remember when I'd last had anything hot to eat or drink.

"Isn't there some kind of professional body to help out-of-work actors?"

"Yes. It's called the National Theatre. I can't get parts there, either." I glared at my feet.

"Oh, Dick, you do have talent, and you're not unsuccessful,'" said Ruth. I knew she had said this before, many times, and yet I needed someone to say it. "But you don't just need talent. You have to have a talent for having talent, too."

That was the kind of gnomic thing Ruth could always be relied on to say. My irritability increased again. She had been through an excruciating divorce herself, when Sam left her. Why wasn't she more sympathetic?

"I'm a failure. Truly. I'm not comparing myself to the eighty-five percent of actors who never get any jobs. They're obviously no-hopers, whereas I do occasionally—just occasionally—get work. But I'll be forty soon, and I feel like I've been beating and beating on this door for twenty years, and on the other side of it is a wonderful party, full of half the people I grew up with, and they aren't even aware of my existence."

"What about the other half?" Ruth asked.

"What?"

"The other half of your peer group?"

"I don't care about *them*," I said impatiently. "They're all very nice people living in Essex or something. They aren't part of my world. Or the world I wish were mine. It's the uncertainty that's killing me. I could wait my whole life and not get the Call. Or it could come tomorrow."

"The call?"

"The Call. The part. The role that takes you above-line. It's what actors spend years waiting for. It's like Harrison Ford and *Star Wars*. Like Branagh and *Another Country*. You go from being nobody to somebody. It *makes* you."

"What would you do if you gave up?"

"I don't know. Be utterly miserable, I expect. The only question is whether I'd be *more* miserable. Howard warned me,

I should have a safety net, I should get a proper job. It's great, isn't it, my wife and children move in with somebody else, my life is in ruins and all my father can say is, now is the time to become a teacher. As if their lives were any better, poor sods."

"How did Georgina get on with him?"

"Oh, Georgie got on splendidly, she does with everyone. Particularly if they can be useful."

I thought about that dinner, long ago, at which my future wife had been formally introduced to my father. Georgina had set out to charm him, and succeeded in flattering the old sod into a semblance of sociability. She had always known she would be a writer, and successful; she is far cleverer than I am, having gone to Oxbridge and so on. Everyone, including myself, wondered why she had chosen me of all people. I suppose that most of the men she knew were frightened off by her air of terrifying competence. I wasn't. I was useless at school, and have such huge gaps in my knowledge and understanding of the world that I seldom dared express an opinion to her or her friends. But I needed her confidence and decisiveness. I never imagined it would one day be turned against me.

It was raining when we left the posh restaurant, and I had been the only one carrying an umbrella. I tried to open it, and couldn't. It was one of those cheap folding jobs, and the spokes had become jammed. The more I struggled and pushed the more it jammed, and of course the more I tried the more nervous I became, with all the food I'd eaten churning around, and Howard sighing impatiently. So after a bit, he turned to Georgina, and said, "This is my son, whom you wish to marry. He can't even open an umbrella." Then he took my umbrella and opened it, as he did everything else, effortlessly.

There had been no room for me underneath. They walked on ahead, laughing and gossiping, while I got wet.

"The thing is, she was always going to succeed, just as I was always going to fail."

Ruth looked at me. "How are you sleeping?"

"Not well."

Before she left me, I hadn't been able to have enough sleep. Now, every night, I found myself writhing as particular scenes or phrases from our life together glowed, as if lit by an infernal heat and branded on my brain.

"She wants to be 'civil.' That's what she said after she left. To be civil, imagine, to your husband, the father of your children. To someone you've fucked. As if I were some sort of gibbering savage."

"It's a period of temporary madness. I know that's no consolation, but you will be sane again. It just takes time."

I was silent. It was like the story: *you must wear out an iron staff and a pair of iron shoes.* I wished I could be strong, like the girl in the picture.

"I found something of my mother's when I was packing."

"Oh?"

"It's a book of fairy tales."

"Have you read them?"

"Just a bit. But it—interests me."

"I see. That's new."

"Yes, well. . . . Boys are hardly ever interested in that sort of thing, are they? I know I wasn't. It's all trains and cars, crashes and disaster. Not romance and wishes."

"They're not always like that."

"I grew up in a generation which had no idea that women were going to be our equals. You were just supposed to keep going no matter what. But now there's no place for us. We're a biological dead end. It's stupid to even keep on living."

Ruth put her cup down. "You're thinking suicide is the answer?"

I said angrily, "Everyone thinks of it, don't they, when things get bad? And things have been bad for me for a long time. I can't really remember when they weren't."

"Yes. Everyone thinks of suicide. There probably isn't a person alive who hasn't considered it, or actively struggled with it. You think, That's when they'll all be sorry. You imagine that death will make you heroic, perfect. Whereas to live is to act, to be in a state of conflict, to do things that are unlovable. That is very hard."

"I know I'm unlovable," I said. "But I don't see why it's so bad to—to remove yourself from the picture. At least that would be more courageous than hanging around whimpering."

"No," said Ruth. She fixed me with her eyes. "If you read fairy tales carefully, you'll notice they are mostly about people who aren't heroes. They don't have special powers, or gifts. Often they are despised as stupid. They are bullied, beaten up, robbed, starved. But they find they are stronger than their misfortunes."

"How? How?"

"By luck, or courage, or kindness."

"Ruth, you must know that in real life, none of those things *work*."

"How do you know?" she said. "Have you tried them?"

Later, when my boxes had been carried up to my old room, I looked out over the back garden. A tall tree scraped its twigs across the red night sky. I leaned my forehead on the icy pane, and watched it. The bare branches flayed against the night, tormented by the wind. I watched the wild, despairing, senseless jerks. The branches were leafless, dead. It seemed impossible that they would ever be capable of regeneration.

T H R E E

I couldn't rest, I couldn't sleep. I couldn't sleep. I couldn't rest. At some point in that first week, these two forces of agitation and exhaustion met and canceled each other out. I switched on the light, picked up my mother's book, and began to read.

THE TWO SISTERS

Long ago and far away, a young widow lived in a little house by the edge of a deep, dark wood with her two little daughters. When the elder of these was six years old, the mother sent for her sister.

"I am dying," said the poor widow, "and I have nothing to leave you except for my two daughters. I beg you, take care of them as if they were your own."

Then she kissed her children, closed her eyes, and died.

Now her sister was not at all pleased at this. "What use are children to me?" she said. "If they don't earn their keep, I'll be rid of them."

But she soon discovered that she was wrong, for as they grew up she found that Bianca, the younger of the two, was very useful around the house. In spite of this, it was Laura, her elder sister, who was her aunt's favorite: Laura, who was as ugly as she was cross and lazy.

I stopped. Why on earth had my mother given the bad sister her own name? Was it a kind of joke? Was this the way she actually felt about herself? Then another thought struck me. Why had the mother in the story died when her elder daughter was exactly the same age as I, the real Laura's child, was when she killed herself? Puzzled, and increasingly agitated, I read on.

> *As the two children grew up Bianca's eyes became bigger and bluer, and her hair more golden, and she became known by everyone around as "pretty Bianca." But the elder girl was dark-haired and dark-eyed, and as plain as only a cross, selfish person can be.*

Somehow, I found myself loathing Bianca. What was it about fairy tales that they always equated the good with the beautiful, the bad with the ugly? Who wasn't cross and selfish some of the time? Besides, what was so marvelous about blond hair and blue eyes?

> *In her efforts to seem more attractive than Bianca, Laura persuaded her aunt to give her a fine pair of red leather shoes to wear on Sundays, and a shawl embroidered with roses. But no fine shoes could hide the fact that her feet were as big as bricks, and no embroidery softened her frowning face. Bianca with her small bare feet and neatly darned scarf had all the young men of the village watching her.*
>
> *"I saw you making sheep's eyes at the blacksmith's son at mass today!" said Laura to her sister one cold December day. Now, if anyone had been making sheep's eyes at the blacksmith's son it was Laura herself. But he hadn't even noticed, because he was too busy looking at pretty Bianca.*
>
> *"I won't stand it, do you hear? I won't!" said Laura.*
>
> *"I'm sorry, dear sister," said Bianca unhappily. "You know there's nothing in the world I wouldn't do to please you and my aunt."*

"Isn't there?" said Laura. "Then go out and pick me a bunch of violets."

"Violets?" said Bianca in astonishment. "Where should I find violets in December?"

"Well, you won't find them by staying here, will you?" said Laura. And she and the aunt laughed mockingly.

So Bianca went out into the snow in her bare feet. Already it was growing dark. Shivering, she ran into the wood.

How long she wandered she could not tell. But just when she felt she could die from cold and misery, she thought she saw a flickering light through the trees. Creeping up on her frozen feet, she saw a large, leaping fire. Round it, each seated upon a stone, were twelve men. They sat in a circle, from the youngest who was a pretty little boy, to the oldest whose hair was as white as cotton grass, and who held a wonderfully carved staff in his hand. But the strangest thing was, from the eldest to the youngest, they all had different versions of the same face.

Bianca crept timidly into the firelight. "If you please, kind sirs, will you let me warm myself for a few minutes by your fire?"

The twelve men looked at her gravely, and the white-haired man said, "What are you doing in the dark wood in this bitter weather, alone and thinly clad, my child?"

"My aunt and my sister have sent me out to find a bunch of violets," said Bianca. The warmth of the fire gave her courage, and she told the twelve men about her cruel sister's demand.

I wondered whether my mother had a real sister somewhere, and whether Bianca was her name. Bianca was the name of the sister in *The Taming of the Shrew*, who seemed as good as she was pretty, but who turned out to be the real shrew of the piece. Was my mother making some sort of feminist point here? That good daughters were just like blank sheets of paper, whereas interesting, cross ones won the laurels? Somehow, I didn't think my mother had liked her relations, whoever they were.

When she had told her tale, the twelve men exchanged glances. Then the white-haired man handed his staff to one of the younger boys and said, "Brother March, will you help this child?"

"Willingly!" said Brother March, and he raised the staff in the air. He murmured some words, though what they were Bianca could not hear through the crackling of the fire. At once, a bright green flame leapt up as he spoke, and the snow began to melt all around it. As she watched, tiny leaves pushed through the bare soil. Then before her eyes celandines and primroses budded and uncurled in the fine grass.

"Quick, Bianca," said the young man. "Look beneath the hazel bush."

Bianca looked. One half of the bush was weighted with snow, but the other, close to the green flame, was showered with yellow catkins. At its roots bobbed a clump of violets. She fell on her knees with delight and picked the tiny purple flowers until there were none left. When she rose and turned to thank the twelve men there was nobody there—nothing but a circle of stones round the dying embers of a fire. The trees were dry and leafless once more, and laden with snow. If it had not been for the violets in her hands, Bianca would have thought she had dreamed it all. She said, "Thank you," all the same, then ran home as fast as she could go, the green fire singing in her veins and the scent of violets all about her.

"Where did you find them?" asked Laura grudgingly.

"In the wood," said Bianca.

"I shall wear them pinned to my embroidered shawl for Christmas Eve. Then all the young men will admire me!" said her sister.

She was wrong, however. As soon as Laura pinned them to her shawl, the flowers drooped and died. The scent was gone. Yet pretty Bianca, oddly enough, still smelled faintly of violets. Laura was so angry when they returned from church that she would not eat a mouthful of dinner.

"I can't live without strawberries!" she cried, and burst into tears.

"Now see what you've done to your poor sister!" said the aunt indignantly to Bianca. "Go out this instant, and don't you dare return without this basket full of strawberries!"

Poor Bianca set off into the dark wood again. It was snowing so hard that she could barely see where she was going. She struggled on and on until she felt she could go no farther. Just as she was about to lie down in despair, she saw a faint red glow through the trees. So she took courage and stumbled on. There, once again, were the twelve strange men sitting round the mysterious fire.

"What are you seeking this time in such bitter weather?" asked the old man, smiling at her.

"Ripe strawberries, if you please, sir," said Bianca.

The old man turned to his companions. "Brother June, will you help the child?"

A fair young man rose to his feet, and took the staff. "Willingly," he said, raising it in the air. His lips moved, and now the flames leapt blue into the air, the blue of summer skies and warm days. The snow melted, and where it had been was a ring of pure white flowers among the green grass. As Bianca watched, the flowers bloomed for a moment; then their yellow centers swelled, and blushed, and became ripe, red strawberries.

"Quickly, Bianca!" said the young man. She fell on her knees and picked and picked until not one was left. Then she rose and turned to thank the twelve mysterious men—but nobody was to be seen, nothing but a ring of stones around a dying fire. "Thank you!" said Bianca, and ran back home with her basket of sweet fruit, the blue fire singing in her veins.

Even Laura and her aunt had to admit that the strawberries were delicious. Although it was Christmas Day, they ate up every one, and left none for Bianca.

"Where did you find them?" they asked suspiciously.

"In the wood," said Bianca. After that, Bianca's aunt and sister did not beat her for twelve days.

On the last night of Christmas, after mass, the blacksmith's son came round and knocked on the door. "May I speak to Bianca?" he said, when Laura opened the door.

"No, you may not," said Laura and slammed the door. Then she shrieked and cried all through dinner.

"I couldn't eat a morsel," said Laura, "not unless it's a fresh, juicy apple."

"You useless girl, Bianca," said her aunt. "Look what you've done. You'd better go out and find some apples right now." And she pushed her out and slammed the door.

Outside, it was bitterly cold and very dark. Icicles hung sharp as teeth from every tree, tinkling like distant bells when the wind blew.

Bianca ran on and on until she saw the glow of the fire in the clearing. There sat the twelve men with the same face, just as before.

"Come near to the fire, my child," the old man said. "What have you been sent for this time?"

"Apples, if you please, sir," said Bianca timidly. "Fresh, ripe apples, for my sister."

"Well, well," said the old man. "Brother September, will you help the child this time?"

"Willingly, Brother December," said one whose hair was the russet of autumn leaves. He rose and took the staff, and once again the fire leapt, its flames twisting gold, the gold of twilight that comes early with the year's turning. "Look up, Bianca," he said.

Bianca raised her head and looked. The tree beneath which she was standing was bare and hung with icicles, all but one branch that thrust towards the jagged flames. As she looked, buds swelled and broke into tiny leaves that sprang like pale green flames. Pink-tipped blossoms foamed between them. The white blossoms held for a moment, then fell on her upturned face. As Bianca watched, tiny apples began to appear in the centers of two flowers. The apples swelled and grew sleek and round, their smooth sides flushing from green to yellow, from yellow to red.

"Quick! Do not let them touch the ground!" said Brother September.

Two large, ripe, juicy apples fell into her hands. She turned, only to find that the twelve men had gone, leaving nothing but the stones and the embers and the bleak winter behind.

"Thank you!" said Bianca, and ran home with the apples, and the gold fire singing in her veins.

Laura and her aunt ate the apples so greedily that the juice ran down their chins. They did not leave so much as a core for Bianca.

"Why didn't you bring more?" said the aunt.

"I suppose you ate the rest on the way home, didn't you?" said Laura.

"I was only given two," said Bianca.

"Given?" cried the others. "Who gave you these things? Tell us at once, or it will be the worse for you."

Then she told them about the twelve men and the great fire; and when she had finished her story, Laura said, "You've done something useful at last. I'll go myself and see what I can get out of them."

Laura wrapped herself up so warmly she could hardly waddle out. But despite that, the frost nipped her and pinched her until she wished she had never ventured into the dark wood. The snow whirled round her head and soon she was completely lost. Then she saw the glow of the fire through the trees. Thinking of all the good things within her grasp, she hurried forward.

When she reached the circle of stones and the twelve men she said, "Move and make room for me, you fools!"

They looked at her gravely.

"What do you want?" asked Brother December, with a frown.

"Ripe apples," said Laura. "There weren't enough last time. Oh, and while you're about it, I want some strawberries, some peaches, some cherries, and some pears as well."

The old man turned to his brothers. "What shall we give her?"

"Nothing but what she deserves!" they replied.

Laura put out her basket expectantly, but instead of a shower of ripe fruit there was a slither, and a drift of snow fell from the tree above and filled her basket, and her mouth and eyes. With a hiss, the twelve men and the fire all vanished. Nothing but a ring of stones remained.

Bianca and her aunt waited, but Laura did not return. After three hours, the aunt said, "Who knows what delicious things she's feasting herself on. I'm going to make sure I get my share!"

She, too, did not come back. When the snow died down, Bianca went to search. She found the circle of stones with the blackened remains of the fire in the middle, and by its side were two dirty, melting piles of snow which might once have been snow men, or even snow women. But as for her sister and aunt, they were never seen again.

Pretty Bianca married the blacksmith's son. They both lived happily ever after, in the house on the edge of the dark wood. The twelve men were never seen again, but it is said that sometimes, in midwinter, a fire can be seen burning, though nobody knows how or where or why.

Had she made it up herself? There was too much about the elder sister being unpleasant to the younger one for it not to have come out of something real. Yet it felt like something I had heard before. Perhaps all stories of this kind had been written before. Or perhaps it had no significance, and I was imagining things.

I looked at the illustration that accompanied this story. It was black and white like the first picture I had seen, drawn with a quick, sure line. Not the line, I thought, of somebody hesitant or lacking in confidence. It was beautiful, too, with a kind of melancholy humor that I remembered from her better-known works. Here was Bianca on one side of the page, shivering outside, and on the other the wicked sister and aunt were laughing together by the fire. When my wife had left me, I had felt just like Bianca, shut out in the freezing snow while Georgie and Bruce laughed inside their warm home. I turned to the front of the book, to see when it had been published. 1965: the year of her death.

There was another drawing, a full-page one this time. Bianca had her back to the reader. She stood with her bare feet apart, but the hair that escaped from under a shawl was dark, not fair. Perhaps this was my mother. The picture was speckled and barred with shadows, impregnated with an eerie sense of the supernatural. The trees seemed to crowd in. The twelve men sat round their fire, bearded like hippies or tramps. Their long shadows stretched out towards me. The fire leapt and twisted. As my eyes drooped, it sent a shower of sparks into the air.

F   O   U   R

For a long time, I stayed in Ruth's spare room without emerging. The sense of having returned to the powerlessness of childhood was overwhelming. I lay curled up in a fetal position, being what my wife had called an "amorphous heap." She had never had any sympathy for these moods; she thought I should just snap out of it. But I couldn't even snap my fingers, let alone my spirits.

Downstairs there was music, laughter, food, company; and I couldn't join it. I hated everyone, myself especially. The sense of failing at everything was like a stink. I was afraid other people would smell it, too. I was rotting away on the inside, worms writhing just beneath my scalp, my tongue blanched, all vile. To get up every morning was a gigantic effort, yet once up, I couldn't keep still. Nor, as I'd admitted to Ruth, could I sleep. The stupor of the previous six months had been replaced by raging insomnia. When I did sleep, for one hour or two, I could not remember exactly what I had dreamed, only that my dreams had been full of anxiety and terror.

What I thought about mostly was killing myself. It was abundantly clear to me that I'd never get another job as an actor. I was unfit for anything else, including fatherhood. Taking myself off would be a relief to everyone, especially myself. I thought of all the different methods I could choose, as if I were in a kind of macabre supermarket. Here were sleeping pills, ideal for a quick and painless demise. I dismissed them as essentially feminine. There was the altogether more violent option of throwing myself under a tube train. However, I didn't want to be announced as a signal failure to half a million delayed commuters. Then there was slashing my wrists in the bath. I found this quite attractive. At least there would be a lot of gore, and it was again supposed to be quite peaceful. A dozen boxes had been delivered and stacked in my room. I rummaged through greasy cutlery in the box marked KITCHEN and found a large, sharp knife. It had been the first serious piece of cooking equipment I had bought when I had moved out of this house and in with Georgie. I had done all the cooking, and the knife fitted into my hand as easily as an extra limb.

I ran a bath, and undressed. I hadn't washed for a long time, and was vaguely surprised by how pleasant it was to lie in warm water. I examined the knife again. A ridge of steel bisected the matte black handle, and there were two silver bolts through it, both functional and decorative. Georgie always insisted on the best. There would be honor in killing myself this way. I pricked my wrist with the point until a bead of blood welled up. It was astoundingly red and liquid, and the pain shocked me. The blood fell into the bathwater, and uncoiled into a faint brown stain. Then nothing at all. I could see my penis floating in the water. That would be the thing to cut, not my wrists. I sat up, and it shrank away into my crotch, as if it knew what was coming. It would have to be my wrists, then.

I lowered the blade, and made a jabbing motion. It hurt a lot. Shit! This wasn't going to be easy. My wrist was now definitely bleeding, but I hadn't sliced open the vein. I tried again, clenching the handle like my resolve. Repeatedly, my other hand jerked away. For a few moments, one hand stalked the other all around the bath. Every time, the hand with the wrist got away just as the blade was descending for the deeper cut. I felt like killing myself out of pure shame at the cowardliness of my flesh. Eventually, I got out of the bath, which by now was cold, and put a Band-Aid on my attempts. There wouldn't even be a scar.

Next, hanging. I got quite far with this one. I found a particularly nasty tie that my stepmother had given me for Christmas, and tied it to the light fitting in my room. But when I kicked away the chair, the bloody fitting came out of the ceiling, and I fell to the floor with a thud. I hoped Ruth wouldn't notice.

It really was astonishing how hard it was. Gas was safe. I could try crashing the car, but it was obvious that I'd never get up enough speed in London, because of all the traffic jams. I had no idea how to get hold of a gun. There was still the option of throwing myself off the roof of Josh's flat at the top of the house. Ten seconds of terror, then oblivion. This idea roused me to some activity again. I checked out the possibilities while his family was away, and the drop was certainly high enough. There was even a sort of roof terrace up there, just to make jumping easy.

I took my clothes off again and sat trembling on the railings, willing myself to be brave enough to jump. It was my fate to jump, I felt. I looked at all the bitter air between where I was, and where the ground was, and imagined what it would feel like, to fall and fall before the final, shattering crunch. The cold air rushed through me. If I did this, it would be something in my wretched life to be proud of. I felt myself pushed forward, closer and closer to the edge. All I had to do was let myself go.

But then I wavered. I couldn't go without writing a letter. I turned, sat down at the kitchen table indoors, and found a piece of colored paper. Then I hunted round for a pen. There were only felt-tips. Well, that would have to do. *Dear.* I stopped. Whom should this be addressed to? My wife? My children? My father? I knew what my father's reaction to it would be. He would point out that I had repeated a verb twice or split an infinitive. I put my clothes back on, crept out of the flat, and lay down on my bed again. I was a failure even at suicide.

How had my mother done it? Had she left a letter? I didn't know. She had simply not been there. At first, I think, I had some memory of her—not of what she looked like but a feeling of her presence. All through my childhood I had believed she would one day miraculously reappear, and that feeling would come back. I can't remember when the truth emerged. The details were always hazy. My father never discussed the facts of her death, just as he had left it to others (Ruth) to explain the facts of life.

I began pacing up and down again. Some kind of energy was returning to me, particularly in the evenings. There was life in this house as there had not been in my own. I could hear people coming and going—patients, friends, relations—Grub playing on the piano, practicing some piece I half-recognized, Josh's children crying or laughing. There was the smell of food, cats, cigarettes, laundry. I heard Ruth's voice on the telephone, or talking to her grandchildren; the murmur from her office where she saw people in the morning, the splutter of her 2CV when she went off to the hospital where she was a consultant.

Ruth was too tactful to force me out, but still attempted persuasion. Every three days (I noted) she would tap on my door.

"Tom is coming over," she would say. "I'm sure he'd like to see you." Or, "We're having a Sunday lunch, come on down."

I wouldn't, but sometimes I promised I would. Occasionally I did, too. That is the worst thing about despair: it is not constant, any more than love is. If only I could really reach the bottom of hopelessness, I could be resolute enough to end my life. But I was still falling.

I had been able to hold on just long enough to reach this house and now it was as if I had no strength left. The heavy winter clouds seemed to have penetrated my spirit, or else I had become one with them, weeping when they wept, tossed by every gust of wind. I had no sense of myself as beginning *here* or ending *there,* only of suffering, and shame.

Half my life was over, with nothing to show for it. That thought was like a stone on my chest. Perhaps I should try drowning myself in the nearest pond or canal. If only I had work. The telephone extension in my room, its white curves those of a woman lying on a bed with her back towards me, remained silent. I turned it off, unable to bear its shrill cries for other people.

Often, I stared at my reflection, trying to puzzle out the mystery of my existence. As I watched my face some thought or expression would suddenly bring my father's features into the mirror. Then I would see that I was the weaker copy of Howard, my eyes a washed-out version of Howard's blue, my bones coarser. Howard's hair had been gold, like that of the girl in my mother's story; mine was a dull stubble. I was the ugly one, doomed to be unpleasant and a failure. Georgina had not understood my agitation when we discovered that our first child was to be a boy, how strongly I wished to break any semblance of repeating my father's life. When Flora followed, I had felt as though some curse were broken.

Except it had not been. Six months after Flora had been born (as far as I could calculate such matters) Georgina had begun the affair, and the little girl whose existence had caused me so much joy and relief had hardly staggered to her feet before she was gone. It was Laura's life, not Howard's, that my own had come to resemble. When I looked in the mirror now, I had glimpses of another face, wild with anger or anguish, sliding off the glass. I longed for this person, yet feared it terribly. I knew it was Laura, rising up through my flesh as though through water, calling me to her in my time of need.

. . .

A T A C E R T A I N P O I N T, I knew I had to look at her book again. One day, when I had been at Ruth's for about a fortnight, I saw what I had missed before. The blank pages at the beginning were not wholly empty. One carried a dedication: FOR B. R.

So this book had indeed been meant for me, Benedick Richard. Beneath the dedication was a poem.

> *A man of words and not of deeds*
> *Is like a garden full of weeds,*
> *And when the weeds begin to grow*
> *It's like a garden full of snow,*
> *And when the snow begins to fly*
> *It's like an eagle in the sky,*
> *And when the sky begins to roar*
> *It's like a lion at your door,*
> *And when the door begins to crack*
> *It's like a stick across your back,*
> *And when your back begins to smart*
> *It's like a whip across your heart,*
> *And when your heart begins to fail*
> *It's like a ship without a sail,*
> *And when the ship begins to sink*
> *It's like a bottle full of ink,*
> *And when the ink begins to write*
> *It makes the paper black and white.*

What was this if not a kind of coded message to me? *A man of words and not of deeds.* I looked down at the long, muddy strip of weedy garden below, and was overcome by another wave of disgust at my life. What was the point of being a man, now? I should be flying like an eagle, not going to seed. I thought of the girl in the picture, and sighed.

. . .

DESPITE MY LACK OF charm or appeal, single women continued to ring up. It was nothing to do with me personally,
I could have warts and one leg, and they would keep on coming.
It must be more obvious to them than to myself, I thought, that
having once married I would inevitably do so again. I didn't
really know any of them. They had all been friends or acquain-
tances of Georgina's, and probably still were. Like her, they deserved better.

Diana "dropped by"—though as she lived in Clapham, there
could be nothing casual about it. I saw her, in her leopard-print
trousers and large, fake pearls, and my heart sank. I knew this
type. What she was really after was someone in the City who could
give her a Volvo and a couple of kids before it was too late; but
she was desperate enough at the fag-end of her thirties even to
take on an out-of-work actor.

"Let's go out for a meal."

"I'm not hungry," I said sullenly.

"What about Marine Ices, then," she said, as if humoring a
child. I had a flash of pity for her, then. She was a perfectly nice
woman who didn't deserve to be scraping the dregs of her generation for a partner. We walked down to Chalk Farm and ordered. She chose a banana split for us both. I wondered whether
this was supposed to be some sort of come-on. Diana talked at
me in a consciously gentle tone, as though I were an invalid,
about people we both knew slightly. The wallpaper boiled with
monotony.

"You've lost a lot of weight," she said, eventually.

"I expect so."

"Have you been working out?"

"Walking. I thought it might help me sleep."

At once, I regretted saying this. Her face brimmed with eager sympathy. I do not want your pity, I shouted silently at her. Just go away. *Go away.*

"It must be so hard."

I shrugged. "You would know." The one thing I knew about this tiresome woman was that she, too, had been dumped. She had lived with a bloke for seven years, then been traded in for a younger model, Georgie said. The usual story.

"Oh, it's not *so* bad, being single, you know." Diana laughed, and the large mole on her cheek bunched, then slid back. I wondered why so many women fail to realize that, as in restaurants, it is the absence of irritants as much as the presence of attractions that counts. The mole had two long hairs sprouting from it. I tried not to stare.

"—Free to do what I like. Whenever I've lived with a man, I found we always ended up doing what *he* wanted." She'd have a decade of resentment stored up behind that vulnerable manner. Any man would run away from it.

"Yes, well," I said vaguely.

She laughed again. Oh, God, she was being feisty. I regretted the brief impulse that had made me accept her invitation. I was feeling stronger, now. Dislike was giving me back some sense of myself.

"It isn't too bad, as long as you keep busy. I do a lot of shopping, and I'm out practically every night—galleries, films, theatre, I sometimes feel like I'm the most cultured person in London! Quite apart from all the parties. The weekends are the worst, aren't they? So empty. Especially on Sunday."

I knew I should say something reassuring but didn't. Why should I? For her, the humiliation of being single and childless would at least be modified by her girlfriends. My loneliness was far worse. I knew people professionally, in the strange, half-intimate way one does when on a job together, but (unless I counted Ruth and Tom) I had no real friends of my own.

Georgina had run our social life, and I had fallen into line obediently, never considering that a time would come when I might need friends of my own. This is the payoff for writing all the Christmas cards and buying all the presents: when a couple split up, the woman knows everyone, and the man is left with nothing but his work. Or in my case, nothing.

"Sundays aren't too wonderful in families, either," I said. I looked at the next table, where a couple were sitting in stunned exhaustion during a brief period of silence while their two small children spooned chocolate ice cream into their mouths. "All you do is have lunch with another family and talk about schools for five hours."

"I suppose it's different for you now," said Diana, archly. Why can't she just behave like a normal human being? I thought. Every one of the fake pearls round her neck was a dead eye, ogling me.

"Why should it be?"

"Well—"

"Look," I interrupted, before she could propose something. "Don't waste your time. I'm not interested in you. Sorry."

Diana swallowed, and gave a wavering smile. "I didn't think you would be," she said, with some dignity. "But I thought we might at least—keep each other company."

Guilt made me cruel. "You'd be better off getting that growth on your cheek removed."

Her hand flew up to it, and she blushed. "Some men say they find it sexy," she said.

"They were lying. It looks like a slug crawling down your face. You want to know why you're single? That's why."

Her face was suddenly taut with rage. She glared at me. This, I felt, was her true face, underneath the syrupy voice and self-deprecation. "Oh, piss off, you arrogant creep! What makes you think you're so wonderful, anyway?"

She rose, clumsily, and ran out, leaving me to pay the bill. I'd told her the truth, and she was too stupid to see it. It was something I'd noticed about these women: they were desperately unhappy, but wouldn't do anything about changing themselves.

R ETURNING TO Ruth's house, I found Tom in the kitchen. "Beer?"

"Yeah."

Tom was the only person who never asked about Howard— possibly, I always thought, because he was sublimely uninterested in the details of people's lives. He was kind, like Ruth, though probably not quite as bright. He was an anesthetist at a big London hospital and about as uncomplicated as any intelligent person could be. Or so it seemed.

"What have you been up to?"

"Finding out about my mother." The words came out of my mouth as if spoken by somebody else. I hoped I didn't look as shocked as I felt.

"Why?"

"What do you remember about her?"

Tom thought. "You had a m-mouse living in your kitchen, and we all had to keep very quiet when it came out. Don't you remember?"

"No. Everything about my life before I was six is a sort of blank."

"She baked a gingerbread house with a roof made of Smarties, and we ate it all up."

"Did she?" I wasn't sure whether I liked this idea.

"She was always making and baking and sewing and things. I used to wish Ruth were a bit more like that, instead of g-going out to work. Didn't she make a theatre out of a cardboard box?"

There had been figures on lolly sticks to move about, and a

red curtain. The memory swam up, suddenly, as though through developing fluid. "Yes! How come you remembered and I didn't?"

Tom shrugged. "Perhaps you remembered in a different way, by becoming an actor."

I shook my head. I knew exactly when the fever had struck. I had been reading *Hamlet* in an English class at school. Everyone else stumbled, puzzling over the strange words. Then it had been my turn, and the language had suddenly woken in me, so that my heart and lungs and tongue and throat were set on fire. Later, I understood that this was why people spoke of Shakespeare as a god. At the time, I had felt like weeping. Somebody had released me from dumbness, from utter isolation. I knew that I could live inside these words, that they would give me a shape, a shell. I had no idea, then, that I would never play Hamlet.

"I found a book of hers for children," I said. "It's interesting. I wonder why people don't take that kind of thing more seriously. . . ."

"It's the same in medicine," Tom said. "The lowest-paid doctors are pediatricians. Yet they're the ones who can make the most difference."

He was godfather to Cosmo—the only atheist among the six. Typically, he was also the only one to remember his birthday and Christmas.

We went to the kitchen, and automatically leaned against the Aga rail as we had when teenagers. It was strange seeing Tom with flecks of white in his hair.

"So—are you seeing anyone?" he asked.

"I've just been out with this girl. Disaster."

"Why?"

"I told her she should have plastic surgery."

He grinned. "What was her r-reaction?"

"Livid. I've no idea how to talk to women. I wonder if I

ever did. I don't fancy anyone. Everybody's too young—or too haggard—or something. And then, I have to think about the children. I don't want somebody like Nell coming along. Tom, is Ruth fed up with me hanging around?"

"No. You know she's not like that. But she *is* worried about you."

I said, angrily, "Yes, I'm not exactly happy."

"You will be. One day."

Ever since Tom had fallen in love with Mary Quinn, he had become tiresomely optimistic. I wondered how long it would be before my friend, like all the other men we'd known, was married.

"Sure. I can say, 'I'm an actor, and in a good year I earn eleven thousand pounds for dressing up as a carrot.' "

I IMAGINED my mother standing in a gleaming Formica kitchen, the powdery blue of clothes detergent, her tiny waist encircled by a mass of frilly, flowery skirts, waiting for my father to come home. Or perhaps she had been a swinging chick, in a lurid miniskirt and white boots. I thought of the girl in the picture I had seen. Where had that face come from? Was it her own? It didn't look like the one publicity photo I'd seen—but then neither did I resemble mine.

Ruth had given me the address of Liz Shaw, someone else who had known her. I had a vaguely unpleasant recollection of this woman, but in a burst of resolution wrote to her, and to my mother's publisher, James Cork. Who else had she known in her brief life? Too few, it seemed. Just like myself.

A letter arrived.

Dear Benedick,

What a surprise to hear from you after all this time. I remember you last as a hulking great teenager peering through the thickets of your own hair, though I've caught glimpses of you occasionally on the box. I am of course extremely busy, but if you really would like to come and talk about your mother then ring and fix a time. I'm not sure I can help.

Regards,
Liz Shaw

I remembered this harpy, now. She had been something in the BBC; one of those women so aggressively middle class her voice emerged through bared teeth.

"I wish I had more arrogance," I said to Ruth, that evening. I thought of Laura, the Laura of the story. "That's what makes people like my father successful."

Ruth knelt in front of the fireplace to push a small silvery button. There was a soft pop, and a yellow flame wandered over the gray lumps in the grate, making them glow like coals. The room warmed.

"You've got your agent. She believes in you, and so do I."

A new idea struck me. "Didn't my mother have an agent?"

"I don't think so. She never mentioned one. Who pays you her royalties?"

"The publishers."

"You could ask them."

I sighed. It all seemed such a hopeless task, suddenly. Why am I bothering? I thought. Even if I discovered why she killed herself, it wouldn't alter the fact that she's been dead for most of my life. Why should it suddenly matter?

Ruth looked at me steadily. "You know, Benedick, that if you really want to find out about Laura, it's the same as psychiatry. You must look at her roots."

"America."

"Yes."

"I could go," I said, doubtfully. "There's money there from her American sales. I've never touched it. We'd meant to use it for a family holiday when the children were older. I suppose I should use it up before Georgie's lawyers demand half. But I've never wanted to go."

I didn't want to say that America had always been a kind of dream, a world elsewhere, for me. I didn't want to find out what it was really like.

"Well, it's up to you," Ruth said. "But you're right, there is a mystery about your mother. Her family didn't even know where she was. I can't tell you how strange I've always found that. I met them after the funeral."

"She had a family?"

"A sister called Lily, and parents. Your father only found out where they lived afterwards, when he was going through her papers. They didn't know she was married and had had a child. It was as if she'd appeared out of nowhere."

I felt my curiosity revive. North of Nowhere, I thought. That's where she came from. "Why was she so obsessed by dark woods? Did she ever say?"

"No. Our conversations were the sort I had with every other mother. Usually, it was about health, because I was a doctor. I never realized how bad things had become for Laura, partly because she didn't talk about herself, and partly because I was at the stage you are now. Totally bound up with small children, I mean."

I looked at her. I knew Ruth too well not to see that she was withholding something from me. "But you knew about her books?"

"Oh, well, none of us really took much notice, I'm afraid, not until the last book came out and became such a best-seller. She'd actually given me a copy of *The Angry Alphabet,* and I hadn't liked it much."

"Why not?"

"It didn't seem to me to really be for children," said Ruth. "It's so full of, well, weirdness. Nobody fully understood then that children like oddity. When I was a child I remember being utterly terrified of the pictures in *Alice in Wonderland.* Laura's pictures have the same sort of feel. Now that we're used to them, they seem perfectly natural. But then—well, people were very uneasy. As for the dark woods, well, I know you've never been to America but have you ever seen pictures of the Carolinas?"

"No," I said.

"There are woods there. That's where her family lived. They're like the deepest, darkest manifestations of the subconscious you could hope to find."

"Isn't absolutely everything a symbol of the unconscious to you lot?" I said, rudely. I didn't like it when Ruth started talking like a shrink, even if that was her job. I've never believed in the talking cure, or whatever it's called, blaming everything on your unhappy childhood.

Ruth smiled. "Well—not absolutely everything. And I'm a psychotherapist, not a psychiatrist. But her woods interest me, too. It's not by accident that people talk of a state of confusion as not being able to see the wood for the trees, or of being out of the woods when some crisis is surmounted. It is a place of loss, confusion, terror, and anger, a place where you can, like Dante, find yourself going down into Hell. But if it's any comfort, the dark wood isn't just that. It's also a place of opportunity and adventure. It is the place in which fortunes can be reversed, hearts mended, hope reborn—"

I said, angrily, "Ruth, I—I've lost—I'm wandering around, not something rich and interesting like a wood, but a scene of utter, fucking *devastation*. I don't want to seem ungrateful; I know how much you've done for me. But this sort of stuff doesn't help. The only thing that will is work, and work is what I can't get."

"I do wonder if you shouldn't try medication. I can refer you—"

"No!" I shouted. "*I do not want any drugs!* I never take drugs, not *ever*. I don't believe in that stuff."

Ruth's needle darted forward, then drew out a long line of thread. "Well, then, why not travel? If it's necessary for you to find out about your mother, what's stopping you? Go to America. You have a family out there that you've never seen. Even if you may not like what you hear, they could give you some answers."

I wondered why she was pushing me like this. Did she simply want me out of the house? I couldn't blame her if she did. "Why? They've never wanted to see me."

"How do you know?"

"There are a dozen ways they could have got in touch. They didn't. You say my mother ran away from them. Why should I go back?"

"It may make you feel less alone."

We sat, gazing into the flames that looked like coal, but were not. The glowing lumps were not fossilized trees but lava, quarried from dead volcanoes. As soon as you switched it off, the heat died away, and all that was left was a dying glow in a pile of gray, powdery rock.

F I V E

O NE SATURDAY MORNING, there was a shrill ringing at the front door. After a long wait to see whether someone else would go to open it, I did.

There, on the wide step, were my children, weirdly etiolated as if in a fairground mirror, each clutching their favorite toy. I stared. Then Flora said, "Daddy, Daddy!" and dived forward in a kind of rugby tackle to wrap her arms round one of my legs. A joy like pain swept through me.

"Where's Mummy?" I asked Cosmo, suddenly afraid. "Is something wrong?"

"Mummy's in the car. She said you'd take us to the zoo. She'll collect us at teatime," he recited, adding, "*POOH, you stink.*"

I had forgotten everything about children, including their honesty, and how vile adults smell to their milky, innocent flesh. "I'm sorry," I said humbly, ashamed. "I'll shower."

"Shave off those nasty bristles on your face, or I won't cuddle you," said Flora.

"OK. Come up to my room."

I did not dare to look towards my wife, as I shrank like a snail back into Ruth's house. I knew she would be watching, tensely. As I closed the door, her car sounded its horn, presumably in re-assurance. I followed my daughter. I was stunned by the way they now looked unmistakably like *people*, by the way they were so utterly familiar yet unutterably strange. How could I have refused to see them? How could I bear seeing them again?

Flora said excitedly as she climbed, "Is this your new house, Daddy? Is this your new home?"

"For a little while. It isn't mine; it belongs to some friends. You've been here before, as a baby."

"When I was young."

"You're young now," I said gently. I was surprised she even remembered me.

"When are you going to come and live with us?"

I didn't know what to say. She had asked this question before, unable to understand why, at the end of a visit, we were not all driving back to Stockwell.

"Can I tell you something?" Cosmo tugged my hand. I stopped, anticipating some disaster. My son whispered, "Flora's growing her hair, right down to her bum."

"That's nice."

"No, it *isn't*. How will she go to the toilet? She'll get the ends dirty."

"I expect she'll have to wear it tied back, then."

I feared for my serious, logical son, as I did not for my daughter, cocooned in her discovery that the world loves those who make it laugh. I found it much easier to love Flora, but then everyone did. Little girls seem so tough and confident now, knowing they'll inherit the earth. Whereas boys are left in a sort of prolonged infancy, lumbering about with dinosaurs, with radio sets, with cars—with anything except what will help them get along in the twenty-first century. I squeezed Cosmo's hand. It lay quite still, a small trapped creature, uncertain whether to run or play dead. The other hand clutched his tiger, Ti-Ti, closely to his chest. I saw this, and sighed. I had forgotten about the dreaded Ti-Ti.

"Here, you can play while I have a shower. Then we can do something together."

At once, Cosmo cheered up. "Dad, Dad, why did the tomato blush?"

"I don't know."

"Because it saw the salad dressing. Is that a funny joke?"

"It's an old one, but yes."

Flora said, "Can I have a puppy, please, Daddy? Please?"

"No."

Cosmo looked around as we climbed the stairs. "Why are there green fingernails growing in that pot?" he asked. I looked at what he was pointing to with a mixture of fascination and horror.

"Those aren't fingers. They're daffodils growing from bulbs." I turned the label to show him.

"This is what they're like when they're grown up."

"They give me the spooks."

"They give me the spooks, too," said Flora, not wishing to be left out.

I looked at the stubby green fingers of a dead hand, poking stiffly out of the earth. Each bud was a pale oval sheath like a witch's nail.

"They're called 'Cheerfulness,' " I said, hopelessly.

When I returned, shaved and shamed into changing my stinking black clothes for fresher ones, they were both squeezed into the only box I had unpacked.

M Y MOTHER's first storybook had been called *The Magic Box*. It had been a story without words, everything being recounted in a kind of cartoon strip. Someone, I forget who, told me this was a radical idea at the time, although now it is more common. The drawings were overly detailed, compared to the spare elegance of her later work, but still had energy and quirkiness.

The story was simple enough. There had been a brother and

a sister, very neat and tidy, the boy in shorts and long socks, the girl in a gingham dress and bunches. They were bored. It was raining outside, and their mother (an unseen presence indicated only by a hand with a wedding ring on it) had shut them in their room. Each sat on a low, buttoned chair. The room was drawn with some detail, from the inlaid clock on the mantelpiece to the fireplace with its curling dog irons. Nothing was quite what it seemed in this bedroom. The clock had a face like that of a funny little man with a thin mustache. Pictures on the walls changed; plants grew from frame to frame and peered in through the open window. Yet the children failed to notice this.

They found a cardboard box, just as my children had done, and climbed inside it. When they shut their eyes and made a wish, the box rose and flew. First along their street, then through the city, with only other children as witnesses to their extraordinary journey, and finally out across the sea to a tropical jungle. There was a wild, romping adventure with animals. Eventually, they returned in time for tea. While they were eating it, an adult threw the magic box away. The last picture was of them finding an even bigger box, and climbing in. A metaphor for the imagination, I supposed. It was out of print.

Cosmo and Flora were quarreling about how much space each was allowed to take up in the box. They could never amuse themselves for long. I wondered, guiltily, whether this was because they had been starved of attention and saturated with treats, or whether, as some people claimed, it was all due to videos and TV. When I had last seen him, Cosmo had still been unable to read. He was now almost six. I wondered if anything had changed.

"Come on," I said in the hearty voice of the ideal father. "We're off to the zoo!"

"No. Shan't!" said Flora, who was now bouncing on the bed.

"Don't you want to see all the animals?"

"We don't want to see animals, we want to play dogs," said Cosmo. "Can I eat your orange?"

I felt the familiar welling up of utter despair. I can't cope, I thought. The children went on laughing and bouncing. How dared Georgie do this to me? She was probably off shagging bald Bruce at this very moment.

"No. Stop it!"

Cosmo, growling, dived onto a pillow and displayed his bare bottom like an Aborigine. I became stern. Their mouths turned down, their eyes filled. The really disconcerting thing was how much better they were at acting than I was.

"Don't want to go out."

"Come *on*," I said, impatiently. I sounded just like Howard. Oh, Jesus, I thought. Can I only be a father by pretending to be mine? The knowledge that they would soon need feeding and cleaning tormented me. "It's a *lovely* day! Don't you want to see the animals?"

"*We*'re the animals," said Cosmo. "Defend yourself, Scar!" He leapt onto me with sudden ferocity.

"Murderer!" shrieked Flora.

They snarled, their hands curled into claws. I saw hatred in their faces and shrank from it. "Come on, Cosmo. Stop that! Come *on*. I'm warning you, Flora. Oh, Christ."

I DROVE to Regent's Park with one eye open. The other was becoming dangerously swollen. The children lolled on the backseat in the manner of aristocrats in a tumbril. At the zoo they got out and, after I had been relieved of an exorbitant sum of money, in. A smell of urine-soaked straw, peanuts, and boredom enclosed us.

"Why are they in cages, Daddy?"

"For the crime of not being human," I said, savagely.

"Why?" asked Flora.

"Because humans hate anything different from themselves."

"Why?"

"I expect because they're scared."

"Why?"

I realized, too late, this was an infant device to keep me talking, not a symptom of intellectual curiosity. "They just are."

"But *you*'re not frightened of anything, are you, Dad?" said Cosmo.

"Well, er—some things."

"Like dinosaurs?"

"Dinosaurs are all dead. They died millions of years before humans came along."

"What's your favorite, favorite dinosaur?" asked Flora.

I racked my brains for a name. "Brontosaurus."

Both children looked aghast. "But you *can't* not prefer T. Rex," said Cosmo, almost in tears. "He's the biggest. He's the fiercest."

"Oh. Sorry. T. Rex, of course. I was teasing you."

"Well, it's *not* very funny," said Cosmo, as if he were the grown-up and myself the child.

Flora had to be lifted up onto my shoulders to see the penguins. Cosmo trailed along, sulking. It was all so slow, so tiresome. I wished I could have the company of another adult, if only to stop myself thinking of how, the last time we had been here, Cosmo had been Flora's age, and Flora herself curled small as a prawn inside Georgina's belly. We had still been happy then. Or so I believed. A voice whispered, *"And when the door begins to crack / It's like a stick across your back, / And when your back begins to smart / It's like a whip across your heart."*

She could not have written those words without knowing what betrayal felt like.

At lunch, the children threw a tantrum at the prospect of sharing a piece of chocolate cake. The area around the table was soon ankle-deep in plastic wrappings, striped bendy straws, broken crisps, used paper towels. There were fake rubber trees dotted all over the place, and pious notices about the environment, and yet here I was with my own personalized version of Agent Orange. It was a relief to leave, even if it meant trudging round more cages.

"Is that Simba?"

"Don't be silly, stupid, he's in Africa," said Cosmo in a patronizing tone.

The lion left his harem and came to stand on the farthest promontory of rock. He was lean and rather moth-eaten. He opened his mouth and let out a sound: not so much a roar as a mighty exhalation. I know just how you feel, I thought. Then, with tired disdain, the lord of the jungle turned his back on us all and slumped behind a tree.

Flora wriggled and squealed. The back of my neck grew ominously damp. I had forgotten about this, too. "Are you potty trained now?"

"I am potty trained most of the time," Flora said, with the dignity of a duchess.

"Oh, *hell*."

It was only after I had heaved the sodden mass into the waste bin and cleaned up the worst that I discovered she had a small backpack containing spare pull-ups. How could a child as articulate as my daughter have so little control over her bodily functions? For the last hour, I trudged round the shop, consenting in desperation to buy a selection of rubbery snakes, insects, and bouncing balls. I didn't have the money for this, but it still found its way out of my pocket. Rage and misery had become a buzzsaw in my head.

They began to fight again. Flora kicked Cosmo. He punched her back. "Daddy! Daddy!" she howled.

"Just don't *do* that! Stop it! Stop it *now*, or I'll smack!"

My hand came down. *Whack-whack.* Other adults looked away as my children shrieked.

Ashamed, and almost weeping myself, I drove back. The marks of my fingers were clear on Cosmo's reddened flesh; the stains of my cruelty streaked on Flora's soft cheeks. Both children were whimpering to themselves. I am a monster, I thought, sweating with guilt and strain.

My wife met us on Ruth's doorstep. She was refreshed and smiling. There was a bright pink scarf-thing round her neck, probably pashmina. I wanted to murder her.

"Hallo, darlings, hop in."

"Mummy, Mummy, Mummy."

Flora jumped into her arms, and nestled there, beaming. "I-love-my-Mummy-I-love-my-Mum!" she sang. All traces of distress had vanished. Cosmo, too, broke into smiles and put his arms around her. The magna mater, back in charge again.

"Georgie, I can't do this again. It's too much for me."

"I'm afraid you have to. They're staying with you every other weekend and for half the holidays. We've both spent a great deal of money thrashing this out."

"I *cannot* cope." I tried to put all the force of my desperation into my voice; it came out as merely petulant.

"Do you know, that's what women think, too? How do you think we manage? How do you think *I* managed? You'll cope because you have to."

All of a sudden, the rage I felt could no longer be contained. My hand lifted again, and was hurtling towards her face. I watched it as though I was serving a tennis ball, saw it arcing towards her, arrive on her cheek with a crack. Then my hand bounced back and we were both reeling. I could see the white mark left by my fingers turn to scarlet, just as it had done on the children.

I was incredulous. I can't have done this, I kept thinking. The palm of my hand stung. She covered her cheek, and leaned back against the car. The children went on playing, oblivious. I reached out to comfort her, and she flinched away.

"Oh, God, I'm sorry, I'm sorry. I don't know what came over me."

"Shut up."

"I'm so sorry, Georgie. Forgive me."

"Shut up!"

She was dry-eyed, fierce; I was the one almost in tears. I had never thought of myself as a man who was capable of hitting a woman, or a child, yet this was what I had just done, three times. And this is the most hideous thing about somebody falling out of love with you. When someone loves you, you show your best self to them, to the world. When you lose that love, you lose your best self, and are shown instead how loathsome and contemptible you truly are. To be seen without love by someone who once loved you is to be made lower than anyone can endure. I had a terrifying understanding that everything I had believed about myself, about my moral nature, had been no more than a thin crust on the surface of the earth. I was a hateful man, the kind of man who hits children and women.

Georgie said, breathing hard, "Every other weekend, Benedick. That's what the lawyers have agreed."

"I TOOK THEM to the zoo," I said, with martyred pride. The other things I had done were fast receding into unreality. A part of my mind was actually exulting that I had hit back at last, that I had struck a blow for manhood.

"In my day, that was what divorced fathers did, too," said Ruth. She was sewing her interminable quilt, while supper plopped and simmered on the stove. I was relieved that for once the house was apparently empty of anyone but ourselves.

"Did my father take me?"

"You came with us."

I took a bright green apple from the bowl on the table. Its

juices were tart, setting my teeth on edge. I thought of the apples given to Bianca in the story.

"How did my parents meet?"

"At a party." Ruth was silent for a moment, absently biting off a thread. "She lodged above a couple of men, Len and Rupert. I forget what Len did, something in the arts, but Rupert designed costumes for the theatre. They lived in a sort of Aladdin's cave—swaths of silk and velvet, chiffon and net, boxes and boxes of fake jewels and sequins and feathers. If you can imagine *Dr. Who* crossed with *The Abduction from the Seraglio,* you may get the idea."

"Were they friends of yours, too?"

"Yes. I loved them. Everybody did. They were the sort of people who bring light into other people's lives. And also brave."

"Why brave?"

Ruth sighed. "You had to be, if you were openly homosexual, then. You could be sent to prison."

"Oh, yes. That kind of thing seems so remote, now."

"More innocent times."

"They sound pretty barbaric to me."

Ruth's needle flashed under the spotlight. "No doubt. Anyway, Len and Rupert are still together, unlike most couples from that time."

"Could I see them?"

"Only if you go to New York. I haven't seen them for years, but we still exchange Christmas cards. I've got their address."

So she *does* want me out of the house, I thought, with a squeeze of panic. "Go on about my parents," I said.

"Well, what can I tell you?"

"Tell me about when they met."

She was silent, thinking.

"We were all very young. I was still a medical student, your father and Sam had just come down from university. There were a lot of parties. The usual sort had candles in bottles and lots of

Valpolicella—probably why so many of my friends are dead of liver failure, come to think of it. But Len and Rupert's were different. They lived in Primrose Hill, which may have been why we all got to know the area. Everybody crammed into a small double drawing room, talking about communism and art and everything in between." Ruth smiled. "People think now that the sixties were the decade of ferment and revolution, but it really all began in the fifties. Or perhaps everyone believes that about his or her own lost youth. Do you?"

I looked at her hand, with its topography of veins and wrinkles, resting on the table beside me. She was becoming old, I thought sadly. I looked at my own hands. They, too, were covered in the fine cross-hatching of use and reuse. Only children are perfect, flawless, unlined. "Dearest Ruth, I don't know. Yes, I suppose the eighties were a kind of revolution for my generation. It did seem fun to be all greedy and conscienceless, for a bit, though personally, I never made enough money to really believe in Thatcherism."

Ruth said dreamily, "What I really remember about their parties is the color. You can't imagine how we craved it. Len and Rupert mixed their own paints. Most people had this dreadful cream on their walls, and utility furniture, and blue lino. You could pick up beautiful antiques and button-back chairs for a few shillings because anything old was considered junk. But getting hold of color was impossible. . . . Anyway, there they were on three floors of the house, and your mother on the top, in a tiny bed-sit."

"On her own?"

"I think so."

"What did you think of her?"

"Well," said Ruth slowly, "I thought she was like Snow White."

I thought of the fairy story I had read, and was immediately intrigued. "Why?"

"Partly the way she looked. Black hair, white skin, red

lips. . . . In those days, there were only two colors of lipstick, like there were two kinds of woman. Either you wore pink, and were girlish and virginal, or you wore red, in which case you weren't."

"What color did you wear?"

"Oh, pink. I was a nice Jewish girl. Laura wore red."

"So she was a vamp." I didn't think the girl in the picture was a vamp.

"Well, there was a kind of innocence about her, too. Perhaps it was because she came from South Carolina." There was a world of metropolitan amusement, tinged with faint disdain, in Ruth's face.

"But you liked her?"

"She was irresistible."

That wasn't an answer. I knew it, and Ruth saw that I did. "She could charm the birds from the trees."

"Did that help when my father left her?"

To my surprise, Ruth had become quite agitated. I asked, trying to keep my questions general. "More innocent times?"

"Ignorant, not innocent," she said. "Sooner or later, it happened to us all. If you were left by your husband, things were pretty bad. It wasn't just being a lot poorer. Somehow the woman always got the blame."

She must have blamed herself, too; that was the only explanation for the fairy story about the two sisters I had read.

"Benedick?"

I jumped. "What was she like as a mother?"

"You could have been advertisements for the ideal family. Oh, we all made our children clothes then, just as we made all the food we ate and washed the dishes afterwards. But she did it better. As if competing, and in a contest she despised. That's why nobody thought she might need help. In those days, there wasn't the culture of complaint there is now."

I thought of my own hopeless attempts at being a single parent. "Come on, Ruth! You're the woman whose sons are notorious for going round in jumpers that are more holes than wool. *You* weren't like that, surely?"

She smiled, and relaxed. "You're right. I was what you'd call a slut, and still am. The laundry gets done but most of my clothes are held up by safety pins and I usually wipe the kitchen table with a kitten."

I smiled. "Was my mother lonely, do you think?"

"There was such prejudice against Americans. No matter what you did, or how educated you were, if you were a Yank you just had to be stupid, coarse, ignorant, and uncultured." Ruth spoke with unusual bitterness.

"Then it must have been hard for you, too."

"Yes. It was. It was so stupid, too. You still thought of yourselves as having an empire, as being superior."

I wondered why she kept digressing like this, away from what I was actually asking her. "So you're saying my mother's suicide was part of a larger picture?"

"I'm just trying to explain, I don't think it was just your father leaving her, or even her own mental condition."

"What do you mean, her mental condition?" I said.

There was a long pause.

"I think there were other things wrong, besides an unhappy marriage," said Ruth.

"Other things? What else did she need? She was married to my father for what, seven years? I should think that's enough to drive anyone to suicide. I know exactly how she feels, believe me."

"I'm sorry, Benedick. The last thing I wanted to do was upset you."

"I'm not upset," I said.

S I X

OUTSIDE, the long exhausts of airplanes grew like the ver-tebrae of some vast, insubstantial deity, then dissolved. In Ruth's garden, crocuses flared blue and yellow, gassy jets from the underworld. Every puddle, every window sema-phored a message to which my pulse quickened.

An orange rotted on a plate beside my bed. I watched the greenish-white of putrescence crawl like new continents across its surface. The relentlessness of nature fascinated me. I thought again about the two sisters, and the twelve men who had been able to command the seasons at will. Ruth brought me meals. She understood that I didn't want to be with people. I ate listlessly, and began to feel stronger again.

What dragged me down were the visits from my children and their world of Kellogg's and Disney and Pampers. By six every evening I knew that all over Britain parents were going through the same hell of trying to cook chicken nuggets with one hand, run a bath with the other, look at a drawing being thrust under their nose, and not drop the pan when kicked in the shins. I could yell, howl, plead, laugh, or cry, it made no difference.

"That's *my* toy. Mine!" Cosmo yelled.

"No, it isn't, it isn't!" Flora yelled back.

"Daddy! She hit me. I'll pay you back, you pig."

"Be quiet, please, both of you."

"Daddy, *Daddy!*"

Flora clung shrieking to my knees.

"Don't *do* that, I could spill hot oil over you."

"Daddy, tell her to give it back. *Give it back!*" my son screamed at his sister.

"I won't, I won't, so there!"

We swayed, all three of us tangled up in the current object of contention, a skipping-rope which one or other of them had been given for Christmas. It had handles painted and carved to look like two figures. One was a king, the other a queen. Each wore a crown of hearts. Cosmo wanted to use the rope as a harness to play horses in; Flora wanted to skip.

"Just stop it, both of you."

They took no notice. Eventually, I put the pan down and shouted, "Stop it, stop it, or I shall go mad!"

My children stopped hitting each other for a split second, then carried on as before.

It was in this kind of desperation that I turned again to the book I had found. The children were seated at Ruth's table refusing, as usual, to feed themselves. The list of what they would eat had now narrowed down to five things: chips, sausages, chicken, pasta, and pizza. Any deviation from this was met with fierce resistance.

("They're not malnourished," Tom said mildly when I asked his advice. "Just let them go hungry until they eat." Like most people without children, he failed to grasp that they would go hungry until two A.M., then wake the whole household demanding dinner.)

"Look, this is a book my own mummy wrote. She did the pictures, too. It's called *North of Nowhere*. Shall I read it to you?"

"What's it about?" asked Cosmo suspiciously.

"Magic. But if you want me to read, you have to eat three pieces of chicken."

"I don't eat chicken anymore, you know that."

"If you want a story, you have to eat."

There was more sulking and fighting. I sank into my own thoughts, only to have a small voice repeat the same question over and over again.

"Are there any animal ones, Daddy?"

"Are there any animal ones, Daddy?"

"Are there any animal ones, Daddy?"

My entire consciousness became a single, silent scream.

"Are there any animal ones?"

I roused myself. "I don't know. Let's see. This one has a picture of a girl on a black horse, Flora, look."

They both came, crowding on either side of me. There was a pen-and-ink drawing of a girl riding on horseback. It was the same as the face I had seen when the book fell open. My heart beat frantically in my throat like a bird trapped in a chimney. She looked proud and sad, and was wearing armor. One arm was lifted against the branch that raked like a clawed hand against her path. The horse arched its neck. Just ahead rolled what looked like a ball of light, spinning and shooting sparks of whirling white.

"Why is she dressed like a knight? Is she going to fight somebody?"

"I don't know. If you want me to read, you have to eat."

"Is that her ball? Is it magic?"

"It might be."

They both swallowed some food, obediently. "OK. Read it. *Please.*"

I began to read.

There was once a king who fell in love with the daughter of a weaver. She was as good and gentle as she was beautiful, but she had two older sisters who were not at all happy at their sister's marriage.

"Why should SHE have all the luck?" each complained to the other. "Why couldn't one of us have married him instead?"

For a short time, the king and his bride were happy together. A month later, however, war broke out. The king rode away to defend his kingdom and the poor young queen was left behind. She missed her husband, but her sorrow and anxiety turned to joy when she found she was expecting a child. Soon after, she gave birth not to one child but to three: a girl and two boys, as lovely as the moon and the stars. The two older sisters pretended to be happy for her, but in reality they were even more envious. Together, they plotted and schemed how to bring their sister to ruin.

When the king returned from the wars, the sisters told him that his queen had given birth to a cat and two dogs.

"Did she?" asked Flora, very interested. "That's nice."

"Don't be so stupid," said Cosmo. "She can't possibly, can she, Dad? Humans have human babies, not animals."

"You have to eat three more chips before I answer."

"OK."

The king, overcome with grief, ordered his queen to be shut up in a tower in the mountains. When his soldiers came to remove her, however, they found nothing in her chamber but a small white bird that flew away, nobody knew where. Everyone believed the queen must have died from shame, and the whole country went into mourning.

"Did she really die?" asked Cosmo.

"I don't know," I said, uneasily. "Let's find out."

In the middle of the night, the sisters had put the three babies into an old bird's nest and sent them drifting down the river that flowed through the king's garden. The wicked sisters thought the nest would soon sink, and that that would be the end of the little princes and their sister. However, the nest had been woven tight and strong, and so it stayed afloat a long time. The babies floated on and on, until they reached the outer edge of the city. That very night, it happened that the king's head gardener was walking in his own gardens along the river bank. Suddenly, he saw something floating on the water from which came a pure, shining light, like that of the full moon. He reached out towards it and there inside were two beautiful little boys and a girl.

Now the king's gardener had no children of his own.

"Surely," he said to himself, "God must have sent me these beautiful children." So he picked up the nest, carried it home to his wife, and brought the babies up as his own.

The princes and princess were so quick and clever that they grew up as lovely in mind as they were in body. The head gardener and his wife were so happy that they did not inquire where they had come from. However, they made sure that each had the best teachers that could be found, and the princess, just as much as the princes, learned how to read, write, sing, paint, ride, and hunt with the javelin and bow.

"I wish I could have teachers like that," said Cosmo. "I'd like to learn to ride and hunt."

"Be quiet!" said Flora. "When are we going to get to the horse?"

The princes and princess loved each other, and when the gardener and his wife died they vowed to live together, free from any ambition.

"What does 'ambition' mean?" asked Cosmo.

"Greed. Keep eating, please."

I could see Flora had lost the thread of the story, but she was still listening.

One day, while the princes were away hunting, an old woman came to the gate, begging for food. The princess welcomed her in, and after she had been fed and rested, showed her around the house and its grounds. The old woman admired everything, but when the princess asked how she liked their home, she answered, "It is beautiful, but it needs three things to make it perfect."

"Good mother," cried the princess, "what are those?"

"The first of these is the Bird of Truth, who can speak the language of men and sing more sweetly than any bird," said the old woman. "The second is the Tree of Light, which can reveal that which is kept hidden. The third is the Water of Life, a single drop of which, dropped into a bowl, will restore health to the living, even if they are at the very door of death."

"Ah, good mother," said the princess, "thank you for telling me of these things. But where are they to be found?"

"My daughter," said the old woman, "the road to these wonders lies before your gate. You only need to follow it for twenty days, and ask the first person you meet where the Bird of Truth is to be found. The Bird, in turn, will tell you where to find the Tree of Light and the Water of Life. But be warned: the Bird is well hidden, and guarded by an ogre who hates her, and keeps her guarded night and day by the Birds of Bad Faith."

Then the old woman went on her journey, leaving the princess lost in thought.

"I bet that old woman is a witch," said Cosmo.

"Why?" asked Flora.

"Old women in stories are always witches."

"No, they aren't."

"Yes, they are."

"No, they aren't," Flora insisted. There was a brief but violent exchange of blows.

"Daddy, Daddy, he kicked me!"

"Tell-tale tit, your tongue will be split, / All the birds in the world will have a little bit!"

"Do you want this story or don't you?"

When her brothers returned, instead of finding her lively and happy she was so quiet that they asked, "Dear sister, are you ill? Has something made you sad? Tell us."

The princess did not answer at first, but at last she told them of the old woman's words. "You may not think these things important," she added, "but I am sure that we shall never be happy without them. Tell me, then, who I may send to find them."

"Sister," said the first prince, "I would not dream of sending anyone but myself. I shall set out tomorrow."

Then the princess became afraid, for the old woman had warned her of the dangers ahead. But the prince smiled at her fears, and to reassure her gave her a knife from his belt.

"Pull this knife out of its sheath every day. If you see it clean and bright, as it is now, you will know I am alive; but if you find it stained with blood, believe me dead and pray for me."

The next day, the prince rode away. For twenty days he went forward, turning neither left nor right, and on the twentieth day he saw an old man, as thin and white as an ear of barley, sitting under a tree at the edge of a great, dark wood. This old man was a hermit who had sat still for so long that his hair touched the ground, and his beard and whiskers covered his mouth in a tangle of white. The nails of his hands and feet had grown until he could neither walk nor feed himself without difficulty.

The prince dismounted, and greeted the old man.

"Good morning, father."

"Why does he call him father? He isn't his father, is he?"

"To be polite." Another disquieting thought struck me. "Does—does Bruce ask you to call him Father?"

"No," said Flora scornfully. "We call him Brute."

I wasn't sure whether or not this was a genuine slip of the tongue.

The hermit answered, but his words were muffled by hair, so the prince asked if he could cut it away with his scissors. The old man nodded, and when the prince had trimmed his beard, and his nails, he thanked him.

"Our nanny does that for us," said Cosmo.

When he heard of the prince's quest the hermit became sorrowful.

"What is a quest?"

"A search. A special kind of looking for something," I said.

"My son, a great many brave men have passed by here and asked me the way to the Bird of Truth. Not one has ever returned. If you have any regard for your own life, go no farther but return home."

The prince would not listen, however, and at last the hermit reached into his bag and pulled out a shining ball.

"Throw this before you, and follow it. At the end of a day's journey through this wood, you will come to the foot of a mountain. Here, dismount and leave your horse. As you go up the hill you will see all around it a number of large black stones, and will hear on all sides a confusion of voices. The voices will say a thousand irritating things to discourage you and prevent you from climbing to the top. Take care not to look around, for if you do then you, too, will be changed into a black stone. If you reach the top of the mountain, you will find the ogre's castle. Here, you must wait until he has fallen asleep before going to the

aviary; but be careful not to touch any of the brightly colored birds in it. Choose the small white bird that is hidden in the corner, which the others incessantly try to kill, not knowing that it cannot die. But if you will take my advice, you will turn back."

The prince thanked the old hermit, but took no notice of his warnings. He set off, following the shining ball, which led him on and on through the dark wood, where thorns and branches tore at his clothes and flesh. At last he came to a mountain, high, barren, and black, made blacker still by the stones with which it was studded. Here he dismounted, and began to walk up. But he had not gone more than three steps before voices began to call out to him, though he could not see where they came from. Some said, "What's that lunatic doing? What does he want? Don't let him pass!" Others said, "Stop him, catch him, kill him!" or wailed, "Fool, beware, turn back before it's too late!"

The prince kept climbing for some time, but the voices became so loud that his courage began to run out. His legs trembled, he staggered, and at last, forgetting the hermit's words, he turned to challenge his tormentors. At that instant, he was changed into a black stone, and so was his horse.

There was an appreciative silence.

"What happened to the ball?" asked Flora.

"It went rolling back to the old man, I expect," I said.

Now all this time, the princess had been anxiously looking at the blade to see how her brother was faring. For twenty days it shone bright and clear, and then, on the twenty-first day, she drew it out and to her horror saw that it was stained and sticky with blood.

"Oh, what have I done!" she cried. "My longing has brought my brother to his death."

"I will go in search of him," said the second brother. "It may be that I will succeed where he has failed."

The princess begged him to stay behind, safe at home, but her second brother would not listen. He gave his sister his own knife, telling her to look at it each day, then rode off down the same road. After twenty days he met the old hermit. Once again, the hermit warned him not to attempt the quest, but the second brother was not to be put off. He followed the ball to the foot of the black mountain. Up he climbed, ignoring the voices that mocked and taunted until he suddenly thought he could hear his brother calling among them. He, too, turned, and was changed into a stone.

On the twenty-first day, the princess took the second knife from its sheath and saw that it was stained with blood. She wasted no time grieving, but told her servants that she would return after a month. Then she disguised herself in a man's clothes, mounted her horse, and took the road that her brothers had taken before her.

"Why did she disguise herself as a man?"

"Well . . . perhaps so that anyone she met would think she was strong."

"Girls aren't as strong as boys," said Cosmo, with satisfaction.

Flora looked at the illustration for a long time. "She is," she said.

On the twentieth day, she met the old hermit, who was sitting under the tree just as before. The princess shared her food and drink with him, then asked, "Good father, what is it that brings you here?"

"In all the time I have sat here, not one person has asked me that question," said the hermit. "Once, I was a weaver, the finest in the land, and I wove so fine a web that my cloths were bought for the king himself. But alas, the king took my youngest daughter as his queen, and from that union came such sorrow that I have abandoned the society of men, and sit in this wild place until such time as the Bird of Truth returns to this land."

"Good father," said the princess, "tell me, I beg you, where I may find the Bird of Truth, the Tree of Light, and the Water of Life."

The old man said, "I know very well where these things are to be found; but what makes you wish for them?"

The princess said, "I wish for them because, though I was contented before I knew of their existence, I shall never now know peace until I find them. Furthermore, my brothers have died in search of them."

So the old hermit told the princess what he had told her brothers. When he had finished speaking, the princess, who was both wise and clever, said, "From what I understand, the first difficulty is getting past the voices. I believe I may use something to help me."

"Daughter, what will you use?"

"I shall stop my ears with cloth," said the princess, "so that however loud and terrible the voices may be, they will make less impression on me."

"Of all those who have attempted this quest, not one has done this," said the old man. "Be of good heart, and follow the shining ball where it rolls."

The princess thanked him, and set off. At last, she came to the foot of the mountain. Very big it was, its hard stony surface baked in the heat of the sun, and as black as a cinder. Here she dismounted, as her brothers had done before her, and stuffed cloth in her ears. Then she began to climb, still following the shining ball.

It was just as well that she had blocked her ears, for the invisible voices were louder than ever. They jeered and jabbered and screamed, saying every kind of rude thing, telling her that she had no business there, that she was too weak and vain and foolish to continue, that she could never succeed where so many men had failed. But she climbed on. It was a long and weary journey, for the mountain was steep and jagged and soon every step caused pain, for first her shoes and then her feet were cut to ribbons. The black rocks stored the heat of the sun and gave no shade. Their shapes were full of menace and horror, and the higher she climbed the louder the voices became. Yet she kept climbing. At last she climbed so high that she came to the ogre's castle.

Its great, iron-bound door was open and she slipped inside. As soon

*as she did so, she heard the noise of a monstrous snoring. The ogre was
asleep.*

There was an illustration of the princess peering through an
open door. The ogre slumped in a chair, with a table beside him.
It was laden with flagons and platters of food. I looked at the food
more closely, and saw, with disgust, that it was piled high with the
bodies of dead babies. I turned the page, hoping my children
hadn't seen this.

*Quickly, she walked along the dark hall, past rooms where monstrous
shadows gathered and grew. At the very end of the hall was the aviary.
The princess entered, and was almost deafened by the clamor of birds,
each claiming to be the Bird of Truth. Very gorgeous they were, with their
plumes of scarlet and emerald, sapphire and gold, all shimmering and
shining like silk so that the eye was dazzled, and their voices were as sweet
as rain, but the princess looked neither left nor right until she came to the
darkest corner. Here, hemmed in by a flock of black crows she saw the
small white bird she sought, shrinking and wounded, but unable to die.*

There was a picture of the Bird of Truth. It looked delicate and
proud. The ugly black birds that surrounded it jabbed with their
hard beaks. Tears rose in my eyes.

"Poor bird," Cosmo said. I covered his hand with my own.

*The princess stooped, and picking the Bird up tenderly, she held her to
her breast and left, followed by the screams of the rest.*

*"Hurry," whispered the Bird. "You still need the Water of Life and
the Tree of Light, but the ogre will not sleep for much longer."*

"Where may I find them?" asked the princess.

*"If you look carefully, you can see the Tree of Light," said the Bird,
"in the woods behind you. Break off a small twig and when you get home
plant it carefully in your garden. The next day you will find a Tree of*

your own. The Water of Life springs from its roots; take a small flask, and when you pour it into a pool, the Water will become a fountain."

It was just as the Bird had said. The princess broke off a twig and filled her flask with the Water, then set off down the mountain. As she passed the first of the black rocks she saw the shining ball stop. She thought to herself that the Water might release the rock from its spell, so she sprinkled a few drops on it. As soon as the Water touched it the stone melted, and there in front of her stood her beloved brother. She then sprinkled the next stone and from it sprang her second brother. Great was their rejoicing, and as they went down the mountain the princess released each and every one of the men imprisoned by the ogre's magic. Soon the air was filled with their voices, and the neighing calls of their horses. Back they rode through the dark wood, until they stood before the old hermit. The Bird of Truth flew at once to his shoulder.

"Father, come with us if you have not forsworn the company of men," said the princess, "for the ogre's power is broken, and none now will pass this way."

So the old hermit was lifted up onto the first prince's horse, and brought back.

When they arrived home, the princess went straight to the garden and the Bird of Truth flew high into the branches of a tree. She began to sing, and the garden was filled with a thousand songbirds, but none as sweet as the Bird that drew them. The twig from the Tree of Light was no sooner planted than it grew into a great Tree itself. The Water of Life the princess poured into a marble basin, and at once the Water bubbled and shot into the air as a fountain of living gold.

Now such wonders are not kept secret, and it was not long before news of them reached the palace, and even the ears of the king himself as he sat silent and mournful in his gloomy chambers. He sent a message to the brothers and sister, saying he would like to visit them. At this, the princess became anxious, lest the king were angered that they had made their gardens more splendid than his.

"Do not fear," said the Bird of Truth. "You will see, everything will turn out for the best."

The day of the king's visit arrived. The moment he entered the courtyard, the king was struck, not only with the grace and beauty of the brothers and sister, but with the mysterious feeling that he had met them before.

There was a picture of the king. I stared at it. I, too, had the mysterious feeling that I had seen him before.

"Why, these three could be my children," he thought, sadly.

It was a portrait of my father as a young man.

The garden soothed his spirit. Great, spreading trees sheltered them from the hot sun, and a delicious scent of flowers filled the air. The fountain sent its golden Water high into the sky, and the Tree of Light cast a soft radiance from its silvery leaves. As the king walked, he became aware that hundreds of birds sang all around them.

"Why are there so many birds gathered here?" he asked.

"My lord, it is because the Bird of Truth draws them," said the princess.

"How is that possible?"

So the princess told him the story of how she had found the three marvels.

"I can scarcely believe it, though the proof is here."

The Bird said, "Yet you believed your queen gave birth to a cat and two dogs."

"Who said that?" demanded the king.

The little white bird cocked her head and looked at the king.

"This is the Bird of Truth," said the princess. "Will you not greet the king?"

"I wish the king and his children long life and great happiness."

At this, the king sighed deeply, and said that he had no children.

"But you do," said the Bird. "You have two sons and a daughter as beautiful as the sun and the moon."

At this, the king grew pale, and asked, "Why is this called the Bird of Truth?"

"Because what I say is true," sang the Bird. "Your queen bore you three children, and they are standing here before you."

Then the king remembered his mysterious feeling that he had met the brothers and sister before, and understood that it was because they reminded him so strongly of himself when young, and his beloved wife. His eyes filled with tears, and he embraced them as a father. They were indeed his long-lost children.

"If only my queen were alive," he said at last to the Bird. "I have done her a great wrong."

"She is alive," said the Bird.

"Where is she? For if my children are alive, she cannot be guilty of the crime of which she was accused."

At this, the old hermit, who had been listening and watching, stepped forward. "No, my lord," said the old man, "she is not."

Then he lifted the Bird into the radiance from the Tree of Light. Its form unwound like that of the finest cloth and in place of the Bird stood the queen, laughing and crying for joy. The king knelt down and asked her forgiveness. And so the queen and her children came home to their rightful place.

And what of the evil sisters? Rather than face the king in his anger, they packed their bags and ran, all the way to the ogre's mountain, and there they stand to this day as black rocks in the baking sun.

THE ASCENT to Liz Shaw's flat was made in a mahogany coffin. It creaked and stank. When she opened her door, the cause was easily identifiable. Several cats were lolling around like dollops of jellied fur. At the sight of me, they ran and hid. Once they had sussed me out as someone who disliked them, I had no doubt they would return to jump on my lap. Cats, like women, have always been good at humiliating me.

"Well, now," said their owner, with apparent affability. "Tea?"

I shook my head. I was surprised at my temerity in turning up here at all, and so, I suspected, was she.

"So," she said now, "what do you want to know?"

"Oh, well," I said. All at once my quest seemed a foolish one. "What she was like. Life in the Crescent."

"Ah. The Crescent. It was wonderful then." She glanced around at her flat. Perhaps she found it as depressing as I did. The smell of cat was nauseating. Ruth had cats, too, but hers were lean and clean and happy. (They were also Burmese, which is the only breed of cat I have any time for.) I wondered whether these wretched moggies were ever allowed out. It didn't seem likely. A kind of uneasy pity for them, and for her, began to creep up on me. Perhaps she saw this. She said with a return to her aggressive manner, "Primrose Hill began to go down as soon as it was discovered by all those fashion people. There was a point when it seemed you couldn't go out the door without that man David Bailey snapping away. Have you ever seen the original *Avengers* series? Diana Rigg's flat was supposed to be in Chalcot Crescent, and it was always filmed with just one car, hers. The only car then was actually your father's. That was Laura all over."

"How do you mean?"

"She always had to *have* things. Telly, washing machine, even a gadget for ironing sheets. She wouldn't make do, like the rest of us. We all used buses and public transport, but *she* had to have a car. Everybody was counting the pennies, but we didn't mind, d'you see? We didn't mind because we were all in the same boat. There was none of this awful greed you have now, and none of the crime and violence. You didn't bother to lock your door at night, you left money out on the step for the milkman. . . ." She puffed on her fag. "It wasn't just Primrose Hill, it was everywhere. There was the NHS and the schools and the public libraries, and they were all wonderful. Now everyone is impatient, acquisitive, spendthrift, and rude. And you don't even know what's been lost."

I was bored by this little homily. People of my father's generation always go on about how greedy people are now. They forget, we have no choice.

"More innocent times," I said.

"Yes. Mothers made their children's clothes, you scoured junk shops for furniture and got everything secondhand, unless you were rich. Your parents certainly weren't, or they'd never have bought a house with a stone tenant."

"A *what* tenant?" I asked, startled.

"Stone. As in millstone. It meant you got a house more cheaply, but you had the inconvenience of having some old biddy living with you, often in the best rooms, paying you a couple of shillings a week. We had two. I'm surprised they weren't mur-

dered, they lived for sodding ever. We waited until the eighties
for our second one to shuffle off her mortal coil. You, of course,
were lucky—your old crock moved off to a bungalow almost at
once. I expect Laura persuaded him. She was good at that."

I let this pass.

"Do you have his address?"

"No, of course not. He'll be dead, now, he was an old man
even then. Anyway, your parents got the whole house, dead
cheap, within a year of buying it, and lived in the bottom two
floors. So then you had tenants—oh, it must have been a regular
little goldmine."

I could hear the envy in her voice. "But they were hard up in
the beginning," I prompted.

"But she and your father *had* to have a new bed, and not just
new either. It was *king-size*."

I said, surprised, "Why not? Why shouldn't they be
comfortable?"

She said, angrily, "I know it's different now. *You* want to have
everything right away. *My* generation saved for our luxuries. The
only thing *we* ever bought on credit was a gas stove."

I almost laughed. Was this what old age consisted of? The
petty resentments about who had what, and when? God pre-
serve me from ever reaching it, in that case. Better the knife and
the rope.

"You seem to know a lot about their domestic arrangements."

"She was spoiled," said Liz, grimly. "Anyone could see that.
Probably had niggers to do everything for her, where she came
from. Have you ever been there?"

At first I was too stunned to answer. Not even Howard had
ever used this word, perhaps the only word that still has the power
to make somebody of my age feel like erupting into fury. Automatically, I shook my head.

"Why not?" she asked, curiously.

"Never had the time."

"I thought time was the one thing actors were always rich in," she said.

I wanted to hit her. Why had I been able to hit Georgie, and my children, whom I loved, and not this poisonous old hag? A cat reached up and stuck a claw into me. I swatted it away, as unobtrusively as possible.

She sniffed. "Dreadful place, America. A country of urban peasants, that's what they are. Take a peasant off the land and you lose everything good about them. She could only peel potatoes backwards—funny, what you remember—though she did keep that house immaculate, I'll say that much. Too immaculate. Primrose Hill wasn't the place for washing whiter than white. It was for artists."

"But she *was* an artist," I said. Her rudeness was a kind of marvel to me. She was like one of the girls in my mother's stories, only able to spit out toads and snakes every time she opened her mouth. Again, the cat stuck a claw into me. I removed it firmly.

"You've never seen anyone less likely," she said. "I mean, if someone is creative, you usually know, don't you? They have a certain look. I mean, look at me. Or you. I suppose you're unemployed most of the time, though."

"Yes," I said. I understood, now, that she was trying to make me angry.

She gave another sniff.

"What is it, exactly, that you do—or did?" I asked, feeling it was time to turn the tables a little.

"I produced children's television programs for the BBC," she said, with immense hauteur.

"What—making cars out of toilet rolls?"

The cat extended its claws and jumped up onto my lap. I yelped. My hostess gave a grim little smile. "I was the one who gave your mother the idea of writing for the children's market. Just push her off if she's annoying you. Not that she ever repaid me."

"Is that why you disliked her so much?"

"That would be convenient for you, wouldn't it? No. We were friends, at first. I took her under my wing, in fact. She had no family over here, and was pregnant with you. Your parents were renting a flat in Fitzrovia, and were desperate to move back to this area—she'd lived round the corner in a bed-sit with a couple of pansies. I told her about the house that was coming up for sale next door to me—I knew the old biddy who owned it had just popped her clogs. I thought it would be nice to have a young family living there."

She smiled, as though she were actually a benign person.

"Must have been mad. The last thing we needed was a baby bawling his lungs out day and night on the other side of the wall. A right little pest you were, too. Scribbled all over my skirtings the moment you got the chance. But I told Laura where to get things, I introduced her to people. She changed from being charming and grateful into the most frightful snob."

Being indebted to someone like this would be unbearable, I thought. She would constantly be reminding you of what you owed, implicitly or explicitly. If Laura had spurned this woman, I only thought more highly of her. "So you knew she was an illustrator?"

"Yes. She was always in a frenzy, drawing. God knows where she found the energy. Of course, in those days mothers thought nothing of leaving a child in a playpen. That's why you all learned to read young, too bored not to."

"Didn't you *admire* her at all?"

"I found her single-mindedness quite chilling."

I thought of how hard my wife had worked to support us while I was unemployed. It was one of the slow poisons that had killed our marriage. She had been single-minded, too. To me, that had been part of her attraction. "If she'd been a man," I said, "would you have judged her so harshly?"

Liz drew on her cigarette, then blew out a long stream of smoke. I was itching for a fag myself, but hadn't brought any. "She just never took any notice of other people's feelings. What really turned me off her was when we met one morning in the street, and I was in tears because my cat had been run over. Do you know what she said? 'What a pity. I'd always thought it would make rather a nice hat.' I've never forgotten that."

I thought of my mother as Cruella De Vil and suppressed a smile. She had obviously been joking, though as I eyed the creature on my lap I thought perhaps not. It was digging its claws into my thighs in an ecstasy of sadism. So my mother hadn't liked cats either. Good for her. In my experience, it is always the most selfish and cold-hearted of people who become mawkish over felines. I suspect it is because they instinctively recognize a nature even more unpleasant than their own.

"And my father? Did you know him?"

"Your father, frankly, stuck to his world and we stuck to ours. Your generation wouldn't understand. *Mustn't complain*—that's what should be on our tombstones. If you were ill or depressed, you took tranquilizers—there was absolutely no expectation that your husband would help. Very different from nowadays. I bet you're expected to change your children's nappies, aren't you?"

I shrugged. Actually, if I was being honest, I had changed my children pretty infrequently. Like most dads, I had dealt with the first nappy of the day, then opted out. Coping with Flora on my own these days was a hideous reminder of just how unpleasant and inconvenient it could be. But I had done the cooking and the shopping during my periods of "rest," and I had not complained.

"Of course, your mother never discussed her marriage; one didn't, in those days. But everybody knew Howard had affairs. He was devastatingly attractive, you know. A big bad wolf. The sort of man who should never get married, but always does."

I was silent. My father hadn't changed. "Did he have affairs with anyone in the Crescent?"

She was longing, I could tell, to claim Howard had slept with her. "Why don't you ask him?"

Liz lit another cigarette, and in the sudden flash of her lighter I had a vision of how she had once been: never pretty, but *gamine*. Too bitchy and strong-willed for Howard, I suspected.

"Look," she said, exhaling, "you have to realize, people did screw around. We drank—my goodness, how we drank!—and there was a lot of behavior that I suppose you'd now call bad—but that was what it was like. Of course, there were a lot of perfectly nice, dull couples who eventually moved off to the suburbs where they belonged, but . . . we were the first to discover Habitat and plonk, you see. We had Japanese lanterns and bookshelves in our alcoves. We had the Pill. We—well, you should look at the cartoons Sam Viner did for *The Cutting Edge*. That was life in the muesli belt." She took another drag and smiled. "Before it all went pear-shaped. The trouble was, Laura didn't fit in."

I wanted this horrible woman to stop, now. I could see the white Bird of Truth surrounded by jabbing beaks. The delicate, innocent angle of her head, one fragile claw raised, unable to fly away. "Except that she was a kind of genius," I said.

"Only as a children's writer. Children are closer to lunatics or animals than human beings."

"At least children grow up," I said nastily. "Unlike cats."

She looked at me with delighted malice. "Quite. But then, cats cause so much less trouble in a divorce."

• • •

I WALKED to my interview for *Jigsaw* in Soho in a fury. I had learned nothing, except that she had disliked my mother. Had Ruth known just how hurtful the encounter would be? I couldn't believe she did. My mind seethed, filling me with a vast energy. It had seemed like a good idea to see Liz beforehand; now I cursed my stupidity. The last thing I needed was to lose my cool.

I jumped onto a double-decker bus, grasping its pole, pale and spiraled like a unicorn's horn. It was one of the old Routemasters. Bright red on the outside, cream on the inside. The roof curved overhead like a shell, and a long wire jingled *ting-ting!* when you pulled it for a request stop. The sort of bus everyone loved and thought of as the quintessence of London; it was now being scrapped as inaccessible to the disabled. I had dim memories of traveling on this sort of bus as a child, and of the feeling of excitement it had given me. I wondered whether my mother had taken me on trips in one. If only I could remember her, if only.

At Piccadilly, I jumped off again in front of Hatchards. Black and gold, it exuded the same air of dignity and propriety as a gentlemen's club; yet its wares were for the most part produced by people who lived lives one step away from the gutter. Although from what Liz said, my parents had scarcely been poor. I paced up and down in front of the windows. When people bought a book, did they ever consider the suffering that had gone into making it? Of course not. Why should they—any more than they did when watching an actor dredging up the thing that made him act? I could see my mother sitting at a table, drawing, her dark hair held back in a bun like a pioneer woman's, pouring out her frustration and her brilliance. *And when the ink begins to write, / It makes the paper black and white.* As though it happened without volition.

I bought some fags in preparation for the inevitable wait. Here was the usual anonymous door, here the stairwell, open the doors and there were the people. The receptionist was too busy flirting into a banana-shaped telephone to do more than scribble my name. People who think acting is glamorous or exciting can never believe that you're treated like dirt by virtually everyone. That's why most actors, if successful, become producers.

There are days when I think that any job, absolutely anything, including mending sewers or picking mushrooms, would be preferable to mine. When you first feel the vocation to be an actor it's like falling in love. Nothing can stand in your way, you're going to conquer the world, become rich and famous. It's only when you start to fail that you see the other side. Georgie used to laugh at all the gushing and flattery that went on at cast parties. Well, you try standing up just once in front of a room of total strangers and singing karaoke, and then imagine doing that for a living. You try it. See how dignified and secure it makes you.

The dingy leatherette sofa, overflowing ashtrays, and faces of the other, rival actors there all filled me with despondency. Each of us was trapped in professional limbo, too old for the juvenile leads but unable to move on to the big, serious stuff. I knew most of them, vaguely. That one talking into his mobile phone had won the Ronson Prize at RADA the year I'd been at Webber Douglas; another had even had a decent-sized part in *Taggart*. The bald bloke who had just gone in looked a thousand times more like a detective than I. I didn't stand a chance. I had to believe I stood one, though.

I waited. And waited. It was better to be called for an interview than not. It meant that the casting director thought that I had once done *something* right. But then, so had these guys. Whether you succeed has nothing to do with talent, and almost everything to do with the way you look. That is the first thing you learn. Georgie told me it was like being a woman. These people would know within about thirty seconds of clapping eyes on me whether I was right for the part, long before I'd begun to speak or read. It was a waste of time after that—yet somehow you had to perform, to try to overcome the odds. Auditions are a chance to seduce them into forgetting what you look like. At least that's the idea.

This room was really terrible, worse than a dentist's. Fragments of the conversation I had just had kept flashing in my mind like shards of broken glass. *Your father was a big, bad wolf.* . . . *She was spoiled.* Sometimes, if they were casting for a big-budget film, I got to hang out in a swish hotel suite. More often it was this. Ritual humiliation. I remembered how, when I had first met Georgina at the Edinburgh Fringe in a production almost entirely populated by Oxbridge graduates (most of whom, annoyingly, had gone on to become extremely successful), the director had drawled, "Oh, I'd love to make a film, but if only I could make one with all my friends instead of having to use ghastly people."

It had dawned on me then that by "ghastly people" the director meant professional actors, the ones like myself.

I glared at a bubbling tank filled with orange fish kissing their own reflection, doubtless installed to improve the *feng shui* of the company. You could never have too much luck. I'd been through this so many times. Pretty soon, I'd sink to the level of simulating sex for beer commercials in cinemas. Oh, let me get this part, and my life back, I prayed.

As the girl continued to chatter on, my temper rose. Everyone was smoking. It was like acting: you knew it was killing you but couldn't kick the habit. The itch to start pacing the room became irresistible.

The murmur of voices went on. How many? At least three. Every ten minutes, an actor came out and another went in. They were all pretty much like myself, mid-to-late thirties, well built, white. Not exactly housewives' choice, but not completely hideous either.

At times like these, when my entire existence seemed to hang by a thread, there was nothing I wouldn't do to work again. You understand at such a moment why actors become whores, why we have painful plastic surgery, why the obverse of becoming a god is being more frail and foolish than any normal human being. All around me there were as many as fifteen frantic little performances going on at once as everyone tried to reassure themselves that they could still *do* it. But none of us were confident that we could, not really. What I had said to Ruth was what I said to myself: nobody's life depended on a good performance. Why couldn't I just see it as a job? Why did it demand so much agony?

I went to the toilet. My heart throbbed, shaking my whole body. I added to the stench, and rage came over me. *Why* did these places never have adequate ventilation, when *everyone* got the runs before an interview? I staggered to my feet and began to bang the window over and over. Oh, bars of my body, open, open. Flakes of thick, yellowed paint jiggled loose.

"Benedick? Are you there?" It was the receptionist. I went on banging. I could hear other voices. Still the window would not budge.

"Are you OK?"

I said, scarlet with embarrassment and exertion, "Just trying to get this *bloody* window free."

"They want to see you now."

"Fuck!"

I punched the window with my fist. Glass exploded everywhere, cutting my hand. The pain was sweet and vivid. Faces crowded the doorway.

"Hey, mate. Chill out," said one of my rivals, oozing concern.

"Are you feeling OK, Benedick? You look a bit strange."

"I'm OK, right? I'm OK."

"You should get that seen to."

He'd probably played a doctor in *Casualty*. In another moment he'd be telling me I was going to be all right.

"You're going to be all right," he said, not missing his cue.

"Just fuck off."

I ran my wounds under cold water and slicked back my hair. I looked pale, my eyes wild, my hair darkened by sweat. Laura's face was looking out of the mirror. I stared at my reflection, until the hand dripping blood began to sting again. Someone brought me loo paper to staunch the flow, and then I followed the receptionist into the room where my fate would once again be decided.

EIGHT

T HREE BORED FACES looked at me. The table in front of them was, as it always is, heaving with half-empty plastic cups of cold coffee. The producer looked about ten years old. The director so thin and nervy he had to be coked to the eyeballs. The casting director, a woman.

"Hi," she said. I liked her immediately.

The others said nothing, only stared. This is the way producers and directors usually behave. I sometimes wonder whether it's a psychological test to see who will break first, or whether they think you are a sort of freak in a show. I could feel my tongue shriveling in my mouth. I wasn't going to be able to speak. It was just like the first weeks at Ruth's. Still they went on staring at me. I stared back.

"We meet again." The woman shuffled momentarily among her pile of CVs and failed to find mine. "I remember your Mercutio at Stratford last year. Very exciting, very physical, almost out of control."

"Thanks," I said, in a whisper. Words came back to me. I cleared my throat. "That's how the director wanted it played."

Not a good answer. Or it might make me sound like just the sort of accommodating patsy they wanted. I wiped my face.

My hand throbbed. I'd probably smeared blood on my forehead now.

"But you managed to bring a sort of anguished thoughtfulness to the part as well."

"Thanks. Anguished thoughtfulness is my specialty." I grinned, unconvincingly. The producer stared at my teeth. Had I remembered to brush them? Shit. No.

"What d'you think of the script, then?"

"Mmm," I said.

It was important not to be too enthusiastic, or intelligent. If you were too intelligent they thought you'd be stroppy. They assumed you were thick, as a matter of course, because what intelligent person would be doing this? If you're ever spotted reading a book or a magazine, or anything with an intellectual quotient above *Viz*, it has to be for a part. On the other hand, if you don't seem interesting, you don't stand out.

"I liked the balance between the two partners. Sort of Mutt and Jeff."

Every bloody cop show had a Mutt and Jeff partnership, so this was safe ground, but producers and directors always thought you were too dumb to notice it.

"Yes. Greg is the foil to Frank, who is wiser, more cautious, conservative—the true hero. Your part, Greg, admires and respects him, but also resents his way of doing things by the book. You're more anarchic."

"He wants to prove himself to him, sort of father and son. But not compromise himself?"

"Right."

I smiled. Gradually, I could feel the smile turning into a kind of rictus. I switched it off.

I loathed their bloody script. But I needed the work.

"So, what have you been doing since then?"

I looked at the faces in front of me, trying to block out the smell of my fear, the pain, a light in the building opposite. I described the part I'd played in the Brit-flick, and suddenly, my voice came out more strongly. I could *do* it. I could see a way to say these banal phrases as though they mattered. I hadn't felt like this since I'd played Mercutio. The nerves pounding through me like electricity through a wire, I was lit up, alive, I was the eagle in the sky. I had an audience again. Then, suddenly, it was time to shut up. I had just enough control to realize that.

Neither the director nor the producer had said a word.

"What do you think?" said the casting director to them appealingly.

"Yes," said the director at last, in a long drawl. "I'm not convinced. Greg's more of a comic character."

My heart sank. "I can do comedy."

"It needs . . . camping up, somehow," the producer said.

At that moment, I had the most extraordinary sensation. It was as though my blood had started fizzing, and the lid of my head flipped open. I just stopped caring. I leaned forward and said, "It's always a one-way street with you lot, it's always what *you* want, never what *we* want, isn't it? We don't have shit for brains, we don't have feelings, we're just puppets on a string. I wouldn't want this part anyway. The script stinks like a week-old fish."

Silence. They all looked at me with identical expressions of astonishment.

"Come, now," said the director. "We don't necessarily mean that—"

"Get stuffed."

I rose, and walked out of the room. The faces of the two remaining actors turned towards me. "You can go home," I said. "I got the part."

Outside in the street, I laughed and laughed. A wig-out, a genuine wig-out, in an audition. I strode through the revolving door of the Slouch Club, where my membership had expired too

recently for anyone to eject me. There, hunched by the granite
bar counter, was Sam Viner.

T HE ONE obvious person, besides my own father, whom I
had not approached for information was Ruth's ex-husband.
It would not be easy under the best of circumstances. For one
hour every day, somewhere between the second drink and the
fourth, Sam Viner was said to be the most charming man in
London. Then he turned into a monster. Yet he still produced
two cartoons for a national newspaper (not counting the half-
dozen rejected ones) five days a week, before returning towards
the bar stool where he now sat, swiveling like a discontented eye.
I could see he was drawing a picture of an enormous frog in a
dinner jacket. It was delicately eating a pair of human legs. He
had often said that if he weren't a cartoonist he would have become a mass murderer. Sam was not to be approached without
caution.

I thought of what Liz Shaw had said. Sam's first success
had come from satirizing Primrose Hill people during the sixties
with *The Cutting Edge*. Their shifting values, trend-setting tastes,
and intellectual affectations had been attached to characters
so similar to individuals in real life that many professed outrage. (This was, of course, nothing to the feelings of those left
out.) He must have known my mother, as well as my father. Perhaps they had even influenced each other. It was worth asking,
anyway.

"Dick!" he said, with morose pleasure. I was relieved he recognized me. "You'll pay your round, eh? A double vodka and
tonic." I nodded to the barman. "I hear you're living with Ruth."

"My wife left me."

"Bloody hell." Sam hated being alone, I remembered. He
had gravitated towards Soho as soon as he left university, mostly

for this reason, a move that eventually ruined both his liver and his marriage. "Who for?"

As always under scrutiny, I felt myself become stupid. Sam is one of those people like my father who are surrounded by an invisible force field. It isn't just my weakness of character that makes me feel this. I've known of people, usually other journalists, who get sucked into his way of seeing things to the extent of becoming alcoholics also. For him the worst crime was being boring or conventional. I said, "A short, fat slap-head."

It was when Sam smiled that you suddenly saw the cruelty in him, amoral and almost childlike in its purity. I admired him for this. He simply didn't care about other people, or his inner life; he was pure mischief. "They're the ones you have to look out for."

"He's her publisher at Slather and Rudge. She says he's going to rebrand her."

"Ah. Like a cow." He nodded at my hand. "Been in a fight?"

"Casting director," I lied.

"That's the spirit. Kick them when they're up."

Our drinks arrived. I poured my vodka over my cut hand, and nearly fainted. More blood welled up, shockingly red, but there didn't seem to be any glass in the cuts.

I said to the bartender, who was eyeing me in a languid fashion, "You wouldn't happen to have a first-aid box, would you?"

A hush fell as I dripped onto the floor. The pattern of crushed peanuts on the carpet showed up the red almost too well. All the women there were wearing pashminas tied round the neck with identical knots. They looked hungrily at my blood. I could almost feel the snick of disappointment when my hand was bandaged.

"Sam—was my mother very upset when my father left her?"

"No, actually, she seemed relieved, much happier and livelier."

I could feel my jaw drop. This was contrary to everything I had ever believed. "Are you sure?"

"Of course, afterwards we all thought it must have been a front. But she was a very strong woman."

I thought of the princess in "The Bird of Truth." Perhaps I was wrong to see her as a cowering dove. Perhaps she had strode up the mountain boldly, ignoring the whispers of discouragement and opprobrium in her ears. I felt my own back straighten.

"Why do you think she killed herself?"

"I don't know. It could be, as I say, that it was all show. But it could have been anger, too. She was a very angry woman, I always felt. Well, you could see that in her drawings."

I winced.

"Mind you, I'd have been less surprised if she'd murdered Howard. She had this streak of wildness in her that I only saw at the end. In the beginning she seemed like every other corn-fed American girl I'd ever met. Yet she changed the way I saw things."

"How?"

"I'd never have done that series about the Crescent if she hadn't made me see how absurd a lot of our friends were."

This was the most interesting thing I'd heard about her so far. "Did she suggest *The Cutting Edge* to you?"

"No. Sometimes she'd say something I could use for a caption. She called one liberal who was always spouting on about the Third World 'the black man's burden.' I remember thinking that was very funny. But it was more the things she *didn't* say. You could feel all this intelligence gathering like a thunderbolt. She didn't talk much, but you somehow knew."

"Can you read so much into silence?"

"Yes. Even your father could. I did a cartoon of him once as a hunter with a gun going off at half-cock in front of her." For a moment, he looked ashamed, yet pleased, like a little boy. Sam's crueler portraits were always excused to mutual friends of the subject as an aberration.

"Are you saying *he* was afraid of *her,* not the other way about?"

Sam sang, *"If all the world was paper / And all the sea was ink / If all the trees were bread and cheese, / What would we have to drink?"*

Nobody in the Slouch even blinked. They all knew, as I did, that from now on the malicious streak in him would grow wilder. I sighed in frustration. What he was telling me couldn't be true.

"She was very angry when he left. She kept talking about needing to go back to America, and about how mean he was with money. Even quarreled with Ruth," he said. "I mean, I've never managed to do that."

"It's not a situation from which many emerge with dignity," I said.

"If she hadn't asked for sympathy, she'd have got more. As it was . . . well, Nell was young and pretty. . . ."

I could see Sam was approaching the aggressive stage, in which he would invite violence as others invite friendship, but I didn't want him to stop talking. "Did you know my mother professionally?"

"Not really." He sounded bored. I had to keep his interest.

"Did you fuck her?"

He perked up, then snorted. "Not my type. Too bloody frigid."

I wouldn't have been surprised if they had had a fling. Sam is said to have been even handsomer than his sons, before drink took a wrecking ball to his face. I've often thought my father's hatred of him was at least partly due to sexual envy and rivalry.

"Did you discuss her work?"

"No," said Sam, shortly. "I didn't even tell her I thought it was good. It wasn't fashionable, of course. People don't want to admit that children are drawn to the dark, that they can make monsters out of a chair and a couple of shadows. I didn't think she needed praise. She seemed so confident. She'd never even gone to art school, she'd taught herself, somehow. She didn't seem to need my opinion."

Again I could see her, striding past the black rocks and their whispers of fear and failure. Yet the whispers had penetrated after all.

"Was she a feminist?"

"No. Very good at being a traditional housewife. You know, doing fifty-seven things with mince while the laundry dries and the bailiffs bang on the door. I think that's almost why your father married her. He thought she'd be the perfect supportive spouse, once he gave up journalism and became a real writer. Does he still bang on about fiction?"

"He mostly seems to think it stopped with Kingsley Amis. I seem to remember him liking some other miserable bugger. Coetzee, I expect."

Sam said, grinning, "He once showed me something he'd written. It was full of this stuff about living in Paris, and having it off with tarts. What was the one he published? *The Laughter in Jakarta*?"

"The Lowland Fling."

Sam snickered. "Jesus. Why do they do it? Give me a good columnist ninety-nine percent of the time. Much less pretentious and they stand their round."

Taking the hint, I ordered another vodka and tonic for us both. Sam went on, "That was her revenge, you see. Off he went, pursuing anyone with a glimmering of talent—painters, poets, playwrights, musicians, film directors, novelists—hoping it would rub off on him and never seeing that the person under his nose was extraordinary."

"Surely that wasn't the only motivation?" I said. He took no notice.

"Of course, what she did was in a marginal field. The vast majority of people supposedly interested in the arts never look at children's picture books. It's only when you've got young kids, or you're into graphics, that you notice."

"What do you think was so special about her?"

Sam was now visibly drunk, his nose like a boiled beetroot. His voice seemed to carry the remaining force of his personality. "The good ones—they're like poetry, indes, indest—oh, fuck. Like a rubber ball. You can throw it against a wall and it will keep on bouncing back. How many times do you reread picture books? A hundred times? A thousand?"

"A lot drive me mad."

"Well, yes. Mice in frilly fucking aprons. The nuclear family living in a suburban semi. The token black person. But the good ones are a kind of visual poem . . . as much a . . . the real thing . . . as . . . . it's—I don't know what it is."

I could see he was starting to lose it. How much time had passed? There were more and more people coming into the club now. My own edges were blurring, too. I looked at my reflection in the mirror opposite, and again my mother's face stared back.

"Come on, it's . . . you know. A short circuit. Children know, we forget. Some don't. . . ."

Then he said, aggressively, "Who the fuck are you, anyway?"

My heart sank. "I'm Benedick Hunter."

"Yes, but who *are* you?"

I said humbly, "Oh, nobody, really. We used to be neighbors in Primrose Hill."

"Just because we've met doesn't mean you're allowed to talk to me. Piss off!"

I slid off my stool, and went.

I HAD LEFT no address for my father to find me, but he did. One day I was summoned to the telephone. I hoped, when Ruth handed the receiver to me, that he hadn't been too brusque. When I took it, a woman's voice said, "Is that Benedick Hunter? Will you hold, please, I have your father on the line for you."

There was a pause, then my father said, "Dick. I've had an interminably tedious time tracking you down. Or rather, my secretary has. Why haven't you left a number for anyone?"

I was silent.

"Dick? You're not *still* sulking, are you?"

"Don't call me Dick," I said automatically. "You know I hate it."

He and Georgie both did this. With a surname like mine it's no joke.

"I've always called you Dick, and I always will," he retorted at once. "What does it matter what I call you? Why didn't you call *me*?"

"I'm homeless, penniless, and in the middle of a divorce. All you ever do is tell me to change careers."

"So you *are* still sulking. I thought so." He sounded almost pleased. I sighed, inaudibly. Neither of us got any pleasure,

I believe, from our encounters, and yet he persisted in trying to run my life, or at least in criticizing it. No turn unstoned, as we say in the theatre. The few people I've ever told about my father thought it must be some kind of adolescent locking of horns. Even when I tell them that he sent me away to boarding school at eight, and cut me off without a penny at eighteen, that I was effectively brought up by my best friend's mum, they insist he can't be a monster. The most dangerous thing about him is that he can make himself seem so reasonable. I wondered if my mother had felt this, too. *I'm leaving you, but it's really all your own fault.* Georgie had said this to me. I was sure Howard had said it to my mother.

As if he sensed my resistance, his tone became more aggressive. "Why have you been going round asking questions about Laura? . . . Benedick?"

I wondered who had informed on me. Not Ruth, I was sure. "I have a right to know."

How was it possible to be nearly forty, and still feel like a little boy when he was angry with me?

"I see. Why didn't you come to me?"

I could have said, Because I've learned never to ask you for anything, or trust what you say, but I thought I had better try diplomacy. "I did. You never gave me proper answers."

"I gave you answers appropriate for your age and understanding, as I recall." The underlying contempt for me in his words was all too clear. His voice became muffled. "Just tell him to go on holding, will you?" Then, to me, "I'm in hospital, didn't you know?"

"No."

"Well, you'd know if you read the *Chronicle*," my father said, as though it were a personal affront that I did not. "That boy of Ruth's, your friend, put me under for the op. That's how I found out where you are."

"So now you've found me," I said. There was a long pause, then I gave in. "Is it serious?"

"Not really, just bloody sore. I've had a hernia. Otherwise, my consultant tells me I've the constitution of a teenager."

In someone other than my father, this piece of vanity would have made me smile. It was probably true, however, so I did not.

"Where are you?"

"The Lister. You can drop off into Fortnum's on the way and get me some Angostura bitters."

"I don't think I'll be able—"

"Why? You're not working, are you?"

"No."

"Thought not. Oh, and Dick?"

"Yes?"

"Don't talk to anyone else about Laura. It's really nobody's business, outside the family."

"What family?" I said; but he was gone.

I WENT, of course. When somebody is unpleasant to me, it only makes me more eager to please him or her. I am never able to say what I actually think of them—assuming I've worked it out.

His room overlooked a park by the Chelsea Embankment. The windows were full of pale spring light. My father lay on his bed, half-asleep, hair disordered, dressed in a blue hospital robe rucked up almost to his waist. Even this didn't cause as much shock as the sight of his exposed legs, terminating in a shriveled, dusty-looking tuber. I stared at it. How long was it since I had seen the thing that had made me? I had a vague idea of it being huge and meaty compared with my own little tassel of flesh, which crawled and shrank even at the memory. My father grunted and woke. The room was suddenly charged with his personality.

"Dick."

"Hi." I always avoided calling him anything. "How are you feeling?"

"I'm on morphine," said my father languidly. "Marvelous stuff. No wonder they keep it away from the middle classes. I can press this button, see, when the pain gets too bad."

"Is there pain?"

I was prepared to pity him, if there was. He saw this and said in his old manner, "Not so you'd notice. Your friend Tom is bloody marvelous. Should have sent you to become a doctor."

"I didn't do the right A levels," I said tonelessly. He watched the TV with flicks of his eyes. The sound was turned down, as some ads were on. We both watched a cartoon of Rapunzel trying to grow her hair for the prince to climb up and rescue her. She drank a lager, and it suddenly cascaded to the ground.

"How's the world of architecture?"

"Theatre."

"Of course, theatre," he said, irritably. "The roar of the greasepaint, the smell of the crowd. Have you brought what I asked for?"

"I don't have the money."

"You don't? Why don't you do some commercials, then, hey? I see all sorts of actors doing those. That's where the money is."

My father's ignorance of the theatre is only matched by his contempt for it.

"I know."

"Too stuck up, I expect. We should never have sent you to that bloody boarding school. That's another thing I blame the Viners for. You'd never have got this acting bug at a good grammar school like mine."

I looked at his face and felt sorry for him. Sometimes I think the only way we can communicate is when we both lose our tempers with each other. It's a more charitable view than the other, which is that he's a wicked old bastard who has never loved me. I was trying to remember that he was, after all, a sick man. He would be seventy next year, and for the first time ever looked old. He asked, "How are the kids?"

"Fine."

He always asked this; not that Howard ever showed any interest in Cosmo or Flora when presented with them in the flesh. He expected doglike devotion merely because he was their grandfather. It never occurred to him, I think, that a child's love has to be earned. The only reason why they even got presents at Christmas or on their birthdays was because my stepmother Nell always enclosed a couple of book tokens for them. They didn't regard these as proper presents.

"Interesting, the way children grow up to be so different from their parents," he mused. "Tom's a splendid fellow."

I felt a surge of anger that my friend should so effortlessly win what I had never had. Howard went on, "Not like his poisonous shit of a father. The day that man chokes on his own vomit in some Soho gutter will be one to celebrate. I could have sued him for that cartoon strip of his."

"What cartoon strip?"

"*The Cutting Edge.* Before your time but—"

"Oh, yes, I know about it," I said.

"I should have taken him to court," said my father. "Bastard."

It always amazes me, the enthusiasm journalists have for suing each other. The one freedom every journalist will passionately defend is freedom of speech, otherwise known as the freedom to be cruel about other people. Yet they are utterly humorless about anyone who does the same thing to them. If actors tried to sue critics for what was written about us, we'd be laughed out of court. I didn't say any of this, of course.

I sat down, unasked. Waves of violence were coursing through me, just being in his presence. The room was as bland as only expensive private hospital rooms can be—lots of stripped blond wood and the general anticipation that strapping Swedish nurses dressed in starched white uniforms would be coming along shortly to give you a massage. It smelled faintly of overripe fruit and the sort of extravagant flowers celebrities send each other to maintain the fiction of their existence. My father followed my gaze.

"Help yourself to some grapes. Or wheatgrass juice. It's from Planet Organic. Nell brings it every day."

"No, thanks."

"Disgusting looking, isn't it? I thought Angostura bitters might liven it up."

Now I felt guilty. I hadn't brought what he asked for, partly because I'd had all my credit cards revoked and partly out of pure bloody-mindedness.

"Why this sudden interest in Laura?"

"I found something of hers while I was packing."

"What?"

"A book of fairy stories. *North of Nowhere.*"

"Oh, those." He waved a hand dismissively, then winced as it pulled on the drip.

"Yes, those. You didn't take her seriously. Why not?"

"*I* was the writer, wasn't I?" said Howard, with a kind of amazement. "I was the one who got a first in English from Cambridge. She was merely doing books for tots. I thought her drawings were mildly interesting, though far too gloomy. I had no idea how ambitious she was."

I stared at him. "Why shouldn't she be ambitious? Because she was a woman?"

My self-righteous tone was undercut by the recollection that this was one of the words I had hurled at Georgie's head. I hadn't meant it as a compliment either. Applied to a man, it is simply a fact of his being; applied to a woman, it is never flattering. I had always known that Georgie was marrying beneath her in choosing me. Most women do; but usually they have the tact not to remind you of this.

"That wasn't the deal," said Howard.

"Neither was infidelity, I imagine," I said. He ignored me.

"Let me tell you, she was very pleased to become my wife." His voice was rising. I was getting to him. "She wasn't earning anything before she met me, she was just a jobbing illustrator drawing ladies in sensible dresses. An *American* illustrator. I gave her the leisure to get on with her own work. Not that I knew she was doing it, until she showed me her first book. And no, I didn't take a handful of kiddie stories seriously. Like every other sane person, I'm resistant to believing in little people with hair between their toes or whatever. Laura, like most of her infantile nation, found fairy tales deep and meaningful. I didn't and don't."

I wavered. For most of my life, this had been my attitude, too. Then I wondered if it *had* really been mine. Howard, like all columnists, had an opinion about everything and it somehow seeped into the very air you breathed. You could ask him what he thought about widgets and he'd come up with twelve hundred pithy words to persuade you that widgets are good. Or bad. But now I was prepared to fight. I thought of the girl in the picture. *She* hadn't been afraid.

"Didn't you see there was something different about her work? Her pictures, even?"

Howard said, "No."

"But other people have. People you must take seriously."

"Oh, for God's sake, you're judging me with the wisdom of hindsight. Why do you think everyone looks back to the fifties and early sixties as the golden age of the family? Because that's what it was."

"Oh, sure. The Ladybird version of British life, all home-baked scones and women doped up to their eyeballs with Valium.

I'm not completely ignorant, you know, despite the school you sent me to. Anyway, what this has to do with my mother and your treatment of her, I can't imagine."

My father said, "It has everything to do with our marriage. Most people, whatever you think now, were happy with the conventional life. She was, too. Except that some worm in her brain made her turn against it."

"Or against you. If she hated you, didn't you give her just cause?"

"No, not in the beginning." Howard fell silent, then said urgently, "Come on, Dick, you know better than to fall for this nonsense. You don't have to be PC with me. They aren't serious people. She wasn't a genius. There are the feminists in their delightful fishwives' ghetto, but the big stuff, the stuff for grownups—women aren't up to it, are they? Unless they're dykes."

I was used to my father's provocations. Often, they were no more than a preview of the column he was writing. I could see the headline now: *WHY WOMEN WILL NEVER BE SERIOUS ARTISTS*. For a while, when I had been trying to like my father, I had persuaded myself that he was parodying what he secretly hated. Perhaps that's how he began. I had been taken once to see Marcel Marceau perform a sketch, in which a man tries on different masks, one of which eventually sticks to his face. It reminded me of my father. Perhaps there was still a decent human being lost in there. But I had given up trying to find him.

"I don't even know where she's buried."

"She isn't. I had her cremated. I scattered her ashes from a rather unattractive vase at the top of Primrose Hill. I can't think of anything worse than rotting in a grave."

"You left me with nothing of her."

He gazed out of the window as if looking at the past. A leafless plane tree etched shadows across his face.

"I thought her obsession with fairy tales was part of her

instability, perhaps even the cause of it. At first it all seemed perfectly natural and proper, a part of her becoming a mother. I quite liked that one about the magic box. Then there was *The Angry Alphabet*. That made me less happy. She'd started doing the same thing as that toad Viner, using real people's faces, people we knew. It seemed unnecessary, embarrassing, vindictive. Why couldn't she just make it up? She drew herself as the Quiet Queen, and me as the Kicking King. I didn't know what to think. And then having the same three women she had as Mostly Mothers in 'M' repeated as Witches in 'W.' One of them was Ruth, did you know?"

"Was Ruth upset?"

"No. She saw it as a joke. But another woman, a neighbor of ours, didn't."

I made a guess. "Liz Shaw?"

"Yes, her. She attached herself to us like a sort of leech. Laura couldn't bear her. Neither could I. But to draw your next-door neighbor and your best friend like that . . ."

"So you didn't like the book," I prompted.

"No. It *was* angry. And repulsive, too. Don't you think?" I shook my head. "The last picture, 'Z,' has the little girl zipping herself into a body bag."

"I haven't looked at it for a long time."

"Well, you should."

"Don't you see anything else? That it was funny, for instance?"

"No. I think the feminists are right, up to a point. Her work *was* about anger. I just don't think she was right to be angry, or that she deserves the sort of seriousness with which she's now treated. She's joined the pantheon of oppressed women artists, and anything about the other sides to her has been whitewashed out. But then suicide is always a good career move."

I couldn't bear his sneering tone. If I were to succeed in topping myself one day, he would at least find an exception to his rule. "That was the story you put about, wasn't it? Impossible to live with, crazy, ambitious—what about your own part in all this?"

Howard glared back. "I suffered, too, you know. She wasn't the only victim. We got married so young, and we had no idea, really, what life was about. We were so happy, that first year. After you were born, that's when it all started to go wrong. When she was down she wouldn't lift a finger. She'd just sit about, not wanting to go anywhere or do anything. Anything, you understand."

"It's called post-natal depression. Lots of women get it."

"It wasn't just that. There were months when she seemed quite normal again. When she was happy, she could stay up all night laughing and talking and dancing. Sometimes it became an embarrassment—"

"Why?"

"Well, I know it's different today, we're all touchy-feely, including the bloody prime minister, but women just didn't kiss people in public then, particularly not strangers. Some people thought she must be drunk. Or on drugs. If I'd been a jealous man . . ."

"But you weren't, were you? You were too busy having it off with Nell," I said.

"She drove me to it."

"Oh, sure. Your wife didn't understand you."

"It's true. *She* was the jealous one. She gave me so much grief over the affairs I didn't have that I thought, What the hell, I may as well do what she's accusing me of. But I didn't, for a long time. She was so vulnerable. I was always aware of that."

"Yes, she was vulnerable, wasn't she? I dare say you didn't take that seriously, either."

I had a vision of my mother lying on her grave in the woods like Snow White, waiting for the prince to kiss her. Only the prince turned his back and rode away on his white horse, and all that was left was a six-year-old dwarf weeping by her coffin.

My father groaned. "I can't make you understand, can I? We stuck it out for seven years. Believe me, I tried. I suffered, too. I used to go to sleep worrying about Laura and wake up worrying about Laura. I was wiped out. She never even saw me as having any existence independent of her."

"Did you see that she had an existence independent of you, though?"

"You're not so clever in your twenties as you are in your sixties, but I did try. I even moved out and stayed with Ruth for a while. Funny, how history repeats itself."

I was startled. "You did? I thought you said you hated Sam."

"He wasn't around too much. He's really spent most of his life in Soho. She's an extraordinary woman, Ruth. I hope you're paying her rent."

I gritted my teeth. I knew what was coming. "I'm a friend of the family."

"That's not good enough. Manners maketh man. She's not a wealthy woman. You aren't her son, you're an adult, you should be paying her something—"

I said, breathing hard, "That's between me and her."

The next thing he would be asking if I'd written a thank-you note to Nell for the appalling tie she always sends me for Christmas. I hadn't even been able to hang myself with the bloody thing.

"No, it isn't," said my father. "If you don't have the money, I'll write her a check. You shouldn't be sponging off other people."

"Oh, for Christ's sake!" I yelled. "I'm nearly forty, and you're still treating me like a child! Just shut up!"

There was a discreet knock at the door. A smiling, round-faced nurse poked her head in. "Everything all right, Mr. Hunter?"

"Yes," we both said automatically, glaring at each other.

"I'm going now," I said, and walked to the door. I could tell from her face that she thought I'd been unpleasant to a sick old man. The failed son of a famous father. This was the only role allotted to me around Howard, so I did the one thing I could do, and left.

EVEN WALKING from Chelsea to Hampstead wasn't enough to exhaust me. The utter blackness of spirits, the rage, the hopelessness intensified. I bought a bottle of vodka on the way back to Ruth's, and drank over half of it. Most days, now, I started drinking vodka as soon as I got up. I was drunk by the time I got to Belsize Park. I threw myself down, fully clothed, on the bed, and stared at the red darkness. A voice welled up like light. Faint at first, then stronger:

> The water is wide, I cannot get o'er
> And neither have I wings to fly
> Give me a boat that will carry me o'er
> And thus will part, my love and I.
> I leaned my back against an oak
> Thinking it was a trusty tree
> But first it bended, and then it broke
> And thus was my false love to me.

The voice faded, and just as I was about to fall asleep, I recognized it and started up. There was a half moon outside, and my room was full of moving dark, the shadows of leaves and branches.

"Mummy?" I whispered. "Laura?"

For a moment the sense of her presence was so strong I thought I could reach out and touch her. I was quite certain she was in the room with me. It was as though she had never left. A feeling of absolute bliss enveloped me, so complete that I thought anguish or loneliness could not touch me again. Then, just as suddenly, a reek came at me. I shrank back under the duvet, terrible visions of my mother as a moldering corpse seething through my brain. I could hear myself whimpering, convinced that at any moment a bony hand would clutch me.

It was only when I became calm enough to switch on the light that I realized the smell came from the orange, rotting on a plate beside my bed.

I COULDN'T find a copy of *The Angry Alphabet* on Ruth's shelves. Perhaps she hadn't kept it. It was still in print, though, and I could remember quite a few of the drawings.

Georgie had never really believed in me as an actor—any more than my father believed in my mother as an artist. When I had been in a play or film I needed someone to listen to my complaints about how badly written the script was, how at five o'clock every evening my nerves were shot, about what a nightmare some actress was. I knew my rants were tiresome, but I needed her sympathy and approval just as much as she needed mine when she had a bad review. Yet where I gave, she only took. I wasn't entitled to grumble. I wondered whether my mother had felt the same. I thought of the desolate figure I had first seen on opening *North of Nowhere*. How unhappy she must have been, to draw herself like that. But of course she must have been unhappy. You don't kill yourself otherwise.

Or perhaps she was, as my father claimed, simply mad. Most men believe this of women, privately, and they haven't been married to Georgie.

She was now insisting that I look after the children full-time, without intermission, for two weeks over the Easter holidays, while she finished a novel.

"Don't you have a nanny now?" I asked.

"She left," Georgie said. "I'm trying to find a replacement, but they're all useless. All the Australians and Kiwis are staying home for the Millennium. I just can't cope." For once, she sounded quite human.

"What about Bruce?" I said meanly.

"He isn't their father. You are. You have to take them. You did it before. They've seen you playing teachers and colonels and the lieutenant of a spaceship—just pretend it's another role."

"That's a cheap shot."

She knew it was. In an altered voice she said, "Cosmo *needs* you. Look, I don't want to go back to lawyers to sort things out. We agreed we would have joint custody. I look after them most of the time, but I need a break. Can't we be civilized about this?"

When I pointed out that almost every time I looked after Cosmo and Flora they inflicted grievous bodily harm on me, she snapped that I was still a lot more capable of controlling them than her seventy-year-old parents. I knew her in these moods. At a certain point in a book, she becomes completely unbearable. A hack called Ivo Sponge once asked me what it was like being married to a novelist.

"Like being the back half of a pantomime horse," I told him.

"I'll take Flora," I said. "I can't cope with Cosmo."

"No. If you take one of them, it has to be him. He needs you, Dick. Sons need fathers. Just do this for me."

I told her I'd think about it. She gave a muffled scream and put the phone down.

"Do you think most creative people are mad?" I asked Ruth, later. She stopped peeling potatoes and looked at me over the top of her half-moon glasses. I sometimes had the suspicion that she wore these as a sort of prop, much as she practiced her quilting. "What do you mean?"

"Well—" I floundered. "Seeing things differently. That's how madness starts, isn't it?"

She said with asperity, "We all see things differently. It's the *degree* that can shade into insanity, or into great insight. But by and large, I'd say that those who are engaged in making a work of art render chaos into order. That is the opposite of madness."

She jabbed the end of the peeler into the potato and twisted out a green eye. I scratched my neck. Most days, I couldn't be bothered to shave, but neither could I face my reflection with a beard. Given the choice, who would want to leave childhood, and exchange a perfect, odorless, hairless body for the monstrosity of adult life? And yet I could remember so little of my childhood, so little of what really mattered, that it often seemed to me as if I had been asleep until awakened by puberty.

"Do you think *she* was, then?" I continued.

"Creative or mad?"

"Well, I know she was the first."

"I don't know. I've asked myself that so often. It's probably the single biggest reason why I went on to become a psychotherapist instead of staying as a doctor."

"Canst thou not minister to a mind diseased?"

"Exactly. Sometimes you can, and sometimes you can't. It's a bitter truth, which most of my profession finds it extremely hard to admit, but in the gravest cases there still isn't anything as effective as ECT. On the other hand, there are types of psychosis that respond to drugs; and other conditions that seem to be lessened or cured by talking. I don't know if talking would have helped Laura."

"Did she talk about herself at all?"

"No. Female friendships were different in those days."

I sighed mentally. Here we go again, I thought. Why did these people insist there was such a great gulf between their time and mine? Was it true, or was it just the difference between youth and age?

"We were all so inhibited that even to say the word 'contraception' was unthinkable," Ruth said. "You never talked about problems, particularly those in your marriage—all that came a decade later, with feminism. If your husband came home and your friend was visiting, she'd instantly get up and leave."

I grimaced. In a similar situation now, as I knew from experience, the husband was the one who crept away, while the women stayed in the kitchen laughing—probably at him.

"But didn't she talk about anything else? Her home, where she'd come from?"

"Not really. She was very reserved, even by English standards. She had such a strong personality, and yet she was so vulnerable, too. I don't think a lot of English people saw that. They expect us to be brash and childish and ill-educated—" She saw my face, and laughed. "Yes, yes, they do! Or should I say, *you* do, as you've grown up an Englishman, bristling with assumptions about other people based on the way they talk and look. I always felt that some shadow lay on her. I think her work was a way of coping with that. She couldn't escape, as I could, into the professional life of a teaching hospital. So she escaped by turning inward."

I, too, had learned to retreat into my head. I had never been any good at lessons, only the drama classes. Again, I felt the sense of closeness to my mother.

"So you think there *were* shadows?"

"There are in everybody's life. Why do you think fairy tales have such resonance? It isn't because we believe in their morality. It's because they dramatize situations, internal conditions, which we feel tremendously, yet can't rationalize."

Ruth exasperated me when she talked like this. I kept feeling that she was trying to shepherd me into some sort of Jungian archetype, instead of answering my questions. I persisted. "What were *her* shadows, then? You must have some ideas."

"No. I don't know what had happened to her, or where she came from. I just knew she'd come from the Carolinas. She was, well, a lady. She used to make me feel like a klutz, now and again." Ruth paused. "But she was horribly poor when I first met her, so poor that I know for a fact she only had one pair of shoes. On the other hand, she had the most beautiful leather valise with her initials on, so there must have been *some* money somewhere. When I met her she was just about scraping a living by her drawing. It was quite a good time then, to be an illustrator—newspapers and magazines used hardly any photographs, so people needed them more. I think Len and Rupert helped, a bit. They knew all sorts of people in the publishing world."

"Did she tell you anything about her family?"

"Not much."

"What did my aunt look like? Did she say anything about my mother?"

"She was quite similar to Laura. Older, and less pretty, very charming, dignified—Southern, I suppose. She had a child with her, a little girl. Her husband had stayed behind."

"Is she still alive now, do you think? What did you say her name was?"

"Lily."

"Where in the Carolinas did she come from?"

"One of those towns, Charleston, I think. I know Laura wasn't quite so amazed by how old everything was as I was, coming from New York."

"Do you know why she came to England? My mother, I mean."

"No. I asked her once, when we were both complaining about how cold it was here, and she just smiled and shrugged. Of course, a lot of my countrymen came to Europe in the fifties and sixties. It was what you did if you were intelligent. Now, they don't want to know."

The water is wide, I cannot get o'er . . . I thought of the song that I'd heard, and shivered. Had she wanted to go back, because my father had betrayed her, but been unable to?

"Why did you all end up in Primrose Hill? Was it just coincidence?"

"It was cheap, close to a park and the center of town, including Fleet Street."

"Cheap? Really?"

"In the late fifties this whole area, including Belsize Park, was a slum. Very different from now, I know. It was actually quite hard to get a mortgage on anything Victorian or earlier. Respectable people were supposed to go off and live in the suburbs. You only lived in town if you were arty, or poor, or both. Camden Town was so run down, you wouldn't believe it. I was thrilled because it was still so like what Dickens described, but it was grim, too. There was a lot of bomb damage, and the houses looked like old women huddled together. There was all this soot from the trains running into King's Cross. Then the Clean Air Act was passed making it illegal to burn coal, and suddenly the air was like crystal."

"Do you feel more English than American now?"

Ruth shook her head. "Every now and again I can feel my accent slipping and becoming like that appalling Grossman guy on TV, but I'm still one hundred percent American. Your mother changed, though. After a while, she sounded completely English. At least to me."

I didn't like this. I wanted my mother's otherness. "So you think she was trying to fit in?"

"Maybe. It's hard to be different, after all. Or it could have been a sort of snob thing. The South is very Anglophile. I don't think any of us realized quite how isolated she felt. You know what it's like when you've got small children. You become very selfish, don't you? Your—"

I interrupted. "But people can be *driven* mad, can't they? It only needs other people repeatedly telling you you're crazy, or just your wife or husband—and you start to doubt whether you are or not. I mean, Georgie keeps telling everyone I'm bonkers. So everyone started treating me as though I am. People believe the more powerful partner in a relationship. That's why I don't believe what my father says. It makes me so . . ."

"Mad?" said Ruth.

I HAD LITTLE DOUBT that my behavior at the audition would have repercussions, but I found it hard to care. The one advantage of depression is that it leaves very little room for anything but itself. Often, it was as if I was fighting for my very existence against an invasive presence that I could only feel, not see. I began to believe, with a part of my mind, that it was an actual presence, that my mother was sitting in the shadows of any room I was in. It was like my children, who firmly believed that their toys were alive. If I turned quickly, I would see her. I yearned to do this, yet dreaded it.

For years I had refused to think about her, and now she dominated my thoughts. Some days, my curiosity about her was the only thing that kept me tied to life.

Yet I couldn't do to my own children what she had done to me. It wasn't just cowardice that had made me draw back from the high jump or the deep cut. I had to save Flora and Cosmo from this. Again and again I would ask myself, Why couldn't she have endured? Even when my father had left her, there was still somebody who needed her. Myself.

When it was my turn to look after Cosmo and Flora, however,

I could understand her desperation all too well. I felt her bones move under my flesh; her rage was my rage at being forced into the groove of routine. I never imagined that I would find myself uttering such timeworn phrases as "Because I say so," or, "I'm going to count to three and *then*—" or, "If you don't eat it, you'll have no pudding."

But I did. An anagram of "parent" is "entrap." At times I was like a wolf in a snare, so desperate I would have chewed off a leg to escape. It didn't help knowing that I was a bastard for feeling this. I was permanently irritable, angry, or in despair; even when my children struck me as comical or endearing I was secretly furious. People try to make you feel bad about admitting to not finding parenthood an ecstatic experience twenty-four hours a day. They forget that children are the closest example of an alien species any adult is likely to encounter. Cosmo and Flora could weep over the imaginary wounds of a cartoon creature yet watch a real animal crawl or gasp its last with utter indifference. Their egoism was even greater than my own. If I asked them to be quiet, or told them that I was feeling ill, they took no notice whatsoever, but went on monotonously repeating some demand or complaint. Their own minor cuts, on the other hand, had to be treated with lavish sympathy and an expensive holographic sticking plaster.

Laura had killed herself when I was Cosmo's age. She had been at least a decade younger than me. How did *anyone* survive it? As babies and toddlers my children had been relatively impotent. Now, not only did they fight each other continually, they had also begun to turn their pitiless gaze onto me. Cosmo would begin sentences with the ominous words, "I love you, Daddy, but—"

They were either deliriously happy or utterly despairing. Often, it was hard to tell the difference. Their laughter sounded chillingly like sobs, and their sobs like laughter. One moment they'd be playing amicably, the next trying to kill each other. Worse still, they were so cavalier about their own lives. It was an irony I alone could appreciate that I so often had to prevent them from effortlessly scoring the goal I was too cowardly to achieve. Their fingers would creep into plug sockets, their legs would carry them to open windows; they would be drawn irresistibly to childproof bottles of dangerous medicine, to running with sharp knives, to each and every method of self-slaughter my own body had protected me from.

"Never, *never* put anything round your neck," I'd say, beneath the very light fixture that I myself had pulled out of the ceiling. Then they would scream, and cry, and demand *why* they couldn't wear their medals from Legoland in bed, and the noise would go through my aching head like a dentist's drill.

Flora's acts of violence usually happened after an episode of *Xena, Warrior Princess* on TV. Cosmo's furies were quieter but more alarming. He would bite his own arm, overwhelmed with frustration, leaving purple bruises. I saw these with deep anxiety.

He was fiercely jealous of Flora, which of course made me even more defensive of her. I had longed for a sibling myself, I couldn't understand why he failed to see what a blessing she was. But they were chalk and cheese. He was an unusually tidy child, always folding his clothes and putting away chairs he used to climb up on things, whereas she was incorrigibly messy. He wanted everything in its proper place; she went with the flow. Worst of all was when he woke up and couldn't find his tiger, Ti-Ti. Then I would have to stumble around at three A.M., searching. The whole house rang like a glass with his screams until they were reunited. I dreaded to think what would happen if this confounded toy, a casual purchase from a motorway service station in France, were ever to be genuinely lost. If only he could be like Flora, who casually bestowed her affection on at least a dozen soft toys called Beanie Babies with the same promiscuity she would no doubt display in later life towards boyfriends. Cosmo was like myself, I thought, faithful to one alone. It was this likeness that made him unbearable.

"I'm so sorry," I said to Ruth every Saturday and Sunday morning. "I hope he didn't wake you."

"I just turn over and think, Thank God they're not mine," she said, smiling. "*Hazak!* Believe it or not, one day you'll look back on all this with longing."

Ruth really was the kindest person in the world, I thought. I knew I should be searching for a flat of my own, now that the money from my half of the house had come through. I couldn't bear it, though. The few one-bedroom flats I could afford were so dismal, so far away, that they sent me into a frenzy of misery.

"Do you think their behavior is normal?" I asked anxiously.

"It's not abnormal."

"I was wondering, well, if it's the effect of the divorce."

"What's important is that you're still a part of their lives. He'll adjust. It's harder for him because he understands more. He's a very intelligent child."

"I know," I said gloomily. "Just impossible to live with."

I longed to be the kind of father Howard had never been for me. I didn't want Cosmo to grow up with the sort of scars I had carried from my own parents. Yet I had no illusions that I was any more successful as a father than I was as an actor.

I would take them to the swimming pool, to the park, to the cinema; I read them stories and all the rest of that stuff; but I was still hopeless. Modern men are not supposed to be bad at fatherhood now, but I am. Even before they arrived I was exhausted; by the end of every weekend I felt poisoned by fatigue. Occasionally, they could be pleasant, clean, charming, funny, and well-mannered. Then strangers would nod and smile and say, "*Oh, how sweet!*"

When they were frightful, of course, nobody wanted to know.

You're marooned on a desert island with two little cannibals, desperately signaling for help, and everyone sails past pretending they haven't seen.

"So, tell me about your new school," I said to Cosmo. We had driven to Primrose Hill for a walk. They were like animals, needing copious amounts of regular exercise every day.

"It's plopsy."

I had no idea what this meant, but it didn't sound good. "What's wrong with it?"

"I just sit and play with a little stone in break time." He looked up mournfully. I hardened my heart. I had seen this expression too many times in Disney cartoons not to recognize it for what it was, a shamelessly manipulative piece of behavior. "The teachers say I should play with the other children."

"Why don't you?"

"Their minds are tame. Mine's like a wolf's."

Something about this remark made me shiver. "Can't you tame it for some of the time?"

"The others say I'm mad."

I said, robustly, "Well, you're not. To be mad is not the same as being different."

His face closed. I tried to think of another question. At that moment, Cosmo darted forward and grabbed a ball out of Flora's hands. "That's *my* ball! How dare you!"

She let out a yell and kicked him. He burst into tears and hit her back. I grabbed them both as they howled and lunged to inflict further damage on each other.

"Beast, you beast, I hate you!"

"Nah-nah-nah-nah-nah!"

"Stop it, stop it, both of you!" I cried.

Flora lay on the pavement in utter abandon sobbing, "He *snatched* it, Daddy, smack him. Smack him!"

"Apologize," I said sternly, bending over my son. Cosmo

rolled his eyes and actually gnashed his teeth. A small snigger escaped me like a fart.

"Don't laugh at me!"

He lashed out. I roared in surprise and pain. Blood spurted from my nose and started to choke me with its warm, salty taste. Both children burst into even louder screams on seeing it.

"It's all right, *it's all right*," I said angrily. "Stop making a fuss."

"I'm so sorry, Daddy, I'm so sorry," sobbed Cosmo, heartbroken. Flora's fat, damp little hand insinuated itself into mine.

"Are you going to die?"

"No, of course I'm not going to die," I said vehemently. They didn't believe me.

What luxury it must have been, once upon a time, I thought, to ignore your offspring if you were a man. Astonishing to think that for hundreds of years, men like myself had simply been able to *walk away* when confronted by any difficulty, and be applauded as masculine for doing so.

The blood was caking my nostrils. The children, reassured, ran off ahead of me, down the hill. Morosely, I followed. Cosmo dribbled the ball. He was as good at this as Flora was bad. Georgie had once written, *Most men would be happier, not to say more dexterous, making love with their feet.*

In the back of my mind, there was still the hope that my wife would come to her senses and return. I didn't blame her for ruining our lives. If anyone was to blame, it was our children. The childless believe the horror of parenthood to revolve around dirty nappies for the first twenty minutes of every day, but what they don't understand is how much worse *everything else is*. When I thought of how Georgie and I had once been able to go to parties, stay up late, get drunk, read, take foreign holidays, and actually make love most nights instead of just having sex, I felt such sadness I groaned aloud. Of course she wouldn't come back. Who in their right mind would want to?

I walked down Primrose Hill for the first time in over thirty years. This park, with its tall trees, was just as it had been when I had flown my kite, hoping to find Mary Poppins at the other end of it; the lanterns stood at the borders of Narnia. Here was the green hill where Pongo and Missus had barked for news of their puppies in *101 Dalmatians*. Here, one snowy day, I was tobogganing on the precipitous slope with Tom behind me and cracked my forehead on the ribbed post halfway down. I still had the scar. The double-decker buses still sailed past the collapsed spider's web of the aviary at the zoo, and on towards Baker Street, where Sherlock Holmes lived. All this had been my kingdom; all this came flooding back as Cosmo and Flora romped across the muddy turf.

The playground was walled, as it had always been, by a hedge of hawthorn. Here, to my dismay, was change. The big brass slide burnished from all the little bums slipping down it was gone, replaced by a monstrous construction in dull steel. The swings where I had scabbed my knees had been moved, and had rubberized tarmac beneath them; the sandpit had grown immense. There were rockers shaped like horses and sea horses, rainbow-painted roundabouts. But the smell of creosote and childhood, the shrieks and cries, were still exactly the same.

My children tumbled and swooped through the chill air. All the other adults here were fathers, too. Were they divorcees, or just kindly husbands allowing their wives a lie-in on a Sunday morning? I felt I should carry a placard on my back saying, SHE LEFT ME. And yet, how could I blame her? I had always been slightly dazed by my good luck in getting her in the first place, the Frog Prince who knows he's really a frog, no matter how many times he's kissed.

We walked back along the little parade of shops. I was enraged by all the changes. This had once been like a street in a French textbook: pub, dairy, bicycle shop, cobbler, greengrocer, ironmonger, post office, chemist, butcher, baker, and another pub. As with all such streets now, it was full of useless shops. The chemist was now a delicatessen; the former butcher's a shop for pampered cats and dogs; the ironmonger's a café. In fact, cafés and restaurants were everywhere, and each one was populated by actors more successful than me, it seemed. I avoided looking them in the eye. There was still the greengrocer, the post office, and that essential requirement for civilization, a small independent bookshop. Otherwise Primrose Hill was hideously trendy.

Nostalgia overwhelmed me. The stones had turned gold when it rained, like those in *Dick Whittington*. Girls once played hopscotch on these stone slabs. *Tread on a crack, break your mother's back.* You could hardly see them now. Every street had cars parked, bumper to bumper—Jaguars, Porsches, Mitsubishi Space Wagons. *Your father had the only car in the street.* In Chalcot Square, where we had played at being Daleks, the straggling bushes and chicken wire had been replaced by ornamental trees and iron railings. All the scruffiness and raffishness were gone, and with them the magic. Or perhaps it still existed, but I couldn't see it anymore.

I walked on, following my children's voices. My footsteps seemed dogged by a faint echo. I went into the library. The smell was immediately familiar, a sweet smell, as though the air were powdered with angel cake mixture. According to large banners, it was under threat of closure. Yet another piece of the postwar socialist paradise in ruins. Light fell in bright slabs on the wooden floors. There was a poster of Miffy the rabbit up on one wall, its colors as pure as hope. Cosmo and Flora played with a table of model dinosaurs while I sat down, exhausted, and tried to gather up strength again. Eventually, we went back out.

"Can't we have an ice cream?"

"A chocolate ice cream? *Please?*"

"We're so near the chocolate shop, Daddy, *please*?"

I hesitated. "I just want to walk down this street."

"Why?"

"Because I used to live here when I was your age."

They looked disbelieving. Impossible to understand that I had ever been a child. I couldn't believe it of my father, why should they of theirs? But they held my hands and walked along the twisted rainbow of Chalcot Crescent, past houses painted every color: primrose yellow, pale blue, leaf green, iced pink. Each was lovingly tended, often with trees and flowering shrubs or creepers, but it was not a place for ordinary families anymore. I could remember so much about Tom's house, from the jumble of bicycles in the hall to the bowl of polished pebbles in the kitchen downstairs. Most of all, I remembered the feeling of ordinary happiness, of rightness. It was this dream that I had tried to re-create with Georgie in Stockwell. The rows of little red wellington boots by the door, the small coats hanging above; the special chairs, the piano, the books, the bright colors, the sweetness, the light. Surely I must have had it in my own home, too?

When I reached the house that had been mine, ours, hers, I stopped. It had changed color, but I still recognized it.

"Was that your old home, Daddy? Was it?"

"Yes."

"It's got a lion on the door," said Flora, with approval.

I looked at the railings, standing up like a row of spears. I could feel something very strange happening. The whole world was turning upside-down and fading. Then everything I saw went white, as white as paper without ink.

THE CHILDREN had no idea that I'd fainted. I used to do stage faints for them when they were younger, to amuse them. They thought it was all a game. When I'd pulled myself together again and driven back to Ruth's, I put them in front of one of the videos she kept downstairs for her own grandchildren. They chose *Dumbo,* and watched it unblinkingly, though they must have seen it a hundred times before. I slumped between them, an amorphous heap again.

"Why are you crying, Daddy?" Cosmo asked. "Is it because they've locked his mummy up?"

"It's only a story," Flora said, reassuringly; then, "*Why* do they lock her up?"

I said, "Because they think she's mad."

"What's mad?"

I thought of what Ruth had said. "It's when you see or feel things differently from other people."

"Like me," said Cosmo.

"Well, not really. The mother elephant gets locked up because she loses her temper at one of the boys who tease Dumbo."

"Nasty boys," said Flora, pointedly, taking her mouth from a bottle of apple juice. "Boys *are* nasty, aren't they?"

"Well, I hope not. I was a boy, once."

"When I grow up I want to be a man like you, Dad," said Cosmo, flatteringly.

Ruth came in. I blew my nose, because it's one thing to be maudlin in front of your children and another to be so in front of another adult. Streaks of blood came out on the tissue.

"Hi. Good walk?"

"Daddy had a nosebleed," said Flora. "Cosmo done it."

"*Did* it," I corrected automatically.

He stuck his tongue out at her. "Tell-tale tit!"

Flora was giggling at Dumbo's drunken hallucinations. "Why does he keep changing?"

"He's drunk alcohol," said Cosmo, primly.

Ruth said, "His dreams are trying to tell him that he can do or become anything. That's what dreams are for. He first flies when he's dreaming, look. He didn't know he could do it before."

I couldn't help smiling at this.

"Is that true, that you can become anything?" Cosmo asked.

"Yes," said Ruth firmly. "That's what Americans believe."

"Do English people believe that?"

I cleared my throat. "No, not really."

"What do we believe in?"

"In irony," I said.

M Y MOTHER'S PUBLISHER, James Cork, was still alive. I had given up thinking he might be, but one day I had a call from him in response to my letter. He had been abroad, he said, but could see me if I cared to visit. The voice sounded so much like a crackly recording of a Pathé newsreel that I found it hard not to laugh. He invited me to tea at his house in Notting Hill.

So I went. Ever since my fainting fit in Chalcot Crescent I had been feeling strange about my quest. What was I doing, really, stirring up the past instead of getting on with my life, or what remained of it? I didn't understand. *North of Nowhere* rested unopened beside my bed. The money had come through from the sale of my old house, and I had gone shopping every day for a week. I knew I should be hoarding it, or investing it until I found the dismal flat in Neasden or wherever, but I decided I deserved some pleasure. My agent still hadn't called. I might as well drive to Notting Hill.

Cork was as creased as a tortoise. A pair of rectangular, gold-rimmed spectacles rested on a blunt nose from which several bristly gray hairs sprouted. He wore a gray cardigan and, incongruously, a spotted bow tie. I wondered whether he had put it on for my visit. His wife offered not only tea but a homemade sponge cake and biscuits. When I refused both, she looked disappointed; she was a small, sweet-faced woman like a wren. I was shown into a large double drawing room filled with the kind of furniture I neither like nor can afford: large ceramic lamps with tasseled shades, gold-framed mirrors surmounted by eagles and ribbons, photographs of famous people in silver frames on a grand piano, glass-fronted mahogany bookcases. It smelled of potpourri and, indefinably, of old age.

Cork pottered around for a bit, and I looked past him, embarrassed, at the private park below. Howard's house (which I had repeatedly been told I would never inherit) looked down on to one that was very similar, if not the same.

"Lovely, isn't it?" Cork said. He gave a wheezy laugh. "We bought this place when we first married. I often reflect that this house is now worth more than I've ever earned in my entire career. Doesn't seem right, somehow."

"Did you own Nutshell?"

"It wasn't called that in those days," he said, with some asperity. "It was James Cork. Nutshell bought the children's backlist. Of course, it was very different from now. All these damned conglomerates run by accountants, what? What?" I wondered whether he was being deliberately affected. His eyes twinkled behind the smeary lenses. "When I took on your mother, we were working out of a tiny office in Charlotte Street, just the three of us, counting the secretary. That was Jane Holly, who became one of the great children's editors, took over the firm eventually, made it what it is today. But we knew every one of our authors, y'know. I'd only publish people I believed in. Mostly, they became friends, even if they didn't all become as successful as your mater. But we took the trouble to carry them, even if they were unprofitable."

"Good for you," I said, as he paused for breath.

"Yes, well. That was our job, to nourish. To nourish. You'd never get one of these whiz kids saying that today, eh? We were always broke, but never too broke to buy somebody lunch. We believed in building an author until those few hundred sales grew by word of mouth into thousands. It was a partnership. Not like now. It's all six-figure advances and onto the remainder pile in eight weeks."

I hadn't come here to listen to his bleatings about publishing. "So did my mother become a friend?"

"Oh, ah, yes, I suppose so," he said, vaguely.

"How did you meet?"

"Oh, at a party somewhere. Damned attractive woman, thought she was an actress, what?" I nodded encouragingly. He leaned forward and said in a conspiratorial whisper, "The wife couldn't stand her. Jealous, you see."

"Oh," I said. "That must have been unfortunate."

He nodded vigorously. "She mentioned she was an illustrator. Well, of course, they were two a penny, but still I said she should drop by, what? And she did. Rather pushy, American, I thought, later. But it just so happened that I had a book that needed a few decorative headings. And when I heard who she was married to, well. . . . She did it well, I must say."

"So her first book wasn't all her own work?"

"Good heavens, no. Illustration has been called an impure art because it interprets a text provided by somebody else. That's how they all began."

"Like acting," I said, interested.

"Quite. In the beginning it was pretty mundane. Yet she captured something unexpected about each book. She had genuine talent. No doubt about that. I loved the dogs and ponies. If I'd thought to buy some, I could have made a tidy sum now. Have you ever seen Gustave Doré's fairy tale illustrations? That's who she reminded me of, but she could knock off anything.

"Then she sent me *The Magic Box*. I wasn't too sure about it, to be frank, thought she was being pushy again. But Jane tried it out on her little girl. Amazing how kids spot the best-sellers. Kids and secretaries, they're always the ones."

I wondered whether he classed secretaries as being adult. "They don't care so much about what other people think, perhaps."

"Too damned right. Of course, it was Jane who really discovered Laura, you know. She was the one closest to her. You should talk to Jane."

"Where does she live?"

"New York. Ah, yes, she's a very big cheese now. She started as my secretary but gradually, well, took over. Stirred up the whole side of that business. Up until the late fifties, y'see, children's authors were almost all men—Ardizzone. Hergé, Dr. Seuss, the Babar man—unless you count the dreaded Blyton. We used to publish a bit of everything, with children's stuff at the bottom of the pile. It was Jane who began to make us specialize."

"Why?"

"Saw into the future," Cork said. "Clever little woman. She began going to Milan, and selling the foreign rights, looking for new markets. Round about the time your mother came to us, there was this great explosion in education and libraries, new markets opening up here and in America and Australia. And the books themselves started to look altogether different, because of changes in printing techniques. Nothing had really changed since the thirties—there were a few beautiful books with illustrations by Dulac and Nielsen, not really for children at all, cost a fortune to produce, otherwise it was all line drawings on cheap paper. Then color became a lot more affordable, and all of a sudden there was Sendak on one side of the Atlantic and your mother on the other. . . . Took a lot longer for her to be accepted, of course."

"They're quite alike in some ways, aren't they?"

"Yes. Both mad as hatters."

He laughed, wheezily. The thick, moss-green carpet and heavy draperies, the curving brass picture lights and cut-glass decanters with silver labels, all oppressed my spirits. Of course this sort of person wouldn't understand Laura. He wouldn't understand me, either.

"Was that how she appeared to you?" I asked. "Did she seem, well, unbalanced?"

"She was a woman, wasn't she? Not like Jane, but still . . ." Cork gave a sigh. "There was something about her eyes. They had this glitter to them. That's why I wasn't surprised, you see, when she did that dreadful thing."

I looked at his own dull eyes, which blinked. I couldn't tell whether he was genuinely sorry. The trouble with acting is that you can never tell when other people are pretending, only when they're acting.

"So she wasn't a friend, despite what you said?"

He seemed startled. "What? No. No, of course not. The wife wouldn't have . . . well, look, she was your mother, I don't want . . ." Cork seemed to withdraw into himself.

"Did you know her, really?"

"I really don't know. How well do any of us know anyone? As I said, Jane's the one you should really talk to. Would you like her address?"

"Yes," I said, though I had no intention of going to New York.

He got up, looking relieved, and shuffled round the various round, dark tables shining like pools of water in his swampy room. When he returned he had a piece of paper in his hand. I rose to leave.

"There you go, Jane's address and telephone numbers. She's still at it, you know. Give her my regards. Remarkable woman, really, even though we didn't see eye to eye on a number of matters, your mother included."

"Why?"

"I didn't really like her later work, if I'm perfectly honest. Too dark for me. I liked the ponies," he said wistfully.

I followed him out into the wide, shabby hall.

"You look like her," Cork said, as I held out my hand. Surprised, I let it fall again. "Do I?"

There was a mirror beside me. Involuntarily, I glanced in it. But however hard I stared, I couldn't see anyone but my own dull self in its depths.

WALKING to my car, I saw my stepmother, Nell. She waved and beckoned. I hesitated, then approached her. I had been dreading this possibility.

"Dick!" she said. "How nice to see you. Do come in. Your father's having his first walk since his operation."

"I wasn't coming to visit him, actually."

"Oh. Oh, do come in anyway. He'll be back soon, and I know he'll be sorry to miss you."

I doubted this very much, but followed her in.

I don't know why I dislike Nell so much—apart, that is, for her having indirectly been the cause of my mother's death. She's a good woman, with the blotchy complexion that good women always seem to acquire. Nell is the sort of Englishwoman who wears a straw hat when abroad, who shops at Liberty and who *really*, *really* *likes* William Morris. Perhaps the most important thing about her is that she's much posher than my father.

"I'm working class," he'll announce to everyone, "but my wife, as you can probably tell, is upper. One of the Ansteys, you know."

Poor Nell would blush. I suppose she loves him; nothing else can explain why she puts up with everything from his infidelities to his bad temper. She had worked on the same paper as Howard, as some sort of sub-editor, when their affair began, but had soon given up once they married. They had never had children. I suppose she's really a sort of housekeeper to him.

Of course, she had tried to be friends. When I had been sent to boarding school she, unlike Howard, had written me letters littered with exclamation marks. She could not have been much more than twenty-five or so at the time. Looking back, I know I should have felt sorry for her. She had been so young, as young as I had been when Georgie and I met. Old enough, though, to know better.

She made tea in a large, dark brown pot. There was always a lot of dark brown in Howard's house. It's a perfect seventies time capsule. The cork-tiled floors, the white eyeball spotlights, the shag-pile rugs and leather sofas are almost trendy again, but they still make my skin crawl. On the rare times I had stayed there, I had slept in drip-dry sheets and eaten off bright orange Formica plates. Howard was comically resistant to change. I still remember his astonishment when his tiny old TV broke down and he at last got a new one.

"You should come and see the picture," he crowed to me. "It's so sharp, it's a bloody marvel. Incredible!"

Nell said brightly, "So, what *are* you doing in this neck of the woods?"

"Seeing my mother's publisher."

One of the satisfactions I get in dealing with Nell is watching the interplay between her desire to do and say the right thing, and a quivering sensibility to her own feelings.

"Oh. Why?"

"I'm finding out about my mother's life and death."

She was skinned by emotion, like a rabbit on a butcher's hook. I wondered if this was the secret of her attraction to my father. Howard was such a bully, it was impossible not to believe he'd fail to enjoy seeing her suffer.

"What good do you think would come out of such a thing?"

"Well, my father is always urging an alternative career on me. Perhaps I could write a memoir."

"Is that what would make you happy, though?" she said gently. My father had never asked me this question. I reminded myself that she had never done anything to help me.

"No, not particularly, but then I often don't get what I want."

She leaned forward. Beside her, a plant holder overflowing with jumping grass dangled like a monster-movie spider. "What *do* you want, Benedick? Is it to hurt him?"

I shrugged.

Her pale blue eyes in their sandy lashes were as earnest as a doll's. "Don't you think he's suffered enough?"

I said, "I think there's something about my mother's death that everyone has tried to cover up. You wouldn't tell me—how could you, seeing you're the one who's most to blame?"

Nell's lips tightened. She no longer looked vague or benevolent. "It saddens me to think that no matter what I do, you still have me cast as the wicked stepmother. Laura's death was tragic, but I don't think our behavior had much to do with it."

"So you admit it had *something* to do with it?"

She paused, then looked at me and smiled slightly. "I've seen you do this role before. The prosecuting barrister in *The Bill*, wasn't it?" I glared at her. "*She* played roles, too, you know, and tried to put other people into them. The wicked ogre. The wicked witch. The prince. The princess. But Dick, people don't behave as they do in fairy tales. I know it would probably be easier to understand if they did, but real people, real marriages, are much more complex than that."

"Are they?" I said. I was enjoying seeing this side of her. She'd never fought back before. Having an adversary was making me feel stronger, more defined. Normally, she was so passive that we both ended up waffling to each other about nothing very much. "It's funny, isn't it, the way it's always people who've done something they should be ashamed of who insist that life has no story. Because if there is a story, you'd have a role in it and it wouldn't be a good one, would it?"

"Why should there be only one story?" Nell asked. "Or only one role?"

This took me aback. I thought of the way my mother had cast herself as the nasty sister in the first tale I had read. I still couldn't understand why she had done this.

"Nobody really sees him or herself as the villain, though, do they? I bet you don't. I bet my father doesn't."

Nell said, "In my story, the villain was somebody quite different."

"Is that why you cut her face out of all the photographs in the album?"

There was a long silence. Alarm, weariness, and some other emotion flickered across her features. "I didn't do that," said my stepmother. I laughed, disbelieving.

"Who did, then?"

"Laura."

I stared at her.

"She did it, I swear. Long before I moved in. She was bonkers, you know."

"If she was mad, who drove her so?"

I could hear my voice rising. Hers rose, too.

"It wasn't us. I realize, you must have blamed me all these years, but it wasn't. What Howard did was the result of her behavior, not the cause."

"A convenient fiction."

"Not fiction, truth." She was almost panting. "Why don't you find out more? You ought to. Nobody liked her, you know, not even that fool Jane Holly. She doesn't remember Laura as she was, just has her down as a martyr. Your parents' marriage was completely dead by the time I came along."

"That's what men always say when they're shagging someone who isn't their wife," I said.

"If you blame someone, why not that woman Ruth, whom you think so perfect and marvelous? She's the one you should blame, she's—"

I shouted over her voice, "How *dare* you talk that way about a woman who's been far more of a mother to me than you have?"

"You know nothing about her, though."

I said hotly, "I do, I've lived with her on and off for most of my life—"

"Did you know she was your father's lover, too?"

I stared at her. I couldn't believe it, and yet it made perfect sense. Hadn't I always felt there was something odd about Ruth and my father?

Nell stood up. "You should ask her. I'm sorry it had to come out this way, but perhaps it's time you straightened a few things out." She paused. "I won't say anything to Howard. Unless you'd like me to?"

I shook my head, speechless, and left.

T W E L V E

I DIDN'T KNOW what to do, so I did what I usually do in a crisis and went back to Ruth's. Luckily, she was out. Grub was giving a recital at the Wigmore Hall, and the whole family would be there to hear him and cheer him on.

Nell's words churned in my head. My father and Ruth had been lovers. It explained such a lot about her persistent interest in him, and yet it couldn't be true. I thought of the support Ruth had given me, and the fact that if Nell were telling the truth my one true friend in my parents' world must now count as an enemy. How was it possible that such a person could be so treacherous? I thought of Ruth's face. She had certainly been attractive enough to me as a teenager. Was what Nell had said true, or the delusion of a jealous second wife? Yet Nell knew, I was sure, about my father's succession of mistresses and never appeared to be in the slightest bit ruffled. Why had she cared about Ruth? She couldn't, surely, be jealous of *my* affection for her.

I couldn't eat, I couldn't sleep. I was back pacing my room like a convict. I couldn't stay in this house now, that much was clear. If it was true that she had been my father's lover, then Ruth had to carry the moral blame for my mother's death. No wonder she had claimed not to be that close to her. Ruth's acts of friendship must have been made as a kind of atonement. I was even more isolated than I had realized. It therefore followed that Ruth could never have really liked me, or cared about me for my own sake. It was all guilt—or worse still, a way of keeping in touch with my father. I had always feared this, knowing that I lived in his shadow, and yet it had never occurred to me that Ruth of all people—Ruth, on whose honesty and generosity I would once have staked my life—could possibly be so duplicitous. I crouched down on the floor and sobbed like a child.

I had no property, no talent, no family, no dignity. When I was able to stand up, I saw my mother's book, the book that had started all this. I grabbed it and it fell open in my hand. Gazing up at me was a picture of a girl in rags riding a white bear across the snow.

I knew at once that it was Laura. The stars streamed in her dark hair, and the earth surged beneath the bear's paws. Behind, its prints rose and fell in the snow; it was racing towards me, its mouth open in a half-snarl.

My despair left me. I began to read.

THE WHITE BEAR

There was once a woman who lived by the edge of a deep dark forest who had three daughters. The eldest of them said, "Mother, bake me some bread for I am going to seek my fortune." So the mother did so, but before giving her the loaf, she asked her daughter, "Would you rather have half the loaf and my blessing, or the whole without it?" The daughter chose to take the whole loaf, for she thought that she might find herself hungry, and what use would her mother's blessing be then?

So off she set, and she soon discovered that she did not need her mother's loaf for she found a husband in the next village. But she chose him without her mother's blessing, and so the marriage did not prosper.

Then the second daughter said to her mother, "Mother, bake me some bread for I am going to seek my fortune." The mother did as she was asked, but when the loaf was ready she asked her daughter the same question: would she take half the loaf and her mother's blessing, or the whole and go without it? The second sister did as the first had done; she, too, found a husband, but being without her mother's blessing was no happier.

Now the third daughter wanted to leave, too. Her mother was very sad to see her go, but the girl was determined. So once again the mother baked a loaf of bread and asked if she would take half a loaf and her blessing, or the whole and go without.

"I will take half the loaf and your blessing, if you please," said the girl. Then her mother embraced her and blessed her, and the girl set off down the road. She did not take the road to the village, for she knew where that went, but chose instead the path that took her through the dark wood.

On and on the road went, and soon the trees pressed in so close that the road became a ribbon of shadow beneath her feet, and the sky a ribbon of light. The girl ate sparingly of her bread, but by the third day she was growing tired and hungry. Still her mother's blessing kept her from evil, and she walked on until she found herself at twilight in the very heart of the forest.

Just then, what should she see come gleaming through the trees but a big white bear. It padded towards her, its coat shining like snow in the moonlight, and when it came near it said, "I'm hungry. Give me something to eat."

"I have little to eat, but what I have you may share," said the girl, and she broke off half of her remaining loaf.

The White Bear ate it, and when he had done so he said, "Are you afraid?"

"No," said the girl, though she trembled greatly.

"Then get on my back, and I'll take you away from this place."

I paused. I needed to get away from this place, too.

The girl got up on his back, and away they went through the dark wood, across wild rushing rivers white with foam. When they had gone a part of the way the White Bear asked, "Are you afraid?"

"No, I am not," said the girl.

"Then keep tight hold of my fur, and there's nothing to fear," said the White Bear.

On they went so deep that there was not a sound except for the far-away sighing of branches high out of sight. The air became warm, and had a scent at once sweet and bitter. They came to a great castle. Its pillars were made of great ivied boles, and its walls of woven honeysuckle and wild roses, all blossoming so that they looked like the most marvelous tapestry in the world. In the middle was a hall, with a magnificent table spread with food, and candles burning.

"This is your home now," said the White Bear, and he gave her a silver bell and told her that if she needed anything she should ring it and whatever she desired would appear. So after the girl had eaten, she grew sleepy and thought she would like to go to bed. She rang the bell, and scarcely had she touched it than she found herself in a chamber all garlanded with flowers with a bed of soft green moss to sleep on. But when she had lain herself down to sleep and put out the light, a man came and lay down beside her. This was the White Bear, who threw off the form of a beast during the night. She never saw him, however, for he always came after she had put out the light, and went away long before the dawn.

For almost seven years all went well, and the girl became very fond of the White Bear, because he was so gentle and kind to her. But still she began to feel sad and lonely, always having to wait until night for company. The White Bear had made her swear that she would never tell another living soul about what happened between them; "or," he said, "you'll bring great misery on us both."

No, she swore, she wouldn't. One day, however, she was sitting outside the castle door when she saw a wise woman go past. It was so long since she had seen another human being that she called out to her, and *they fell to talking of this and that until the girl said, "I shall be grateful to you all my life if you can tell me what is the matter with my true love. Why is he a White Bear by day and a man by night?"*

"How do you know he's a man?" asked the wise woman. "You've never seen him; perhaps he's a hideous troll. My advice to you is to take this bit of candle and flint and hide them in your breast. When he's fallen asleep, you have a good look at what you're in bed with."

So she took the candle and flint, and hid them in her breast. When night fell, the White Bear came to her as before. As soon as she could hear he was sleeping, she got up and lit the candle, letting its light fall upon him. There lay beside her the handsomest prince that eyes ever beheld, and straightaway she loved him so much that it seemed to her she must die if she did not kiss him that very moment. So she did; but even as she kissed him three drops of hot wax fell on his shirt, and he woke.

I was puzzled. Surely if this was a story about my parents' marriage, she should have found a monster in her bed?

"What have you done?" he cried. "If you'd but held out three more days, the spell would have been broken, and I should have been free. There is a troll witch who enchanted me so I must be a White Bear by day and a man by night; but now all ties are snapped between us, and I must leave you and marry her daughter instead."

The girl wept and pleaded, but it was in vain, for go he must. Then she asked if she might go with him. No, she could not.

"At least tell me the way," she said, "and I will seek you—that I may surely be allowed to do?"

"There is no hope, not unless you wear out an iron staff and a pair of iron shoes in searching," said he. "The troll witch lives in a castle which lies East of the Sun and West of the Moon, and there, too, is her daughter the princess with a nose three ells long, and she is the one I now must marry."

This was the very story I had started to read the day I left my own home—and here was the picture of the girl, or woman, who haunted me, her great sorrowful eyes burning into my memory. It was this story that had come to me in my darkest hour, and now it was here again. It had to be a sign. My hands were shaking.

Then the girl fell into a deep, deep sleep; and when she awoke there was no prince or castle, only a little patch of green on which she lay and the great dark wood all around. By her side was the same bundle of rags that she had brought with her from her mother's home.

When she had rubbed all the sleep and the tears out of her eyes, she went to find a blacksmith, and asked him to forge her a pair of iron shoes and an iron staff. Then she set out on her way, and a long and weary way it was. She wandered over seven seas and seven lands, over cruel rocks and plains of mud, but on she went and never looked back. At last, wearied with her long journey and overcome with sorrow, she reached a house.

Now, who do you think lived there? The Moon and her mother.

The girl knocked at the door and begged to be let in to rest a little. The mother of the Moon felt a great pity for her, and took her in and nursed her. And while she was here, the girl had a little baby.

A cold, sick feeling crept over me. There was a story behind this story. I knew this as you know things in dreams, with a certainty that had nothing logical about it.

The Moon came in, and her face was half-bright, half-sorrowful. Her long silver hair was like mist, and on her back she carried a bow and arrows. The Moon asked the girl, "How is it that you, a mere mortal, have managed to come so far?"

Then the poor girl told her what had happened, and how she would never see the prince again until she found the castle that lay East of the Sun and West of the Moon. The Moon wept, because she, too, was parted from her lover the Sun, and doomed to follow him forever across the sky.

"It is for this that I cover my face for two weeks out of three," she said. Then the Moon gave the girl a roast chicken to eat, telling her not to throw any of the bones away, and a little silver nut which she was to crack only at a time of great need.

"But where am I to find the castle?" asked the girl.

"I know not," said the Moon. "Ask the Sun. He travels farther than I."

When the girl had thanked the goddess for her hospitality, she set out once more with her baby and her gifts tied to her back and her iron staff in her hand.

On and on she went, over deserts vast where the sand was so heavy that for every two steps forward she fell back one. She had to cross plains of flint, which cut even through her iron shoes so that her feet were always bleeding. She came to high rocky mountains and had to jump from crag to crag. Often she came to a precipice across which she could not jump but had to crawl around, helping herself along with her staff. Only the blessing that her mother had placed upon her kept her from evil.

There was a drawing to accompany this passage, which expressed suffering more clearly than any words. The girl's hair was bound up in a kind of turban, her baby swaddled on her back, asleep. My mother had drawn herself in profile. She was bent with extreme weariness but grasping her iron staff. One delicate foot was placed on a black rock.

At last, close to death, she reached the palace of the Sun. The mother of the Sun opened the door, and took pity on her. Then, having given her food and drink, she hid the girl and the baby.

"The Sun will be angry if he finds mortals here," said the mother of the Sun. "Wait until he has rested."

"But how is it possible for the Sun to be angry?" asked the girl. "He is so beautiful and so good."

"In the morning," said the Sun's mother, "he stands at the gates of Paradise, and he is happy and smiles on the world. During the day, however, he sees all the evil deeds of men, and that is why his heat becomes scorching; but in the evening he stands at the gates of Death, and this makes him sad and angry. From there, he comes back here."

In came the Sun. His skin hissed and glowed, his curling hair crackled heat, but his face was grim and red.

Two long, thin drawings accompanied this part of the story. One was of the Moon, who was drawn as a tall, elegant woman in long flowing robes, with a crescent on her brow; the other was of the Sun, a beautiful young man in a kind of short toga with a crown of rays on his head. I recognized neither.

"Mother, I am weary. Fetch me some supper," he said. So the mother of the Sun fetched him some supper and listened to his tales of all that he had seen that day. At last the Sun became happier, and his shining face turned fair and bright again. Then his mother led forward the girl and her baby and told him all about the White Bear and her search for the castle that lay East of the Sun and West of the Moon. But the Sun knew no more than the Moon, and told the girl that her only hope was to go and enquire of the Wind.

"He travels everywhere. If he doesn't know where it is, you'll never find anyone in the world to tell you."

Before the girl left, the Sun gave her a roast chicken to eat, advising her to take care of the bones, and a little gold nut which she was only to open in a time of great distress. So she thanked the Sun and set out again, with her baby growing ever heavier on her back.

Now she met with even greater hardships than before. She came to mountains all fissured and cracked, out of which flames would flare up; she passed over fields of ice. Her shoes were worn as thin as paper and her iron staff was blunted by the time she reached an enormous cave in the side of a mountain.

Here, the mother of the Wind took pity on her. When she heard that the girl was looking for the prince who lived East of the Sun and West of the Moon, she shook her head.

"Wait here and be rested," she said, "but I do not know if my son can help you."

In came the Wind with a blast of air. He was huge and cloudy, and his hair and beard swirled everywhere in long streamers of cold. The feathers on his wings rang and chimed like ice as he sighed.

Yes, said the Wind, he knew well enough where to find the castle that lay East of the Sun and West of the Moon.

"Once in my life I blew a tiny leaf there," he said, "but it tired me so, I couldn't blow a puff for days afterwards. But if you really wish to go and aren't afraid to come, I'll take you on my back."

Yes, said the girl. She must and would get there in any way possible, and as for fear, she wouldn't be afraid.

"Very well then," said the Wind, "but you must sleep here tonight for we must have the whole day before us if we are to get there at all."

Before she slept, the Wind gave her a chicken, the bones of which he warned her to keep, and a little nut of diamond, telling her to take great care of both and only use them in great need.

Early the next morning the Wind woke her and puffed himself up and made himself so big and angry it was terrible to see. Off they went, high, high in the air with the girl and her baby just a tiny speck in his long glassy hair.

Down here below the woods roared and were thrown down; houses were flattened; the seas were piled high into black waves and great ships foundered.

There was a picture of the Wind stretched out across the sky, his cheeks puffed out and his hand straining forward. He was balding and powerfully muscled, and I was certain had been drawn from life. I wondered whom she had used as a model. If you looked carefully you could just see the tiny figure of the girl hanging on to his hair. The black sea pitched and heaved beneath him, ripping the ragged sails of galleons. It was a wonderful drawing, a celebration of chaos unleashed upon the world.

So on they tore—no one can believe how far—and still they went madly over the sea until darkness fell and the Wind became more and more weary. Eventually he grew so out of breath that his wings drooped, and the girl's heels touched the crests of the waves.

"Are you afraid?" he asked.

"No!" said the girl, holding her baby tight; and at this the Wind was so pleased that he just managed to throw her up onto the bleak and barren shore of the castle that lay East of the Sun and West of the Moon. With a clatter, her iron shoes fell off, and her staff shattered. She slept, and the sea quieted.

There was a picture of the castle. It was half in bright light, the sun blazing fiercely down upon it, and half in shadow with only the thin crescent moon to give it definition. All around the castle, the sea dashed itself against the jagged rocks. The drawing was no bigger than a large postage stamp, but extraordinarily detailed, with the asymmetry of nightmare.

Next morning, the girl sat beneath the castle window and began to play with her baby; and the first person who saw her was the Long Nose who was to have the prince. She leaned out of her window sniffing and snuffling and said, "What do you want for your baby, beggar?"

My mother had drawn the Troll Princess with great care. Her long nose curled like a piece of apple peel. She was festooned with jewelry that only made her ugliness more grotesque. It was a drawing steeped in malicious wit, yet try as I might I couldn't see a trace of the face I would have expected. Long Nose looked nothing like Nell, or, indeed, like Ruth.

"It's not for sale," said the girl, but she could see the Troll Princess's eyes glowing red at the scent of the baby's milky skin. In desperation, the girl felt in her pocket. What should she pull out but the silver nut. It fell on the ground.

Crack! Out of the nut flowed a dress as silver as the moon, all covered with silver embroidery as fine as cobwebs and shimmering with stars. When Long Nose saw the dress, she forgot all about her desire for the baby.

"What will you take for the dress, girl?"

"It's not for sale," said the girl, "but if I can get to the prince who lives here and be with him tonight, you shall have it."

"You may come if you can climb up," said Long Nose. "There is no stair, as you see."

The girl looked and it was true, there was no way up. The sides of the castle walls were sheer against the sky. She almost wept, but then she remembered the chicken bones and said to herself, "There must be a reason why I was given these to take care of."

So she took the bones out of her bundle, and placed two ends together. To her surprise, they stuck tight, like the rungs of a ladder. Step by step the girl climbed, until she was close to the window. But just as she got to the very last rung, she noticed that there were no bones left. What was she to do? Without the last rung, the whole ladder was useless. Where was she to get another bone?

Suddenly, an idea came to her. Taking a knife, she cut off her little finger and placed it as the last step. Then she was up, and inside the Troll Princess's castle, walking towards the prince's room.

But Long Nose had given him a sleeping draught, and though the girl shook him and called and wept, she could not wake him up. She sang:

> "Seven long years I lived with thee—
> The iron shoes I wore, the baby I bore,
> My finger as bone I cut for thee—
> Wilt thou not waken and turn to me?"

But still the prince slept on, and thought he heard the wind murmuring and sighing in the trees of the wood where he had lived as a White Bear. Though the girl wept, she could not make him stir. Next morning, as soon as day broke, Long Nose came and drove her out.

So once again she sat down to nurse her baby: once again the Troll Princess asked to buy it and in desperation the girl pulled out the gold nut from her pocket.

Crack! Out slid a dress as brilliant as the sun, all rayed with gold embroidery like the waters of the dawn. The Troll Princess wanted this one, too. Once again the bargain was struck.

Again she climbed the ladder of bone, and again she sang and wept. But the drugged prince did not stir, and at dawn she was driven out.

Now there was only one nut left, the diamond given by the Wind. The girl cracked it and out spilled a dress made of every feather in the world: kingfisher blue, duck green, robin red, peacock gold. Once again she bargained with Long Nose and once again she climbed the ladder of bone.

In all this time the Wind had been waiting to grow strong again, and had seen what was happening. So he sent one of his long locks streaming through the prince's window, and it knocked over the sleeping draught that the Troll Princess had made for him. The prince lay down but was unable to sleep, and when the girl came in and sang:

> "Seven long years I lived with thee—
> The iron shoes I wore, the baby I bore.
> My finger as bone I cut for thee—
> Wilt thou not waken and turn to me?"

*he heard, and turned to her. When he saw all she had suffered his heart
was moved by so much love and pity that he wept.*

*"I have been in a dream, bewitched to make me forget you. But you
have come in the very nick of time, for tomorrow is to be the wedding
day. Now I shan't have to marry Long Nose. I'll ask her to wash the shirt
that has three spots of wax on it, and say I'll only marry the woman who
can wash it clean in the black caldron. She'll say yes, but that's no work
a troll can do. Then I'll call you. If you can do it instead, all her power
over me will be ended."*

So there was great joy and love between them all that night.

There was a drawing of them both. They were fully dressed, but lying in each other's arms, gazing at each other as I now gazed at
them. It was the most beautiful picture I thought I had ever seen.
Joy and love, the two things that had gone out of my life, were here.

*The next day, the prince said to Long Nose, "First of all, I'd like to see
what my bride is fit for."*

"Yes," said the troll witch and her daughter.

*"Well," said the prince, "I've got a shirt that I'd like to wear for my
wedding, but it's got three spots of old wax on it which I must have
washed out. I've sworn only to take as my bride the woman who can
wash it clean."*

*This seemed no great thing, so the trolls agreed, and Long Nose be-
gan to rub away as hard as she could. But the more she rubbed, the bigger and blacker the spots grew.*

"Ah!" said the troll mother. "You can't wash, let me try."

*But the more she scrubbed, the blacker the shirt became until it
looked as if it had been dipped in soot.*

*"Ah!" said the prince. "You're no good for anything. There's a beg-
gar girl outside the window, and I'll be bound she can wash better than
any of you. COME IN, GIRL!" he cried down.*

So up the girl climbed, and in she came.

"Can you wash this shirt clean?"

"I don't know, but I can try," she said.

And no sooner had she dipped the shirt in water than it was as white as snow.

"I will marry you, and you alone," said the prince.

Then the old troll witch was so angry she burst, and Long Nose also, and all the other trolls, too, like foul bubbles on a marsh—at least, they've never been heard of again. But the prince and his bride and their little child were blown far, far from the castle that lies East of the Sun and West of the Moon. Yet still it stands there, across the seas, for any-one to find who may.

I had found out what I was to do next.

"WHAT'S GRAY and has a big trunk, Dad?"
        "An elephant?"
        "Wrong! A mouse going on holiday."
I laughed.
"Dad, Dad, why is an elephant wrinkled?"
"Tell me."
"Well, have you ever tried to *iron* an elephant?"
Assured of my undivided attention, Cosmo had blossomed. I remembered this person with shining eyes and dancing feet: this was the way he had been before everything went wrong.

I hadn't intended to take my son with me; I wasn't due to have the children until after the Easter weekend, but Georgie had rung me. "I was wondering if you could take the children earlier," she said. "I've just had to sack the new nanny. Bruce can't cope."

"Tell Bruce to keep his hair on," I said. "Oh, I forgot—he hasn't got any, has he? Of course I can take the children, but they'll have to come with me to America. I've got a flight booked for Friday."

There was a long pause while she digested this. "I don't think Flora could do that," she said cautiously. "She's too young. But Cosmo—could you really take him? How long are you going for?"

"A couple of weeks," I said.

She was so desperate, she even paid for his ticket. Poor Cosmo. Nobody wanted him, any more than they had wanted me at his age.

I had told Ruth I'd decided to go to America the day after my meeting with Nell. She had reacted as though I were making a great step forward in therapy. I didn't tell her I was going because of a fairy story, or because I couldn't bear to live under her roof anymore. She wanted to believe I was getting better. I was plied with names and addresses of people we could stay with, advice about what to see and where to go. Even before I was landed with Cosmo, I knew it would be impossible to stay with any of them. Now I had a credit card again, I wanted to have some fun. I told Ruth I would stay in a hotel.

"Give Len and Rupert my love and tell them to visit soon. I may ring them myself. You'll find Len particularly interesting. He's really big in Hollywood now, but I know he spends as much time as he can in New York."

"But will they be able to tell me about my mother?"

She hesitated. I watched her struggle with her desire to conceal from me her own involvement in my mother's death.

"They knew her before I did. You should meet them anyway. Who knows, they might be able to help you find more work. But you should get to know them. You're doing the right thing."

I held myself stiffly as she put her arms around me and hugged. She felt it and drew back, looking at me quizzically. Georgie always claimed that knowing what I was feeling was like tracking the spoor of a wounded animal in the jungle, but Ruth was usually more perceptive.

"There's something else," she said, then paused.

"What?" I could hear the grudging note in my voice.

"I've got your aunt's address and number, too. In case you might want to make a visit. I know you won't have much time. . . ."

I didn't tell her that, if I had read my mother's fairy tale correctly, this was exactly where I should go.

"Best call them when you arrive," she said. "It'll cost a lot less."

So there I was, sitting on the train to Gatwick with my son. I couldn't believe it was so easy. The last time I had been in a plane, my son had been a baby. After that it became too stressful. Cosmo held Ti-Ti up to the window and pointed out features of passing interest. I glanced at the dirty, furry face. It did look curiously expressive, its button eyes shining with what seemed like a gleam of intelligence. We rattled through scraggy woodland splashed with primroses. Cosmo murmured, *"Tyger Tyger, burning bright, / In the forests of the night."*

He had probably heard it on one of his cassettes. To Cosmo and Flora, everything was perceived through the medium of fiction. Where I lay gasping for some relief, beached by the realization that my life and indeed that of everyone else was without plot or meaning, they swam like amphibians between fantasy and reality. Their T-shirts, their cups, and no doubt their dreams swarmed with cartoon characters and Manichean dualities. They had Wallace & Gromit toothbrushes, Peter Rabbit bowls, Tintin jumpers. When I saw my children talking to themselves or drilling imaginary holes in the walls with their toy toolkit I realized that what Liz Shaw had said was almost true. Lunatics were children in adult bodies.

Cosmo drew something out of his rucksack with a smile. "Promise you won't be cross?"

"No."

He interpreted this as a yes. "I've stolen the skipping-rope. When you get tired, I can be your pony and pull you along."

"Chance would be a fine thing," I muttered, but his delight still made me laugh. Why shouldn't we play horses? I'd done sillier things than that to entertain grown-ups, after all.

Cosmo was disappointed that we were not flying to America

in a giant peach borne aloft by seagulls. He expected trains to have the faces of Thomas the Tank Engine like those on his Galt train tracks, and was deeply frustrated by the speed at which they passed.

"Will we see the Fat Controller soon?" he asked.

I pointed out that a six-foot wooden model of a man in a top hat would be rather peculiar in real life. Tom had told me about a disastrous scene last Christmas at his hospital when the actors playing the Teletubbies had visited sick children in costume. Nobody had considered what the reaction of these tots might be, coming round from anesthetic to see a gigantic mauve Tinky-Winky bending over them. Parents whose offspring had suffered postoperative trauma were now suing the hospital.

"We're becoming more and more like Americans," he said gloomily.

"But Tom, you and I *are* American—at least partly," I pointed out. It had always surprised me that he didn't feel this more strongly. Now that I knew I was finally going to America, I felt liberated, elated, as though some drug were fizzing through my veins. I told Cosmo I could make the clouds go away.

"Do it," he said, excitedly.

I pointed my finger at the sky. "Begone," I said, in my deepest voice. "Let the sun shine." The clouds parted. "See?" I said.

Cosmo did not find it at all strange that I was going on a quest because of a book of fairy stories. All he cared about was that we were being, as he put it, "boys together." Flora hadn't minded about being left nearly as much as I had feared (or hoped) for the same reason: she and Georgie could be "girls together." I wondered, as we slipped through the suburbs, how long my son's good behavior would last. Tom had prescribed some tranquilizers to give him before the flight, just in case.

He was bouncing again. "Dad, how did the potato cross the sea?"

"Did it turn into a french fry?"

Cosmo looked at me reproachfully. "It turned into a *chip*. Is that funny?"

"Very. Did you think it up yourself?"

"No, I saw it on children's TV. Is there children's TV in America?"

"Lots and lots. Much more than in England."

"Great!"

Everything at the airport was delightful. The moving paths that made us feel as fast as Superman, the model of an air balloon with two figures who mechanically raised and lowered their telescopes, the cars he could climb into that shuddered and tilted when Cosmo posted twenty-pence pieces into them.

It was intoxicating to be leaving England, with all its adult cares, behind. Cosmo and I descended a spiral ramp, circling a vast silver cone ribboned with falling water. At the bottom, gold and silver coins glinted in a shallow pool fringed by plants.

"Is it a magic fountain?" Cosmo asked.

"I don't know. It might be."

"Look at all the coins, Dad. Does it make money?"

"No. People throw money in for luck. Or to make a wish."

"Can I throw some in?"

I gave him a handful of coins. Money was like wishes: useless unless spent. I remembered this too late when I found to my dismay that our seats were not together.

It was an American airline, packed with American students. None of them were prepared to give up sitting with their friends. Cosmo clung to me when he understood, terrified of separation. I pleaded with them. "Look, he's only a little boy. This is his first flight. He's frightened."

Blank stares of indifference. They chewed gum, bared their braces, and shrugged. I couldn't believe people could be so selfish. The airline staff were equally unhelpful. "I'm only doing my job. Wait and ask one of the other passengers," snarled a steward.

I said to the student in the next aisle, "He gets airsick, you know." (Later, when Cosmo vomited over her, I felt a surge of pleasure. It *served her right,* just as it served the nasty, selfish sister in the fairy tale right that she was turned into snow.)

Eventually, the passenger on the other side of me relented, and we were able to sit together. The plane began to move. The film of our lives speeded up, and up and up.

"Oh, wow!" said my son. "There are all these toys outside, little cars moving, and a patchwork blanket and they're shrinking. Oh!—oh, it's all melted." He stared out of the thick window, then asked, "Are those things icebergs?"

"They're clouds."

"Can we get out and walk on them?"

"It looks as if you could, doesn't it? But you can't."

"Jack does. In 'Jack and the Beanstalk.' The giant has his castle up here."

I shook my head. The clouds did look remarkably solid. "You'd fall through. Clouds are just water vapor, like steam."

He turned to me. "I don't believe you."

"Well, what do you think they're made of?" I asked, curious.

"I think they're made of dreams."

"Well, how do you explain rain coming out of them?"

Cosmo said, "That happens when the dreams are sad." The boiled sweet he was sucking rattled against his teeth. His eyes met mine. "When people don't make them come true."

We played noughts and crosses on some paper. Then I showed him how to play hangman.

"I win, I win!" he said, putting the noose round the neck of the stick man for the third time. After a moment he said, "But it's dangerous to put something round your neck."

"OK," I said. "Let's draw a pair of scissors, shall we? Snip, snip. There. He's safe."

He looked out of the window. "Are we in heaven?"

"No."

"Where is heaven, then? Is it farther up?"

"Farther up, the air gets thinner and thinner. Then there's just space."

"So where's heaven?"

Howard had told me that heaven didn't exist. For a long time I had hoped he was wrong, that if I caught an airplane I would see my mother walking about on the clouds. But he had been right, as usual. I said to my own son, "It's somewhere else. I don't know where."

He had no memory of the other flight he had taken. Indeed, my son had so little recollection of any events that I considered important, I wondered why I tried to do things with him. Why bother to give Cosmo and Flora a wonderful birthday party or even make sure they had matching socks, if they would forget it? I had heard people talk about their happy childhoods with incredulity. Did they really remember them, or was it a kind of comforting myth? If I could be certain that my presents ensured lifelong adoration and gratitude, it would be worth it. As it was, I knew it would all go into the trash can of the cortex, just like my own memories of my mother.

Yet the curious lightness of heart that had come over me at the prospect of flight from my normal life persisted. I was full of joy at the beauty and vastness of this aerial landscape, at its strangeness. Nothing could really harm me anymore. I had left all my troubles behind, I was traveling North of Nowhere to the other half of my inheritance, my motherland.

Cosmo had fallen asleep with a coloring book called *What's Wrong with This Picture?* open in front of him. It featured children playing in a world that looked perfectly normal but had TV sets swimming with fish, teapots in trees, and beaches on which peacocks pranced. What was around us was no less marvelous. The tinkling trolleys of booze bottles shrunk to a tenth of their usual size, the tiny tube of toothpaste, the palm-sized TV screen on the seat in front—were we giants, or babies? We ate with disposable knives and forks off molded plastic trays like those on highchairs, were given miniature white pillows on which to place our heads. For hours and hours we sat in the vivid twilight, chasing the sun as it vanished over the curve of the world.

My head rang with angelic chimes. When I looked out of the window I saw the gold-tinted clouds slowly sculpt themselves into a form. The North Wind was flying with us, his mighty wings like glass. He blew, and the red seat-belt signs came on, warning us of turbulence. One hand was stretched out, pointing towards America. His bald head shone.

But even as I looked, the North Wind melted slowly away, falling and shrinking until there were only a few wisps of pink in the thickening air.

W HEN I WOKE it was hot, and dim. The plane thrummed. Cosmo stirred and shifted. I could see beads of sweat pearling his face. I tried to ease some of his clothes off, and he cried out, "Mummy, Mummy!"

A lump of dread formed in my throat. It was natural that he should love her more than me. How could I have thought I'd cope? He wanted his mother. All children did. For the first time, I felt a glimmer of sympathy for what Howard must have gone through after my mother's death. Even if he had been a hopeless father, he must have had a hard time.

Ti-Ti had fallen to the floor. I bent, awkwardly, and put the toy into my son's grasp. At once he quieted. I sighed with relief.

The tiny pillow was sweaty. My legs pinged from cramp. I looked past my son, out at the twilight. There was nothing to see, only the faint reflection of the cabin inside with all its sleeping, stinking cargo. Mile after mile of dusk. I was making the opposite journey that my mother had taken, far below, more than forty years before.

As if in answer to this thought, the evening sky was suddenly lit up by a million lights—lights suspended hundreds of feet up in the air, lights of diamond white outlining walls and towers and spires and streets. I was looking at America.

E VEN AFTER we landed, the earth continued to buckle and tilt. Cosmo was too sleepy to notice the outline of Manhattan through the vast windows as we filed slowly through Customs. It was just evening here, almost as though our journey had been accomplished in no time at all. For us, though, it was the middle of the night. Cosmo was sunk in the profound slumber of infancy, impossible to rouse. I had to carry him propped up on top of our baggage, with my arms around him. The hotel was supposed to have sent a car for us, but after an hour's wait I realized it was never going to arrive. So much for the service economy which we were supposed to emulate on the other side of the Atlantic.

"Cosmo, wake up, look!" I hissed as our taxi bounced along. "It's the Brooklyn Bridge! It's *New York*! Look, Central Park!" These names, remote and magical, were suddenly real.

"Why is the driver sitting in a cage, Dad?" Cosmo asked, yawning.

My eagerness to spring out and examine this legendary city was so strong I felt I could jump out of my skin. "Wake up! Look, I've brought you thousands of miles to see this country and all you can do is loll about."

My son's eyes rolled back into his head. The taxi drew up at the door of our hotel.

F O U R T E E N

THE HOTEL LOBBY had half a cherry orchard arranged in a monumental marble vase. The lift was lined with beveled mirrors and had an ornate bench upholstered in red velvet. The TV in our room was concealed inside an antique walnut cabinet. Cosmo woke, investigated it, and found the Nickelodeon Channel. This was his idea of bliss.

The bed was seven feet wide. I had never seen anything like it. I knew I was reacting like the most naïve tourist, but it was no use suppressing my amazement. It reminded me of when Cosmo was born: I kept looking at his tiny hands and remarking on how perfect they were. I felt as though I, too, had become a child, and that this was why everything around me was once again so big. We bounced around the bed as though it were a trampoline. Then we used the shower. It was like standing under Niagara Falls. So *this* was why people went on and on about them, I marveled.

"We're being boys together, Dad, aren't we?" Cosmo said, after he had stuffed himself with fish-shaped biscuits and Tropicana orange juice.

"Yes," I said, and for the first time felt like a real father, the sort you see in films.

I rang the numbers Ruth had given me, and got the answering services for both. I opened a window. The grinding throb of traffic was amplified by sheets of metal laid down over large holes in the road. Every time a car went over them, the metal thumped like an erratic heartbeat. We went out and ate pizza in a place overlooking a vast, curving brown skyscraper.

"Is it made out of chocolate?" Cosmo asked, awed.

Whump-whump! A white stretch limo went over the metal sheet.

"Brown marble, I think," I said; but I wasn't sure. Anything was possible. One building had trees growing up one side of it; countless others were slabs of mirror, multiplying this city with wavering illusions of itself. Everything was melting and fusing, past and present, now and then. So much still looked as it must have done when my mother was alive. The fire hydrants and rubbish lorries, the street lighting and many of the apartment blocks were pure fifties. To Cosmo, I was astonished to find, it was much more familiar.

"I've seen it all in *Oliver,*" he explained kindly, as I took him for a walk the next day in Central Park. Despite jet lag, he still had to be walked.

"That's set in London."

"No, it's not. It's about a kitten that nobody wants, and he meets a really cool dog called the Artful Dodger, and this little girl. Then a baddie called Sykes kidnaps Oliver. . . ." He prattled on while we walked.

Ever since we had stepped onto the airplane I knew something strange was happening to me. Perhaps it was that I had lost all sense of proportion. My eyes kept traveling up edifices, stopping at the expected cutoff point, then forced to travel the same distance again. The traffic lights flashed messages at me. *Walk, Don't walk.* I was in my mother's world now, a world in which animals could talk and objects think; I was infinitely small and yet infinitely free.

"I want to play," said my son.

The children's playground in Central Park was crisscrossed with broken yellow tape announcing this to be the scene of a homicide. For once, I was glad Cosmo couldn't read. He cringed away from the scene in *Snow White* in which the huntsman draws his knife to murder the heroine; the idea that real people could actually do something similar to each other was so far mercifully distant.

We went under the yellow tapes. There wasn't anyone to stop us, and my son needed to climb frames and swing, to run and slide into a sandpit. Without exercise, there wasn't a chance he would sleep. Cosmo flung himself into a round of solitary games, crossing a river full of crocodiles by jumping from one log to the next, climbing the rigging of a pirate ship, calling commands and instructions. He was full of courage or bravado.

I sat down on a bench, and felt something hard in my jacket pocket. It was my mother's book.

"What's that?" Flushed and bright eyed, he came to look.

"A book of stories. You've had one from it."

"Read me another." He settled down beside me expectantly.

"OK," I said.

L O L L Y   A N D   T H E   G I A N T

Once upon a time—

"Daddy? Why do fairy stories always start with 'Once upon a time'?"

"They don't. They start with 'The check's in the post.' "

I snickered at my own joke. Cosmo looked blank.

"But this story—"

I said irritably, not wanting my performance to be interrupted, "Just listen."

Once upon a time, there was a woodcutter and his wife who had so many children and so little food that they decided the only thing to do was to get rid of their three daughters.

"That was very wicked of them," said Cosmo. "*You* wouldn't do that, would you, Dad?"

"No," I said.

"Sons are more useful than daughters," said the woodcutter's wife. "Besides, they're the eldest."

The woodcutter was very reluctant to let any of his children go, but at last he was persuaded. Whatever happens to them in the wood, he thought, abandoning them can't be as bad as letting the whole family starve.

So the next day, the woodcutter took the three girls into the dark wood, gave them a last slice of bread, and left them.

"Do people really do things like that?" Cosmo asked uneasily. He shifted closer.

"No, of course not. It's only a story."

The three girls ate their bread and walked until they were utterly worn out and lost. Soon they would have lain down and died in each other's arms. But just as it was getting dark, they spied a small light beaming through the trees. It came, as they hoped, from a chink in the window of a house. So Lolly, who was the youngest and also the cleverest, went and knocked on the door.

"Is that a picture of her?" asked Cosmo.

"Yes."

There was Lolly knocking at the door of a big white house. Behind her was a clearing, and a white gate overhung with great shaggy trees. The girl had the same face as the one I had seen

{ 165 }

riding the White Bear and the North Wind, but she was younger. I knew my mother had drawn herself, as a child. The house, too, looked oddly real, like something out of an old photograph. It didn't look like an English house, I thought suddenly. The walls were made of wood, not brick or stone, and there was a kind of porch running down either side of the front door. There were louvered shutters on the windows. Where had I seen this kind of house before?

"Go on," said Cosmo.

A big woman came out and asked who she was and what she wanted.

"My name is Lolly," said Lolly. "We're lost and need something to eat."

"Eat!" said the woman. "My husband's a giant, and he'll eat YOU before you can say 'slice' and 'knife.'"

But Lolly was so tired and hungry, she went on begging and begging and at last the woman let them all in. She sat them down and gave them bread and milk; but hardly a bite had passed their lips when there came a great thumping. It was the giant come home, and he sniffed and said—

"I know! I know!" said Cosmo. "Fee, fi, fo, fum, I smell the blood of an Englishman."

"That's not quite right," I said.

"Fee, fi, fo, fash,
I smell the blood of a little lass—
Be she alive or be she dead,
I'll grind her bones to make my bread."

"Now then, don't take on so," said his wife. "I have a surprise for you."

She showed him the three young girls, and the giant and his wife laughed and winked at each other. Then the giant sat down and had his supper, but in between bites he looked at Lolly and her sisters.

Now the giant had three daughters of his own. They were much younger than Lolly and her sisters, but being giants they had already grown to the same size. The giant's wife put them all six in the same bed. So Lolly and her sisters thought they would be safe. But before he went to bed, the giant hung three chains of gold around his own daughters' necks. Then he patted the heads of the three homeless girls and put three necklaces of rope round theirs. Only Lolly noticed this, and thought about what it could mean.

"What does it mean?" Cosmo asked, anxiously.

"The giant is going to do something bad to them in the dark," I said.

"What?"

Soon the other five were asleep in the great bed, but Lolly lay awake, listening. At last she got up softly and changed over, one by one, the necklaces of gold and rope. So now it was Lolly and her sisters who wore the chains of gold, and the giant's daughters who wore the rope. Then she lay down again and waited.

In the middle of the night, the giant came tiptoeing in and felt very cautiously with his finger and thumb for the rope. And when he had felt them round his own daughters' necks, he dragged them out of bed, and took out a big knife. Then he cut their throats, one after another, as they lay sleeping.

"Ho!" he said. "That's my breakfast."

Then he went away to bed, chuckling.

Cosmo's eyes were wide. I had his complete attention now.

As soon as it was quiet, Lolly woke her sisters and they slipped out of the house and never stopped running until morning.

At dawn they found they had come to another house, a great grand house with a thousand windows and a lake with swans floating on it.

This was the house of the king. In went Lolly and her sisters, and straight up to the king to tell him their story. When it was finished, the king said, "Ah, Lolly, that thing's done, and done well. But I could tell you another thing, and that would be better. Go back and steal the giant's sword, and your eldest sister shall have my eldest son for a husband."

Lolly thought of the chains of gold which she and her sisters had carried out of the giant's house, on which they could live well; but she thought, too, of how her own mother and father had set their lives at naught: and she said she would try.

"What's 'naught'?" Cosmo asked.

"Another word for nothing. In those days, people thought sons were worth more than daughters."

"Flora isn't worth anything."

I said, "Of course she is, and so are you."

"But you love me more, don't you? You've taken me on holiday with you and not her."

That very evening, she made her way back through the dark wood to the giant's house. She listened at the window, and heard him having his supper; and while he was eating it she crept into the house and hid under his bed.

In the middle of the night, when the giant and his wife were snoring like a hundred pigs falling down the stairs, Lolly climbed softly up onto the giant's bed, and unhooked his sword from the nail in the wall. It was big and heavy, and when she came to the door it rattled in its scabbard. Before you could say "slice" and "knife," the giant woke up.

Then Lolly ran, and the giant ran, and they both ran, and at last they came to a great chasm. Lolly plucked a single hair from her head, and it made a bridge. Lolly ran over it on her thin little legs to the other side. But not the giant: he was too heavy. He shook his fist and shouted, "Woe betide ye, little Lolly, / If ye e'er come back again!"

But Lolly just laughed and said, "Twice again old fee, fi, fo, / I will come to trouble you."

Then Lolly carried off the sword to the king, and her eldest sister married the king's eldest son, and there was great rejoicing.

"Well," said the king, when the wedding was over, "that was a thing done and done well. But I know another, and that's better still. Steal the purse that lies under the giant's pillow, and I'll marry your second sister to my second son."

Lolly looked at the second son, and laughed, and said she would try.

Back she stole through the dark wood to the giant's house. This time she hid herself in the linen closet. Sure enough, the giant looked under his bed in case Lolly was hiding there; but he didn't think to look in his smelly clothes, where she lay hardly breathing, and waiting.

There was a picture of the giant peering under his bed. He had a very big bum. Cosmo laughed.

In the middle of the night, when the giant and his wife were snoring like two express trains, Lolly got out of the linen closet and felt a little way under his pillow. The giant stopped snoring, and she was still as a mouse until he started again. Then Lolly slid her fingers in a bit more. The giant called out that there were robbers; but his wife said, "Lie easy! It's them bones you had for supper, old man."

Then Lolly pushed her fingers all the way in and felt the purse. But as she drew it out, a piece of gold dropped out and clinked on the floor. At the sound of it, the giant woke, and before you could say "slice" and "knife," he was up.

Now Lolly ran and the giant ran and they both ran. They ran and they ran through the dark wood until they came to the Bridge of One Hair. And Lolly got over on her thin little legs, but the giant stayed for he couldn't and wouldn't. Then he cried out across the chasm, "Woe betide ye, little Lolly, / If ye e'er come back again!"

But Lolly only laughed and said, "Once again old fee, fi, fo, / I will
come to trouble you!"

So she took the purse to the king, and her second sister was married
to the king's second son, and there was great rejoicing.

"Well, now," said the king when it was over, "that was a good thing
done and done well. But I know a better yet, and that's the best of all.
Steal the giant's ring from off his finger, and you shall have my youngest
son for a husband together with half my kingdom and the whole of my
kingdom when I die. For Lolly, I can think of nobody as brave and clever
as you."

Now this was a very difficult thing to do, but Lolly looked at the
youngest prince and he smiled at her, so she laughed and said she would
try.

Off she went through the dark wood, and this time she hid herself in
the chimney while the giant and his wife had supper. Then they went to
bed, and when she heard them snoring like alligators in the swamp—

I stopped.

"Go on," said Cosmo. "Is the giant's ring his wedding ring?"

"Maybe."

"Mummy doesn't wear hers anymore. But you do. Why do
you?"

When she heard them snoring like alligators in the swamp, she crept out.
The giant's hand had slipped over the edge of the bed, and hung down so
that she could see the gold ring on his finger. Slowly, very slowly, Lolly
pulled it until it began to slip down the giant's puffy finger. At last the
ring came off, but at the final tug the giant woke. Before you could say
"slice" and "knife," he'd grabbed Lolly's hand.

"Ho! Ho! Ho!" he shouted. "I've caught you now, little girl." He
glared down at her. "Once too many is never again. If I'd done all the
bad things to you that you've done to me, what would I be getting?"

"Why," said Lolly, thinking quickly. "I'd bundle you up in a sack

with a cat and a dog and a pair of scissors and a needle and thread, and I'd hang you up on the wall and go off to the wood and cut the thickest stick I could find, and I'd beat you to a jelly. That's what I'd do!"

"And that, Lolly," said the giant, beaming at his own cunning, "is just what I'm going to do to YOU."

So up he got and fetched a sack, and a cat and a dog and a pair of scissors and a needle and thread, and he hung her up on the wall. Then away he went to the wood to cut a thick stick.

As soon as he was gone, Lolly began to sing out in a clear, happy voice, "Oh, if only everyone could see what I can see!"

"See?" said the giant's wife. "What can you see, Lolly?"

But Lolly only said in her clear, happy voice, "Oh, if only everybody could see what I can see!"

At last the giant's wife begged Lolly to take her up into the sack so that she could see what Lolly saw. Then Lolly took the scissors and cut a hole in the lowest corner of the sack, jumped out, and helped the giant's wife in. Next, fast as she could, she sewed up the hole with the needle and thread. The giant's wife could only see stars, the sack was so dark. No sooner had Lolly finished than the giant came in with a great big stick. When he saw the sack he let out a bellow of rage, rushed at it, and began to bang away without mercy. The giant's wife shrieked that it was his own wife he was hitting, not Lolly, but the cat and the dog made such a howling and a screeching that the giant couldn't hear a word.

"That's really mean on the cat and dog," said Cosmo, indignantly. "They hadn't done anything bad, had they?"

"I expect the giant mostly thumped his wife," I said. "She was a lot bigger."

Lolly crept softly out from behind the door, and the giant saw her. He gave a roar, and Lolly ran, and the giant ran, and they both ran and ran through the dark wood until they came to the Bridge of One Hair. And Lolly skipped over it with the giant's ring but the giant couldn't go any *farther. He cried after her in a dreadful voice, "Woe betide ye, little Lolly, / If ye e'er come back again!"*

But Lolly waved her hand and called back over the chasm, "Never again, old fi, fo, fee, / Will I come to trouble ye!"

Then off Lolly ran, and she was married to the king's youngest son and given half the kingdom. And she invited the rest of her family to the wedding feast, and they all ate and ate until they were hungry no more. So the giant and his wife were left behind in the dark wood, but without his sword or his money or his ring they had no more power, and every-one forgot about them. But everyone loved and remembered brave Queen Lolly, who had saved them and their children from the cruel gi-ant and his wicked wife.

There was a long pause while my son digested this. "Why didn't the giant die?" Cosmo asked. "He was bad, wasn't he?"

"Bad people don't always die."

"They do in stories."

I thought of my mother, who had died; and how so many people had tried to persuade me she was bad, or at least mad. "Well, not in this one. I expect losing your power is much worse, because then nobody would be afraid of you anymore. Come on, let's go back to the hotel."

"Why?"

"I'm waiting for somebody who knows a lot about stories to call."

JANE HOLLY was not quite as easy to meet as Ruth had assured me. For one thing, she still ran Nutshell, the publishing house specializing in children's books, and for another she had just got back from abroad. I left a message with her secretary and on Len and Rupert's answerphone. I had planned a few days in New York anyway, spending the fairy gold left by my mother.

Cosmo and I went shopping and sightseeing. The moment you become a parent you also become a tourist. We went to FAO Schwarz, the zoo, and, lastly, Ellis Island. We got out of our taxi to take the ferry close to the UN building. My son gazed at it, open-mouthed. "That's where the Rescuers work," he said.

"Who?"

"They're these little mice from all around the world, they save children in trouble. It's in a Disney video."

"Don't you ever get bored of seeing everything through Disney?" I said.

He stuck his chin out in a way that reminded me painfully of my wife. "I *like* Disney."

"Of course you do, but they're just cartoons. People don't really have those huge eyes and tiny noses, do they? Animals don't talk and sing, do they? Look at the world as it is."

"There's Mickey Mouse walking along the street," said Cosmo.

"No, it isn't," I said irritably. "Stop making things up."

"Yes, it *is*!"

I looked where he was pointing and was mortified to see a man dressed as Mickey Mouse ambling along the bottom of Wall Street. "Don't look at him."

"Why?"

"Just don't. It's just a man in a Mickey Mouse costume. He'll be a beggar or something. Look at the river instead."

"Why should I?"

"Just *look*. Isn't this fantastic?"

My mood of joy was intensifying by the hour. I was thrilled by everything, by the glittering towers of steel and glass, by the blue sky and crystalline waves. I felt reborn. The mistiness, the grayness, the despair of England were all gone. To think that I had spent so many hours considering suicide! Why, it was absurd! I couldn't understand what had been going on in my mind.

He wanted to run around under the trees. So we played at giants. I chased Cosmo across the coarse grass.

"Fee, fi, fo, fum!" I bellowed, pursuing my son. He shrieked and giggled. I rolled my eyes and roared, *"Ho! Ho! Ho!"* I did my Brian Blessed imitation. He shrieked again. When I caught him, I swung him about upside-down, then threw him up in the air and hugged him.

People stopped and beamed at us. In some corner of my mind, I knew that this extravagant thespian personality wasn't mine, and yet because this is the way adults normally behave towards their children, nobody found it strange.

GULLS BOUNCED in the air, graceful and mechanical as mobiles. Their voices were American, keening and calling, squawking and whistling.

"Every time I see this view, I want to say, Thank you, Grandpa, for coming here," said one elderly man fervently to his companion, gazing back at Manhattan as the ferry churned across the water.

Cosmo asked, "Why are you laughing, Dad?"

"Just something."

The island came closer. I pointed out the distant Statue of Liberty to Cosmo. As we went past, the teenagers and other Americans stopped talking and hopping about, and clapping and whistling.

"Can we go to see that lady?"

"She's like a lot of them, not so pretty close up."

"Is she a giant?"

"She's supposed to be Liberty. That's another word for freedom. That's what a lot of the people who came to this country were looking for."

"Why did they want freedom?"

"So that they could be happy. It's written into their Constitution that Americans have the right to be happy."

"What's a constitution?"

"How you are, or should be."

The torch in the statue's vast hand blazed, a bud of light. I wondered what it would be like to climb up inside her, as you were able to do, and walk around inside her head, looking out. I wondered if people seemed like thoughts or dreams to her. We walked round Ellis Island, looking at all the names of those who had made the passage to this land of hope. I wondered whether my mother's family had been among them. *Give me . . . your huddled masses yearning to breathe free.* Who did not yearn to breathe free, to start afresh?

"So is everyone who lives here happy?" He looked up at me.

"They're happy if they have money," I said.

"Do we have money?"

"We have some over here. Not back in England. At least, I won't have any back in England."

"Why can't you live here?"

Why not indeed. I had already noticed how much cheaper everything was—that a dollar bought as much as a pound. But a lot of stuff, food especially, was of a standard that appalled me. Neither of us could eat the bread (a sort of light, disgustingly sweet, spongy stuff) or drink the milk. The pizza was unspeakable, thick tasteless slabs covered in a peppery sauce. You could see who the poor people were here: they weren't thin, as they are in fairy tales, but fat—monstrously inflated on junk food. I was thin, so there was no question of being mistaken for one of the unlucky. Nevertheless, I could feel the imperative to spend as a constant pressure in the atmosphere, like thunder building up. Whenever we went out or came into our hotel I tipped the doorman twenty dollars. I tipped everyone. I was more popular than I had ever been in my life.

JANE HOLLY was tall and elegant, her fine white hair cut with razor-sharp precision, and what looked like a silver coffee bean dangling from each ear. She was dressed in sculpted white linen that made her resemblance to a priestess irresistible. Everything in Nutshell was self-consciously cool and modern, from the glass elevator that whisked us up into its offices to the person who owned it. White flowers, each like a scroll of paper, filled large glass vases in the reception room. Cosmo, fascinated, went up to one and touched the thick yellow pistil.

"Don't touch those, honey," said the receptionist, with a hint of acid beneath her gleaming smile.

"Why not?"

"You'll spoil them. Mrs. Holly will see you now, sir."

There was something almost too English about Jane Holly; the sort of idealized Englishness that foreigners like but which never really exists at home. I thought that was probably part of her cult. She charmed Cosmo immediately by talking to him first.

"Can you read yet?"

He shook his head and hid behind me.

"Never mind. My grandchildren can't, either, and one of them is six. I'm sure you will soon. But I bet you're good at drawing and coloring in." He nodded, and a small smile crept across his features. "I've got just the thing, then."

She gave him a book of medieval letters to color in, then made tea. I looked at her shelves, which were as brightly colored as everything else was minimalist. There were many books I knew all too well: anthropomorphic animals, chubby infants, witches, spaceships, dragons, castles—the usual panoply of childhood. How could anyone devote his or her life to it?

We were so high up above New York, I could see clouds floating by. The Chrysler Building looked like a palace of crystal and gold.

"This isn't what you expected?"

"No," I said. "I suppose, if I'm honest, I was expecting a sort of cottage. Or burrow."

Jane laughed. Even her small teeth were white. I didn't doubt that she'd acquired them here.

"Yes. Hardly anyone cares about children's literature, even though half of all books sold in this country and the U.K. are for children. You're not supposed to write for them or notice them, if intelligent. If you publish them, you're supposed to be all fluffy and hopeless at sums."

She moved Cosmo to the big window. I knew he'd be absorbed in coloring his new book, deaf to our conversation, but Jane, obviously, didn't want him interrupting us.

Then I said, "As I think I told you, I'm investigating Laura Perry's life." It felt strange, calling my mother by her name.

"I see. Who's your publisher?"

"What?"

"I assume you're going to write a biography?"

"I'm trying to find out about my mother for myself. I hadn't thought of publishing anything. I'm an actor, not a writer."

Jane picked up her cup, inhaled its scent, and sipped. It was bone china, so fine the light shone through it. I thought of Nell back in London and her overlarge mugs; of Ruth and her cups of mud.

"She's one of the major children's authors. You should think about it. I have a lot of friends in this town, and though I don't publish biographies I know the best people to go to. Plenty of actors have shown they can write, look at Shakespeare."

"*O God, I could be bounded in a nutshell and count myself a king of infinite space, were it not that I have bad dreams,*" I said.

Jane looked startled. "Yes. That's why I chose the name for my company. People assume it must be something to do with squirrels or smallness. How strange that you should understand."

"What are your bad dreams?"

"I have a great many. One of them is guilt over your mother's dying as she did. So many of us got divorced in the mid-sixties, it was a kind of epidemic. Even so, to learn she'd killed herself— I still remember the shock. She was on the brink of becoming, well, what she is now, after an extraordinarily productive year. And she never knew. That's what I find so tragic. It all came too late."

We were both silent. I thought about my own failures. Jane said, "Have you visited your relations?"

"No."

"Aren't you curious? I was. She would never talk about her home or family."

"I'm more interested in her life in London."

"I'm not really the best person to tell you about that. I didn't know her socially. Of course, I was only James's secretary then, but I did see her once at a party, with your father. Our worlds overlapped only very tangentially. They were a striking couple. She was very glamorous, very . . . it wasn't just that she was beautiful. She seemed to have more vitality than everyone else there. Perhaps it was that she was one of the first Americans I had then met. Oh, England and the English! Whenever I go back there I find I've forgotten how small it is—not just physically, but its whole outlook on things. And how small it makes its people."

I didn't like this. Although I was half-American, I didn't think she should disparage her country of origin. No other nation does, why should we?

"So you feel at home here?"

"Yes. If you work, this is the most wonderful place in the world."

People always said this about New York. I said skeptically, "Wasn't England? After all, that was where you started."

"You wouldn't understand," she said. "It was such a struggle to have a career, even with a good degree from Oxford. The BBC only accepted graduates, but they had to be men; one publisher I went to for an interview made no secret he gave candidates marks out of ten for their looks. He actually let me see mine." She grimaced. "I think James gave me a job because he fancied me. Not that he did anything about it . . . any more than he did with your mother."

I raised my eyebrows. "Oh?"

"He liked to think of himself as a lady's man. Not that he did much—a bit of patting and panting. But it was demeaning."

"I know about that kind of thing, you know," I said. "Being an actor."

"It was more to do with being a woman," said Jane. "If you

were bright you were expected to spend your life hiding it. I remember my mother saying that I'd never get a husband if I got a degree, but that if I were so foolish as to go to university, I shouldn't graduate without being engaged. Which, like a fool, I did. But then you couldn't get a job in publishing unless you were unmarried. You couldn't even have a bank account in your own name once you were married. It makes me so angry, even now, to think of it."

I tried to imagine what this must have been like, how someone like Georgie would have coped. "Was it the same for my mother, do you think? Was she angry?"

"Yes, I think so. After all, there was that extraordinary alphabet she drew. She was so subversive, underneath the domesticity. When I was with her I kept finding I was looking at things, noticing them, in a completely different way. She had an extraordinarily powerful presence—it was like suddenly finding yourself under a magnifying glass. Enlarged and clarified, but also scorched."

I thought about this. It didn't make her sound a very comfortable person to know. "How did other people react to that?"

"Poor Jamie! He was terrified."

"You were fond of him, in spite of the groping?"

"Yes, I suppose I was, really. Though I also resented the way he behaved. In the end, I made him see that it wasn't good business. One of the old school of publishers, four-hour lunches and hopeless at marketing. Have you met him?" I nodded. "He couldn't spot a good manuscript to save his life. The children's books were really just a sideline; he had no idea that there might be serious money in them. It was all terribly fusty and genteel. Nothing had changed since before the war."

"But you found my mother. Or did she find you?"

"Oh, she found us. Illustrators were always hawking their portfolios round. You'd hear them trudging up the stairs—it was one of those narrow old buildings in Soho, riddled with rot and probably held together by about three nails." She looked out through her plate-glass windows at the urban geometry, and sighed. "She'd done a lot of hack work, greeting cards. The usual stuff. Illustrators all looked up towards the real artists like Minton and Mervyn Peake. But I could see she was good. I was amazed when I heard she was Howard's wife."

"Yes, I gather most people were. Was he as well known then as he is now?"

"Oh, almost more so. He, Ken Tynan, Mark Boxer, Sam Viner—there was a whole generation of them suddenly sweeping through the media—and he was dazzlingly handsome. Is he still?"

"Yes," I said. "His hair has gone gray, but that's about it."

"After a certain age, men look ridiculous with hair," said Jane. "They don't know what to do with it."

"He's always raking it with his fingers. The tousled look," I said.

Jane laughed. "I thought your mother rather frightening, too, at first. Then, when we went out for lunch together, she was so different."

I felt the protean nature of my mother reassert itself. "How?"

"She was much gentler, softer—as if she'd lost a shell. Almost like a child herself."

"So you liked her."

"Of course. She was delightful. Some of the things she said shocked me—like about the uselessness of the Royal Family and the British Empire. Everyone intelligent sees that now, but back *then* it was unthinkable. I expect she was lonely. Most of the women I knew were so terribly *good,* all on their first marriages, with small children, and utterly miserable but not admitting it."

I couldn't imagine this self-possessed woman being a domestic drudge, even then.

"What saved me was work. I was jolly good at my job, and I

knew it. So, I must say, did James, although he never thought to offer me a pay rise. He'd spend more on one lunch than I could feed into my gas fire for a week. But it didn't matter, because I loved it all. Still do."

It was strange, I thought, the way all the women I had interviewed about my mother spent at least as much time describing their own lives as hers. But Jane had seen more, or told me more, than anyone. I liked her. In an odd way she reminded me a little of Georgie—that peculiarly English mix of sternness and humor.

"Most people don't seem to have liked her very much."

"Didn't they?" said Jane, dismissively. "More fool they."

At last, I exulted, I had someone defending her, describing the person I knew she had to have been.

"You look so like Laura, you know."

"Do I? James Cork said so, too."

"Yes, when you smile. But like your father, too."

The thought of Howard fell across me like a shadow. How angry he would be, I thought, when he found out what I was doing. "What did you think of *him*?"

There was a long pause. "If you want my honest opinion, I thought he was an arrogant shit."

"Was she unhappy with him?"

"How could she *not* be?" said Jane, explosively. "That man— that *MAN* . . . if anyone is to blame for your mother's death, it's Howard."

I leaned forward. "Tell me."

"She absolutely adored him, and he went off with that silly little girl. It's so wicked, men doing that when they have a wife and child. I heard he married her after your mother's death. Are they still together?"

I nodded. Jane said, "Poor Laura! I suppose she was a romantic."

"Why did she write fairy tales?"

"I've no idea. No, that's not true. She said something once that I've never forgotten, that it's children's authors, not poets, who are the unacknowledged legislators of the world. I think that's what she wanted to be."

I said, slowly, "Unacknowledged, maybe; but legislators?"

"Yes. What is the law but a vision of how life should be? Isn't that what the fairy tale—which was originally for adults as much as for children—is deeply concerned with? With justice? What is the phrase every parent hears most often from a child? *It's not fair.* That is what women feel, too, but it's only recently we've had the guts to say it aloud."

I said, skeptically, "Are you saying that all fairy tales were written by women?"

"There's a lot of evidence that points that way. Men like the Brothers Grimm and Perrault simply collected what had been dismissed as old wives' tales. Those whose authorship is known were always by women, practically without exception—but Laura was one of the first to do a collection of stories about heroines. She wasn't given credit for it at the time, that fell to Angela Carter, lucky enough to belong to the generation that came after, but—"

"I've been reading *North of Nowhere,*" I said, interrupting. "I wondered whether she wrote them herself or just found them. Do you know?"

Jane clearly didn't like being interrupted, but said, "I think a bit of both. That's what makes *In a Dark Wood* so remarkable. As far as the stories went, I know she did some rewriting. 'The Bird of Truth,' for instance, is a version of one told by Scheherazade in *The Thousand and One Nights.* 'Lolly and the Giant' is Scottish, and usually called 'Molly Whuppie.' "

"I've just read that one to my son. We liked it, didn't we, Cosmo?" He had wandered back again, bored.

"I liked the giant with the big bum."

Jane said, "She was really more of an illustrator than a writer. I think the pictures were what interested her most. I remember one other thing she said about picture books; they were visual poems. I've always liked that idea. People are still so supercilious about them—they're barely even reviewed. Even when they become classics, most people have no idea why they work as they do."

The tension in my body made it tremble. "Did you know that she used real people as models?"

"Why, yes," said Jane. "She used me."

I wasn't somehow surprised. "Did she? Where? Were you upset by it?"

"You probably can't see it now, but I'm pretty sure I was one of the three mothers that become witches in *The Angry Alphabet*." She smiled. She, it was clear, had not been offended. "And I was the Moon in 'The White Bear.' I was very flattered to be that, of course."

"You didn't mind being a witch, too?"

"Good God, no. We all have multiple selves. I probably am a sort of witch, though a good one, I hope. I was happy to be seen as both. Will you draw me some witches, darling?" she said to Cosmo.

"Were you in Sam Viner's cartoons, too? You know, in *The Cutting Edge*?"

She shook her head. "I wasn't in *that* circle. That was more of an in-joke, like his *Felix* cartoons."

"My father wasn't happy about it."

"Oh, yes. I remember your father actually ringing me up and berating me when *The Angry Alphabet* came out."

"I'd have thought fairy tales far more innocuous than a newspaper cartoon."

"I expect he thought he could bully me," said Jane dryly. "Or perhaps he was outraged at being depicted that way by a woman."

I said, defensively, "I don't have much to do with him, you know."

"Why?"

"I can't stand his views. He thinks my mother was mad."

Jane smiled derisively. "But of course. Artists are nearly always called that. Some are genuinely so. What they do isn't the product of being nice, or even particularly sane. They're running over the Bridge of One Hair, like Lolly."

I looked blankly at her.

"Trying to connect the inner world with the outer. That's what makes them so crucial to a society. It's also what makes them suffer so deeply."

I wondered if my mother's work deserved this praise. The drawings were (as far as I could tell) very beautiful and had moved me, but something about Jane Holly's fervor made me skeptical.

"Did you commission her to write and illustrate her own books right away?" I asked.

"Oh, no. No! That would be like giving an untried actor the lead roles straight out of drama school. No, in the beginning, as I said, she illustrated other people's words. All the same, I don't think James would have agreed if I hadn't pushed him."

"But you liked what she did?"

"Of course. To be working within a tradition and yet so completely modern—it's not often you get that. There are a few who've had it, people like Sendak, and Edward Gorey, and Errol Le Cain, people you won't have heard of but who to me shape our culture as surely as any modern artist. Think of what Beatrix Potter did to the vision of the English countryside, for instance. . . . But there are still very few who have that quality, that extra dimension of the imagination. It isn't always something parents want, is it? There are still the misguided souls who teach their children to sing 'Three *kind* mice.' Then they're surprised when their children grow up and join the Moonies." The silver drops in her ears winked. "All true art is subversive. But often, what parents are looking for is reassurance."

"There's nothing wrong with that, is there? Not every child wants to walk on the wild side."

"Oh, no. Not at all. They're superb at best—I only wish I had someone like Shirley Hughes or Jill Murphy on my list. You've got to have a balance—and God knows there are all those horrible things like *Goosebumps* waiting down the road, so better pack the reassurance in while you can. But it's those who push at the known world, instead of celebrating the idealized status quo, who go deeper and further. They produce the books that people go on remembering all their life. Sometimes it's just particular images. I found for years that when I was having a bad time I could summon up a vision of the road to paradise. I had no idea where it came from until quite recently, when I picked up *Mrs. Tiggy-Winkle* for the first time in fifty-five years and reread it, to my grandson. Then I saw that it's the picture of the path the little girl takes up into the mountains."

I couldn't tell her that I was here because of just such a drawing in my mother's book. I still had enough self-control to know how crazy that would sound. "It's true, they do have this feeling of recognition about them," I said.

"*Exactly.* Unacknowledged legislators, remember?" Jane sipped her tea again. I had the feeling that she was giving me a version of a speech she had made many times before. "The great children's writers and illustrators are not unlike the great adult ones, even if they still portray a belief in the triumph of imagination and beauty which the adult world has lost. Often, they aren't particularly commercial. They don't all get their artwork turned into wrapping paper like Jane Ray, or made into soft toys like Babar or, God help us, turned into Disney videos."

Cosmo looked up at this. "I *like* Disney videos," he said, stubbornly. He held his drawing of a witch. She had earrings like Jane's, I noticed.

Jane smiled at him. "Of course you do. But one day, you won't. You'll find out that reading and using your imagination are more exciting. At least, I hope you will."

"Why?"

"Because otherwise, my darling, I'll be out of business."

I sighed. Tension was building up in me again. My legs kept twitching with the need to get moving. "But my mother's books are pretty frightening, too. I don't know that all children could really understand them."

"Do you? Are childhoods so happy? What about your own?"

"I can't remember much of it," I said, awkwardly.

Jane looked keenly at me. "Did you know she'd killed herself?"

"Not for a long while. I think I thought she'd just left me."

"That must have been terrible for you."

"I don't honestly remember much. I don't think I want to."

"I don't know how you can tell a child their mother is dead," said Jane. "I don't know if there's any way which is less painful. She did love you very much, you know."

"Who's dead?" Cosmo asked anxiously.

"Nobody you know," I said. "We're just talking about people who lived a long time ago."

"Once upon a time?" he asked, his features smoothing as he repeated the comforting formula.

"Yes," Jane said. "Once upon a time."

S I X T E E N

Icouldn't sleep for more than a couple of hours. It didn't matter. The girl in the picture watched over me. I could see her behind my eyes. I knew she didn't love me as I loved her, but it didn't matter. She showed me by a thousand small signs that she was there. When I looked out of the window of our suite I could see three small thorny trees, still leafless but covered with white fairy lights. Every few seconds, these lights would suddenly start swarming, flicking on and off one after the other; then stop again. Cosmo would stare at this phenomenon, fascinated. It looked as if some thin, glittering snake were caught in the bare branches, writhing frantically before subsiding in exhaustion.

I ordered room service or raided the mini-bar when necessary, and didn't impose any routine on my son. Why bother? Routine was one of those pointless things other people did, knowing that the next day they'd have to do it all over again. Cosmo, being tidier than myself, carefully folded his clothes at night and chose clean ones, but I didn't. I was beyond such trivia.

Cosmo was sitting on the floor, watching cartoons when his mother rang.

"Hallo?"

I was breathless from bouncing on the bed. Once I started I found it so exhilarating it was impossible to stop. Cosmo didn't mind. We had bounced together for about an hour, then he got tired and slid off while I continued. I had now been bouncing for most of the day, and was still delighted by the sensation.

"Dick? It's me. Why haven't you called?"

"Were you expecting me to?"

"Yes, of course. Is everything all right? You sound rather odd. Your voice keeps coming and going. How's Cosmo?"

"He's fine. Not too jet-lagged. This is the most amazing city—"

"Can I talk to him?"

"Why not? On the other hand, why?"

"Dick, I want to talk to my son. Is he there?"

"*Over here, over there, / I do wander every where, / Swifter than the moon's sphere, / And I serve the Fairy Queen—*" I bounced, then said, "Hey, Cosmo. It's Mummy. Do you want to talk to her?"

He nodded and took the receiver. As usual, he forgot to say anything, but stood there, holding it, a puzzled expression on his face. "I can hear her voice," he said. At once, the insect whine coming from the earpiece changed tone. He began to smile, and nodded.

"She can't see you," I said, halfway up to the ceiling. "You have to say 'Yes.' "

"Yes, Mummy," he said obediently.

The conversation went on for quite a while. He only said yes and no. Eventually, he said, "Bye," and put the receiver down on the bed. I picked it up, although my wife's voice was still coming out the other end, and put it onto the bedside table. It amused me to think how much money it must have cost Bruce. After a while, of course, we were disconnected.

"Everything OK?" I asked. He nodded. "Not missing her, are you?" He looked at me. "We're being boys together, remember?"

"I want to go to the park."

"Don't you want to do some more bouncing?"

"No, I want to go to the park. I want to see the horses."

The telephone rang again. Before I could stop him, he went over and picked up the receiver. "Mummy?"

I jumped down. He was listening, the shut-in expression back on his face. "It's some man."

I AGREED to meet Len and Rupert in a restaurant that evening. Cosmo had fallen asleep in the afternoon, clutching his tiger's tail in both hands, and was only awakened with difficulty. I endured the ear-splitting screams and cries until he calmed down and agreed that coming out was preferable to staying in with a babysitter provided by the hotel.

"Taxi, sir? Or would you prefer our limo service?" asked the doorman. I pressed another twenty dollars into his hands, and chose the limo. He beamed and tipped his hat. Whenever I came in or went out of the hotel, people now smiled and sprang to attention.

The limo swished through the streets.

"You're not frightened, are you?" I said to Cosmo.

He shook his head, but held tightly on to Ti-Ti. He had a glazed, sleepy look in his eye, and half his hair was standing up because I'd forgotten to brush it. He looked very like Flora. I reached out and stroked his hair as though it were fur. "Look, I'm sorry I was a bit cross with you. It's just that I'd like you to do things like get dressed more quickly, OK?"

"I'm trying," he said.

"I know you are. Very."

"This is a funny place."

I said, "Do you remember our old house? The one we lived in when we were all together?"

Cosmo nodded, slowly.

"What do you remember?"

"There were trees at the end of the garden."

"That's right," I said, pleased.

"They had leaves like green hearts. And when we left, the leaves went yellow, and fell down."

I hadn't even noticed. "There'll be new leaves there, now. It's spring."

We were both silent. We would never be there to see the trees again. It didn't seem to matter, but I was sorry for him.

"Will there be other children here?"

"No. Just grown-ups. Sorry."

We had arrived at our destination, a plush Italian restaurant. There was another gigantic urn crammed with blossom, just like the one back at the hotel. Did they order them all as a job lot? I wondered. Were there orchards somewhere with nothing left but bare trunks?

The columns supporting the roof were painted silver and gold; there were tiny clusters of halogen lights twisted round each one. The floor was black and shining, reflective as still water. Cosmo was a little afraid of stepping out onto it, and so was I. A waiter shimmied forward to ask us what we were doing here, then led us to a table where two men sat.

"Hallo," said one. "How good to see you at last. I'm Len, and this is Rupert. Come and sit down."

Cosmo hid behind me. The bald man who had spoken beamed at him. "Are you Cosmo?"

"Yes. This is Ti-Ti."

"Hallo, Ti-Ti. Come and see the fish. Do you like fish? These are really special." He took my son's hand and led him away without a backward glance.

I said to Rupert, "This is the first time in a week anyone has taken him off my hands."

He smiled faintly. As tall and thin as Len was short and round, he was exquisitely elegant in the way I slightly despise.

"I haven't seen you since you were a baby," Rupert said, offering me a glass of champagne. We sat down on soft, squishy, black leather banquettes and made awkward conversation. I never know how to behave with gay men, even though the theatre is full of them. I'm always worried about sending out the wrong signals, and having a pass made at me. All straight men feel this, secretly. (When I mentioned it to my wife she said caustically, "You should be so lucky.") I found myself wishing Georgie were there.

My son came back and said, "Dad, look, there's a groovy kind of table with lots of cakes. Can I have one?"

"After you've had some pasta."

His mouth turned down. "Don't want nasty pasta. Want cakes."

"Don't talk like a baby," I said angrily.

"You know, you look so like your mother," said Rupert. "Cosmo, too."

"I have absolutely no memory of her at all. That's why I wanted to see you."

"We remember her very clearly, don't we?" said Len. They exchanged glances, and in that moment I saw that, despite superficial differences, they had grown alike in the way that all couples do over time; and I envied them. Georgie and I would never have looked like this, I was sure.

"How did you meet?"

"Someone at the Chelsea Arts Club, was it? Or the French House?"

"No, no," said Rupert impatiently. "She came in response to an ad we put in the *New Statesman* for a lodger."

Len's brow cleared. "Of course she did. We had this little flat at the top of our house, you see, just one big room and a lav, and she took it. Bloody freezing in winter, I should think, but she never complained. We felt ever so intrigued about her, didn't we?"

"Why?"

"Well," said Len, enjoying himself, "she was beautiful, but didn't seem to know anyone. I don't think she'd ever even used a broom before, somehow. And there she was living out of a tiny suitcase. But we never found out much about where she'd come from, not even when we all became friends."

"How did that happen?"

"Oh, because we made the effort," said Rupert. "We could see she was one of us, you know."

I asked sharply, "What do you mean?"

A flicker of amusement passed over Rupert's face. Len said, "Someone creative."

I was reminded of the appalling Liz. "Do you think creative people look different, then?"

"Oh, yes. There's a spark in the eyes. That's what we look for, isn't it?"

Rupert nodded. He was the quiet one, the introvert, I thought; he played the same supportive role that I had done with Georgie. Or perhaps it was just that, like almost every beautiful man or woman, he had never needed to learn the skills that lesser mortals do, of how to make themselves pleasant. (Was this also what had been wrong with my mother?) Len, being ugly, had learned this. I recognized his bald head and big nose at last. He had been the model for the Wind. I wondered whether he was aware of this.

"It took a long time to break the ice. She was having ever such a hard time of it with no contacts, going round the magazines and publishers. We could see she was good, and I had a friend on the *Radio Times,* which always needed illustrators in those days. So we took her under our wing, you see."

"I see. That was very good of you."

They beamed. I found myself liking them both. Our pasta arrived. Cosmo eyed his dubiously. He put a forkful into his mouth, then immediately spat it out again. "It's disgusting!" he said loudly. The pristine white cloth was spattered with tomato sauce.

A waiter materialized. "Is everything to your satisfaction, gentlemen?"

"Take it away!" said my son. "I won't eat it, it's *yucky*. I want some cake."

He banged his fork on the table. The other diners looked round, then away again. I stared back at them fiercely. If they thought this was embarrassing, they should try being in rep. I had once toured in a play that required me to shoot somebody with a gun onstage. One evening, I'd opened the drawer where the gun was supposed to be and found there was only a hat. So I'd beaten the other actor to death with a felt hat.

"What is it you do?" Len asked.

"I'm an actor."

"What have you been in?"

"Not much, for the past year."

They looked at me sympathetically. Of course, I thought, they were in my world, this would be drearily familiar to them.

"Who's your agent?"

I told them, with a brief résumé of my career so far.

"That doesn't sound so bad," said Len. "You know, it sounds to me like you need a new agent."

"I'd change if I could get a better one," I said. I knew they were just being polite.

Len took a piece of paper and scribbled a name and number on it. "Why don't you look up Lottie when you get back? She's an old friend. It's worth a try."

I couldn't believe any of these old people would be able to do something for me. "Tell me more about my mother."

"We thought she was extraordinarily gifted," said Rupert, smiling. I was almost certain, allowing for all the accretions and depletions of time, that he was the model for my mother's drawing of the Sun.

"All our friends adored her."

I felt a throb of pleasure. This was very different from what people in London had told me. I had another glass of champagne. "Did they? Why?"

I lit a cigarette. Before I'd even taken one puff, there was a general ripple of outrage. The waiter hurried over and said sternly, "Excuse me, sir, but this is a strictly no-smoking establishment."

"*Bugger,*" I said crossly, stubbing my cigarette out. Then I remembered who I was with. They didn't blink. I had the feeling they were laughing at me. "Sorry."

"Forget it," said Len.

"You were telling me about my mother."

"She was such fun. So beautiful," said Len, again. "Like Joan Crawford, you know? Tremendously stylish."

"Ruth said she reminded her of Snow White."

The two men exchanged glances.

"Ruth was very generous to Laura," said Rupert.

I must have shown how surprised I was, for he said, "You know she was engaged to your father before?"

It took a moment to understand what he was saying. Then my face must have shown my astonishment. I shook my head, and the thoughts in it whirled like snow in a paperweight.

"All ancient history."

"I'd always wondered—"

"So my father went from one to the other." And back again, I thought. I couldn't blame either of them, in that case. I should have guessed. Thank God I hadn't said anything to Ruth. "What is it about him that has so many women falling for him?"

They looked at each other, and grinned. I couldn't believe it. Of course, I thought. My father had charmed them. They didn't know what it was like to be cross-questioned every day of the holidays about the precise nature of my friendship with Tom.

"You don't choose friends for their views," said Len. "We know he's a dreadful bigot."

"It all worked out fine in the end. Ruth and Sam were much better suited."

"Until it all went wrong," I said. "You know about that?"

They both nodded.

"Ruth told us. She was used to seeing the headlights of his car come in through the basement window onto the opposite wall every evening. Then one night, the headlights came in a foot lower and she went out and found he'd bought a red Porsche."

I hadn't heard this version of the Viners' divorce before. Cosmo woke up enough to say, "I've got a Porsche. A silver one. My nanny gave it to me." Then he yawned. "Daddy, I've got ginger beer in my feet."

"Straighten your legs out."

He settled back down. He had traces of chocolate all round his mouth.

"Poor little fellow," said Len.

"I expect he'll grow up to judge me, too," I said. "His mother and I are divorcing."

"I'm sorry to hear that," they both said; sounding, for once, very American.

I asked, "Did you see the books my mother did? The collection of fairy tales?"

"Yes. She sent us a copy. Poor woman, she drove herself so hard."

"Did you notice that she used real people as models?"

"Did she?" said Rupert, vaguely.

"Some of them were quite cruel."

Len gave a quizzical smile. "Why should she have been kind?"

"Why shouldn't she?"

"Fairy tales are pretty cruel."

"Why do you think she was drawn to them? Was she like that? Everyone either black or white, with no shades of gray?"

"I don't know. She was a passionate woman, I think," said Len. "But I'd say it had more to do with her cast of mind. Most artists—painters, poets, playwrights, filmmakers—have something they desperately want to communicate yet also need to keep hidden. Sometimes they don't even know what it is. Perhaps it's that which makes them what they are."

"Why do you think they want to keep it a secret?" I was skeptical about this theory. "I mean, why not just come out and say it? Or shut up about it?"

"I don't know. Because art is produced out of feelings of shame and worthlessness, as well as curiosity, joy, anger, and excitement? It took me years to come out. I don't think that's entirely unconnected to the work I do," said Len.

"Did my mother go to university? An art college?"

Len frowned. Rupert shrugged. "I don't know." They looked questioningly at each other.

"I think she must have done," Len said slowly. "It was far more common then than it was for English girls. But whether she had been to art school, I don't know. You can see a lot of influences in her early work. But then she found her own style."

"Why do you think she topped herself?"

There was a slight pause. "I don't know. We came over here when you were about two. We assumed she couldn't cope after your father left her."

"Did she seem depressed before then? She lived in your house, you must have known."

Len sighed. "You can live in the same house and sleep in the same bed, and still not know. If we knew what the person next to us was really thinking and feeling we'd probably all kill ourselves—or each other."

I thought again of Georgie saying that knowing what I was feeling was like looking for spoor in the jungle. And she wondered how I could possibly want to say the same lines, again and again, not understanding that I could only show my feelings when I pretended they were real.

"She was happy when we knew her," said Len. "Do you

remember that party? She could have danced all night, like Audrey Hepburn in *My Fair Lady*."

"But that was because she'd just met Howard, don't you think? We felt like fairy godfathers. It was love at first sight, wasn't it?"

"Ruth was the one who suffered. I've always wondered whether she didn't marry Sam on the rebound, you know."

It was like trying to find my way through a fog of platitudes. I said, "It's just that I can't understand why she wrote, or rewrote, all those stories about women who survived and triumphed, only to kill herself."

"Perhaps they were what gave her the courage to commit suicide," said Rupert.

I hadn't thought of this possibility before.

"Are you going to visit her family?" Rupert asked.

"Yes," I said. "Yes, I am."

"We used to wonder what they were like."

"*Pure* Tennessee Williams, I'll bet."

"Have you been to the Carolinas?" I asked. "Or the rest of the South?"

They nodded.

"Savannah's beautiful, just beautiful. It was laid out by the same architect who designed London's parks, apparently. One could weep, thinking about how much of it was torn down. But it's very creepy, too. The South is one of those places, well . . . you see why it has the writers it does. Positively festering."

"We always felt bad about not making it back for the funeral, didn't we?" said Len. Rupert nodded.

"Have you ever been back to England?"

"Oh, yes. But I'm afraid it's changed too much. We prefer going to other parts of Europe. Or the Far East."

"Don't you miss things about England? The sense of irony?"

Len looked at me. "Irony is just a means of suppressing your feelings," he said.

THE WORLD yielded before me now like water. I fished out the addresses Ruth had given me, found my aunt's telephone number, announced my arrival in America, and was booked on the plane to Charleston by the following afternoon. It was very easy. By the time I had finished explaining who I was there was no question about not staying. Aunt Lily gave me directions in a clear, drawling voice. So I shaved, packed, and paid. The doorman and the manager himself came to wish us *bon voyage*. I pressed another fifty dollars into each hand, and was waved off as if we were royalty.

We had many more bags by then than the two with which we had arrived, but nothing would part Cosmo from his FAO Schwarz giant panda bear, new bow and arrows, Furby, and Playmobil pirate ship. Nothing, that is, except the dead-eyed U.S. security guards who, despite my son's screams, also insisted on putting Ti-Ti through the X-ray machine to see if it had a bomb inside.

"Why can't you just bend the rules a bit?" I said angrily. "You can see the bloody thing's a glove puppet."

"I'm only doing my job," said the one closest to me.

Cosmo's screams mounted as his toy was carried away on the conveyor belt. He stretched out his arms, with tears flooding down his cheeks like something out of a Victorian morality painting. The giant panda got stuck.

"I'm sorry, sir, this will have to be checked in," said the guard.

"I don't want it anyway," my son wept. "I only want my tiger."

The guard's mustache quivered. "Hang on, son," he said. I saw to my amazement that despite Cosmo's appalling behavior he was actually feeling sorry for him. The wretched Ti-Ti was put into his hands. By the time we had walked twenty meters it was all forgotten.

"Read me a story," Cosmo said, as we waited in the airport for the flight to Charleston. He had great dark circles under his eyes. He was munching a packet of crisps. Once again, I'd forgotten to give him breakfast.

"OK. What do you want?"

"A story from that book."

I turned the pages of *North of Nowhere*. "Here's one called 'The Wild Wood.' " I sighed internally. Another bloody wood. "Are you sure you wouldn't like Babar? Or Pugwash?"

"No. They're for *babies*."

Cosmo settled himself on the hard, gray seat of the lounge, wriggling, then became still.

Long, long ago there was a dark wood that no man dared set foot in. Strange stories were told by those who ventured there: of a great ruined house with ragged people swarming over it like bees; of a dwarf who rode a black cat as big as a panther; of a fire burning and children dancing round it, all of whom vanished when approached. Once a woodsman, bolder than the rest, struck his axe into a tree. There was a shriek, and a stream of blood poured out of the cut. The terrified man ran away as fast as his trembling legs would carry him. After that, nobody dared go near the place.

I stopped so that Cosmo could see the dramatic picture that accompanied this tale. It depicted a man staggering back, axe in hand, with an expression of horror on his face, watching black blood gush out of the cut he had just made in a tree. The tree seemed to writhe and claw at him, its bark twisted and knobbed into the approximation of human features, screaming with pain. All around loomed other trees, the boles twisted and hung with creepers or ivy. The ground was scattered with toadstools. If you looked hard you could see the figure of an old man in the shadowy background.

"I don't like that one," said my son. "It's spooky."

"It's just a picture," I said, in the way that adults do. "It's all made up."

Yet the trees and the blood seemed to flicker in the corner of the eyes with that strange, febrile life my mother managed to put into her drawings. I wondered if my aunt would be able to tell me how Laura had learned her remarkable skills. Somebody must have taught her.

A mile or two from the wood there was a village, and in this village lived a man, his daughter Anna, and her stepmother. Anna was a good, quiet girl who only wanted to live in peace, but this the stepmother would not allow. She beat her and yelled at her all day long, gave her the hardest work to do and only just enough to eat. Her father did nothing to stop his wife. All in all, she made Anna's life a misery.

One day, Anna went out with the other village children to pick strawberries. They wandered on and on until at last they reached the edge of the dark wood, where the finest strawberries always grew, splashing the grass with their bright color. The children filled their baskets, then threw themselves down and ate as much as they wanted. Suddenly a cry went up from one of the older boys: "Run! Run away as fast as you can! We're in the wood!"

All the children sprang to their feet screaming, and rushed away—all except Anna, who had wandered far into the wood and found a bed of strawberries under the trees. She heard the cry but stood undecided. "After all, what does it matter?" she thought. "What lives here can't be worse than my stepmother."

Looking up, she saw a little black dog come trotting towards her. It had a silver rope round its neck, and the rope was held by a young girl, the same size as Anna and dressed in green silk.

"I'm so glad you didn't run away like the others," the girl said. "Stay with me here and be my friend, and we'll play wonderful games every day. You'll have as much as you like to eat and drink, and nobody will beat you. Come."

She held out her hand and Anna took it. Deep they went, and still deeper, into the wild wood. There were fruit trees laden with blossom and fruit, brightly colored birds swooping in and out of the branches, violet butterflies with wings as large as Anna's hands. Great trees were twined around with flowering vines; from their branches hung moss like white stars. The air was both sweet and bitter, and the grass was as soft as velvet. In the middle of the wood was a white house, and before it stood a lady in rich garments who turned to Anna's new friend and said, "Who is this you've brought me, Elsa?"

"I brought her back to be my friend," said the girl. "Can she stay?"

The lady said nothing, only smiled and stroked Anna's cheeks and asked her if she would like to do so.

At this, Anna knelt down and kissed the lady's hand, sobbing, "I have a stepmother who beats me all day long, and a father who cares nothing for me. I beg you not to send me back, she will half-kill me."

The lady smiled and said, "Fear nothing."

Then they went into the house, and Anna did not know which way to look, it was so fine. Everyone was dressed as if for a wedding, and the table was piled high with food and fruit. A little old man rode in on a black cat, came forward, and bowed to the lady.

"Do you see this girl?" she said, pointing to Anna. "I wish to adopt

*her for my daughter. Make me a copy of her, and send her to the village
in her place."*

*The little old man bowed again, opened a basket, and took out some
clay. Under his hands a doll as large as a baby began to form. When it
was finished he bored a hole in the doll's breast, and put a slice of bread
inside where the heart would be. Then he took a snake out of the basket
and forced it into the hole, stopping it up with a plug of clay.*

"Ugh, gross! I hate snakes," a voice piped.

I looked up. A crowd of children had gathered, and they were
sitting on the ground. Much to Cosmo's annoyance, I showed
them the picture. There was the little old man with his basket on
the ground. A slim black snake writhed in his hands. I could almost see it lashing this way and that as it approached the doll
Anna. Beside her stood the real Anna, and behind them, shel-
tering her own daughter with one arm and her adopted child
with the other, the Lady of the Wood. All were dressed in flowing, almost medieval robes, and all were lovely; but the face of
the child was all too familiar. She was younger than the girl in
"The White Bear" and "The Bird of Truth" but I could see the
same dark hair and fine features.

Or was I imagining the resemblance? How much could I
really see from a few lines reproduced in a book? I looked at the
picture again. The full moon shone down, through the densely
hatched trees. There was something particularly disturbing about
the doll and the man and the snake, but it took a moment to see
what this was. Then I saw the doll's face. It looked exactly like the
flesh-and-blood child beside her, but her mouth was open. The
snake's head was being forced not towards any hole in her chest,
but in the direction of her mouth. A shudder went through me.

"I've got a doll," said a little girl. She held it up for inspec-
tion. "She does wee-wees when she has a drink."

"Don't interrupt," I said, irritably.

"Now," the old man said to the lady, "all we need is a drop of the maiden's blood."

At this, Anna grew white with terror, for she thought she was selling her soul to the Devil.

"Do not be afraid," said the lady. "We do not want your blood for any evil purpose, but to give you freedom and happiness."

When Anna nodded, she took a tiny golden needle and pricked her finger so that a single drop of blood welled out onto the tip. The lady gave the needle to the old man, who stuck it into the heart of the doll, promising that the next day they would all see what a fine piece of work it was.

When Anna awoke the following morning, she was in a soft white bed in a room of her own. A beautiful dress was lying on the back of a chair, and a maid came to comb her long hair.

But nothing gave Anna as much joy as the little pair of embroidered slippers that matched her dress, for until now she had been forced by her cruel stepmother to run about barefoot.

By this time, the doll had grown as big as Anna, and was wearing Anna's old clothes. Nobody could have told the difference between them.

"Don't be afraid," said the Lady of the Wood, noticing the girl's start of terror at this. "The doll can do you no harm. It is for your stepmother, so she may beat it instead of you. Unlike you, the doll can never feel any pain; and if she and your father do not mend their ways, it will soon give them the punishment they deserve."

From this time on, Anna's life was that of any ordinary, happy child. She had no cares or troubles of any sort, and as the years went by her old life seemed like a bad dream. The Lady of the Wood loved her and cared for her, and Elsa was her playmate. Every evening there was a feast, and every morning peace.

But what of the doll? When it came to the stepmother's house, the stepmother gave it such a beating that it would have killed a real child.

As the doll could not feel, it made no difference, which of course only en-
raged the wicked woman more.

I looked up. The children listened, round-eyed; their parents,
too, were spellbound. I showed them the picture of the stepmother, her face contorted with fury, beating the doll in the
porch of a house. The doll was very obviously a doll, its face
blank, but the stepmother seemed not to have noticed. The
background looked familiar; I was almost sure it was the same
house as that in "Lolly and the Giant," the house made of white
clapboard.

The stepmother's temper grew worse and worse. She beat the figure day
and night, and always the doll stood there, not making a sound or shed-
ding a single tear. If the father tried to interfere, he was beaten also.

One day, the woman became so mad with rage that she seized the
figure by its throat. Out darted the black snake from the doll's mouth,
and bit the woman's tongue so that she fell dead without a sound. That
night, when the woman's husband came home he found her body all
swollen and disfigured, but the girl was nowhere to be seen. There was
nothing except a slice of bread on the table.

The man's cries brought his neighbors running, but when they were
asked what had become of the man's daughter, they shrugged and said
that they had heard a great noise from the house that day, as every day,
and thought nothing of it. The body of the dead woman was laid out for
burial, and then the tired husband sat down to eat. He picked up the
piece of bread, and put it in his mouth.

"Uh-oh," said one of the older boys. "Big mistake. I bet that
snake is gonna get him now, too."

"It serves them right," said a girl. "If I had parents as mean as
that, I'd want them dead, too."

"Honey!" said her mother, shocked. She stood up and said loudly, "I don't think I like this story, mister. Come on, Donna."

"No!" said Donna. "Stop bugging me. I want to hear what happens next."

In the morning the father, too, was found dead and swollen. So the wicked woman and her weak husband were buried, and nobody was any the wiser that the real Anna was in the dark wood alive and well.

"Told you!" said the boy.

She lived there happily for many years, growing into a lovely young woman; but Elsa was just as she had been the day they first met. Anna learned many things in the wild wood that she would never have learned in her own home. But Elsa much preferred childish games.

"What a pity," she began to say, "that you've grown too big to play with me anymore."

So there came a time when Anna was summoned to the lady's room.

"Dear child," she said, "the time has come for us to part."

Anna flung herself down and buried her head in the lady's lap. "What have I done wrong, to be sent away?"

"You have done nothing wrong," said the lady, "but you are a mortal child, and will soon be a woman. We look like men, but are not. Now it is time for you to rejoin your own kind. You must go away from here, and find a husband to live happily with until you die. It is very hard for me to part with you, but so it must be."

Then the lady took out a golden comb and gently pulled it through Anna's hair, so that she fell asleep. When she awoke, she was a bird. She flew high into the air, and higher still, until she flew across the ocean and found herself in another country, way above a forest. She felt a sudden sharp pain, as an arrow pierced her breast, and was tumbling down,

*down, down, out of the air, to land as a woman at the feet of a prince
with a bow in his hand. . . .*

"I can guess what will happen next," said Cosmo, disgustedly.
"She'll marry him, right? They always end up getting married."

I had a quick look at the last paragraph. "Yes, and they all live
happily ever after. Look, our flight is being called. We'd better
go. Sorry, everyone."

The children got up, reluctantly, and wandered back to their
parents.

"That was a creepy story," said Cosmo.

"It was, wasn't it?"

"I didn't like the girl. She didn't *do* anything, not like Lolly
and the giant."

It was true, I realized. What it was really about was the revenge
worked upon the girl's parents by the doll—the doll that looked
just like the daughter, and my mother, but who had a snake in
her heart.

I LOOKED DOWN past my son's head at the vastness of America,
and could not comprehend it. Cities and industrial wastelands
went on and on for miles, then suddenly stopped and were
abruptly replaced by what looked like impenetrable wilderness.
As we climbed higher in the thrumming plane only the division
between sea and land was discernible: both equally unending,
immense.

"Are we still in America?" Cosmo asked, pressing his tiger's
battered nose to the porthole.

"Yes. We're traveling south. It'll be a lot warmer there."

"Warm enough to swim?"

My son adored swimming. In water he discovered an ease and
confidence that was never his on land.

"I don't know. Maybe. We're going to see my aunt Lily, your great-aunt."

"Does she have children?"

"I don't know. If she does, they'll be grown up, maybe with children of their own. Are you missing Flora?"

"A bit."

I thought of my daughter briefly, her spirited sweetness, her smallness. She had never seemed more remote. "We've bought lots of presents for her."

"But when are we going to go *home*?"

I began to talk about how marvelous America was, of how it had been discovered and settled. Privately, I was suddenly seized with anxiety about having my son with me. My aunt might have a house like my mother-in-law's, crammed with porcelain and crystal that any child under twelve could be guaranteed to smash. I hadn't mentioned Cosmo on the phone. I wished, not for the first time, that I hadn't brought him.

As soon as the plane landed, however, I knew I had come to the right place. This was another America. I collected our baggage, then looked for a car-rental firm. Cosmo, like someone in a trance, walked out and sat down on the rough grass by the airport entrance. He began picking daisies with intense concentration.

"Here, you guard the baggage. I'm just going to rent us a car."

I walked away, and it occurred to me how easy it would be simply to leave him there, to keep on walking. I found a Hertz counter and rented a white Oldsmobile, then went back. My son sat, his head bent. He looked up and grinned. "I've done you a daisy chain. Do you like it?"

"Daisy chains are for girls," I said.

His face froze. "I'm sorry, I'm sorry, Daddy, I didn't know."

"Never mind. I can pretend it's a crown."

I put out a hand to take it, but he threw it away, stamping his foot. I was saved from another tantrum by the arrival of the car. Immediately, he was fascinated. I packed the boot and the backseat, fiddled about with the mirrors, and then we were off, following the directions my aunt had given me.

The gears were automatic, which gave a strange, gliding sensation to everything. I still couldn't believe I was here, retracing my mother's journey. How much had everything changed since her time? The yellow school bus trundling along the highway looked exactly as it must have done forty years ago.

"Dad! Dad! That's Lowly Worm's bus!" said Cosmo, delighted. This was a cartoon character of which he and Flora were very fond, principally because nothing frightening ever seemed to happen to him.

I drove on and on, my foot on the gas pedal. It was like driving a toy car, with none of the changes and attentiveness to rhythm that a gear shift requires. The looking-glass feel of driving on the right-hand side of the road added to the dream I was in. Here were long, low supermarkets and franchises. You couldn't tell where one place stopped and another began until they began to repeat themselves. In between were shabby trailers, their wheels sunk deep in the grass. People sat out on the steps, looking at the infrequent traffic with the patience and sorrow of animals. Every now and again, we passed a tiny white Baptist church with a sharp steeple and the name of its pastor written up in prominent letters.

Behind these ribbons of development soared trees, dense and verdant. I kept looking for gaps, for *views* through them, but there were none. It was either suburbia, or the wild wood, with the woods apparently untouched by human hand. I remembered what Ruth had said: *The woods there are like the deepest, darkest manifestations of the subconscious you could hope to find.* Had she visited my relations? Of course, I thought, the Viners had had holidays in America. Perhaps one of them had been in the Carolinas, I couldn't remember. Even as I followed my aunt's directions, I noticed that the signs of human habitation were flagging. Occasionally there were meadows, as lush as any in England or France, but increasingly the trees were closing in. There were cypress and myrtle, with birds of prey circling above them, but most of all there were oaks of some sort. They looked magnificent, yet the branches were all hung with what looked like gray rags, fluttering like ghosts hanging up to dry in the breeze. They were too many to be bits of motorway rubbish, as I at first assumed. Yet this deathly decoration did little to lessen the fecundity of the place. The trees had white jasmine and scarlet trumpet vines twined round their trunks, and all along the verges wild flowers the same color as bluebells frothed and bobbed. The air that came through the window was both bitter and sweet.

"How much longer is it until we get there?" asked Cosmo, the whine creeping back into his voice.

"Not long."

"Dad, why did the chicken cross the road?"

"That's an old one. To get to the other side."

"Why did the dinosaur cross the road?"

"I don't know. Same reason?"

"Because chickens hadn't been invented. Is that funny?"

"Here's the bridge over the river, look."

We crossed a wide, shining expanse of brown water. I glanced to one side and saw a log suddenly sprout legs, lumber to the water's edge, and slide in. "Look, look, an alligator!"

"Where?"

"There! Too late, you've missed it."

The woods grew denser and darker. The trailers and tiny churches petered out. We crossed over a railway line, and the great trees sent their branches twisting over us, branches that did not arch and spray like European trees but which writhed like the letters of a foreign language. The road became bumpier and more potholed, and the ugly loops of thick black cable dangling from post to post gave way to slim pylons. At last, just when I was becoming convinced that I had taken a wrong turn, I saw a small sign saying "To Magnolia House." Five minutes later, I drove through some large wooden gates set in a dense, thorny hedge. The sweep of a drive encircled a great tree with shining coppery leaves and creamy flowers like bowls. The magnolia, presumably.

My mother's home appeared. It was a long, two-story house of white wood with a veranda supported by white pillars running the length of it. There were shutters on the windows, painted a faded blue and closed against the glare of the afternoon sun. It looked as if it were sleeping; the silence when I braked was like some viscid substance rushing into a breach. For a moment, I held my breath, and so, I think, did Cosmo. Then a small breeze rustled the leaves overhead, and a wood pigeon said, "Coroo, coroo," in a soft, mocking voice.

We got out and went up the steps. On either side sprouted bright green ferns, every tiny leaf of which trembled as we passed. I pressed the doorbell. Cosmo slipped his hand into mine. I felt its small warmth in my own. There was a long pause, followed by light footsteps. Then the door opened.

E I G H T E E N

I RECOGNIZED HER instantly. It took a moment for my eyes to adjust to the stream of dazzling light in which she was framed, and then another moment to understand that the old woman I had expected was young.

I had seen her on white paper in black ink, as a child, as a girl, as a young woman, and now as she was before me. Her face was as familiar as my own. The dark hair flowed like shadows around her head and shoulders. I had seen her waking and sleeping, richer and poorer, in sickness and in health. It was her image that had called me here, across the skies, across the seas. It was for her I had come.

I thought, for another wild moment, that my mother had been here all this time, all of my life miraculously preserved in this strange place. Such a wildness of grief and joy rushed through my body that my heart rose like a bird about to take flight. Then she smiled and said, "Hi. You must be cousin Benedick. I'm Rose."

She put out a hand, briskly. I took it. It was warm. She was a real American girl—or woman, for as far as I could tell she was about the same age as myself. She wore jeans and a white T-shirt, not the medieval drapery of my mother's drawings. Yet I would have known her anywhere.

"You look surprised."

"Yes—yes, I am. I was expecting my aunt. Lily Gardener."

"Mom's resting. We weren't sure what time you were arriving, and we have a wedding to prepare for the day after tomorrow."

"A—a wedding?" I said stupidly. "Are you getting married?"

She laughed, a strange, silent laugh. Her teeth were small and white and even, like a child's. "Me? Oh, no. No, a couple who're flying in tomorrow. They're having about a hundred and twenty people for the ceremony, and we're catering for them. We run a guest house here, didn't Mom say?"

I saw at once how to handle this. "Then you must let me help you. I'm a cook as well as an actor—I can do it all for you, just show me where everything is."

A smile like the moon grew across her face. "Oh, no. That wouldn't do at all."

"Yes, yes, it would. I love cooking—"

"Who is this?"

I had forgotten all about Cosmo. He was standing there twisting his T-shirt in his hands, staring. It crossed my mind that he looked half-witted. "This is my son, Cosmo. Say hallo, Cosmo."

"Hallo."

He ducked behind me. I said, my anger barely suppressed, "He's a bit shy. Stand *still,* Cosmo. I'm sorry, he had to come too."

Cosmo stuck his tongue out. I could feel Ti-Ti being pressed into the small of my back.

"Never mind. We'll get acquainted later. We love children. This old house needs them. Come, I'll show you to your rooms."

We were standing in a wide hall, its walls and floors of wood, though the walls were painted white. Framed black-and-white photographs of people in hats and white clothes hung on them. I looked around. The air streamed gold with motes. A clock ticked and chimed. At the bottom of the stairs was a large brass gong. Farther along was a pair of doors, facing each other. At the end of the hall were french windows giving out onto another veranda, some kind of terrace, then a long series of steps leading down to a puckering expanse of bronze water.

"You like it?" said Rose, following my gaze. "My mother's work. Gardener by name, gardener by nature. It's her hobby. Mine, too." She looked ruefully at her hands. "Though we also do the other stuff around here."

"What a wonderful house. I wasn't expecting anything like this. Is it very old?"

"It was built in the 1860s. The style is Gothic Revival. All heart of pine—should last forever if it's properly looked after. Not very old by European standards, I know, but here it's historic." She had told people this many times before, I could tell.

"Have you been to Europe?" I was following her up the stairs. Her long dark plait bumped against the waistband of her jeans. I had always laughed at the idea of falling instantly, desperately, consumingly in love, and now it had happened to me.

"No." She turned and looked down at me, as though this were some sort of challenge. "Well, once, as a child. But I don't remember it. Otherwise, I've never been out of America."

"But that's terrible," I said. "You shouldn't just be stuck away here in the backwoods."

"Have you ever been to America before?"

"No."

She smiled. "Then we're even, I guess."

Cosmo trailed behind. "What is heart of pine?" he asked.

"What?" I turned to him irritably. He repeated his question. "I don't know. Ask—"

Rose opened a door at the top of the stairs. "Heart of pine is what it sounds like. It's the heart of a pine tree."

Cosmo stared at her. "I didn't know trees had hearts."

"Oh, they do."

"Do you cut them out with a knife? Like in *Snow White*?"

"No, with a saw. It's not like a human heart. It's like a tree within a tree. The kind of pine you normally buy is softwood, you see; but right in the middle, right at the core, a pine is hard. It's one of the hardest, toughest woods you can find—which is just what you need in a climate like this, with rain and heat and insects. But it means that one tree will only give you about three planks, and to cut down a whole wood just to make one house costs a sackload of money. So people hardly ever did it, even long ago when this family was rich." She looked around. "Well, do you like it?"

I followed her gaze. There was a magnificent antique bed with four dark posts carved to resemble cobs of maize rising up at each corner. It was spread with a pink chintz bedspread. On each of the top two pillows was a chocolate in a black paper doily. (Cosmo moved purposefully towards these.) The two windows were festooned with more pink, shrouded by net and some sort of wire mesh, as well as the branches of a great tree outside. Between them was a kidney-shaped dressing-table, also draped in pink, with a small padded stool beneath it. There was a TV bracketed to a wall and a number of lamps in fringed shades illuminating the whole.

"It's great," I said faintly. "Very—very—"

"Pink?"

I laughed, and she did too. "It's Mom," she said. "She wanted to make it look right for the guests. All the rooms have been booked for a wedding on Saturday. It's lucky we had two left. Come, I'll show you the rest. Cosmo can have the room across the passage."

Cosmo's mouth turned down. I knew he would want to sleep in the same room as myself, as he had done at Ruth's and in New York, so I said heartily, "That's nice. Big boys like sleeping on their own, don't they?"

So he said nothing, clutching Ti-Ti to his chest. I glanced at its squashed, blurry face and again had the uneasy feeling that a gleam of intelligence came from its plastic eyes. Cosmo's room faced the garden, and the water.

"Is that a river?"

"The good ol' Edisto itself. Well—a tributary."

His room, like my own, was stuffy and airless. I moved to the window. "Does this open?"

"Sure. But there's air-conditioning."

I said, "I'd rather open it. I must have fresh air, you know. Everyone English does."

It took a little work. She came over to my side to help. The window was finally released, and swung back, trailing broken webs in its hinges.

"That's better," I said, breathing deeply. I could smell the wild, bittersweet scent I had smelled before. If the women my wife had tried to fob me off with had put this on their skin, I wouldn't have objected, I thought.

"Uh-huh. Wait until evening."

"What happens then?"

"The insects come out to play." She laughed silently.

My son said, "Dad, can I swim in the river?"

She turned to him. "Not unless you want to be eaten by a 'gator."

"What?" he said rudely.

"She means, an alligator. No, you can't swim, I'm afraid. Alligators eat little boys."

Rose gave him her wide, white smile. "But there's a Jacuzzi."

My son forgot to be hostile in his enthusiasm for swimming. "What's that?"

"It's a hot tub. Don't you have them in England?"

"Yes." I wouldn't have been caught dead in a Jacuzzi, but added, "It's like an extra big, round bath. It's hot, and it bubbles."

"It bubbles your troubles away," said Rose, turning to leave. "I go out there at the end of the day with a glass of Zinfandel and look at the stars. But it's best not to stay in too long, or you get dizzy."

There was nothing about the way she spoke that could give you any idea of how enchanting she was. I had probably worked with actresses more beautiful. But it wasn't even to do with the way she looked.

She left us. If I didn't see her again immediately, I wouldn't be able to exist, I would be blotted out, I was already blotted out. I flung myself facedown onto the bed, inhaling her scent, grinding my hips into its softness. I tried to remember my wife's neat, handsome head, her somewhat mannish elegance, her poise. Surely I had once loved her as deeply as this, before she had made me suffer so much?

"Daddy? Dad?"

"What?" Reluctantly, I turned to my son.

"Can I go and play?"

"Yes, of course," I said, annoyed not to be alone with my voluptuous thoughts. "Just don't go near the water."

"Or the witch's caldron."

"What caldron?"

"The jack-thing. The one *she*—"

"Who?" I asked stupidly.

Cosmo said in a whisper, his finger pointing downwards, "The one who showed us to our rooms."

I sat up abruptly. "Rose?"

Cosmo looked at me, his eyes wide. "Can't you see, she's a witch?"

I BLAMED MYSELF. I had read him too many stories from my mother's book, and like all children he had confused the real and the imaginary. I was angry with him, and frightened, too. Ever since I had arrived in this country I myself had become less and less sure.

"But of course you can't see she's a witch," he said, earnestly. "People who're under a spell never can."

"Don't be ridiculous," I snapped. "I am *not* under a spell. My cousin Rose is—is a very beautiful woman, that's all. It just took me by surprise. Why don't you go off and explore?"

He clung to me. "Come, too."

I shook him off. "I need some rest."

I didn't need rest, of course, I never needed rest these days, even when my head felt as if it were full of scratchy cotton wool. Life was too beautiful, too exciting, with all the things to do and places to see. But first I had another matter to attend to, something shameful, but as necessary as scratching an unbearable itch.

"Off you go."

"No. No! I don't want to go on my own."

He sat down on the bed beside me and put his arms around me. I could smell the sweetness of his breath, see the pure, living white of his eyeball, the flushed curve of his cheek. His small, lean body was not the one I wanted, but its innocence drained the hardness from me.

"Read to me."

"I've read you too many stories. You should learn to read yourself."

"That's so boring. I'll never read as well as you."

"Yes, you will. It's just practice. Everything is practice."

"Is acting practice?"

I was silent for a moment, remembering. Even my vocation seemed less important. "Some is. You have to learn your words, other people's lines, and moves. It's like a kind of dance. You feel for what is beyond the words, above the words. You have to be awake, but in a dream. I suppose it's like anything creative. You can't do it unless you find something that comes from within. Finding that thing every day is very hard. The hardest thing in the world, really."

"Do you have it?"

"It's just a question of finding the right parts."

Very gently, he reached up his hand and stroked me on the cheek. "I know you'll find it again."

I put my arms round him.

I WOKE with a start to find Cosmo gone. There was a faint indentation where he had lain beside me, nothing more. I felt a sudden jolt of terror, pure and unreasoning. Why had he left, when he had been afraid? Had someone taken him away? Had he woken and decided to explore on his own?

This last I quickly found to be the case. At the bottom of a series of shallow steps was a wide bowl of lawn. There my son glided to and fro on a swing suspended from a massive tree. When I came closer I saw he was gazing out at the river with a dreamy, excited expression.

"Hallo. I thought I'd lost you to an alligator."

"Can you see it?"

"Where?"

"It's over there. Behind me." He swooped past with birdlike grace. "I thought it was a log at first."

"How do you know it isn't?"

"I looked," he said, smugly. "Hey, Dad, what do you get if you cross a camera and an alligator?"

"I don't know."

"A snapshot!" Then the dreamy expression returned. "Look, Dad, look, I'm flying."

I had loved swinging, too, as a child. I could still remember the feeling, the exhilaration of traveling up and up and up until it seemed I could touch the sky with the tip of my toe; then the terrifying downward swoop, everything rushing away, the breath pressed out of my lungs, before the re-ascent. I felt giddy just watching him.

"D'you like it here?"

He considered as he glided past again in the warm evening air. "It's better than New York," he called back. "There's grass and trees and things. Even if there's also *her*."

I decided to make no response. As he returned I asked, "Would you like some supper?"

"Yes. What's an alligator's favorite game?"

"Snap." He looked disappointed. "Yes, what?"

"Yes, *please*."

"And then shall we try the Jacuzzi?"

"I saw where it was," he said, slowing to a halt. "Shall I show you?"

He led me up the steps again, his small legs appearing and disappearing like the light of an evening star. The stairway was lined with dense, shiny green shrubs bearing pink and red flowers. Camellias. I'd never seen such luscious abundance. Halfway up was a small, round fountain bubbling out of a tall mound of mossy rock. The sound it made was almost inaudible. I had passed it before without noticing.

"There's a goldfish, look." He pointed, and I saw the flick of a large fin and body, curiously leprous, its orange scales blotched and blurred with white. I bent over, and glimpsed a face wavering in its surface, a face that smiled and grimaced and stretched and vanished in a sudden gush to a dark dazzle; a face I didn't recognize as my own.

"Come *on*," said Cosmo impatiently. I was dragged up, almost to the level of the veranda. There were more flowers here: red lilies growing on thick fleshy stems, four blooms to a stem. I had only ever seen them in pots at Christmastime before. Each trumpet seemed to glow with an unearthly light in the setting sun, as if filled with blood. I bent and sniffed. For all their luxuriance they, too, were quite without smell.

A steady, rhythmical plopping noise came from behind a shrub. I saw another round pool, larger than the fountain and black-rimmed, its waters milky with motion. A green towel was spread to one side, and a figure was immersed up to the shoulders in the pool's steaming contents. My body jerked forward, even though I knew in the same instant it was, once again, not the person I expected to see.

She rose out, cautiously and gracefully, offering a hand at the end of a lean arm, its skin as withered as chamois leather. "Benedick," she said. "I'm so glad you found us. Won't you join me?"

N I N E T E E N

I T ' S N O T O F T E N that an elderly aunt you've never met before asks you to join her in a hot whirlpool. I declined. I was straining my ears and eyes to catch a glimpse of Rose. Cosmo was another matter. He forgot his hesitations and immediately stripped and stepped in.

"It's hot! It's hot! It's lovely!" he squeaked.

"Of course it's hot," said my aunt. "That's why we had it installed. It's a great help with my arthritis."

We studied each other for a moment while Cosmo splashed. She had been and still was a handsome woman with the kind of sharp features that often age better than small ones. All the vitality of her face seemed to have sunk into its deep wrinkles and run like liquid into her pale eyes. It crossed my mind that my mother, had she lived, would have become not unlike her, with her dark hair turned to pewter, and her skin hanging in soft folds from her jaw. Dead, she remained perfect, preserved in the crystal coffin of her youth.

"So," she said. "You found us. I didn't think you'd take so long about it."

There was some note, not exactly of reproach or of resignation, in her voice that made me ask, "Did you expect me to come before?"

"Yes. That's why I gave your Jewish friend my address." I didn't like the way she said that. Well, what did I expect in the South?

Aunt Lily continued, oblivious, "We've kept in touch, over the years. I haven't seen you since my poor sister's funeral. You were a little boy then."

Again, I felt the strange mixture of nausea and excitement. "I don't remember," I said. "Were you very alike?"

"Alike, yet not alike," she said. Her voice was deep, a little hoarse: an old woman's voice. "She was the pretty one, you know. I was considered clever, though I never did anything with it." She sighed. "Families always divide sisters in this way. Or perhaps we divide ourselves. The nice one, the nasty one, the one with small feet, the one with the long nose. Every minute difference made large. Small wonder so many grow up to hate each other."

"Did you? Hate each other, I mean?"

"Sometimes. She was the younger by five years. It's always easier to be the baby of the family. She said it was harder, because she always had my castoffs. But we loved each other, too. We were each other's best friend. Well, who else was there, out here?"

"Did you grow up here?"

"Yes. But not at first. In the beginning, we lived in Charleston, in a fine, big house." She sighed again. "It's time I got out. Especially if I'm going to tell you about the family."

She pressed a button and the milky bubbling stopped at once. The pool became black and still, faint wisps of steam curling up into the overhanging trees. Next, my aunt grasped a stainless-steel handle and heaved herself up. Her figure was remarkably good, but the skin hung around her lean frame in loose pleats, like silk. She has nothing to do with me, I thought, repelled. Then I saw her hands. Their fingernails were identical to my own, oval and slightly striated, like acorns. I had never thought that fingernails could be inherited. But they can, like everything else.

"Come on, Cosmo."

"He looks so like her," she said, patting herself down tenderly.

"Like who?" he asked. I glanced at him, and in that instant saw so much of Georgie, I drew breath. Then it passed. I would never get used to the way other people look out of children's faces, as though we ourselves are only peepholes for the past.

"Like your grandmother, Laura. I was her sister, which makes me your great-aunt."

"My great ant?" he repeated, puzzled.

"*Aunt,*" I said. It was quite hard for me to understand her accent, too.

"Daddy, I need a towel."

"Damn. I'll get one from your room."

"Don't worry," said my aunt. "I've a spare, on that chair. If you don't mind?"

Cosmo nodded, then grinned. She put out a hand as knobbed as the roots of a tree. "Will you help me?"

She slowly put on a toweling robe, then grasped a thick black stick with a rubber tip. I picked up the wet towels, and Cosmo's discarded clothes. There was an almost regal procession away from the terrace.

"This is an extraordinary garden," I said.

"Thank you. My grandmother planted the camellias. All different, as you see. They don't breed true from one generation to the next, you know."

We walked up to the veranda, past two white wicker chairs and a table, to the hall.

"Here. And here. Let me see." Aunt Lily put on some wire-rimmed glasses, then said, "That's a picture of Lolly and myself, when we were children. Lolly was her nickname."

Like Lolly and the giant, I thought. So I had been right all along: the fairy stories did have something autobiographical about them. But what was the truth, and what fantasy? I looked at the photograph intently.

It was a black-and-white print, an enlargement of one taken by a professional photographer, I guessed. The two sisters wore identical gingham dresses and sandals, and had their hair drawn back in pigtails.

"We were Lily and Lolly," said my aunt.

They sat on the front steps of a house, and grinned the gap-toothed grin of childhood. I looked at their faces. It was true; one was prettier than the other—finer in feature, more alert, the more perfect combination of genes. Aunt Lily's face was subtly longer, coarser. It was like my own two: Cosmo is attractive, in the way that all children are at his age, but Flora, despite almost identical features, is the pretty one. I thought about the two sisters in *North of Nowhere*. From Bianca to Lily was no great leap of the imagination. Whatever my aunt said, they had been rivals.

"Where did you go to school?"

Cosmo, bored, wandered off to tap the gong. I thought I'd better ask as many questions as I could before he came back.

"At the same convent my Rose went to." I must have shown my surprise, for she said, "We're Catholic, didn't you know? Weren't you raised that way yourself?"

I thought of the strictly nondenominational services at my progressive co-educational boarding school, and shook my head. "My father hates religion," I said. *Bong!* went the gong. "I don't think I'm even baptised. Was my mother religious?"

"We all went to mass," said Aunt Lily shortly. "These are my sainted father, and mother."

"They're handsome. Rather alike," I said, after I had looked.

"First cousins. There's always been a lot of intermarriage in Charleston society. We were cut off for so long down here. It's changing now, but for people of good family . . ." She gazed at the faces, then glanced at me. "I myself was married to a gentleman from Savannah."

The antiquated phrase dropped from her lips with perfect ease. I remembered someone saying of my mother, "You could see she was a *lady*," and understood it now.

"Oh. Is your husband—?"

Bong!

"Don died twelve years ago."

"I'm sorry. You must feel terribly alone, stuck out here in the middle of nowhere," I said.

My aunt made a faint grimace. "That's our wedding day. Lolly was my bridesmaid. She was sixteen years old."

She looked very tired, suddenly. I walked along and saw the black-and-white photograph. How distant they seemed, those people in fifties suits and dresses, and how young. My mother wore a little crown of white flowers in her dark hair and a fitted jacket over a dress with a full skirt. She could have been a model, apart from her grin. I thought she looked tense, despite her smile. Her thick hair was cut in a long bob, artificially curled and swept to one side of her face; her lips were dark and her teeth white and even in the rounded features. Beside her, my aunt was a woman. Her husband was less easy to make out. All I could tell was that he was tall and dark. His face was bisected by a deep shadow. It seemed familiar, despite this.

"Very handsome," I said, again.

"All along this wall, you can see our family. We go back five generations. This used to be a hunting lodge, built by Judge Perry. He became a senator, you know, in 1910, when the family still had money. Then when Poppa had to sell up in Charleston, we moved here. Used to own all these woods around here, too."

Bong!

"Quiet, Cosmo! I should think it must cost a fortune to keep an old house like this going. Did you sell the woods as well?"

She nodded. "Leased to a logging company. Timber's what's left, now that nobody will plant cotton out there." Aunt Lily gestured towards the swampy river. "Timber and tourism. People use us as a venue for weddings, too. There's one the day after tomorrow."

"I'll help you," I said eagerly. I had visions of ravishing Rose over the vol-au-vents. "I cook, you know, as well as act. Just let me sort out Cosmo's tea—"

She inclined her head. "That would be greatly appreciated. Rose carries most of the burden of the work, but even she tires these days, poor child."

"What was my mother like? Was she a happy person?"

"Sometimes. She was very intense," said my aunt. "She drove herself. I remember, even as a child, she would do drawing after drawing, but she was never happy with them even though they were far better than anything anyone else of her age could have done."

"Did anyone teach her?"

"Our father was very artistic. He gave us both some lessons. I think he taught her how to do linocuts and lithographs. I was never any good, but Lolly had inherited his talent. He'd wanted to be a painter, but of course that was unthinkable for someone of our position, so he did it as a hobby. He was the most delightful man." She sighed again. "Poor Poppa. He used to dream of traveling to Europe. We all had passports for the day when we would vacation there, but Momma was never well enough."

"What was wrong with her?"

"Nerves. She suffered a lot from her nerves. Neither of them was a very placid person. I never cared for art; Lolly inherited that. She did art history as part of her degree at college."

"How old was she when she left home?"

"Twenty-one," said my aunt.

"Did she go to London straightaway, or did she travel around a bit first?"

My aunt seemed not to hear. "I must get dressed now, if you'll excuse me."

I was left to inspect the photographs. My excitement was once again turning into frustration. Nobody was willing to talk about this mysterious woman who had been my mother, and yet she was everywhere. So much of her home was familiar to me from her drawings. I wondered whether Aunt Lily had seen *North of Nowhere*. There was something faintly familiar about her face, too, though I could not pin it down. Perhaps it was the resemblance to Rose. I stopped. But that was impossible, of course.

"I'm hungry," Cosmo whined.

"Be quiet. I'm thinking."

Rose was my age, possibly younger. My mother could never have seen her—unless Aunt Lily sent photographs of her niece, and those would only cover the first few years. I looked again at the smiling face in the photograph, and walked on until I found another of my mother as a girl. She was seated in the very swing that Cosmo had just been trying out. I was right, the resemblance between them was astonishing. It could have been a younger version of Rose, but for the style of the white dress. My mother had been drawing herself, putting her own image into her stories over and over again.

Even though I had been sure all along that she had been doing this, the proof took me aback. Why had she done it? It wasn't vanity, I was sure. Painters did this sometimes, I knew, putting themselves in crowd scenes much as Hitchcock had appeared in his films. Was it a kind of joke? Or could it have been something even stranger, the knowledge that I would one day fall in love with her exact image, thirty-three years later?

Cosmo yanked my arm. "I'm *hungry*. I want some supper."

"Let me look at what's in the fridge."

THE KITCHEN was the cleanest I'd ever seen, and very modern. The broad wooden table was scrubbed and bleached white; there was even a blue light tube attached to the ceiling to repel insects. A stainless-steel fridge the size of a wardrobe was installed along one wall, humming with icy power. With some effort, I opened it. Inside was more food than I would have considered possible for one house to hold. There were gallons of milk, whole sides of pink meat, frankfurters like great long fingers, bars of butter like gold bullion. Whatever else was happening here, my aunt and cousin weren't starving.

"It's *giant*," whispered my son.

"What do you fancy? Bacon and eggs? Cheese on toast?"

"Nothing meaty," he said. "I don't know where it's come from."

"Oh, Cosmo, for heaven's sake!"

"Can I help?"

"No!"

"Yes."

Rose was there. We smiled at each other, and I could feel myself going red. She took over, moving with a graceful economy that made me want to stop her, now, and again now, to fix her image on something more durable than memory. I watched her, and all the while I talked and talked. I told her that I was about to be divorced, about my life as an actor, and about the book of fairy tales that had brought me here.

"Have you ever seen it?"

She shook her head. "No, I don't think so. I had a copy of the famous one, of course. We're quite proud of her."

"You know what happened to her."

"Yes. I'm sorry. It must have been so sad for you. I wish I'd known her."

"I wish I had, too. I don't remember her. All I've got are her books, and the money from them. I don't expect she thought she'd leave much, but that's what made it possible for me to be an actor."

"She left me some money, too, you know. She must have been a fine person."

"Yes. The extraordinary thing is how much you look like her drawings. Wait! Wait! I'll show it to you."

I bounded out of my chair, and up the stairs, searching for the book. When I found it, I bounded back down again.

"Here. The girls in it all look just like you. Look!"

But when she looked, she smiled and said in a puzzled voice, "Well, I guess a little bit."

"Yes, yes," I insisted. "They do. Perhaps you can't see it, but I do. You have the same hair, the same shaped face and figure and everything."

Rose laughed. "Nobody's ever said I was a fairy tale princess before."

"But you are," I said passionately. "Here you are, slaving away like Cinderella for somebody else's party—"

"Which will pay us very nicely, thank you—"

"And living here alone in the backwoods—"

We both stopped. Then Cosmo sucked up a strand of spaghetti with a loud, rude noise. Rose and I jumped. I turned to my son. "Bath and bedtime for you," I said abruptly.

"Oh, Dad!"

"Come on. You can watch a bit of the Cartoon Channel if you're good."

"I want a story from that book." He looked at it pointedly. It was obvious he didn't think it should stay anywhere near my cousin.

"OK."

L ATER, when he was bathed and tucked up beside me in the great bed, I put my arm around him. Impatience was crawling over me like a rash. "If I read you a story, will you let me go downstairs?"

"Yes."

I found the next story. It was the last one.

THE   STOLEN   PRINCE

Once upon a time there was a great wood that was said to be enchanted. It was old, and when the wind blew you could smell sweet scents on its breezes. But nobody who could help it went there. Deep within the trees there lived a witch. She appeared to be a beautiful young woman, but she was old, and her heart was as black as a rotten oak. She loved to trap both beasts and men with her snares, and once she had caught them she bound them to her with spells as strong as strangling ivy. As soon as she had tired of them, she turned them into trees.

Cosmo stirred in my arms. He was looking at the picture that accompanied this opening. "Look. It's the house here," he said.

The drawing was of a great heaving mass of trees, shadowed and blurred, twisting and writhing. Over to the right there was a small patch of light where a figure—child or adult, it was hard to tell—was climbing over a picket fence. Behind it were the walls of a house.

"It's not necessarily here," I said.

"It is." He pointed to a roof just visible in the background. "That's *this* house. The one made with the hearts of pine trees."

"Hush."

Beside the wood, in a great white castle, lived a princess.

Cosmo sighed. "Why do they *always* live near woods?" he said. "Why not on a mountain, or by the sea?"

"Well, people do live near woods, don't they? We're next to one here," I said. "Also, there used to be a lot more trees everywhere than there are now. The more people there are, the fewer trees. The trees get cut down, and fields and villages and towns are made in their place."

"But why are they always there in *stories*?"

"To tell you that we live on the edge of mystery," I said, wearily. "Now, be quiet if you want me to go on."

Although she lived right beside it, the princess had never been into the wood. It had been foretold at her birth that if she ever ventured within it, she would be in danger of her life. Instead, she played all day in the large walled garden full of flowers and pretty things that the king and queen had had placed there. But the prettiest thing of all was the princess.

Cosmo made a disgusted noise.

She had many wonderful toys, but the one she liked best was her golden ball.

"I know this one," said Cosmo. "She loses the ball and a frog finds it for her if she promises to let him eat her food and sleep in her bed. She doesn't want to, but he follows her back and her dad makes her keep the promise, and when she does he turns into a prince. I don't want that one."

"Wait and see," I said.

One day, when she was just sixteen years old, she was throwing her golden ball high in the air when to her dismay a gust of wind came out of nowhere and it fell onto the other side of the wall.

"The birds fly over the wall—why shouldn't I?" she said to herself. So without telling anyone what she was doing, she searched for a place in the wall where she might climb over. Soon, she found a place where a tree had sent one of its boughs over the wall, which she could climb as easily as if it were a stair.

Inside the wood, everything was still. Not a breath of wind stirred the wild roses that grew in tangled clumps around the great old trees. Not a bird sang. The princess wandered on, deeper and deeper, searching for her golden ball until she was quite lost. The sun was sinking and she was becoming quite frightened when she came upon a strange little house in a clearing.

Just as the princess was about to knock on the door, a handsome young man came out to the well to draw water. The princess came up, and was about to greet him when he put a finger to his lips.

"What brings you to this terrible place?" he asked. "Don't you know that a wicked witch lives here? If she finds you, she will make you her slave, just as I am."

Cosmo shivered, and leaned closer to me.

"Shall I go on?"

"OK."

The princess told him that she had lost her golden ball, and the young man said, "If I find it for you, will you promise to marry me?"

The princess looked at him, and forgot her golden ball. She thought to herself that she had never seen anyone as handsome before. "I will," she said.

"It's not that love stuff again, is it?" Cosmo asked. I gave him a quelling look.

Then the young man fished her ball out of the well and said, "If you love me, you must be brave enough to withstand the spells the witch has put on me. Tomorrow at midnight, there is an hour when the witch will come out to dance beneath the full moon. I will dance with her, and if you catch hold of me and keep hold, I can be saved. But the witch will try to frighten you with her magic. You must keep tight hold of me, no matter what I become. If you can do so until I regain my true form, I will be free. If you fail, then you, too, will become her servant, even as I am."

The princess swore she would do as he asked. The young man went back inside.

"What kept you so long?" asked the witch.

"There was a wild beast by the well. I didn't want to disturb it," he answered; and the witch seemed satisfied.

The princess found her way back to the castle, and waited for the next night to come. When everybody was safe in bed, she stole out and over the wall again. The full moon showed her a path through the enchanted forest, all the way to the witch's house in the glade. No sooner had she hidden herself behind a tree than the door opened. Out came the witch, shining with a cold, unearthly beauty, and the young man.

Three times they bowed to the full moon. Then the witch took a silver flute from her bosom and began to play it, and as she played she danced. So, too, did the young man. They danced and they danced, turning this way and that in the moonlight; the witch's long hair streamed behind her like clouds at sunset, and the princess, watching in the shadows, almost forgot to seize the young man as he passed by.

But she gathered her courage, and seized him by the arm. As soon as the princess did so, the witch shrieked and the music stopped. Then the witch pointed at the young man, and all at once he was changed into a lion. The lion roared and clawed the princess's back. She could feel its hot breath on her face, and its cruel claws, but still she clung on. Then suddenly the lion was an eagle, screaming and jabbing at her with its talons and beak, trying to fly up into the sky. Still she clung on, though her arms and face were torn and bleeding. And now the eagle was cold *and slippery, a great snake that was trying to crush her to death. The princess shut her eyes, and grasped him more firmly.*

Cosmo had dived under the bedclothes. "It's too scary, it's too scary," he whimpered.

"Shall I stop?"

His head came out. "No."

Then the snake was gone. In its place was a bar of red-hot iron. She gripped it, though it burned her hands with a terrible pain, and staggered to the well. With her last strength, she plunged the red-hot bar into the cool water. A jet of hissing steam went up into the air, and an explosion of sparks. The witch shrieked again, and both she and her house vanished. All that was left was the young man for whom the princess had suffered.

"I am yours and you are mine," he said. "I was a prince of a country as great as yours, until the evil witch stole me away and put a spell on me."

Together they found their way out of the wood to the king's castle, where they were married. And from that day on, the wood was a place of terror no more.

Cosmo's eyes were closing.

"Can I go now?"

"OK. Just don't—don't—"

"What?"

He muttered something unintelligible. I eased my arm out from under his head, and crept across the creaking floorboards. Then I was free.

EXCEPT IT DIDN'T happen as I had hoped. My aunt sat there like some sort of duenna, while Rose cooked dinner. I couldn't even offer to help. It was like those dreamlike periods you have between sleeping and waking when you feel you could die from desire. But I had to sit, reeling and writhing in the study while Aunt Lily showed me photograph album after photograph album of her confounded family. Having been so eager and curious about my relations, I could not have given a fig about which second cousin it was who had grown tobacco and ended his life with a shotgun, or who was dancing the cotillion with what great-uncle. All I wanted was the chance to be with Rose, alone.

"Now tell me about yourself, young man," said my aunt. "You recently played Malvolio, I hear."

"Mercutio," I said, irritably. "You know, the one who dies in *Romeo and Juliet*."

"I should think that'd be kind of exciting."

"It was. I got the best reviews of my career for it. But I had a little accident."

Both women leaned forward.

"What happened?" asked Rose. "Did you kill someone?"

"No, no. But I got too much into the part, it's a wonderful part and . . . well, they thought I was out of control because I wounded the actor playing Tybalt."

"Were you fighting with real swords?"

"Real, but not sharp," I said.

"Say something from your part," said Rose. "I want to hear it."

"He may not remember it," said Aunt Lily.

I shook my head. "Once you've learned a part you never forget it." I turned to my cousin. "This is the Queen Mab speech. It's why actors want to play Mercutio. It's about falling in love." I held her gaze:

> O, then I see Queen Mab hath been with you.
> She is the fairies' midwife, and she comes
> In shape no bigger than an agate stone
> On the forefinger of an alderman,
> Drawn with a team of little atomies
> Athwart men's noses as they lie asleep;
> Her wagon spokes made of long spinners' legs;
> The cover, of the wings of grasshoppers;
> Her traces, of the smallest spider's web;
> Her collars, of the moonshine's watery beams;
> Her whip, of cricket's bone; the lash, of film;
> Her wagoner, a small gray-coated gnat,
> Not half so big as a round little worm
> Prick'd from the lazy finger of a maid.
> Her chariot is an empty hazelnut,
> Made by the joiner squirrel or old grub,
> Time out o' mind the fairies' coachmakers.
> And in this state she gallops night by night
> Through lovers' brains, and then they dream of love;

> O'er courtiers' knees, that dream on curtsies straight;
> O'er lawyers' fingers, who straight dream on fees;
> O'er ladies' lips, who straight on kisses dream . . .

"That's so beautiful," said Rose, when I paused. "I don't under-stand it all, but it's just beautiful. It's like a tiny picture in a book."

Aunt Lily, who had uttered a deep, short laugh at the mention of lawyers, was also smiling at me. I was staring at my cousin's lips.

The lips said, "Is there more?"

I nodded. No actor could resist an invitation from such an audience:

> O'er ladies' lips, who straight on kisses dream,
> Which oft the angry Mab with blisters plagues,
> Because their breaths with sweetmeats tainted are.
> Sometime she gallops o'er a courtier's nose,
> And then dreams he of smelling out a suit;
> And sometime comes she with a tithe pig's tail,
> Tickling a parson's nose as a' lies asleep,
> Then dreams he of another benefice.
> Sometime she driveth o'er a soldier's neck,
> And then dreams he of cutting foreign throats,
> Of breaches, ambuscadoes, Spanish blades,
> Of healths five fathom deep; and then anon
> Drums in his ear, at which he starts and wakes,
> And being thus frighted swears a prayer or two,
> And sleeps again. This is that very Mab
> That plaits the manes of horses in the night;
> And bakes the elflocks in foul sluttish hairs,
> Which once untangled much misfortune bodes.

This is the hag, when maids lie on their backs,
That presses them and learns them first to bear—

"I think," said Aunt Lily, "that we had better have our dinner before it gets cold."

We had dinner in another large, airy room next to the kitchen that gave onto the garden. It was floodlit with green spotlights, like the moment when the Demon King appears in a pantomime. The meal was the best I had had in America. That is, it actually tasted of something.

"We make our own bread," said Rose, when I lavished compliments on her.

But I had no interest in food. My hunger was all for my cousin. I tried to feel for her with my foot under the table but became tangled up with my aunt's black stick. Confound the old hag! If only she would leave! They were talking about the wedding. Bare round plastic tables were folded and stacked all along the wall. Tomorrow's job would be to erect and cover all of them, and put up a mini marquee. In addition, Rose and Aunt Lily were making canapés and lunch for the wedding guests.

"You must let me help," I said. "Truly. I'm an old hand at this sort of thing. I did all the cooking when my wife and I had parties. All I need is some virgin olive oil and ciabatta, a few pimientos and aubergines, some pesto—"

"We don't have anything like that here," said Rose.

"But Charleston will. I'll go tomorrow," I said excitedly. Ideas were cascading through my mind. I planned menu after menu. They would never have eaten such a meal in their lives.

"Well, if you're sure," she said uncertainly. "It would be great to have some real help in the kitchen."

"Of course I'm sure," I said. "Leave it all to me. You've cooked me dinner—I'll cook you a banquet."

. . .

Once again, I couldn't sleep. After transferring Cosmo to his own bed, and taking a shower, I only felt more excited and restless. I shaved. The bristles fell into the sink like iron filings released from a magnet. She must have felt what I had felt, I thought. The power of my desire would draw her to me, as irresistibly. For hours I paced up and down, up and down, up and down. I couldn't stop. Although it was the middle of the night, I heard what sounded like a distant telephone shrilling. The moonlight coming through the windows was all mottled and speckled by the great tree outside, by the silvery moss hanging between its leaves. The scent of honey and lemon, her scent, the scent of a world North of Nowhere, flooded over me. I could hear the miniature whine of a mosquito circling my head. I leapt into the air trying to catch it. They're like critics: you wouldn't mind them sucking your blood if they didn't make such a song and dance about it. Some other insect got to work. It sounded like small teeth gnawing. I looked up at the thick, white-painted beam traversing my room from one end to the other, bracing the walls. A large moth banged repeatedly against the wire mesh in the window. How long would this beautiful old house be able to withstand the life that was swarming over it all year long?

The tapping came again. "Benedick?"

"Who is it?"

"Rose."

"Rose!" I flung open the door. Her hair, undone, fell in long ripples to her waist. "Rose, oh, Rose." I caught both her hands in mine and drew her to me. "I knew it, I knew it—"

She said, with a kind of dry laugh in her voice, "Your father's on the phone."

"What?"

I stopped. She stepped back. She was wearing a long white cotton nightdress, its buttoned-up collar edged with lace. I was suddenly aware that I was wearing only the bottom half of my pajamas. She said, carefully looking at my face, "He's calling from London."

"Oh, shit. Shit, shit, *shit*. Tell him I'm not here."

"I already said you were."

I groaned. "Why can't he just leave me *alone*?" I felt like a teenager again, thwarted and embarrassed. My father's genius for bad timing had never been greater.

Rose said, "The telephone's in the hall. Or I can transfer it to your room. I wasn't sure whether or not to wake you."

"No. No!" If I took the call in my room, she would go back to hers. "I don't want to wake Cosmo."

I didn't want to go, but I went.

"Dick?"

"Don't call me that."

My father ignored this, as usual. "What kept you?"

"Perhaps you've forgotten a small thing called a time difference?" I said. "Most people are asleep over here."

The Demon King lighting had been switched off. My father cleared his throat.

"Oh. Of course. Sorry. Just thought I'd call and see how you're getting on."

"Fine, thanks."

"Met your Aunt Lily?"

"I'm staying in her house, as you know."

"Haven't seen her since the funeral."

I said, with all the cold reproach I could put into my voice, "You never told me I had an aunt. Or a cousin."

"Didn't I? Must have slipped my mind."

No, it didn't, I thought. You just never wanted me to come over here. Why not? Had he thought his power over me would be more absolute if I had no other family? (He was much too snobbish to have stayed in touch with his own, needless to say.) My impatience to get back to Rose was boiling over.

"Why have you called?"

"I just wanted to find out how you're getting along. Lily's had a lot of troubles in her life, I don't want you upsetting her—"

I couldn't believe the insolence of it, especially from a man whose mistresses, laid end to end, would probably stretch around the world.

"Oh, and I haven't, I suppose?"

"Not like hers, no."

"You think I'm going to go blundering around as if—? You thought you'd ring up to spy on me?"

"Don't speak to me like that. How *dare* you—"

"Just fuck off out of my life, will you?"

I slammed the receiver down. It seemed to reverberate with rage. My hand stung as if electrocuted. Then, standing in the shadowy hall, I laughed. At last I'd said what I'd always wanted to say to him. Tiresome, obtuse, meddling sod, I muttered. He wasn't going to win this one.

A clock chimed three. Rose came down the stairs.

"Is everything OK?"

"Yes," I said, looking up at her. Her hair fell to her waist. *If hairs be wires, black wires grow on her head.*

"You sounded angry."

"My father."

She came down another step, so that our eyes were level. "Difficult?"

"Aren't they always?"

We exchanged smiles. She didn't have to describe what life was like with her mother. I could see what Aunt Lily was like. People nearly always get worse with age.

"They're just another generation," she said. "It's hard for people to grow old and let go."

"Have you always lived here? At home, I mean?"

She looked startled, then shook her head. "Oh, no. I went away to college. Georgia. That was a lot of fun." She sighed. "And I lived in Atlanta for all the years I was married."

"You're *married*?"

"Divorced."

"Oh." I couldn't help smiling. It wouldn't have made any difference, but it was still a relief. "What happened?"

She said blankly, "I couldn't have children."

"Did that matter?" I asked. Rose looked at me. Her face had become quite still, like a mask. "I can't believe that anybody who knew you would think it did for a single second."

"Thank you. Yes, it did matter, unfortunately. To both of us." Rose smiled slightly. "Chester tried to pretend it didn't, but it did. I could see him just hurting and hurting and yearning for kids of his own. It wasn't his fault he couldn't have them. So one day I just left and came back here. Wouldn't see him, or open his letters or answer his calls. He's remarried, now. They have two little girls. They're just great."

Her voice faded. I could see she was almost crying, but determined not to.

"That was very brave of you."

"I guess it was, wasn't it?" She turned away from me.

"What sort of a name is Chester, anyway?" I said. I was delighted by the way I was able to say exactly what came into my head. I had never been like this before. "One of those stupid macho names that makes it sound as if you spend all your life on a bench press."

She laughed, and shook her head. "He's a nice guy. It just wasn't meant to happen."

"Was that recent?"

"Seven years ago."

"My wife left me, you know, about eighteen months ago," I said, wanting to show her that I, too, had suffered. "For somebody else. Besides Cosmo, we have a little girl called Flora. I've hardly seen her since she was one. We're getting divorced. If it's any consolation, it's worse when you have children."

"You still wear your ring, though, I noticed."

There were streaks of white in her hair near her temples, and a fine web of lines across her face. She was right, she wasn't a figure from a fairy tale, and yet a glamour lay about her that made her infinitely alluring. Perhaps she was used to fending off strange men, running a guest house like this.

"Do you have a stereo?"

"A what?"

I said impatiently, "Something that plays music."

"Oh. Sure. In the lounge. Why?"

"Come with me."

We went into what she called the lounge. It was a vast, shabby, white and cream rectangle with delicate plaster moldings and big windows swagged and draped in white damask. There were two sofas facing each other in front of a fireplace with curling dog irons, and a leather armchair, but otherwise, apart from some portraits on the walls and some large pots of ferns, it was almost entirely bare.

"It's hopeless, really, isn't it? Trying to keep it all going," she said, surveying it. "I started repainting it last month, but I haven't had the time or the energy to do it properly." She gestured towards some pots and a ladder in one corner.

"Do you break even?"

"Barely. But so much needs mending, and I can't get any help."

"What about all the people in trailers?" I said. "They don't seem to have much work."

She looked shocked. "Oh, no. I wouldn't employ one of them. I don't mean they're bad people, but . . . they're drifters. Eugenie's husband used to help, but he was different. Her family's always worked for us, but her children have all moved away. The American dream even comes true for black people, these days. It's just families like mine that're left high and dry."

"Can't you sell it?"

"I expect I'll have to, one day."

"One day?"

"One day when my mother passes away. She's so much happier since I came back. I don't know what she and my father did before, once I quit home. He spent a lot of time at the country club, I guess, checking out all the pretty girls. But running the guest house has given her a new interest in life. Not that it's without its problems. We only take couples, now, or families. I'd worked in tourism before, in Atlanta, so I had more of an idea than most. It'd help if we could put in a swimming pool. That's what I often think. If only we could afford a pool."

"You feel you're trapped here."

"Sometimes. I do love it, though. I'm not really a big city person, and I love the birds even if I'll never be into the garden the way Mom is. I don't have any special talents, not like you. I always thought I'd be happy having a pretty ordinary life somewhere. Only that hasn't happened. I don't know why I'm telling you all this. I guess it's because you're family. I hope not to sell before my mother goes. She loves this house."

"So did my mother, I think. She put bits of it in all her

drawings, you know. Even those dog irons in the fireplace. I recognize such a lot."

"Did she? I love it, too. Though sometimes—" Rose stopped.

I looked out through the french windows, at the great trees. They looked like something from another world. "What *is* that stuff dangling down?"

"It's a kind of moss. It doesn't do any harm."

"They look like rags. Or ghosts."

"Oh, ghosts. The South is full of those." Rose moved lightly over to a corner where an antiquated record player stood. "This is what we have."

There was a collection of records. I found an Elvis Presley album, and put it on. The sudden noise made us both jump. Then I began to dance.

It was wonderful, wonderful, oh, so wonderful. The air rushed past my body and face. I was laughing and whirling and spinning round the room. Every cell in my being had leapt into life. I held out my arms to her. "Come on. Let's dance."

She shook her head. "I'm not very good at dancing."

I could see all that she had been and could become, this woman who was so like and unlike my dead mother. When you fall in love with someone you see them through a palimpsest of all their former selves. It's as if you've always known them and always will, as if time itself has collapsed.

"Come *on*."

"Aw, shucks," she said, embarrassed.

"You can do this. Don't worry."

So she came into my arms, and out again, spinning and laughing. Her nightdress belled out like a great white flower. Our bare feet stamped, our arms moved, our bodies swayed; we were young again, possessed by the music. How long we danced for in that strange, empty place, I don't know. It seemed like hours and hours. The wooden floor rebounded beneath our feet. We were without thirst or hunger or fatigue.

The moonlight poured across the veranda, through the great french windows, and we were quicksilver, we were something other than flesh and blood. She was so sweet and light and small, it was like holding a bird. I could have broken her neck, or tossed her up into the sky. My hands burned through her thin cotton robe. I caught her and held her—

"Daddy?"

Cosmo was standing in the doorway. I said in the voice of an ogre, *"Go back to bed."*

"Daddy? I'm frightened."

He raised his arms to me, expectantly. He looked very small in his striped blue pajamas. I said harshly, "If you've come down without me, you can go back up, too. This is grown-up time, can't you see?"

His mouth turned down. "But I *want* you. I'm frightened. It's spooky, and there are funny noises. *Daddy.*"

"I'll take him," said Rose. She had stopped dancing as soon as he appeared. "Will you come with me?"

He shrank away from her when she held out her hand. "I don't want you, you smelly old pooh," he said. "I want my dad."

"How dare you be so rude," I said. I continued dancing by myself, and turned my back on him. "Go back to bed, you *rude* little boy."

Cosmo opened his mouth, and out of it came a scream so loud it obliterated the music. The volume was astounding. "No! I want you. *I'm not leaving without you!*"

"Oh, for God's sake."

"It's high time I went back to bed, anyway," said Rose, and yawned. She switched the record player off with a decisive movement. "See you guys later."

I carried my son back upstairs, seething. He refused to walk, and lay as heavy as lead in my arms. But when I put him down, he wouldn't let me go, clutching me with the panicky grip of someone drowning. "There's *ghosts* here," he said in a whisper.

"Don't worry," I said. "There aren't. It's just an old house."

"I can hear them."

"I won't leave until you're ready."

"Promise?"

"I promise."

"Dad?"

"Yes?"

"What's the difference between a man bitten by a mosquito and a man going on holiday?"

"Tell me."

"One is going to itch and the other's"—he yawned, hugely—"itching to go."

I waited a long time until his breathing became regular. He looked so innocent, tucked up under the white quilt. You never, ever love your children so much as when they're asleep. I went out into the corridor that divided our rooms. It was long and shadowy, and the wind, which had been imperceptible until now, blew down it making the white curtains flap and the tree outside go tap, tap, tap on the glass. I didn't think Rose would come to my room again that night; and I was right.

TWENTY-ONE

THIS WAS HOW we came to be driving to Charleston the next day, after another sleepless night. Aunt Lily had asked me to buy them a couple of things while I was in town, and I planned a wonderful surprise for her. It was time somebody gave them some help, I thought. I had seen Rose doing the laundry at six A.M.; she was hoovering the entire house while we had breakfast.

"I'll be back after lunch," I said to Aunt Lily. "Everything's under control."

So we got into the Oldsmobile and drove off, through the gates, along the avenue of trees, through the woods, over the river, and past the blue-flowered verges, the trailer vans, and the chapels and supermarkets.

"What do you get—" said Cosmo.

I groaned. "Do we really have to have another one? Where do you pick them up, anyway?"

My son said, relentlessly, "What happens when you put a snake on a car window? You get windscreen vipers. Is that funny? Is it?"

I reached forward and switched on the radio. An explosion of sound suddenly made us jump. I turned it down, my heart hammering, and switched channels. It was strange hearing nothing but American voices. I still couldn't get used to it, even though I'd grown up hearing them all my life. A woman's voice sang:

I gave my love a cherry that had no stone.
I gave my love a chicken that had no bone.
I told my love a story that had no end,
I gave my love a baby with no cryin'.
How can there be a cherry that has no stone?
How can there be a chicken that has no bone?
Who ever heard a story that had no end?
How can there be a baby with no cryin'?

We both listened for the answer.

Now a cherry when it's bloomin', it has no stone,
A chicken when it's pippin', it has no bone,
The story of I love you will never end,
A baby when it's sleepin' there's no cryin'.

Her voice, plaintive and sweet, sounded so like the one I had heard singing in my bedroom at Ruth's house I thought it must be another dream. Then Cosmo asked, "What does she mean, about love being a story that has no end?"

"Well," I said, "I suppose you could say that love doesn't have an end if you have a baby, because they grow up and have children themselves, and so on. It's a riddle about babies."

"But you and Mummy had us, and you don't love each other anymore, do you?"

"It's different with children," I said.

"What happens when I grow up, then?" He turned to look at me, accusingly.

I said, "I'll always love you, and so will Mummy."

Cosmo began kicking the seat in front of him. "I'm bored," he said again.

"Don't *do* that."

"Why not? If you loved me you'd let me do it."

"No, I wouldn't. If I didn't love you I'd let you go on, and then we'd have a crash and you could be hurt or killed."

He stopped kicking, and glared mutinously out of the window. "Why can't I sit up in front with you?"

"Because it's against the law."

"I don't believe you. If that witch were here, she'd be sitting next to you, wouldn't she?"

"Yes, because she's a grown-up. She's not a witch. She's your first cousin once removed, Rose."

"I can't wait to be grown up," said my son fiercely. "It's only grown-ups who are free."

I was free, I was free, I thought, my foot pressing on the accelerator. The ridiculous car surged forward. I've always liked speed. Acting is a bit like that, it makes you feel you're going fast, that life is accelerating. You're never bored, not for an instant. It's a different world. This was a different world. Nothing could catch me, nothing could hurt me. I could drive off the top of a mountain and be unscathed. *And when the dust begins to fly / It's like an eagle in the sky.* I was soaring through this dazzling air, following the road far beneath me where the insect whine of a police siren was closing in fast.

CHARLESTON was the sort of town where you could have a wonderful life, I thought, after the traffic policeman had written me out a ticket for speeding and wished me a nice day. Cosmo had waved and smiled at him as we drove off at a more sedate pace. Like all small boys, he was a natural fascist, deeply impressed by uniforms and guns.

"Can I have a gun, Dad? Can I?"

"No."

"Not a real one, just a toy one."

"I'll think about it."

"You won't think about it. You never think about me, just about yourself."

Charleston was idyllic. How was it possible for any American city to be ugly when they had this as an example? Even the modern buildings had a tactful, restrained feel to them. In place of the fun-fair bustle and vulgarity of New York there was the sort of civic pride that made it almost European in feel. It had parks, broad streets, cafés, markets; it was alive in a gentle, benign way that was utterly foreign to New York.

"Can I have a basket for Ti-Ti?"

"What?"

"That black lady is making baskets."

He dragged me over to where a group of women were seated, weaving twigs in and out. They were got up in some sort of costume, I noticed vaguely.

"No, of course not. That's for tourists," I said automatically.

"Aren't we tourists?"

"No," I said, "we certainly are not. My mother, your grandmother, came from here. Charleston is in our blood."

I wished I knew which house my mother had been born in. It was as hot as an English summer. We were now in the old part of town. Light bounced off buildings, spattering the shaded sidewalks like paint. These exquisite constructions of painted wood were like delicate doll's houses, set down by a tender young giantess in semitropical gardens. Flower beds overflowed with spring and summer flowers. I walked fast, and everywhere I looked I thought I could see Rose. It was she who sat on the high, fretted balcony, watering the luscious ferns; Rose disappearing just ahead down a long avenue of flowering trees, her light figure going into a shop. I started after each mirage, dragging Cosmo by one arm. We came to a big street, along which traffic flowed with glossy people-carriers and spotless Jeeps. I went out into the middle of the road with my arms spread. The traffic parted like the Red Sea before Moses.

Cosmo said, "My feet are hot."

"OK. I'll buy you some sandals."

We found a shoe shop. The saleswoman, who was immensely fat, bent down and measured my son's feet. He regarded her hair, rising up like a soufflé of spiders, with open astonishment.

"What kind of sandal are you looking for, honey?"

"I don't know. Strappy ones, I suppose."

"I'll see what we've got."

She rolled away and came back with some sandals made out of black webbing and rubber. Cosmo put on first one, then the other, and walked to the mirror. "Wow! Look, they flash red lights when I walk!"

He did a little dance, and I caught him up in my arms and spun him around. The saleslady laughed, then she was dancing, too, clapping her hands, the rolls of her flesh surging as she sang, *"We're going to rock around the clock tonight / We're going to rock, rock, rock 'til broad daylight!"*

Her voice was astonishingly beautiful. Her face was transformed. She could have been singing in church, or in an opera house.

Cosmo beamed. "Are these magic shoes?" he asked.

"Don't know nothing about that, honey. They's fifteen dollars. Thank you, sir."

"Show me some more shoes in his size. What about those? And those? Hey, Cosmo, how about some trainers?"

"Mum never allows me to wear trainers. She says it's bad for my feet."

In the end, we bought ten different pairs of shoes for him, including one with Mickey Mouse faces.

"But I thought you hated Mickey Mouse, Dad," said Cosmo.

"Let's get some for Flora, too, shall we? What's her size?"

"Eight, I think. She'd really like those pink and purple ones, too. And some trainers. Oh, and what about those silver boots?"

The saleswoman, delighted, offered us a discount. I waved away this dismal American preoccupation with saving money, and gave her my credit card.

"Where you from, young man?" she asked, as the electronic till chirred and beeped.

Cosmo said, "I'm from London. That's in England."

"Uh-huh? That's a long way from here. You take care, now. These here are good shoes. They'll shine in the dark."

Cosmo brightened. "I'm afraid of the dark," he said. I shifted impatiently.

"Have a nice day. Don't go getting yourself lost."

"I won't," said Cosmo, and skipped out, making the red lights in his heels flash again.

Everywhere there was light and life, bright new leaves on the colossal evergreen oaks like points of flame when the breeze blew off the sea. We watched ungainly white pelicans land and take off in the waves, and I told Cosmo about pelicans, and how Shakespeare had believed they would wound their breasts with their beaks rather than let their young starve. In the Gap, I bought some more new clothes, clothes I had never dreamed of wearing before—lime green, scarlet, royal blue, egg yellow. I cast off my dismal blacks and grays in the changing room.

"That looks great, Dad," said Cosmo.

He loved seeing money spent. We stopped and bought him another ice cream and a Coke.

We came across three fountains. Each was a marvel of modern design. One consisted of four arcs of water jetting into the center, a shallow dip in the pavement that was clearly intended for children to run through on hot days. They made the air full of rainbows. Cosmo, delighted, ran in and out of them. I was so deeply touched by the kindness and thoughtfulness of the people who dreamed up such a thing that tears rose in my eyes. Cosmo became tired; I, too, was tired, with my fizzy head, but I couldn't stop. The formal flower beds shimmered with color. I could smell Rose's scent, the bitter and the sweet.

The streets were full of leisurely, elegant people going to work after their lunch break. My eyes stung in the strong light. They all had ordinary lives, they had jobs and dinners and a good night's rest. Why couldn't I eat? Why couldn't I sleep?

"You don't need to do those things," I heard Rose say, "now that you've found me."

I came across the health food store that my aunt had told me about. They promised to deliver all I wanted, including a case of organic wine. On into a stationer's, where I bought two hundred staplers because I thought they would be perfect symbols of the union we were about to witness. I explained all this to Cosmo, as we wandered back towards the car.

"They're really pretty colors, Dad, like little bugs," he agreed. "Are we going to get party bags, too?"

"Why not?" I said generously. "We can give them their slice of wedding cake in it, and a balloon."

We found a toy shop. It was a matter of moments to buy two hundred party bags, although we had to have several patterns because, as the charming lady who owned it explained, this cleared out her entire stock.

"Look, don't you think Flora would like this doll?" Cosmo had found a cloth doll of Little Red Riding Hood. She had long dark plaits, and a simple, smiling face. When turned upside-down so that her skirt and cape were reversed, the doll changed into her grandmother.

"And look what's behind the granny's bonnet." He slid it over the doll's face, and a grinning gray wolf's head appeared. For no reason that I could understand, a chill went over me.

"I don't know. Are you sure?"

"Yeah. Look, Ti-Ti's talking to them."

I didn't like the doll. Wasn't there something sinister about each face? Red Riding Hood looked stupid; the granny cruel, the wolf sly.

"OK. We'll buy that, too."

"Can I have a gun?"

"A water pistol."

"Great!"

"And look at this ball. It shines when it bounces."

"OK."

There were two little girls in the shop. One was white, the other, younger, was black and the same age as Flora. Approaching them timidly, Cosmo asked, "Is she your sister?"

The white girl said scornfully, barely glancing at the other, "No, she's our *foster* sister." The foster sister smiled, too young to know she was being despised.

Cosmo's lips trembled. I said, "My son could hardly know that, could he? He was only trying to be friendly."

She looked at me blankly. Then she said, "You talk funny," and turned her back.

Cosmo fell asleep in the car on the way back, which was a nuisance because I wanted to talk to him. It was as if this strange land had liberated a perpetual motion in my inner self. Everywhere I saw radiance, sparkle, shine, the dancing of light on wings and water, the metamorphosis of branch and leaf into birds that darted and soared, whistled and dipped, and I was at one with them. The blades of grass springing out of the rich earth were as hairs on my body; I was a walking tree, a dreaming cloud, I was the eagle in the sky, I was the lion at the door. Everything exulted with me, made fresh and vivid and new.

I carried my son in, past the opulent, trembling ferns, past the luscious red flowers, through the veranda, and up the stairs to his small room. Even this looked familiar. After a moment, I realized why. The cream-colored patchwork quilt had exactly the same pattern as that which Ruth was always sewing. The boxes went tumbling through the white air, always open, always empty, turning into stars, turning back into boxes, a continual cascade of shapes.

Twinkle, twinkle, little star / How I wonder what you are?

Who had taught Ruth this design?

I drew the curtains, and looked at my sleeping son. This had always been a child's room, I thought. It had a rocking chair, and some battered old bookshelves above an equally battered child's desk. I put the water pistol, the doll, and the shining ball on it. There was a sampler on the wall over the bed, depicting a child's version of a house, two trees, and a family. *God bless this house* said the words in tiny stitches. The initials LP and the date 1950 were stitched at the bottom. Had this been Laura's room, or Lily's? I wondered where Rose slept, and if she had had this room, too.

The books on the shelves were those of an American childhood: *The Wizard of Oz, The Return to Oz, White Fang, The Little House on the Prairie, Little Women, What Katy Did, Huckleberry Finn.* Lower down, there were picture books: *Where the Wild Things Are, Bedtime for Frances, Goodnight Moon, In a Dark Wood.* All had been well thumbed. My hand hovered over the last title. I hadn't looked at it for such a long time. Perhaps I would read it to Cosmo tonight.

Then I saw something disgusting. Above the bookshelves was a large crucifix, made out of some sort of black wood with a miniature Christ stuck to it. Every muscle and sinew of the pale figure had been carefully carved to depict agony; tiny trickles of red paint dribbled from the wounds. Loathing rose in me. I yanked it off its nail and wrenched open the window. The next moment, it was sailing through the air, head first, falling down,

down, down—and then the loop of beads to which it was attached caught in a branch, and its descent was suddenly halted.

Aunt Lily and Rose had already started preparing hundreds of vol-au-vents made of semi-frozen puff pastry. They were filling each with a disgusting-looking pink mush made of crabmeat and minced mushroom.

"Hello, Benedick," said my aunt. "Your wife called while you were out. She asked for you to call her back."

I shrugged. "If she wants to talk to me, she can call again herself," I said.

"We've just heard, Eugenie's feeling bad again. She won't be able to help us," said Rose, waving at all the unprepared food. "It's one of those loaves and fishes situations. I'm afraid you'll have to make your own dinner tonight."

"Fear not!" I said. "Don't you know you're talking to a cook? Behold, I shall provide a feast."

Even as I prepared to take over, a white van drew up from the delicatessen in Charleston. I ushered the man in, tipping him lavishly after he had carried in all the boxes and bottles. The two women did not seem as enthusiastic as I'd expected them to be.

Aunt Lily placed a hand on my arm. "But Benedick," she said, "all I asked for was some flour."

"Oh, don't worry," I said. "I've paid for it all." I saw the relief on their faces. "It's my treat. I thought you'd better stock up. That's the trouble with women, you never stock up. My wife was just as bad. Every autumn I'd tell her we had to get enough firewood in to keep us going through the winter, and every winter she'd place her faith in the central heating system which would then be guaranteed to break down."

"But this must have cost a fortune," said Rose, an anxious

frown making waves on her brow. "We thought you'd go to the Piggly-Wiggly."

"Don't worry," I said again. "Honestly. It's my present to you. Just in the nick of time, too."

Then they were all smiles, laughing when I showed them the party bags and the staplers.

"Hey!" said my cousin. "That's cool. They'll really like it."

I am a good cook, even without the equipment that I'd left behind at Ruth's. Sometimes I've thought that if my father and Georgie had encouraged me to turn to this, rather than teaching, I might have given up acting after all. All afternoon, I made canapés. I tossed pancakes, roasted peppers, skewered chicken, marinated lamb. I was invincible, indestructible, the Captain Scarlet of catering and cuisine. When Cosmo materialized, yawning, I roped him in, too. He likes doing things. The sun came down in warm shafts, and all the windows were open. At the bottom of the garden the great river glittered like hammered bronze. From time to time birds would rise or fall into its embrace.

"I wish we could go out in a boat," said my son, looking out.

"You can," said Rose. "I'll take you."

Cosmo scowled at her.

"Say thank you," I said, as I chopped vegetables with lightning speed.

"I don't want to go with *her*." He pushed violently at the table. My concentration and my knife both slipped.

"Oh, no!" cried Rose in dismay. She ran to fetch the first-aid box.

I held out my hand, indifferently. It was only a shallow cut. "You'll find my blood is blue," I said.

She laughed, as though I had been making a joke. I could feel her breath on my hand.

I said to Rose, "Won't you kiss it better?"

She looked up, smiling, then blushed.

"I'm sooo *bored*!" said Cosmo, kicking the table again. "I want to go *home*. When are we going to go home?"

"Oh, for heaven's sake," I said angrily. "Just shut up, will you?"

"Don't tell me to shut up." He burst into tears. "I hate you! I hate you! You stinking fish head!" He ran out into the garden.

The telephone rang. Aunt Lily went to answer it. "Magnolia House, may I help you? Oh, hello, Mrs. Hunter. This is Lillian Gardener, Benedick's aunt speaking. No, surely. He's right here."

I sighed, loudly.

"Dick? Why haven't you called?"

"I've been busy. Affairs of state," I said. I could hear the echo of my own voice as it bounced back from the stars. Love was like starlight, I thought. You could see it even when the star itself had died.

"How's Cosmo?"

"Fine. He's outside."

"I've been terribly worried, not hearing from you for over a week. I thought we agreed, we'd talk every day."

"Well, we've been moving around. No time for that sort of thing."

"Can I talk to Cosmo? I've been missing him. I want to hear his voice."

"He's right at the bottom of the garden."

"Well, call him back."

I left the receiver on the table, wandered into the kitchen to pour myself a beer, then returned, humming. "Sorry, I can't seem to find him. He's off running *through bush, through briar,* in the usual manner. You should see the countryside round here, it's quite—"

Georgie's voice sharpened. "Is he really all right? I know I'm being neurotic, but you do sound strange."

"I'm perfectly all right. Never better. We're having a terrific time. This is such a fantastic place—"

Again, she interrupted me. "I just really want to hear his voice. Flora wants to speak to him, too, don't you, darling?"

I could hear her small voice chirping in the background.

"He's fine. You can ask my aunt, if you like."

She sighed. "Give him my love, then. Say I can't wait to have him back. What time will you be arriving tomorrow? I can come and meet the plane."

"Oh, don't bother," I said. I could hear my voice distort again.

"What do you mean?" said my wife, in an altered tone.

"You're not getting Cosmo back," I said. "We're staying on."

TWENTY - TWO

I HAD NO INTENTION OF going back to England. I understood that now. Georgie had humiliated and bullied me in the
past, she had no insight into what she had done to us all, she
was an evil from which my son had to be protected. I thought of
Flora with sorrow. I couldn't rescue her from the tawdry London
world, but Cosmo and I would stay in America, with Rose, in the
white house by the wood. *They got married and lived happily ever after.* The
ending little boys despise. They want the quest to go on forever,
the hero to continually prove himself against apparently insur-
mountable odds.

I was alive as I had never been before. I could hear every tiny
leaf as it rustled on the tree, the calls of birds, the creak of wood,
the humming of the great steel fridge that contained all the
canapés.

"Everything OK?" my aunt said, as I came back into the
kitchen. They were all seated round the table. "Lemonade?"

"It's really yummy," said Cosmo. He had forgotten all about
calling me a stinking fish head.

"I'm sure it is." I could hear the bubbles fizzing against the
glass. It was unbearably exciting, like fireworks going off.

Rose yawned and stretched. The breath thrummed in her
throat. I envisaged it rushing down into the million branches of

her lungs, the alveoli swelling like fruit with precious oxygen, the oxygen being released into her blood.

"We've done it all, way before time. You're amazing, Benedick, I've never seen anyone work so fast. Cosmo was a real help, too." She turned to him, smiling. "Tell you what. Would you both like to come out in the boat with me? It's cooler now, and I could do with some air."

Cosmo considered. "Only if you show me the baby turtles?"

"Sure."

He ran on ahead, towards the jetty. Rose and I went down through the garden, past the flamelike flowers. The great red lilies on their fleshy stems trumpeted my joy to the four corners of the earth. The loveliness of this green bowl of grass and trees and water made me want to weep. No wonder my mother had longed to return.

"Oh, if only everyone could see what I can see," I said. "If only they could."

"What?" asked my cousin. "What can you see?"

"Beauty," I said. "If people could see what beauty exists in the world, there would be no more cruelty or suffering. Don't you think cruelty is caused by ugliness, and ugliness by what is outside nature?"

I had so many thoughts in my mind, they were like the branches of a great tree. I wanted to follow each and every one of them, all the way to the finest twig.

"I've never met anyone like you before," Rose said.

"I've never met anyone like you."

The air throbbed with insects.

"Oh, I'm nobody special," she said.

"Only somebody special would say that."

She gave a little laugh, as though I were making her uncomfortable. She never lost sight of herself. That was her one defense. Perhaps she thought I said this kind of thing often.

"Perhaps you think I say this kind of thing often," I said, immediately. "I don't. My wife said I never talked to her, and I didn't. I couldn't. But I'm different now."

We came out of the soft turf, onto the bleached wood of the jetty. I could smell the river, its sluggish flood and lush green. I wanted to take my shoes off and squelch my toes in the bank, to feel the luxuriance of mud. Cosmo was standing looking down, slim as the statue in Ruth's front garden.

"I can see some little fish. Tiny, silvery ones," he said.

The rippling radiance all around us was almost too bright to bear. It seemed to go through my eyes, into my brain, my soul, my heart. I was being altered by its radiation, inexorably. A flat-bottomed boat was moored here, a torrent of yellow honeysuckle falling half into it. Rose jumped in lightly, then held out her hand for Cosmo. He took it, jumped, then it was my turn. Her grip was strong. I was moved, again, to find how rough the skin of her hands was. I stepped into the boat. It bucked and rocked, as if alive. At once, Rose stepped forward to brace me. For a moment we stood close. I could feel her body, the tension in it like a coiled spring. The boat rocked again. She seized the jetty to steady us. Gradually, the rocking subsided, but the pulse it had set off did not.

"I'll paddle," she said.

"Oh, I'm sure I could give you a rest."

She shook her head. "No. It's best I sit up front. You look after Cosmo. Remember, there are alligators in these waters."

"Will we see any?" my son asked.

I watched her bend and stretch against the burnished water, the energy in her coiling and uncoiling, the long feathering ripple of water from her oar. How miraculously quick and skillful she was, steering us off down the river! I could have done it myself, but I was in too much ecstasy. I knew her secret. She wanted me, too, as badly as I wanted her. Faces and words can lie, but bodies can't.

We seemed to float on and on between wood and water, gliding on a mirror. All around, a tall tangle of trees plunged endlessly into their reflected trunks, rooted in the sky. There were clouds in their roots, and little fish in the sky darting and flicking; I couldn't tell where one element ended and another began. To swim is to fly, to fly is to swim, there was no division. Every tree was a giant, its writhing branches frozen in the act of launching a thousand shuttlecocks of bristling green fern. Tiny birds darted and swam free from cages of thin reeds. All was silent except for the swirl and plink of water. We pushed forward.

"I can't see any baby turtles," Cosmo complained, suddenly.

"Oh, for goodness' sake, Cosmo, stop whingeing."

My son said, "Adam and Eve and Pinchme went out in a boat to swim. Adam and Eve got drowned, so who was left?"

I knew the answer to this one. "Look at this, look. Feel its mystery, the great green gloom. You'll never see anything like this again. This is like the great forests the dinosaurs lived in, this is the very cradle of life—"

"Oh, shut up," said Cosmo. "You're always talking at me, always telling me off and lecturing. I *still* haven't seen any baby turtles," he said accusingly to Rose.

She raised her paddle, and put her finger to her lips. "Look over there, in the sun. It looks a bit like a stone, sitting on that rock over there. See it?"

"Yes," he breathed. "Can I touch it?"

"I'll bring us a bit closer, but it'll dive down when we get close."

The boat glided towards the murky greenish gold. Light shafted through the thick foliage. We saw the long reptilian neck sticking out, the hump of its shell, the creased head. It reminded me irresistibly of James Cork. Then it must have seen us, for it was gone.

"Oh!" said Cosmo, disappointed.

"Look, look," said Rose. "There's a big white crane, see?" Something vast and white took off from the water, silent as a ghost, and soared out of sight. "I love those birds. They're so powerful, so pure," said Rose. "I used to dream of flying away on one of them when I was a little girl, like the Marsh King's daughter."

"Why did you want to fly away?"

"Oh—because Momma and Poppa quarreled a lot, I guess. It made me very unhappy."

"What did they quarrel about?" Cosmo asked.

"His girlfriends. And his spending. He went through most of Momma's money, as well as his own. All my family has been terrible with money—gambling, mostly. My grandmother was the worst. She would ring up at four in the morning to tell us she'd just bought a horse in Virginia, that kind of thing."

"And had she?"

"Yes. She loved horses. Treated them better than her children, from what I hear."

"Daddy doesn't have girlfriends," said Cosmo. "But Mummy's got a boyfriend. He's called Brute. His breath smells of boiled eggs."

"Uh-huh?" She glanced at me and smiled.

"Can I have a swim?" said Cosmo.

"No," said Rose. "You can't swim in this water. You can fish in it, boat in it, and look at it, but that's all." She turned and looked at him over her shoulder, smiling. "I know, it's tough. But there's still the Jacuzzi."

Cosmo rolled his eyes.

"I'd like to go in the Jacuzzi," I said. "Later on."

IT WAS TIME to put Cosmo to bed. My life revolved around putting him to bed, and getting him to eat, I thought resentfully. Even now, the habit was too strong to break. He was reluctant, after his sleep in the car earlier in the day, but I insisted. I planned to repaint the drawing room once he was in bed. Everything I needed was still there. I wouldn't ask Rose or my aunt; it would be a surprise for them when they came down in the morning.

Putting Cosmo to sleep never took less than an hour. Sometimes, the only way I could get him to stay in bed was to promise him a sweet on his pillow for the morning. Sometimes I had to lose my temper. Today, I gave him some of the knockout medicine Tom had given me for the plane.

"I want a video," he said.

"You can watch one cartoon on TV."

But he was satiated with cartoons. "I want some hot chocolate and a cuddle and a story," he said, in his most babyish voice.

I sighed irritably. "Stay there. If there's no chocolate, will milk and honey do?"

"Yes. But I would *rather* prefer chocolate." He was a very English little boy, so polite. You wouldn't think he had such a temper.

"I have to go now," I said, returning. "There's a lot to do."

"No. Want picture book."

I took down the battered copy of *In a Dark Wood*. I hadn't seen it since my own childhood, and yet the pictures were instantly, uncannily familiar. Each page had only a few lines of text. The words weren't the thing you remembered; it was the pictures. In her last book, my mother had pared her art down to something nobody could forget.

Here was the narrator with her mother and her baby sister. It was almost like a photograph—for this book, unlike all the rest, was in color, with a hyper reality about it that added to its dream-like quality. The mother looked very like my grandmother. The baby, a plump child in a nightdress, was standing up to touch a gigantic red lily with four trumpets. The narrator stood beside her. She, too, wore a nightdress but was clearly older. *My mother said, I never should / Play with the gypsies in the wood.* . . . All had wide, staring eyes as though sleepwalking. Two ducks swam in the far-off river. In the hazy space between land and water two sheep were huddled, with a lamb suckling from the one in front.

"There's a wolf creeping up on them," said Cosmo, pointing. "Look there, in the shadows."

In the next picture, the elder girl reached up to pick an apple from a bough above her.

"Can you see the gypsies?"

"No. Yes, I can. They're dancing, aren't they?"

In the sky, an owl's face made of streaky clouds brooded. By the next page it had dissolved. The two girls were in a bedroom. I recognized this. It was the very one in which I was sitting, right down to its bare wooden floors and patchwork quilt. The window was open. The narrator had eaten the apple, and was bored. She was in disgrace, her mouth turned down. She looked just like Rose, with her long, dark hair caught back, neither adult nor child. The baby was crying. She was hideous. The elder girl took her chubby hand. In the next picture she led her down the stairs. Cosmo yawned, and his eyes drooped. Step by step the two girls walked through the trees. *The wood was dark, the grass was green.* . . .

The pictures swam into each other, completely meaningless. I was desperate to get up and go downstairs. I saw the gypsy girl Sally try to snatch the little sister, but it didn't make any sense. By then, my son was asleep. I slipped my arm, inch by inch, from under his head, and ran downstairs.

I had expected the house to be empty, and it was. My aunt had retired. A blue-and-white-striped marquee had been erected at the end of the hall, adjoining the breakfast room. Beyond it, I could see the velvety Carolina sky, not black so much as a deep violet. The warm air was like a great damp cloth pressed over the face. What it would be like in real summer I could barely imagine. I stepped out through the french windows, and out into the garden. The leaves of the camellias gleamed like great slanting eyes.

I walked down, and the scent came at me in waves. All around, the great boles of the trees were twined with flowering honeysuckle, and with roses just starting to open. My cousin's head was floating in the Jacuzzi. The water bubbled and slurped, and for a moment I hesitated. Her hair was spread all around her, and her eyes were closed. There was a thick candle wavering beside her, a half-empty bottle of wine and a glass. I could have stayed and watched for a long time, but she looked up, and smiled.

"Hi."

"Hallo. I was wondering whether you still had a body."

She sat up, slightly. "You must be beat, too."

"Actually, I was just about to start repainting the drawing room."

She laughed her silent laugh. "Why don't you come on in?"

"I don't have any swimming trunks," I said.

She gave me a long, mischievous look. "You have underpants, don't you?"

"Yes. Sure. Absolutely."

"Same thing."

She was wearing a swimming costume. I could see the thin bootlace straps as her shoulders rose out of the frothing waters, the points of her small, high breasts. Her knees rose up before her like two white water lilies. She put her arms around them.

I took my shirt off. Then my trousers. I could feel myself reddening.

"Tell me something."

"What?"

"Why is it guys always take their socks off last?"

"Because we have cold feet?"

"Do you?"

"Do I what?"

"Have cold feet?"

"I expect so. I'm a hotbed of cold feet."

She laughed at this old joke. I dipped a toe in the water. It was faintly fizzy. I stepped down onto an invisible step, then all at once lost my balance, slid down, and was submerged. I felt her hand grip me, as it had done in the boat.

"Hey! Are you OK?"

"Yes, yes," I said, gasping. "Never better, thanks." The water bubbled and kneaded. I moved my spine so that the stream of unending pressure could work away at a sore spot I hadn't even realized existed. "This is—it's just—wow," I said. "I had no idea these things were so good." I spread my arms out around the rim. The light of the candle fluttered. Above us the sky swarmed with stars.

"We put it in for the guests, but I guess we get more use out of it than they do."

"Do you mind, having people in your home?"

She laughed. "No. Not at all. What else is there to do out here? It'd be different if my father had kept the house in Charleston, but here, you get to long for company. I used to wish so much for somebody to play with when I was a child. A brother or a sister, particularly. Mom and Dad gave me a dog, but even so, I must have been one of the few kids to really look forward to school. I enjoy meeting new people, and cooking and keeping house."

"What are they like?"

"We get all sorts. Honeymooners, big shots from the city, foreigners. We've had our busiest time, but you'll see how different it is when it fills up."

"I could stay here all night."

"But then the drawing room wouldn't get painted," she said seriously.

"It will be."

She stared at me. "Are you serious? My God, you are. Leave it. You're our guest. You've already done enough."

"I had rather crack my sinews, break my back, than you should such dishonor undergo while I sit lazy by," I said. She didn't recognize this, of course. My memory kept tossing up fragments of plays I had been in.

"Why did your wife leave you?"

I looked at her, surprised. To me it was perfectly obvious.

"Forget it. Forget I asked. Stupid question, it's none of my business, I know."

"No. We're family, remember? You can ask me anything, and I'll tell you," I said. "I'm not used to talking about my feelings, though. Georgie thinks it's because of my mother. Or perhaps I'm just a classically repressed Englishman."

"I'm so sorry about what happened to her. And to you. I've always had my mom. I don't know what we'd do without each other."

"You're lucky."

"I know. When I feel blue, I remember that." She sighed. "I just don't get it. You're such a great guy. You're kind, good-looking, clever, successful, you're a terrific cook, a fantastic father. . . ."

So she gave back to me the self I had lost, when I least deserved it.

"Well," I said. "I suppose my wife, or ex-wife, doesn't agree."

"You're still in love with her."

"No. Not anymore. That's what coming to America has done for me, among other things. But I was in love with her, and I always loved her more than she loved me. When someone like that leaves you for another person, it makes it much harder.

Particularly if they blame you for their own change of heart, instead of accepting some of the responsibility."

"Yes. That is mean," said Rose.

"I suppose I seemed successful or glamorous or something when she met me, because I had a good part in a West End show. Or maybe it was just that I'm a couple of years older than she is, and that seems like a lot in your twenties. Then we had children and I suddenly couldn't get any work, just when we most needed the money. So she worked a lot harder, started writing romantic novels, and her career took off. I stopped being successful at just the time she started. It changed our relationship, the balance of power. All the things she'd liked about me became unbearable to her. She started an affair with this other man. And then she left me."

"She sounds like a hard person," said Rose.

"She's a mixture. I suppose I had the soft side first," I said.

"But now?"

"Now?"

I could see the white wedge of her face, the dark hair falling around her shoulders. She was the girl I had traveled North of Nowhere to find, she was Lolly and the brave sister, she was the princess who had saved me from my wife the witch, she was Bianca and Laura, my mother.

"Now," I said. "There's only you."

And so there was great joy and love between us all that night.

You wouldn't think something that is so much to do with bodies in the end turns out to happen in the mind. But it does.

I slept for a little by her side, but not for long. The enchantment was running too strongly in my veins. I couldn't sit still. I had promised I would paint the drawing room, and so I would. I had the paint and the brushes; it was a ridiculously easy task that the two women would never accomplish on their own. I would perform my task overnight, like a genie or a magician. Imagining their tearful gratitude, I was filled with pride.

I worked with the doors wide open and the sound of the crickets cheeping in the dark like a rusty wheel. The paint was pure white, white as snow, white as the moon, white as a sleepless night. I love paint, the sharp clean smell of it, the way it dries so smooth and fresh no matter what is underneath. My hands became clumsy paws, white and thick. Up and down the tall ladder, ten times, a hundred times, three hundred times. The cheeping stopped, and a cold mist rolled up from the river. Little by little the night turned gray, and just as I was putting all the brushes away to soak, the walls flushed the color of flesh. I turned to look.

The sun was coming up. Long, sharp shadows went knifing across the lawn towards the river. I could see every blade of grass. Except that it was not grass, but some sort of short, thin-leafed plant with a tiny flower glittering like a bead of blue dew. Even the grass here was different, as strange as if I was on another planet. The moss hanging down from the branches had turned to silver fleece. An elegant bird hopped around between the great boles of the trees. It was the Bird of Truth, but it was gray, not white. It stopped, and gave a curious chuckling cry like unearthly laughter.

"That's a mockingbird," said Rose, yawning. She had a toweling robe wrapped round her.

"I've never seen a mockingbird before," I said. "Except in a picture."

She yawned again. "Sorry. I must shower before the guests arrive. Ow! These darn bugs have bitten all down my legs." She turned and walked away. She hadn't even noticed the wonderful white room I had made for her.

TWENTY - THREE

ALL AROUND ME people now busied themselves preparing for the wedding, and none of them existed. The two bridesmaids, buxom, giggling girls who painted each other's nails and tweaked each other's elaborate hair arrangements, were not real. The round tables with their crisp white tablecloths, the striped marquee, the florid garden, the elegant white house, were so much paper and ink. It was very funny. I found a bottle of wine in the fridge and opened it because it was the same as the wine I had drunk with Rose the night before. By the time I'd finished it, the whole world was shining like a diamond.

Cosmo found me. His hair was standing up on end, and he had got himself dressed in odd socks; "Just like you, Daddy," he pointed out. "Can I have some breakfast?"

"Yes," I said vaguely, but Rose wasn't in the kitchen. I could hear her voice in the trees, whispering to me that I must give everything up for her. I looked at my hand, and saw that I still wore the wedding ring my wife had given me. It came off easily. I threw it into the Jacuzzi. It was still bubbling, like a pan of milk about to boil over.

"Daddy. Daddy? *Daddy!* I'd like some toast, please."

Cosmo was used to repeating his requests over and over until

I responded. Eventually, it became easier to do as he asked. The knives in the kitchen all whispered to each other.

"Look sharp."

"Cut to the chase!"

I wandered out onto the veranda.

Aunt Lily was sitting there. Bunches of cut flowers and leaves were being jammed into some green, spongy stuff that somehow held them upright.

"Good morning, Benedick," she said, raising her eyes. "Aren't you going to shave?"

"I painted the drawing room," I said, grinning.

"Indeed you did. You might have taken the curtains and the portraits down first."

"I've better things to do than watch paint dry."

Her lips tightened. "I know it was kindly meant."

Carefully she snipped off a lurid pink camellia and set it floating in a glass bowl. I watched, fascinated, as the semicircles of its petals perfected each other in their reflection. They were like Rose and myself, two halves of one whole.

"You like Rose, don't you?"

"I'm in love with her."

She looked shocked. "But you've only been here three days!" she said. "You can't be serious."

"How long does it take?"

"Does she feel the same about you?"

"Of course she does," I said belligerently. "Oh, I know. She's beautiful, marvelous, perfect. You're her mother, you should know."

Aunt Lily was silent. "She is all those things. But she isn't for you."

"What do you mean?" I stared at her. She looked so dignified, with her wave of pure white hair swept up into a chignon. Authority sat on her like a second skin. She was like my father,

I thought: used to getting her own way. "This isn't some anti-British thing, is it? I'm not like my father, I assure you. This is it, for me. It was meant to happen. Oh, don't worry, I won't take her away from you. I'm quite prepared to live here."

Aunt Lily was agitated. "How far has this gone? Benedick? *Benedick!*"

"Can I play with you now, Dad?" said Cosmo.

"That's our business," I said. I couldn't stop grinning. I reached into the tub full of ice and popped open a champagne bottle. "Your health."

"Benedick, listen, you must listen—"

"We're two people on the verge of middle age, we can make our own minds up. Look, in a couple of months my divorce will be through. *It was a lover and his lass, / With a hey, and a ho, and a hey nonino, / With a hey noninonino.* Don't worry. Everything's cool."

She gripped me fiercely, and stared into my eyes. "I need to talk to you both as soon as this wedding is over. And then I want you to leave."

"Leave? What, this house? Why? We've only just arrived."

"I'm sorry to say it, but you should never have come," she said.

T HERE WAS NO accounting for the vagaries of another generation. I had too much to do. Cosmo was buzzing round me like a fly.

"Can I have one of those shirts? I thought only girls wore pink flowers."

"It's one of my new ones. Let's play chase," I said. "I want to see the lights on your flashing sandals."

He darted off, and I followed, bottle in hand, swigging as I went. We chased each other round and round the garden. He was quick and surprisingly agile. I threw the bottle into the river and took his water pistol from him. We doubled back, racing up the steps and almost colliding with an elegant, matronly figure.

"Aha, the mother of the bride," I said, sweeping her a low bow. "Ravishing, quite ravishing."

"I don't believe we've had the pleasure . . . ," she said, puzzled.

"Benedick Hunter, actor and cook, at your service." I burped again. "I prepared the veritable banquet that you will consume later. The serving wench was poorly, so I stepped in to save the day."

"You did?" she said, flustered. "That's very kind—I must find Barbara. Have you seen her?"

I hadn't a clue who Barbara was, so I waved upward. "Inquire within," I said.

I caught sight of Cosmo. I had his water pistol in one hand, and grabbed a fresh bottle of champagne with the other. "Hey, Cosmo," I shouted. "What's the difference between a bad hunter and a constipated owl?"

"I dunno."

"One can shoot but can't hit, the other can hoot but can't—"

He ran away, shrieking as I squirted, then he chased me with it. We were both breathless with laughter. Eventually, he became winded and collapsed on the grass.

"Come on, come on!"

"I can't. I'm tired."

"You can't possibly be tired. You're thirty-three years younger than I am. Have you ever had champagne? Try some."

He swigged. "It's like lemonade," he said, then made a face. "I like lemonade better."

"I can drink and drink and not get drunk," I said.

"Come on, stupid." He sprang up, laughing, and I chased him again. Eventually, I caught him in a rugby tackle.

He rolled over and bounced on my stomach, tickling me with Ti-Ti. "You're such a *great* Dad," he said.

"That tiger really does need a wash."

"No, he doesn't. He mustn't be washed, ever. It would hurt his eyes."

"OK, don't worry."

"I wish you could always be like this."

"Why not?" I said. "America is a state of mind."

THE WEDDING GUESTS had been slowly filling the house all this time, but we paid them no attention until Rose came down the steps. She looked flushed and embarrassed.

"Hi. Er—Benedick, the ceremony's about to begin," she said. "I could really use some help in the kitchen again. If you wouldn't mind?"

"Of course not, my adored one," I said. "We don't want to spoil these merry peasants' day, do we, Cosmo? Come along."

We went up the steps.

"Are you OK?" she asked, in a low voice.

"How could I not be?"

She waited until Cosmo darted ahead. "It's just—I haven't dated much since my marriage ended. I don't want you to get the wrong picture. We hardly know each other, and now you're being so strange. I just didn't want you to think—"

A tinny recording of organ music started to play "Here Comes the Bride." "Christ, *I hate that fucking tune!*" I roared. Several people murmured above us.

"Benedick!" she hissed, then started to giggle. "You *mustn't.* They're paying me three thousand dollars for this. It's somebody's *wedding.*"

We had reached the level where the fountain played. I grabbed her, and drew her along the shallow terrace, out of sight.

"Don't—don't—"

It was as though our skin was on fire. All around us pink and white blossoms fell like confetti. Even as I watched, the centers swelled into apples that flushed from green to red.

"No," she said softly. "Not now. We can't."

The apples wavered. I blinked.

"I don't care. I know, your mother disapproves. She hated mine, I think."

"Poor Laura. It was like they could never forgive her for something," said Rose.

"Leaving, I expect."

"For years I didn't even know she'd existed. Didn't know you existed, either."

Above us the voices droned on, vowing eternal fidelity and all the usual rubbish. I had once made the same promises. It was incredible that anyone should go on believing them.

"Do you want all that?" I said, jerking my head. "Vows in white nylon?"

"I'm old-fashioned, I guess."

"You're the way people ought to be, but aren't. Not in London, at any rate."

"Look," she said, "we have the same hands."

It was like driving an American car. All the usual gearshifts, the brakes, were gone, and there was only this dreamlike exhilaration of movement.

She was less surprised than me. At any rate, she detached herself, and went back to oversee the wedding breakfast.

I followed. These people were necessary to her, so I was utterly charming to them. It was so easy. They were impressed by the most trivial thing about me, my being British. Or perhaps it was just their good manners. When I said I was an actor, one man immediately asked, "An actor, huh? So how much do you earn, in a good year?"

It crossed my mind to ask him in turn how many times he had sex with his wife, but I could see he had no idea how rude his question was to somebody English. I said, modestly, "About one hundred thousand dollars."

"Doing pretty good, huh?"

"Oh, yes," I said airily. "Actually, I'm going into the directing side of things now. That's why I'm in America, to scout out new talent."

"You are? Are you going to Hollywood?"

"I expect so," I said. "My godfather lives there. He's a very important man in the film business."

It was delightful the ease with which all these lies and half-truths rolled off my tongue. From then on, I was treated like royalty. Actors and film people *are* that, in America; it's only in England we're treated like dirt. I told them that I had been in *Brideshead Revisited,* which some of them remembered from *Masterpiece Theatre* (true); had recently acted in both *Notting Hill* and *Shakespeare in Love* (untrue); knew Sir Anthony Hopkins and Julia Roberts *intimately.* . . . They were so willing to be impressed and bamboozled, and I was drunk with my own prolixity, with the champagne. I loved them all. I talked and talked. My tongue was moving so fast that it developed a mouth ulcer. Even when I served canapés, I talked. I was the life and soul of the party, and I had lost all sight of myself, of that inner person who had, through all this, been bound to me by a single hair.

I danced with the bride, all in white and silver, I danced with her mother, I danced with the bridesmaids. I danced with Rose. It was like holding a cloud. I was flying higher and higher. I don't think I've ever been so happy. Then my aunt seized me and held on to me with a grip I couldn't break. I was dragged off, with Rose following, into the white room I had painted the night before.

. . .

I SUDDENLY SAW who she really was. It was like the doll I had bought Flora, with the wolf's head hiding under the granny's bonnet.

"It's you, isn't it?" I said to her. "You're the Troll Princess from 'The White Bear.' I should have recognized your nose."

"That's the way Lolly saw me. My little sister with the cruel eyes."

"What did you do, to make her hate you so much? Did you steal her prince?"

"No," she said. "She stole mine."

Rose was looking at me with an expression full of concern. The noise of the disco throbbed across the walls of the house. Everybody else was outside. "I don't understand what you're talking about," she said. "What's wrong? Mom? Benedick? Why are you both acting so strange?"

Aunt Lily said with cold anger, "Oh, there was all kinds of nonsense about how Don had made a big mistake and only discovered it too late. That was her story. She was very good at telling tales. The truth was quite different. He never was able to resist a pretty young girl, especially one living under his roof. But it didn't mean anything. I was the one he'd chosen, not her.

"We had a lovely antebellum house near Forsyth Park in Savannah. I was waiting for a baby, you see. That was what happened when you got married, I thought. We would get the house and the garden just right, and then the baby would come and we would be so happy. I even had a nursery decorated for my child. Eugenie's husband carved the crib. It had white ribbons and satin bows. I made up a store of baby clothes. Blue for a boy, and pink for a girl. But the baby didn't come and didn't come.

"And then Lolly came to me and said she was going to have my husband's baby. She said they had been lovers ever since she'd come to live with us. She was in college there, you see."

"I don't believe you," I answered. To Rose, I said, "She's lying, can't you see?"

"What did you do?" Rose asked.

"What could I do? Abortion was illegal in those days, and we were Catholic. In any case, it was too late. She knew that. So I told her what to do."

"You did?" I said sarcastically.

"Yes. I've always had to take charge, because of Momma. She came back here, and I pretended I was the one having the baby. I padded my clothes out and tried to put on weight. My husband and parents went along with it all. What else could they do? It was the fifties, when nice girls from good families were supposed to get married if they got into trouble with a boy. In our case, that simply wasn't possible. I wasn't going to cause a scandal and divorce my husband simply because Lolly had made a fool of herself over him. . . . And I so wanted a child.

"I gave out that I had to have a lot of rest, I stayed in the house and when it was time, I came back here as well. It was quite easy, in those days. Home births were common, and the doctor we called out didn't know which sister was which. I even lent her my wedding ring." She smiled bitterly. "When the baby was born, I took her. And she was mine. It didn't matter that it was my sister who had felt her kicking in her womb, that it was my sister who gave her milk from her breasts while mine were dry. She was mine. My daughter, Rose."

She put out her clawlike hand to grasp her. The Troll Princess had gotten the baby after all. The witch had kept the prince. The giant had caught Lolly. The voice in my head chanted:

And when the door begins to crack
It's like a stick across your back,

{ 282 }

And when your back begins to smart
It's like a whip across your heart.

Rose covered her face, briefly. Then she put her hand up to cover the troll's and said gently, "How hard this must have been for you. And for her, too."

She was so infinitely gentle, always, and so kind. Even to the monster, who had just ruined both our lives. Then she looked at me, and the knowledge and pain of all that had passed between us flooded into her face.

"What happened to—my other mother?" said Rose, after a pause. She had become even whiter. "Did you send her away?"

Lily shook her head. "No. Though perhaps it would have been better if we had. Poor Lolly. I had hoped, you see, that we could find a way . . . I was so angry with my husband. I didn't realize. I thought perhaps the two of us could live together and share you. She loved you as much as I did. At least, that's what I thought."

I didn't believe her. She was only acting. The slyness welled up from the cracks in her face. Only I could see the truth.

"What did she do?"

"She took you out into the woods when you were just one year old, and left you there."

"No!" I cried. The pieces of my life, and my mother's stories, whirled into a terrible new shape. "I don't believe you! You're a liar, a liar, a troll! You mustn't believe her." But although my lips moved, no words came out.

My aunt spoke only to Rose. "We thought you'd both disappeared. My husband had come back; we'd gone out to Charleston. He never liked confrontations, poor Don, but he wanted to try and patch things up. It took a while to realize you were missing, but by evening we had the police out, everybody looking. We thought you might have fallen into the river, been bitten by a snake, anything. It was the most terrible day of my life."

"But you found me," said Rose.

"Yes. You were tucked up in Lolly's cardigan, at the bottom of a tree, with an empty bottle. God knows how much longer you'd have stayed. But my sister was gone. She'd left you there alone, rather than let us have you, and she ran away to England. That's what I can't forgive her for."

"WHEN ARE WE going *home*?" Cosmo asked, the whining note creeping back into his voice. "I'm bored."

"Go away, Cosmo, I'm busy." I was sweating. I could feel my terror rising up like a great, sticky black wave. I had lost Rose. I began to sob.

"Don't laugh at me!" he said.

I ignored him.

"I miss my mummy." His lips began to tremble. "I don't like you being busy all the time, and not paying me attention."

> *And when your heart begins to fail*
> *It's like a ship without a sail,*
> *And when the sail begins to sink*
> *It's like a bottle full of ink.*

The ink was rising up around me, and I was sinking into it. I said with the fierceness of desperation, "I do things with you every day, don't I? I give you baths, I clean your clothes, I put you to bed, I do everything for you."

"No, you don't, you don't!" Cosmo screamed, stamping his foot. "You aren't my mummy, you're just my *daddy*." He burst into tears, hugging his Ti-Ti. I could see it glaring at me.

Tyger Tyger, burning bright,
In the forests of the night—
Tyger Tyger, burning bright,
In the forests of the night—
Tyger Tyger—

"Shut up! Shut up, shut up, shut up. I'm too tired. You know I can't bear it. You know this is killing me." I shook him, and his sobs increased. "Just go away! Stop hanging on to that filthy toy and *grow up! Grow up! Grow up!*"

Cosmo shrieked again as Ti-Ti was seized from his grasp. I marched along the corridor and flung it into the washing machine. He beat against my legs with his fists and feet.

"Give him back! Give him back, or I'll hate you forever!"

"No," I said sternly. I was falling out of the air, but I still had my authority as an adult. "You won't get what you want by behaving like that."

"*Please* give him back. *Please!*"

"You can have him back when he's clean again. Now leave me alone."

Cosmo trailed off, and I sighed with relief as his sobs diminished. I knew what I had to do now.

I took the skipping-rope, and looped the end with the king handle over the big beam in my room. Then I made another loop. The queen handle dangled beneath the knot, her painted face quite blank beneath its crown of hearts. I stood on the frilly pink stool, and put the noose over my head. Then I kicked the stool away.

T W E N T Y - F O U R

I HUNG by my neck and my neck hurt. My tongue was coming out as though I were vomiting up my life. I couldn't breathe. Wasn't this what I'd wanted? Light flickered across my eyes, then dark, then light again. Bang-bang-bang went the blood in my brain. An intolerable noise. It sounded like somebody walking down a long, long corridor. I knew it was death coming to fetch me.

The door opened, and I saw my mother.

"Benedick," she said.

"I want to be with you," I said. I knew she understood.

"Is that what you want? To be lost, too?"

"But you weren't lost for long," I said. "You were found again."

"I cannot be recalled," she said.

Her figure wavered and shrank. It was Cosmo standing there. He looked up at me, uncomprehending.

"Daddy?" he said. "Can I have Ti-Ti back? I promise to be good."

All at once, I was running, my feet drumming on the hard air. I went down the steps, across the garden, through the white gate. The path heaved and twisted, wriggling away in the dim light. My mother floated ahead, a flickering white form. Sometimes she looked like a woman, sometimes she looked like a child, sometimes she looked like a white bird. The trees were black bars reaching between heaven and hell. They groaned and roared, stretching out long skinny claws to stop me.

"That's *my* skipping-rope!" Cosmo's voice screamed. *"Give me back my rope!"* He dragged the stool I had kicked away, put it under my feet, and climbed up onto the bed. "I can't get it off you," he said angrily. "I can't reach. It's my toy. Get it off. *Please.*"

I wanted to stand up again, but I couldn't. I sagged, half-fainting, and the noose tightened again.

"I know this game," he said, brightly. "It's Hangman, isn't it? Like we played on the plane. I'm going to get some scissors. I'll ask Rose."

And so I hung there, a creature of white paper and black ink after all.

I was wearing a hospital robe and lying on a high hospital bed, and my father was sitting on a chair. There was a bowl full of fruit, and flowers, and newspapers. Howard was reading one of them. He wore bifocals now, I noted. His eyebrows stood up over the tops like hairy caterpillars.

"Hallo, Dick," he said.

I wondered what he was doing there.

"How do you feel?"

"Strange," I said. My voice came out in a whisper. My throat still hurt. I was floating on a great pool of calm. I could see trees, but they were a long way off. A mist kept rising up out of the pool to blot them out.

"You're full of drugs," he said. "You've been ill." Then he added, "Thank God you had the sense to take out medical insurance before you came over here."

I wasn't sure whether he was real or not until he said that.

"Where is he?" The dreadful anxiety submerged in my pool started to surface. "Where's Cosmo?"

"He's absolutely fine. He's back with his mother. Don't worry, Dick old chap."

"My name isn't Dick, it's Benedick," I said.

"Benedick," said my father. He came over and gripped my hand. I was surprised to see that his eyes looked weary and blurry, almost as though he cared. "Bloody silly name, but if it's so important to you. . . . It was her choice, you know."

"You've never talked to me," I said.

"I'm bad at talking," he said simply. I gazed at him in mild astonishment. Howard never admitted he was bad at anything. His entire being was founded on the belief that he was brilliant at everything. "We will talk, but first you must rest."

I had to be dreaming.

I rested whether I liked it or not. They wouldn't give me back my clothes, and I couldn't read or watch television. The injections wore off, and I began to feel strong and powerful again, like a caged animal. I started to pace about my room, as I had done at Ruth's. I was entrapped, the wolf in the snare, and I had lost my son. My dear son, to whom I'd been so cruel. I didn't know what to do or where to go, only that I had to be free. I had to escape.

They wanted me to take some pills, but I wouldn't. They tried to trick me with some medicine in an orange drink. I spat it out. I turned into a lion, then an eagle, then a burning iron bar. In the end, they had to hold me down and give me another injection.

All I could do after that was shuffle around in my hospital pajamas. Other people were there, some young, some old, some in between. I was trapped between the past and the future, facing both ways. I looked in the mirror and saw a man like a garden full of weeds. His hair was long and lank, his chin covered with stubble, and his expression cretinous. I stuck out my tongue. He stuck out his tongue, too. I touched my nose. He touched his, at precisely the same moment. I winked; he winked back.

"Oh, no, no, no," I said.

He mouthed the same words. The old man was myself.

My sense of wretchedness increased. The drugs I was made to take increased the space between my thoughts, so that I was walking down a long avenue instead of struggling through a million tangled connections. I could count each thought, one, two, three. . . . It was like driving across the plains of France, that endless sense, not of peace but of emptiness. When I slept I thought I was falling into the clouds, endlessly. When I woke, I felt weary, not refreshed.

And so it went on. My father came every day. We still didn't talk much. I had a vague sense that he was afraid of me.

One day he brought me an envelope with a British stamp on it. Inside there were two sheets of paper. One had a small, multicolored, thunderous scribble. My wife had written, *with love from Flora.*

The other was a drawing of a man. He had blue eyes that overlapped each other and a smiling red mouth. The top of the head was covered in brown bristles. On the jumper, a big red heart was drawn. The arms were outstretched. Written beside it in straggling capitals were the words *DAD* and *LOVE, COSMO.*

I tried to write them both a letter. My father lent me a pen, but when I attempted to form letters on a piece of paper all that came out were letters as crude as those of a child. When my father left, I wept. All the tears I had kept inside me came out. The sheets were soaked. I couldn't believe I was ever going to be well again.

A PSYCHIATRIST came to interview me. She wasn't nearly as clever as Ruth. I could see she was cold and rather irritable.

There were some boring, predictable questions about my boring, predictable life. I could talk quite rationally, but then I was an actor. She told me I had been suffering from something more than ordinary unhappiness. That the reason why I had been unable to sleep and eat, and had spent so much money, was because I had manic depression.

"I have every reason to be miserable," I said. "My wife is divorcing me, I have no job, I have no house, and the woman I love turns out to be my half-sister. Don't you see, in the circumstances, that I've never been more sane?"

"Those are organic reasons," she said. "But your illness predates most of those."

"I don't want your pills. I don't believe in them. I've never even taken pills for headaches, why should I take them for heartache?"

She was brisk. "Fine. It's your choice. You'll get better for a while—just as you did before. But the next time you crash, you'll go down so deep that you're unlikely to be saved."

"How do you know that?" I thought she must have been spying on me.

"Because that's what always happens with manic depression. It's a pattern, a cycle. You're either unbearable to other people, or you're unbearable to yourself. In between, there are periods of apparent normality, of transience between the high and the low. During the highs you will spend money you don't have, drive too fast, and eventually become psychotic. But the one will follow the other, as sure as night follows day. There is no cure for it, but lithium carbonate will make it easier—if you don't kill yourself first."

"I don't believe you," I said.

"That's your choice. I'm stopping the injections now, so you're going to start to feel less dopey. Whether you take medication is up to you. You're going to have to choose. Every day, you're going to have to choose, even when you start to feel normal again. You will never be normal."

"I don't believe in your pills," I said. "And I don't believe they'll work."

"Oh, they'll work. If you're lucky," she said.

It didn't help that my father was there. I supposed I should have been touched that for once in our relationship he had actually cared enough to fly out to see me. But it seemed as if he had come especially to torment me, to triumph over me in my weakness and hopelessness.

"How are you?" he'd ask every day. It was as automatic as his asking after the children.

"How do you think?" I said.

"Ah. You sound as if you're getting back to your normal self."

"Do I have one?"

"I don't know. I used to be so worried about you."

"You? Worried about me?"

"Yes. You were the one who found her, you see."

It took a while to understand what he was telling me. "You mean, I found her *body*?"

"Yes. She hanged herself. You lived with her body for three days."

"I didn't know."

"Didn't you? I thought that's why. . . ." His eyes were looking strange again. "I've never understood why she did it. If she wanted revenge on me, why take it out on you, too?"

It was a relief when he went away. I didn't want to see him. I didn't want to see Rose, either.

But she came.

"I wasn't sure if this was a good idea," she said.
   "It couldn't get any worse."

"Oh, I don't know." She was silent a moment. She had brought me a bunch of flowers from the garden, and the scent was like another memory, so powerful that I could feel myself weeping.

She lifted her eyes to mine. I could see the expression in them. No amount of drugs could stop that.

"I didn't understand that you were ill."

"Neither did I. Lunatics never do, I'm told."

"I suppose it must have been catching, then."

"It's in the family," I said.

A new dread had begun to form. I had learned a lot more, not from the shrink but from her assistant. I knew, now, that there was a strong hereditary link to my illness—if I really was what they said. I was terrified that my children, my poor, innocent children, might have inherited it from me, as I had done from my own mother. I thought of all Cosmo's eccentricities, of how he had said that his mind was wild, not tame like other children's. I thought of his moodiness, his imagination, his precocity. How much of this was normal, and how much the early symptoms of disease?

"I don't regret it," she said. "Even if it was crazy. We didn't know. If we'd known, it would have been a sin, but we didn't."

It was important for her to make this clear. I wondered what Aunt Lily, with her sterner faith, now felt. Would the confessional absolve her?

Rose was watching me. She was still lovely, but the fierce, weird beauty I had seen in her face was gone. I understood enough now to know that my passion for her had been a part of my insanity. Yet I still loved her. My sister was not particularly bright, not gifted, not sophisticated, but good, just like the girls in my mother's stories. Good, and beautiful. How my mother must have loved her daughter, I thought, to have imagined her so obsessively! Or perhaps it was guilt. She had abandoned both of us, in different ways.

Rose laughed a little. "Oh, it was something, you know! To hear someone talk to me as you did. It made me feel better than I've felt for years. It gave me confidence again. Women always dream of having a man say all those things, and they never do. I guess it's only if they're going crazy that they do."

"We think them, even if we don't say them," I said. I could feel the dumbness of my sex creeping back on me, the shame of making a fool of myself belatedly asserting itself. Before it overwhelmed me again I said, "Rose—you deserve all the things I said. Even if neither of us are what we thought we were. Don't give up."

"I don't quit easy," she said, "nor should you. You owe your son. He saved your life, you know?"

I had wanted to save my son, and instead it was he who had saved me. How much of this he understood, nobody knew. He had gone down the stairs and had told Rose that he needed scissors to cut me down from some rope. All because of the game we had played on the airplane. Just two strokes of a pencil to save a stick man had saved me. You never know what a child remembers, and what he forgets.

I supposed, lying there, that it was all horribly funny, but I had lost, or mislaid, my sense of humor. I could only find irony, that national characteristic of which I had been so proud. Len was right, I thought. It was just a way of hiding from feelings.

I didn't think I could cope with feelings again.

BUT MUCH OF THIS was the drugs, too. It was terrifying, to lie there and wonder how much of what I had thought was myself was ever really me. I was still trying to navigate across a boiling black sea on a thin slick of oil. Beneath me the waves heaved, trying to break the surface. All my life I had tried to escape from myself, and now I had to work out who I really was. I could see myself living like the White Bear in the castle East of the Sun and West of the Moon, half bright, half dark. There were huge attractions to this existence. For as long as I was on the bright side, I would be filled with confidence, I would have no money worries, I would for a time act brilliantly, the way I had done my Mercutio. Looking back, all the parts I had played well, like the confidence I'd had when I met Georgie, had probably owed their success to being manic. Mania had enabled me to act, just as I suspected it had enabled my mother to work so hard in the last year of her life. While I was high I would be happy. In ecstasy, even. Then I would crash. There would be the blackness, the utter despair, the listlessness, the loss of identity; and I would want to kill myself. Maybe next time I would succeed. Maybe next time, Cosmo wouldn't be there, or would come too late.

Or I could take the pills. Lithium wasn't addictive, I was assured. It would stabilize my moods. But it would also leech the magic out of my life. I would return to having no story, no destiny, no conviction; just endurance. You know when you set out as an actor that you're going to need courage. What nobody tells you is what that costs. But perhaps it's the same for every profession, for every person.

I thought of what Jane Holly had said. *We all have multiple selves.* Was this true for the sane, as well as the mad? I had been so proud of being spiritually superior to Bruce—but what if my inner life were simply a manifestation of my illness? How, too, could I know for certain that my former friend didn't possess such a thing? Who can tell, really, what goes on in the heart and mind of another human being? The heart of another is a dark wood, too, always, no matter how close you are to them. What if Bruce the balding should happen to have a soul too?

I thought of the people I had questioned when trying to find out about my mother. I had been so ready to dislike and condemn them, but it was really myself I had been disliking and condemning. You're either unbearable to other people or you're unbearable to yourself, the psychiatrist had said. What if I were both? Every day I swallowed the pills I was given, an act of faith in something I didn't believe in. Nothing seemed to change, although my appetite began to return. Well, I wasn't so tired, I reasoned; I didn't have Cosmo to look after anymore, just the sleep for which all parents crave. It didn't necessarily mean that they were right and I was nuts.

There were other patients there. I started to notice them. Some were quite silent. Others twitched and talked to themselves. You wouldn't necessarily notice their madness at once. There was a fat young girl in her early twenties, a photographer, very plain. She seemed quite normal, just a bit slow. We talked.

"I don't think they'll let me out for a while," she said, conversationally.

"Why not?"

"In case I try—" She showed me her arms. They were notched with fine, horizontal scars. One wrist was still bandaged. I thought of my own attempts with the knife in the bath. She had been braver than me, many times.

She gave a sweet, sad smile. "You know."

Even when you're mad yourself, it's hard to get over your fear and loathing of other mad people. It was a much better hospital than any I would have had with the National Health (as my father pointed out), but it was still vile.

You never think, before you arrive in the place in which I now found myself, that all you've ever learned is a part of that struggle to survive. Everything I'd ever read, every part I'd played, every picture I'd seen or music I'd loved, was locked in battle with the cloud of unbeing. Perhaps I'd always lived inside this cloud, perhaps that was what had made me so unsure about everything except my need to act. I longed to go back to being the eagle in the sky and the lion at the door, because then I'd had no doubts. But perhaps doubts are what make you an adult. Some people, I learned, had months or even years of being high before the crash came. It was so unfair that mine had only lasted a few weeks.

UNFAIR, UNFAIR, that's what children cry. It takes such a long time to comprehend that fairness never happens except by the most improbable chance, that you are almost always going to be disappointed. That success, if it comes at all, arrives when you least expect it. The rules of law are an adult response to an essentially unfair universe. If an adult complains of unfairness, he's told to grow up.

It struck me that everything that was most admirable about human beings is, in fact, created by childishness. Imagination, curiosity, loyalty, optimism, a sense of fairness, love—all the qualities my son had shown me. Rose was right: I owed it to him, and to Flora, not to pass on the curse of my mother's suicide. It had poisoned my life, and poisoned my father's; it had loaded Nell and Ruth and Lily with an irremovable sense of guilt.

"It was such a dreadful time, before and after your mother's death," said Howard. We were talking more easily, now. "I was grateful you couldn't remember finding her body. I was trying so hard to forget it myself, you see. I was horrified, furious at the way she hadn't thought more about you. It seemed to me like the most selfish and vindictive thing a person could possibly do. But I suppose she was just too far gone, poor soul. Perhaps she should never have had children. I don't know.

"I wish I'd listened more. She told me there was something wrong with her. I didn't believe her."

"Why not?"

"I thought she was just being melodramatic."

"I thought her stories were about you. About your life together," I said. "But it was all jumbled up with the past. Did you know she'd had a child before me?"

He shook his head. "No. I didn't know until Lily told me. She was so young when she had you. I suppose if I'd known what to look for I might have realized. But she was so slim, before she became depressed."

"Well, you would know," I said dryly.

"Poor Nell," he muttered.

"Why did you marry her?"

"She was in love with me and . . . I thought she would be a good stepmother."

"You should have married Ruth," I said.

He stared at me. "*Ruth*? She'd never have looked twice at me. Not once she met Sam."

So this was why he had hated Tom's father, I thought. Not because of the cartoon strip, but from sheer jealousy, or wounded vanity.

"Laura never really loved me, you know," said my father. "Perhaps in the beginning, when we first married. But when I left her she made it pretty clear it was a relief. That wasn't why she killed herself, I'm sure of it."

What was it, then? Guilt? Longing for the daughter she'd left behind? I wondered whether I'd ever find out. I knew, now, how the dark could rise up and overwhelm the mind, without reason.

THE PILLS made me very thirsty, and so I had to drink a lot. Often I had to get up in the middle of the night, just as Georgie had done when pregnant. The water would slide down my throat, and every time I felt it I was reminded of what the rope had felt like. The idea that this was what the rest of my life would be, assuming I chose to stay sane, was not exactly attractive. I still didn't believe the lithium would work.

I came out of the bathroom one afternoon and found a nurse there with Aunt Lily.

"Go away," I said at once.

The nurse held her by the elbow. They both looked at me.

"Please, Benedick. I need to talk to you before you go back."

The psychiatrist and my father had agreed that I could fly home. I had spent thirty days in the bin, and my insurance policy was running out, apparently. I would be heavily sedated (they were terrified of being sued) and in a wheelchair, but I would be going home.

"He mustn't be upset," said the nurse. "If he doesn't want to see you, I'm afraid you'll have to go, ma'am."

My aunt put out her withered hand. "Just a few minutes, in private."

She was still able to bend people to her will, I noticed, because the nurse left. I sat on the edge of the bed.

"I feel so bad about all this."

I dropped my guard, then, because she said she was sorry. "Don't be. I invited myself, after all."

"I knew you'd come, one day. I should have told Rose long ago. But we've always been so close, and I was afraid of losing her."

"You won't," I said. "I found someone else, you know, to be my mother when my real mother died. You've met her. Ruth."

"I still don't know whether I did the right thing, you see. She wanted her back so badly," said my aunt. "Lolly wrote to me before she killed herself. But by then Rose had spent nine years with us. It was unthinkable. And she had you, whereas I had nothing if I lost her."

"I wasn't enough," I said.

My aunt leaned forward. "No. No, it wasn't that. Think if you could have your own son back, but not your daughter. Half your heart would be broken, wouldn't it? Wouldn't it?"

"Yes," I said, "though as things stand, I'll probably lose them both. I can't see Georgie letting me have either of them now she knows I really am mad. Just as she always said."

"You've had a breakdown," said my aunt. "That's different. I've never met your wife, but I've talked a lot with her on the phone, sorting out Cosmo's return. I don't think she'll be as harsh on you as you may think."

"But what about Cosmo?" I said. "What will he feel about being with a father he's seen raving at him, and dangling at the end of a rope?"

Aunt Lily smiled at me. "He probably won't think it so strange," she said. "Children forget. If he remembers anything, he'll feel proud. It's not many sons who can be the father to the man."

"**W**HERE are we going?"

"To Hampstead Heath?"

"Why is it called that?"

"It's named after a famous hamster, stupid."

Georgie and I laughed.

"No, we're going to Primrose Hill."

Cosmo's voice piped, "Can I have a dog, please, Dad? Can I?"

"I don't know. It depends. I might be away, working."

Nothing happens the way you expect it to. I had returned to Britain owing £20,000 on my credit cards and expecting to find my career in ruins. But the British film I had acted in had found a distributor and gone on to win a prize at the Venice Film Festival. My performance as the cross-dressing drug dealer had actually been singled out for praise ("a superb performance by Benedick Hunter," *Daily Telegraph*). It was so long since anyone had said anything good about my work that I couldn't quite believe it, but my father saw it. He was almost embarrassingly proud. My agent had started to ring me again, too. The disastrous audition for *Jigsaw* was barely mentioned.

"I did hear that our Benedick had taken divorce rather badly," she said, and that was that.

Because of the Brit-flick, I had been given a job in a car advertisement. All I had to do was get into a car and drive away, but it was enough to pay back all the money I had spent when manic. I was getting off pretty lightly—as Ruth didn't fail to point out. I felt so well again that I thought perhaps I could stop taking the drugs. I had stopped for a while, only to collapse into mania again. So that was that. All I had was a life sentence of raving lunacy culminating in suicide should I stop taking my pills. The spell on me, unlike those in my mother's stories, would never be broken.

But while I was becoming manic, I rang Lottie Lang, the agent Len and Rupert had suggested. She took me on, and had already had a miraculous effect on my career. I had played Leontes in *The Winter's Tale* at the Donmar, and Frederick Wentworth in a BBC adaptation of *Persuasion*.

People said that I was acting better than I'd ever done before. I no longer bothered to work out what I was supposed to be feeling or thinking, I just said my lines. I understood that I could be the blank sheet onto which an audience could project its own dreams and desires. Perhaps that is all an art, or a craft, is—learning not to care. I didn't care. I was working again.

It was this, I think, as much as the lithium, that made me better. It meant that I hadn't been written out of the story of my life. People say that life has no story, that to believe it does is a symptom of madness, and I had thought this, too. But I knew I couldn't go on living without some version of the truth. Every version has its blessing and its curse. I had told my new agent about being a manic depressive, and she had just laughed.

"Darling," she said, "if you took every actor who was manic depressive out of this profession, there'd be no unemployment. And probably no great performances, either."

I had taped the cutting from the *Telegraph* to the bottle of lithium I had to take every morning. The pills looked exactly like the contraceptives my wife had taken. I wondered whether the critic who had written those six words about my performance would ever realize what power he had over my life, death, and hope of happiness. Probably not, any more than my mother could have known what effect her book of fairy tales would have on me. My trip to New York had had one other result. Jane Holly was reprinting *North of Nowhere*. I told her to send all the money to Rose, to help her build the swimming pool she so wanted. I would use the income from my mother's estate for a new end.

It was as warm as the Carolinas. Georgie was driving. Bruce had given her a car with air-conditioning and automatic gears. I wondered if her relationship with him felt like mine had, so briefly, with Rose. Perhaps it did. Money makes such a difference to anyone's life. It, too, is a kind of magic.

"Oh, please, Daddy."

"We're desperate for a dog," said Flora.

"What about your toy animals? What about Ti-Ti?"

"He's just a toy tiger. I'd rather have a *real* pet."

Ti-Ti stared at me from Cosmo's backpack. His eyes, bleached by detergent, now looked quite blind.

We got out of the car and began to walk up Primrose Hill. It no longer filled me with nostalgia. The world, like the mind, constantly renews itself. The past makes way for the present; and yet it lives on, in fragments, in people and places. The children bounced ahead, barking and calling to each other. Cosmo, in a bossy voice, read out all the prohibitions on the signboard: NO CYCLING, NO MUSIC, NO SKATEBOARDS. It was a little like when he had started to talk: one week nothing, the next, a torrent of words. Something had just clicked in his brain, as it had clicked in a different way in mine, and the new world of reading had swung open. I could barely remember his intense anxiety over it all, how he had ground his teeth and bitten his arm. He had raced through picture books and a year later was now on what he called "real books." I wondered whether he'd ever read *North of Nowhere* to himself.

"Let's chase the shining ball to the top of the hill!" Flora cried. We followed our son and daughter. It was so familiar, walking side by side again. Not a consolation, nor a desolation, just a space in which it was possible to live.

"Getting on together, aren't they?"

"Yes, thank God. It's been like this ever since you and Cosmo were in the States. I think they missed each other a lot more than they realized."

We had started to climb the hill. It was rippling with grasses, a long surging wave of movement. I stared at them and thought, What would I be seeing if I weren't taking the pills? Would it be bringing me ecstasy, or terror? The grass swayed like water moving to the ends of the world.

"I used to wish you were dead," she said suddenly. "I'm sorry. I'm glad you aren't."

We passed a couple coming down the hill. The woman looked vaguely familiar. She paused, briefly, and I saw it was Diana, the woman I'd last seen running out of Marine Ices.

"Hallo," said my ex-wife.

"Hi," said Diana. She raised her eyebrows quizzically.

"How are you?" said Georgie, smiling. "You look terrific."

"Thanks," said Diana. She ignored me pointedly.

I looked at her while they chatted, in the way that people in London do, promising to meet up again, before kissing the air. It was true, something about her was different, but I couldn't think what.

"Did you notice?" said Georgina after they'd walked on. "She's had the mole cut off her face. No wonder she's got a new boyfriend."

"Has she?" I thought about it. "You're right. I told her to have it done. She was furious with me."

It was still a novelty to me to be able to laugh so easily and naturally again.

"You're different, too," said Georgie.

"I suppose so."

We stopped and looked up. Far above us, above the figures of our children toiling up the green hill, kites whirled and swooped in aerial geometry, whirring as the breeze caught them. Up and down and round and round, looping the loop, soaring and plunging, the fine lines that held them like great fish taut in the hands of the fliers. If I could hold on to myself like that, I thought, if I could still fly but remain anchored, stabilized, sane. I had to try. It was never going to be pleasant, but I knew, now, that I might be worth saving, if only because of my children.

They watched the kites, open-mouthed. Would they remember this? Cosmo had forgotten everything about America except seeing the Statue of Liberty and eating a lot of ice cream. He knew, vaguely, that I had been in hospital for a few days, and that he himself had traveled back from Charleston in the company of an air hostess all by himself. Otherwise it had all been erased. There were mercies in infant forgetfulness, I thought, just as my aunt had said. Or perhaps it would resurface again, months and years later. Who could say? I remembered seeing my mother in my aunt's house, as vividly and completely as if she had never died; and I dreamed of her, too. *I cannot be recalled,* she said. Sometimes she was young, sometimes she was as old as Aunt Lily, and sometimes she was the girl in the stories whose face I had given to Rose.

"It's funny about that book," said Georgie. "The one you say started you off. I read them, too."

I turned to her. "You did?"

"Yes," she said, almost apologetically. "I liked them. Well, you know women like fairy tales more often than men do. I wonder why?"

"Perhaps you're just the wiser sex," I said. "That's what Ruth would say."

"Dear Ruth. I used to be rather afraid of her, you know. I think she always knew it wouldn't work out. I used to think she was a sort of witch."

I was back living with Ruth, but not for much longer. I had found a flat of my own, even if it was tiny, somewhere not too far from Georgie and the children. This was the last time I'd be able to visit North London for a while.

"No," I said. "It's stupid to think of people like that. People are too much of a mixture. You can't force them into archetypes."

"I know," said Georgie, "but one still does it."

Ruth and I had had many talks since my return. She knew now what I had suspected after my meeting with Nell, and my lack of trust had hurt her, perhaps because it came quite close to the truth.

"Did you honestly believe that all this time, I'd really cared so much for Howard?" she said indignantly.

"Well, you did at one time, didn't you?"

"Benedick, you of all people should know how much we all change. Sure, your father and I were crazy about each other for a time, when we were young. Life isn't perfect. You don't get it right, first time."

"It's strange, isn't it?" I had said. "People talk about fairy tales as though they offer a vision of perfection, but they don't. It's only offered at the end, when the story is over. While the story is happening, it's pretty grim."

Ruth had been rather put out by this.

"Ow," said Georgie. "This bloody baby's kicking."

"Do you want to stop and rest?"

"I'll be OK."

"Do the children know?"

"Yes. It hasn't sunk in, at least not with Flora. Cosmo's quite excited."

"Is he?"

"Of course, he'd prefer a dog."

We had climbed to the very top of the hill, now, and the whole of London lay below us, stretching away to the South Downs. A steady breeze blew. The sound of the wind in the leaves made me think of Aunt Lily, and of Rose. It was a pity they hadn't been able to make it for the ceremony, but it was going to be very small. I waved to my father, Ruth, and Nell. They were coming up the hill behind us, talking to Rupert and Len.

"Look," said Cosmo. "There's someone's name the same as ours on this bench." He pointed.

"Yes, darling. That's why we're here," said Georgie.

There was a new bench just over the hill with a plaque on it.

"It's to remember my mother, your grandmother, by," I said. "The one who did the book I read to you."

Cosmo traced the letters with one finger.

In memory of Laura Hunter, artist, wife, and mother. 1938–66. "And when the ink begins to write, / It makes the paper black and white."

"Tell us a story about her," he said.

We sat down on the bench. Its wood was pale, unstained as yet by time and grime. What could I tell him about the woman whose genes they now carried? Which version of the truth would they understand? What could I tell him of the blessing and the curse that might be theirs?

"Once upon a time," I began, "there were two sisters who lived on the edge of a deep, dark wood."

ACKNOWLEDGMENTS

NOT ALL of the people who helped me can be named. I am, however, indebted to Greg Battle, Lucy Bird, Lorna Brook, Gillian Cohen, Zelda Craig, Susannah Fiennes, Eleanor Fizan, Katharine Frankfort, Shirley Hughes, Andrew and Juliet Lawson, Kate Little, Ian Mankin, Nick Myers, Emily Patrick, Kate Saunders, Liz Stoll, Pip Torrens, Amanda Vickery, Fay Weldon, and Jenny Wright. I would particularly like to thank those who have suffered from manic depression—either as patients or as relations—who recounted their experiences with honesty and courage. I would also like to express my admiration and gratitude to the Manic Depression Fellowship for its work in encouraging a better understanding of this fascinating yet terrible illness, and to Alan Garner, Tim Lott, Nicola Paget, Kay Redfield Jamison, Anthony Storr, and William Styron for their insights into it. I am also grateful to Ellen Handler Spitz, Alison Lurie, Marina Warner, and Maria Tatar for their writing on fairy tales, much of which informed this novel. I am particularly indebted to Andrew Lang's fairy tale collections. I hope readers familiar with the conventional versions of "East o' the Sun and West o' the Moon" will forgive the liberties I have taken with it in order to suggest aspects of Laura's struggle with her past.

In America, I would like to thank my agent, Emma Parry of

Carlisle & Company, for her unstinting enthusiasm, and Nan Talese of Doubleday U.S.A. for making one fairy tale come true. Lorna Owen and her team have caught out my errors concerning American culture with humor and sensitivity. Unlike Benedick, I love America but still know too little about details that Americans take for granted.

Fourth Estate has shown me exemplary patience and support. Mary Chamberlain, Howard Davies, Katie Owen, and in particular Christopher Potter have combined tact with inspirational suggestions. So, too, did my agent, Giles Gordon.

I also wish to thank the newspaper and magazine editors who kept both my spirits and my income from sinking too low during the period of writing. They make it possible for novelists like myself to continue. Roger Alton, Sarah Baxter, Lola Bubbosh, Jason Cowley, Suzi Feay, Justine Hancock, Martin Ivens, Gerald Jacobs, Rosalind Lowe, Brian MacArthur, Eleanor Mills, Terri Natale, Justine Picardie, Maggie Pringle, Hilary Robinson, Sarah Sands, Nancy Sladek, Erica Wagner, Auberon Waugh, and Peter Wilby have all been my benefactors.

Lastly, as always, my beloved Rob, Leonora, and William for being who they are.

A B O U T   T H E   A U T H O R

AMANDA CRAIG was born in 1959 and is the author of *Foreign Bodies*, *A Private Place*, and *A Vicious Circle*, which is currently being developed as a film by Sharon Maguire, director of *Bridget Jones's Diary*. She lives in London and writes regularly for *The Times*, *The Sunday Times*, and the *New Statesman*.

A NOTE ABOUT THE TYPE

The text of this book is set in Mrs. Eaves,
a historical revival based on the design of Baskerville
and designed in 1995–1996.

*"In translating this classic to today's digital font technology, I focused on capturing
the warmth and softness of letterpress printing that often occurs
due to the 'gain' of impression and ink spread."*

Zuzana Licko (type designer)